"Have you always been this much of a skeptic? Or do babies make you that nervous?"

"Come on," Eric said. "You waltz into my life with some wild story about a sister I never knew I had? Wouldn't you have some doubts, too? A desperate woman looking to find a decent home for her babies can come up with a very convincing lie."

She leveled him a look that would have made most men back off in a hurry. "I personally guarantee that if you don't want to raise the girls for any reason at all, they will always have a good home—with me."

The intensity of her words brought him up short. This woman was not fooling around. "You want to adopt the twins?"

"With all my heart." A fine sheen of tears appeared in her eyes, but she didn't let them spill over.

"Then why did you bother to track me down? I never would have known otherwise."

"Because I promised I would."

Montana Instant Family

CHARLOTTE MACLAY
&
TERESA CARPENTER

Previously published as *Montana Twins*
and *Baby Twins: Parents Needed*

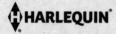

ISBN-13: 978-1-335-47372-1

Montana Instant Family

Copyright © 2022 by Harlequin Enterprises ULC

Montana Twins
First published in 2003. This edition published in 2022.
Copyright © 2003 by Charlotte Lobb

Baby Twins: Parents Needed
First published in 2007. This edition published in 2022.
Copyright © 2007 by Teresa Carpenter

Recycling programs for this product may not exist in your area.

For questions and comments about the quality of this book, please contact us at CustomerService@Harlequin.com.

Harlequin Enterprises ULC
22 Adelaide St. West, 41st Floor
Toronto, Ontario M5H 4E3, Canada
www.Harlequin.com

Printed in U.S.A.

CONTENTS

MONTANA TWINS   7
Charlotte Maclay

BABY TWINS: PARENTS NEEDED   241
Teresa Carpenter

A multipublished author of more than fifty romance, cozy mystery and inspirational titles, **Charlotte Maclay** lives in Southern California with her husband of fifty years. They have two married daughters and five grandchildren, who Charlotte is occasionally allowed to babysit.

Books by Charlotte Maclay

Harlequin Western Romance

Montana Twins
Montana Daddy
Courtship, Montana Style
At the Rancher's Bidding
With Courage and Commitment
Between Honor and Duty
With Valor and Devotion
Bold and Brave-Hearted
In a Cowboy's Embrace

Visit the Author Profile page at Harlequin.com for more titles.

Montana Twins

CHARLOTTE MACLAY

Chapter 1

"**I**'m going to be a father."

Still stunned by the news, Sheriff Eric Oakes sat down heavily in the swivel chair behind his desk, trying to figure out how it had happened. Or if it could possibly be true.

His brother Rory, who had just come into the office, looked at him as if he'd lost his mind. "You're kidding."

"Twins. Girls."

"Hey, I didn't even know you were seeing anyone. How come you're keeping secrets from—"

"No, it's not like that. It's like—" He was stammering almost as much as the woman who'd called him with the news a few minutes ago. "They're my sister's kids." Three months old, the woman had said.

Rory frowned, and a hank of his dark hair slid across his forehead. In a futile gesture, he shoved it back into place. "Have you been nipping at that bottle you keep in your bottom desk drawer? You don't have a sister. Two brothers, me and Walker. Unless ol' Sharpy has had a sex change I don't know about—"

"No, that's not it." Eric pushed back from his desk, stood and paced across the room to look out the window onto the town of Grass Valley, Montana, located not far from the Canadian border.

Small was the only way to describe the town.

Rory's veterinary clinic was down a side road a block away, across from Doc Justine's medical clinic where Rory's bride, Kristi, worked as a nurse practitioner, helping her grandmother, the long-time town doctor.

On the main street there was a garage with rusty old heaps parked around it, a drugstore that sold more ice cream than prescriptions, and a general store. The saloon with a tattered banner that announced "Good Eats" was the only place that ever drew a crowd, except for the nearby church.

Crime wasn't a big issue in the community. A few Saturday-night drunks to fill his two jail cells now and then. Traffic accidents on the highway that called for him to respond. Occasional reports of cattle rustling or adolescent vandalism. A safe place to live.

And to raise kids, he thought as a lump formed in his throat. He'd always wanted children. A family of his own.

He turned back to his brother. "Some woman called a couple of minutes ago, a Laura somebody from Helena. She says my mother had another baby after she abandoned me." It was no big deal to tell Rory he'd been dumped by his mom. Rory's mother had done the same thing to him. That's how they'd both ended up at the

Double O Ranch as foster kids to Oliver Oakes, who'd eventually adopted them and another kid, their brother, Walker—nicknamed Sharpy because he'd once shot himself in the leg. Walker was running the ranch nowadays.

"According to this woman, my sister's name was Amy Thorne, and she had twins a couple of months ago. Then she died." Still incredulous about the phone call, he shook his head. "She wanted me to have the babies. Be their dad. Apparently I'm their only living relative."

"Somebody's putting you on."

"I don't know. This Laura person sounded pretty legit." Except she'd been nervous, stuttering and stammering as she tried to tell her story.

"No, it's got to be some kind of scam. Did she ask for money? Child support?" Rory hooked his hip over the corner of Eric's desk and crossed his arms. His Native American heritage sometimes gave him a brooding look, but since discovering that he had a son and his recent marriage to the boy's mother, Kristi Kerrigan, Rory had been all smiles. Until now.

"The whole phone call kind of caught me off guard," Eric said. He was still shaken, half disbelieving the news yet wanting it to be true. "But no, she didn't say anything about money." Not that he could remember, at any rate. "She's going to bring the twins up here tomorrow."

"And just hand them off to you?"

"I don't know. She said something about interviewing me." Which didn't make a whole lot of sense. Either he was the twins' uncle or he wasn't. And if he wasn't, that woman wouldn't have bothered to call and make him identify himself by his birth name, Eric Johnson. A name he hadn't used since he was fifteen and Oliver Oakes adopted him. Eric had celebrated his thirty-second birthday last fall out at the ranch. Walker's wife, Lizzie, had baked the most lopsided cake he'd ever seen—not that he or anyone else had cared. Devil's food with chocolate frosting was hard to beat whatever the shape.

He shoved his fingers through his hair, shorter than Rory's, more brown than black and several shades lighter. Now that he was trying to explain this baby situation to his brother, it sounded pretty damn crazy. Maybe it was a hoax. One of those adolescent games when a kid calls someone and asks if their refrigerator is running. When the victim says yes, the kids giggle and say you'd better catch it before it runs out the door. A silly, harmless prank.

But his caller hadn't sounded like a kid. More like a woman with a sultry voice who hadn't wanted to call him at all.

And the story of his mother, who had run through boyfriends like water through a sieve, sounded legit, too. She could have gotten pregnant again.

God, could it be that all these years he'd had a sister who he didn't even know existed and now she was dead? He'd never have a chance to meet her. Or talk to her. Why hadn't she come looking for him sooner?

Or could that call have been nothing more than a cruel trick? The woman the same kind of person who would abandon her own kid?

Tears stung at the backs of his eyes as memories assailed him. He'd been ten years old and standing in the parking lot of a fast-food hamburger joint. Looking for his mother and her current boyfriend. Looking for their car. He knew where it had been parked. It wasn't there anymore. He'd had to go to the john. They'd left without him. God, he'd felt so alone. So hurt.

How could any mother do that to a kid?

He hadn't had a sister then. He'd been an only child, crowded into the back seat of the car along with everything they owned, and making it a point to stay out of reach of his mom's boyfriend. The guy had big meaty fists, Eric remembered that. And he knew how to use them.

A sob rose in his throat.

The office door opened to admit a current of fresh spring air along with Rory's wife, Kristi, and their son, Adam.

Swiping the back of his hand across his face, Eric struggled to pull his emotions back under control.

"Hi, Uncle Eric." The dark-haired five-year-old made a beeline for the nearest jail cell and began to swing on the door, peering out through the bars.

"Where did I put that key?" he asked, playing the game he and the boy had started recently. "I've caught me a monkey and I need to lock him up."

The youngster giggled and made scratching gestures under his arm pits. "Hoot-hoot-hoot."

Kristi stood on tiptoe to brush a kiss to her husband's cheek. "Ted Pomperan is at the clinic with a dog that cut its foot."

"Okay, I'll be right there. Eric's been telling me he's going to be a daddy. Twins, he says."

"Girls," Eric added. If the tale was true.

"You're kidding!" Kristi whirled toward him, her eyes widening. "I certainly hope you plan to marry the woman."

"Well, no. I mean, I don't even know the woman. She just called a couple of minutes—"

"I'd say you know her plenty well enough if she's going to have your babies," Kristi insisted.

Adam piped up. "Does that mean I'm gonna get some more cousins?"

"She's not going to have my babies. They're already three months old. And they might not even be—"

"So she hadn't told you she was—"

"Rory!" Eric came around the desk, caught Rory and Kristi by their respective elbows, ushering them toward the door. "Go take care of your canine patient, and in the meantime will you please explain the situation to your wife so she doesn't think I've committed some mortal sin."

"I'm not sure I get the picture myself," Rory complained.

"Neither do I. With luck, when the woman shows up tomorrow with the twins, I'll be able to figure out what's going on." *Assuming she comes at all.*

Rory opened the door for his wife.

"You be nice to the woman, Eric Oakes," Kristi admonished him. "If she's had your babies, she'll be feeling very vulnerable and unsure of herself. I know that's how I felt when I came back to Grass Valley and had to face Rory and tell him about Adam."

Exasperated, Eric said, "Talk to her, bro." He eased them out the door, closing it behind them and drew a deep breath.

Incredible. Was he really about to become a father of two baby girls?

Which reminded him that he didn't know squat about babies and diapers and bottles or any of that stuff. How the hell was he going to manage if it came to that?

Turning around, his gaze landed on Adam, who was still behind bars.

"Your folks just left."

The boy lifted his shoulders in an easy shrug. "The door locked itself. I can't get out."

"Right." He headed for the ring of keys hanging on a peg behind his desk.

Not only did he know little about caring for babies, he wasn't all that sure he'd be able to handle a couple of girls Adam's age when the time came. And God help him, when they became adolescents, his goose would be cooked.

If they were his nieces and he was about to become their daddy.

"I don't know how you can give away those sweet little babies." Barbara Cavendish shaded her eyes against the morning sun as Laura loaded the twins inside her SUV for the trip to Grass Valley.

"It's what their mother wanted. Amy made that abundantly clear." A knot formed in Laura's throat at the mere thought of handing the twins over to a perfect stranger, even if he was their only living relative. And she fully understood that in her mother's heart, she'd already claimed the twins as her grandchildren.

Laura tried for a brave smile as she adjusted Amanda's

car seat, then reached across her to the second car seat and caressed the blond fuzz on Rebecca's head. She'd never seen two more beautiful babies, small for their age but absolutely perfect in every way. She desperately hoped that once their uncle Eric met the twins he wouldn't feel the same way about them as she did. There was no law that said he *had* to raise them. He could easily reject the idea once he realized what it entailed.

"You know I loved Amy as if she were my own child," her mother continued. Barbara Cavendish had taken Amy into her home and heart as an abused foster child when the girl had been only ten years old. Laura had become her big sister—a role she'd loved and continued as best she could after Amy had moved out on her own. "I'm just not sure she was thinking clearly, wanting to give her babies away to a complete stranger when she knew you—"

"Her half brother, Mom."

"Who she didn't even know existed until she rummaged through that shoe box of things her mother left her. I wish you hadn't hired that private detective to find the man."

In more ways than Laura could count, she wished that too. "I promised Amy I'd follow her wishes if I could."

During Amy's last trimester of pregnancy, it had become clear she wouldn't be able to continue working as a waitress, and the complications of Amy's diabetes made the pregnancy high risk. She was told she could die.

Not wanting to burden Laura's mother, who tended to be overly protective, Amy had moved in with Laura. Soon after that she'd discovered she had a half brother—the twins' only living blood relative.

Then the worst had happened. Amy slipped into a coma before she gave birth to the twins. Only the doctor's quick action, taking the babies by cesarean section, had saved them. Amy had given her life for the children she never had a chance to hold.

Preparing for that contingency, she'd left written instructions for Laura to follow, signed and notarized, as binding as any will. Find Amy's half brother, if she could. See if he'd be a suitable daddy. If not, Amy wanted Laura to raise her babies. In the end, the decision would be Laura's.

It had taken the private detective three months and several thousand dollars to locate the man. Five hours from now, give or take a little, Laura would actually meet him.

"In spite of the rocky road she'd traveled, Amy believed families ought to stick together," Laura told her mother. "I suspect you were the one who taught her that."

"I don't know, dear—"

"Mom, I have to do this. I gave my word of honor." Straightening, she rested her hand lightly on her mother's shoulder, trying to reassure herself as much as her mother. "Chances are a sheriff in a town like Grass Valley has a beer belly, chews tobacco and has only a passing interest in the offspring of a woman he never knew. I'll have an easy decision to make—he obviously won't be a fit father for the twins—and my conscience will be clear."

Failing that, her last, best hope would be that Eric Oakes wasn't married—at least the detective hadn't uncovered any evidence of a woman in the picture. Amy had been adamant that she didn't want her babies raised by a single father. She didn't trust any man that much.

Laura hugged that thought tightly to her as she kissed her mother goodbye and climbed in behind the steering wheel of the SUV. Amanda and Rebecca were already her life, the children of her heart.

Because she couldn't bear children of her own, they were her one best chance to be the mother she longed to be. They could ease the ache that had been with her since that terrible accident when she'd been sixteen years old—an accident that had been her fault. Oh, she hadn't been driving the pickup truck filled with a half dozen cheering high school friends when a speeding car crashed into them.

But climbing into the back of that truck after their team had beaten the town rivals *had* been her idea. She'd carry that guilt with her forever.

Her hand trembled as she twisted the key in the ignition. Anxiety about what would happen in Grass Valley dried her mouth like a summer drought turns a prairie to dust.

The early-morning sky was a pale blue, the air crystalline clear. The temperature would probably reach seventy-five degrees, typical for July.

Normally she loved driving across Montana during her time off from teaching high school history and government. She'd even been known to go hiking on her own or camping with friends. But this trip—and what might follow—she dreaded at a deeply personal level.

She could lose the babies she had come to love with the intensity that only a mother could possess.

* * *

As she'd expected, six hours later and three stops for diaper changes and bottles, she discovered Grass Valley was little more than a wide spot in a very narrow road.

Laura slowed as she entered the town. Eric Oakes had told her to meet him at his house, so she cruised past the few buildings that lined the main street, noting a couple of women visiting in front of the general store. An older man coming out of the saloon waved at Laura—probably mistaking her vehicle for someone else's. She caught sight of the sheriff's office, a short, stout building that wouldn't even intimidate a jaywalker.

Then she saw the quixotic roadside mailbox, a prisoner in a bronze striped uniform escaping through the roof of the jail. Eric had said she'd have no trouble finding his place.

Drawing a deep breath, she turned into the long driveway leading to a two-story house. Modest by most standards, the best feature was a porch that stretched the full width of the house and was positioned to catch the morning sun. Two wicker chairs promised comfort while watching the sun rise.

A big cottonwood tree shaded portions of the front yard, and beyond the house stood a small barn and corral. A pair of sorrel horses raised their heads to check on her arrival.

Laura didn't want to think about how much Amanda and Rebecca might someday want their own horses or have a swing hanging from a sturdy tree branch. Her townhouse didn't have room for a corral, and the trees were mostly poplars, impossible to climb much less swing from.

When she pulled to a stop, a man came out of the house, the screen door bumping closed behind him as he walked down the steps toward her with an easy stride. Tall and lean in his khaki uniform, he wore a badge pinned to his broad chest and a pager on his belt that was no larger than a trim size thirty-two.

She'd really been counting on a beer belly.

Checking first to see that the twins were still sleeping, she got out of the car.

"Afternoon," he said in the same clear baritone she'd heard on the phone, a tone that held a note of caution.

She nodded. "Sheriff Oakes." His hair—the color of a sand dune after a rainstorm—was cut short, probably to tame the natural waves rather than from any desire to appear military. Crinkles fanned out at the corners of his eyes, as though he'd spent a lot of time squinting into the Montana sky—or laughing. His face was tanned, his jaw square, his lips set in a firm, skeptical line.

"Most folks just call me Eric. We're pretty informal around here." He glanced toward the truck. "You've got the twins with you, Ms...uh... I didn't get your whole name."

"Laura Cavendish. They're in their car seats."

"I wasn't a hundred percent sure you'd show up."

"I said I would."

"Well, let's take a look at 'em." He gestured toward the back seat.

She bristled. "This isn't like picking out a good horse, you know."

His pale-blue eyes narrowed and darkened with suspicion. "I didn't think it was, Ms. Cavendish. But they are my nieces, aren't they?"

"Apparently." More than anything in the world, Laura wished they weren't—wished the detective had made a mistake and traced the wrong man. But he'd assured her that wasn't the case.

"How did you find me, anyway? Johnson is a pretty ordinary name."

"I had your date and place of birth from your sister, which I gave to the detective I hired. Since I knew you and she hadn't been raised together, we guessed you had landed in the foster care system somewhere." The tricky part had been getting ahold of the adoption records. Laura hadn't asked the detective how he'd managed that.

He cocked his brow, then edged closer to her vehicle, peering through the tinted side window. "So you're pretty sure I'm the right guy."

"Yes." She swallowed hard. If she simply got back in the truck and returned to Helena, no one would question that she'd done as Amy had requested and decided their uncle wasn't suitable. The twins would be hers. "But if you're not interested in raising them—"

He grasped the handle and opened the door. Laura held her breath as he leaned inside.

"Oh, my God." He spoke as though his words were a whispered prayer and filled with awe. "They're so little."

Through the crack, Laura saw him tenderly slip his finger into Rebecca's hand. The baby closed her tiny fingers into a fist around him and opened her eyes, looking up at Eric with her bright blue eyes. A bubble escaped her lips.

"Hey, Tinkerbell," he said softly. "This lady says I'm your uncle Eric. Whadaya think, huh?"

The magical exchange between the big, rugged sheriff and his tiny niece was so powerful, Laura's throat closed down tight, and she almost couldn't speak. "That one is Rebecca. The other one is Amanda."

"How do you tell 'em apart?"

"Rebecca's left eyebrow arches a little more than Amanda's does and her ears stick out a tiny bit more. She's also more wakeful than her sister." Somehow, from almost the first moment following their birth she'd been able to tell the twins apart without checking their ID bracelets. The hospital nurses had been amazed. "Other than that, they're identical."

"I'll say."

A light breeze ruffled Laura's hair, shifting it along the back of her neck, and she felt a chill run down her arms. "I think we ought to take the girls inside. They're still a little fragile."

He backed away from the truck. "Oh, yeah, sure. Come on in."

"You get Rebecca, and I'll go around to the other side to get Amanda."

"You want me to—" He blanched as white as if she'd asked him to pick up a deadly snake. "I've never held a baby that tiny before. I'm not sure I know how."

He'd better learn how in a hurry if he expected Laura to even consider leaving the twins in his care for as little as two minutes—forget the rest of their lives.

"Here, let me." She edged past him, acutely aware of what a big man he was. His aura expanded around her, stealing inside her personal space, leaving her feeling slightly breathless. Unsnapping the car seat harness, she lifted Rebecca and gave her a quick kiss.

"Come on, Becky. Meet your uncle Eric." She held out the baby to him.

He hesitated.

"She won't break as long as you don't drop her."

"I won't," he promised.

She laid the baby in his arms. "Keep her head propped up. Don't let it fall back."

He looked as awkward as a boy at his first dance, standing as stiff as a robot, not knowing quite what to do with his hands, his expression frozen with fear. Even so, Laura saw he was gentle. His big hand cradled the back of Rebecca's head, his arm held her firmly against his chest.

Not that that meant he'd be a good daddy for the long haul.

"Now, hold her carefully," she warned him again. She hurried to the other side of the SUV, quickly extricating Amanda from her car seat. The infant stretched and yawned, then let out a tiny cry of complaint. "Sorry I had to wake you, Mandy. You're fine, really you are." She grabbed the oversize diaper bag and rejoined Eric, who hadn't budged. "We were going inside?"

"Right." He eyed Laura, then looked down at Rebecca. "I was wrong before. She's not Tinkerbell, she's *Stinker*bell. And I think she's leaking."

"Oh, dear." She stifled a smile at his horrified look. "Well, let's get her inside, and I'll change her diaper. That probably means Mandy is about to let loose, too."

Eric didn't look at all pleased with the prospect. His easy walk that she'd noted earlier turned to a tiptoe race up the porch steps. Despite that, he took the time to hold the door open for her.

An officer of the law and a gentleman—shades of the old west.

For a bachelor's place, the living room looked neat, and the heavy leather couch and recliner gave the room a masculine flavor. In lieu of any feminine touches, there was an overflowing bookcase stuffed with mystery, adventure and science fiction titles, a big-screen TV and a stereo sound system that would rival an outdoor amphitheater. It looked like a case of a boy with plenty of expensive toys.

Noting the row of huge silver rodeo trophies on the mantel above the natural rock fireplace, Laura suspected Eric's music of choice would be country-western. She wondered how he was at two-stepping. Not that she was an expert. Just the opposite. But the dance had always looked like fun.

Holding Amanda in one arm, she pulled a receiving blanket from the diaper bag with her free hand and spread it on the center cushion of the man-size couch. She put Amanda down and reached for Rebecca.

Eric passed her the baby, thinking how odd the situation felt. A woman in his house and two tiny babies so small he could probably cradle one in each hand like a football if he wasn't so darn scared he'd drop one.

No question, he was going to need a crash course in infant care if they had any chance of surviving under his roof after he was on his own with them.

A father ought to know *something* about taking care of his kids.

If indeed he was a relation at all. He had the feeling he should be waiting for another shoe to drop, one that resembled a complicated con job intended to raid his bank account.

How could anyone know how much he'd always wanted a family of his own?

He watched Laura's swift, confident movements as she changed the babies' diapers. Her head was bent over them, allowing her hair to slide forward, hiding her face behind a ginger-blond screen. Her hairdo was practical, only long enough to reach the angle of her jaw, one of those styles that brushed into place with a few strokes or little more than a shake of her head. But it seemed to shine in the reflected light of the room as though someone had turned a golden spotlight on her.

Her clothes were practical, too. A businesslike navy jacket over a light yellow blouse and navy slacks. Sensible shoes. A long way from a femme fatale or what he'd imagine a scam artist would wear.

She dressed as primly as every social worker he'd ever known as a kid, but something was different about her. When she held one of the twins, murmuring sweet, loving sounds, her smile glowed from the inside out. She had some kind of a special connection to these babies. Eric wasn't sure what.

Granted, he wasn't a big-city cop. But he'd had a fair amount of police training and pretty good instincts. Despite her very attractive packaging, this woman was hiding something.

"Except for knowing my birth name, what other proof do you have that these babies are any relation to me at all?"

Chapter 2

Laura's head snapped up, her eyebrows arched in surprise at his question. "Trust me, Sheriff Oakes, there is no reason in the world why I would lie to you about that."

"But that doesn't mean what you're saying is true. How well did you know the woman who said she was my sister?"

"Half sister. You and she had the same mother. I've known Amy since she was ten years old."

"That long?" The more a witness talked, the more likely they were to get their story confused, if they were lying. Eric wanted this woman talking. He wanted the truth.

Rebecca started to fuss, and Laura picked her up, holding her against her shoulder, patting her back. "My mother took Amy in as a foster child when I was about twenty and going to college. I was still living at home, so I was around a lot."

Something dark and painful rose in Eric's chest. "Where was her mother?" His mother, if what she was saying was true.

"Amy was being both abused and neglected. Child Welfare removed her from her home and placed her with my mother for her own safety. It was the best thing that could have ever happened to Amy."

God, remembering what had happened to him as a kid, Eric could believe that. "Where is her mother now?"

Laura softened her voice slightly. "She died about five years ago. I'm sorry."

A muscle flexed in his jaw. "I see. You realize I can check your story, don't you?"

She made an impatient sound and plucked a baby bottle from the diaper bag. "Be my guest. The detective's business card is in the truck. And my mother would be happy to give you the name of Amy's former case worker."

Either she was telling the truth, as she knew it, or she was a damn good actress. But the whole story could still be a scam.

Eric sat down on the arm of the couch and watched while Laura slipped the bottle into Rebecca's hungry mouth. She did it with such ease, he guessed she'd done it a thousand times before. Probably. He also noted she wasn't wearing a ring, which likely meant she wasn't currently married.

"What about the twins' father? You know where he is?"

"She never gave me his name. I'm not sure if I knew who he was that I'd go looking for him. She'd gone off with him about a year ago. From what she did tell me, he was abusing her. After she got pregnant, she ran away."

"Smart woman. But if he knew about her pregnancy, he could still show up and claim his parental rights." Eric couldn't think of anything worse than losing his own children. But he couldn't imagine abusing a woman, either.

"I think it's unlikely he'll show up, whoever he is."

"If Amy knew I existed, I wished she'd tried to find me sooner. I might have been able to help." With a restraining order…or something a little more personal and persuasive.

"She didn't know about you, not until shortly before her…death." Her voice caught on the word and her chin trembled slightly as though experiencing a painful memory. "She was going through some old papers of her mother's. That's how she…we learned about you."

Amanda began twisting and turning on the couch like an eel. Almost immediately she registered her displeasure about something. Eric didn't have a clue what.

"There's another bottle in the bag," Laura said. "Mandy's has a blue top. Can you feed her?"

Panic spiked him in the chest. "Uh, sure, I guess."

He found the bottle, gave it a little shake as he had seen Laura do, then stuck it in Amanda's mouth. She started sucking eagerly.

"It would be better if you picked Mandy up and held her while you were feeding her. Cuddling is important to an infant's emotional and intellectual development."

"Right." His brow tightened into a frown. It looked so easy when Laura held and fed Rebecca. In contrast, he didn't know quite where or what to grab on to, and it irritated him that Laura sounded like a baby-care expert.

"You do this for a living?" he asked. "Taking care of babies."

"Bigger babies." She smiled slightly. "They can cry louder. I'm a high school history and government teacher."

"Oh." Adjusting his position, Eric picked up the baby, bottle and all, cradling her in his arm. She looked up at him with big blue eyes, trusting him as though he could walk on water.

God, did he dare believe these two babies were really related to him? That they were family? That he had a legitimate claim to be their father and raise them?

"What makes you so sure these records you're talking about weren't forged or something."

"Have you always been this much of a skeptic? Or is it that babies make you that nervous?"

"Come on, you waltz into my life with some crazy story about a sister I never knew I had? Wouldn't you have some doubts, too?" Less than a year ago a woman had shown up at his brother Walker's house with a baby in tow and claiming to be his new housekeeper. A totally phony story, which had worked out well in the end, he admitted. "A desperate woman looking to find a decent home for her baby can come up with a very convincing lie."

She leveled him a look that would make most men

back off in a hurry. "I personally guarantee if you don't want to raise Rebecca and Amanda for any reason at all, they will always have a good home—with me."

The intensity of her words brought him up short. This woman was not fooling around. "You want to adopt the twins?"

"With all my heart." A fine sheen of tears appeared in her eyes, but she didn't let them spill over.

"Then why did you bother to track me down? I never would have known otherwise."

"Because I promised Amy I would."

That simple truth, stated with such conviction, had more power than anything else she could have said. She wanted to be the twins' mother. She loved them. Eric was standing in her way. And still she had kept her word to a dead woman—her foster sister.

Removing the bottle from Rebecca's mouth, she lifted the baby to her shoulder again, rubbing her cheek against the infant's blond, fuzzy little head and patting her back.

Assuming the twins were related to Eric, did he have any right to take them away from a woman who so obviously loved them even if it had been their mother's wish that he raise the pair? What the hell had made her—or him—think he was qualified for the job?

Rebecca gave a very unladylike burp, and milk drooled down her chin.

"I brought along the box of records and snapshots Amy discovered. It's in the back of my truck." She laid the baby back down on the couch and wiped the dribble from her lips with the edge of the blanket. "If you'll watch the twins, I'll go get it. Some of the pictures are of you and your mother."

That news drove the air from his lungs. He had nothing of his mother except memories. Some good, some bad. All of which he had tried to repress because the very last memory was of her abandoning him.

Laura managed to get outside before her chin began to wobble again. She didn't want Eric to see how strongly his interrogation had upset her. It had taken all of her courage to come here to fulfill Amy's wishes. She didn't appreciate being treated like a common criminal. Given a choice, she'd be happy if he decided he wasn't related to the twins, didn't want them around.

But her damn conscience demanded she give him all the information she had before he made up his mind about what he wanted to do.

Sometimes being honest really stank!

Grabbing her slender briefcase from the front seat, she went around to the back of the truck and lifted the hatchback. Her suitcase, baby paraphernalia and a crib filled the back of the SUV. Tucked to one side was a shoe box from a discount store that had long since gone out of business. She took that and a small quilt, carrying them inside.

She found him gazing at the babies but couldn't quite read his expression. It was softer than when he looked at her, more relaxed with at least a trace of awe.

Please don't take my babies away from me.

He looked up at her.

"This is the box with the snapshots and Amy's birth

certificate. You'll note the similarity of your mother's name and hers."

Eric held the box in his lap unopened for longer than necessary while Laura busied herself by spreading the quilt on the floor and laying the twins down one at a time. He wasn't sure he wanted to know what was in the box. For the most part, he'd put his childhood behind him. He'd grown up. Whatever faults his mother had had, he didn't dwell on them now.

He didn't want to reopen wounds he'd spent most of his life trying to heal.

One of the babies made a singsong sound, and he realized he had to see whatever Pandora had in mind for him.

The snapshots didn't appear to be in any particular order. A young blond girl in a ponytail standing in front of a pickup truck. The twins' mother, his half sister? A younger version of her on a tricycle. He felt no recognition, no connection.

He picked up the birth certificate and examined it. Amy Maria Thorne, mother listed as Millicent Karen Thorne.

Eric swallowed the tightness in his throat. His mother must have finally found some guy to marry her. She'd been listed Millicent Karen Johnson on his birth certificate. Unmarried.

And then she'd abused and neglected her daughter—just as she had neglected and allowed a hamfisted man to abuse him.

He caught his breath at the next snapshot, he and his mother standing in front of a roller-coaster ride. He'd been maybe seven or eight at the time.

"I remember this." His voice sounded rusty, his throat was dry. "We'd gone to a county fair. It was the first time I'd ever ridden a roller coaster and some guy with a camera…"

His throat shut down entirely. He couldn't speak, and it felt like someone had tightened a band around his chest, screwing it down hard.

He stood. He had to get away from Laura. Couldn't let her see how upset he was.

With a vague wave of his hand, he fled the room.

Why had his mother abandoned him? What had he done that was so wrong?

Sitting back on her haunches, Laura watched him leave. His obvious pain had brought an ache to her own chest. From what she'd just seen and what Amy had told her, Eric's wounds were fully as deep as his sister's had been.

Smiling down at the twins, who were now chewing on each other's fingers, she silently vowed she wouldn't leave them with Eric until she made sure whatever damage his mother had done to him emotionally hadn't left him so severely scarred that he was incapable of giving the twins the love they deserved.

If she decided to leave them here at all.

When he returned, his strong, masculine features were tightly under control, and he held himself erect.

"You've convinced me," he said. "Amanda and Rebecca are my nieces. We're blood kin, and I'll give them the best home I know how."

Fear and adrenaline drove Laura to her feet. "It's not that easy. I'm not going to simply hand the girls over to you."

"Why not? That's why you tracked me down, isn't it? It's what my sister wanted, right?"

"Not exactly. First, I have to—"

The doorbell chimed, but before either of them had a chance to react, the door opened.

"Hey, Eric, are you home?" a female voice asked.

Laura's heart sank. If Eric had a woman in his life who could be a good mother to the twins—

A young woman with reddish hair swept into the room followed by an equally attractive blonde.

"Oh, look at those sweet little babies," the first one crooned, kneeling beside the quilt on the floor. "Look at their tiny pug noses. They're adorable."

Laura bristled, her protective instincts rising.

Frowning, Eric muttered, "What are you two doing here? And since when do you use the front door?"

"Since we knew you had company and we came to see the babies, of course," the blonde responded. "And to meet the woman you've been seeing on the sly." With a welcoming smile, she extended her hand to Laura. "Hi, I'm Lizzie Oakes, Eric's sister-in-law. And that's Kristi fawning all over your babies, Eric's other sister-in-law. We're both upset he's been keeping you a secret from the family."

Laura gaped at the woman before finally taking Lizzie's hand. "I think there's been some misunderstanding. Eric and I haven't been—"

"You don't have to pretend with us," Kristi said, playing peek-a-boo with Amanda. "We're certainly not ones to cast stones."

"Neither of us," Lizzie agreed. "We just want to

make sure Eric is prepared to do the right thing. A woman shouldn't have to—"

"Ladies!" Eric barked, causing both babies to twist their heads around searching for the source of that unpleasant sound. "This is Laura Cavendish, who I just met today. And those two babies, who you think are so cute, are my nieces, which is no doubt why you think they're cute. Family resemblance."

Jaws agape, both young women stared at Eric.

"What sister?" they said in unison.

"Half sister," he admitted. "Laura, who knew her when she was growing up, brought the twins here so I could meet them. I'm very grateful for that." He acknowledged her with a nod. "And it is my intention, based on my sister's wishes, to adopt the twins and be the best darn father I know how to be."

"Oh, my…" Kristi murmured.

"Well, then," Lizzie said. "Congratulations. You'll be a terrific dad."

"Excuse me, but it's not that simple," Laura told them. She'd been aware via the adoption records the detective had uncovered that Eric had two brothers. She hadn't expected to be assailed right off by two sisters-in-law, however.

"You're right," Kristi agreed, placing a kiss on Rebecca's forehead before she stood. "Among other things, I don't think Eric has a lot of experience with babies. I know he'll be grateful if you could stay here with him for a few days to help him get the hang of things. Unless you have a husband to get home to."

"No, I don't—"

"That's a terrific idea." Lizzie shot a conspiratorial look in Kristi's direction.

Eric stepped forward. "Now wait a minute—"

"You've got that extra bedroom where Laura can stay," Lizzie said. "And the room on the south side will make a wonderful nursery. Sunny and warm in the winter. The babies will love it."

"Trust me, you'll need a lot of extra help at first," Kristi added. "Why, I remember when…"

Laura's head spun as the two women pointed out the importance of having someone on hand who knew how to handle infants. They, the women insisted, didn't have time to help him out. They had their own families. Laura suspected the whole deal was a matchmaking scheme. On the other hand, she wasn't about to leave the twins in Eric's care just yet. Maybe never. In order to give him a fair chance at proving himself, she needed to give him some time with the babies. Maybe he'd hate all the inconvenience enough to forget being a father.

Driving through town, she'd noted Grass Valley didn't offer a whole lot of options for temporary housing. She hadn't considered that problem before she left home, and now she had nowhere else to stay except with him and the twins, because she sure as hell wasn't going to leave them.

"I think staying here is a fine idea," she announced.

They all turned toward her. Eric shook his head. Lizzie said, "I think it's perfect, too. Would you like us to help bring in your luggage?"

"No, I'm sure Eric will be more than happy to do that for me." She gave him her stern schoolmarm look that had been known to wither a whole gang of adolescent boys. Managing one man shouldn't be all that difficult.

Lizzie and Kristi appeared pleased they'd accomplished whatever it was they'd set out to do.

"We've got to be running along," Kristi said.

"Just wanted to welcome you to Grass Valley," Lizzie added. "Eric's a great guy, by the way."

Laura smiled weakly. The man had certainly developed a fan club among his sisters-in-law. She wondered what their spouses thought of that. And knew their views wouldn't sway her about leaving the twins with Eric if she wasn't one hundred percent convinced it was the right thing to do.

Given how much she loved the babies, it was hard to imagine she'd ever be willing to do that, despite Amy's wishes.

She swallowed hard, telling herself she didn't know enough yet about Eric to seriously consider handing over the twins' custody. His worthiness to be their father could take days to determine. Maybe even weeks.

She nearly groaned aloud. Surely it wouldn't take that long to discover some fatal crack in his paragon-of-virtue image.

He managed to escort his sisters-in-law out the door, then returned to the living room.

"I'm sorry about the misunderstanding. Those two are really great people but they do sometimes jump to conclusions."

"It's all right." She knelt and draped a light blanket over the two sleeping babies. "The fact is, you've jumped to a conclusion, too."

"What's that?"

Pulling some papers from her briefcase, she handed a copy of Amy's notarized instructions to Eric.

"Amy was abused most of her life, not just by the man who fathered the twins. The one thing she asked me to do before I relinquished the babies to you is to make sure you had a wife who could love them like a mother should."

He stared at her in disbelief, then quickly read through the papers.

"This makes you the final arbiter of whether or not I get custody."

"That's true." The attorney she and Amy had hired had carefully crafted Amy's last wishes so that the custody decision about the twins would be Laura's and hers alone.

"And she wanted me to have a wife."

"It was her very strong preference. She had good reasons to—"

"That's crazy!"

"Those were her wishes." She gestured toward the legal papers in his hand. "This is what she wanted. I intend to fulfill her request as best I can."

"Then I guess that makes it you and me against each other."

"If that's how you see it. I see it as doing what's best for the twins."

Chapter 3

"I'm going to need some sort of a changing table."

Sunshine streamed through the window of the designated nursery, but the room itself looked bare, the only furniture the crib Eric had hauled upstairs. There ought to be a border of teddy bear ballerinas dancing along the top of the walls to match the bumper pads and crib sheets Laura had chosen for the twins. An overflowing toy box would fit under the window, a pair of desks in the corner for when they got older, a two-sided easel for painting.

"Seems to me we're short one crib, too," Eric commented, checking that the crib was solidly held together. "They should each have their own."

"For now, they're all right in one. In fact, I think they like it better that way. They seem to want to cuddle as if they were in the womb. When I take them back home—"

"The way I see it, they are home. Right here."

"Yes, well…" For a man who'd only lately learned about the twins, he had certainly developed a possessive streak. Or maybe he was challenging her because he was innately competitive. Given the number of rodeo trophies on the mantel downstairs, he wasn't one to give up easily. "That's yet to be determined, isn't it?"

"A court might decide my claim has more merit than yours, given my relationship with the twins."

"You're welcome to consult with an attorney." She and Amy had already done that. In general, the mother's wishes would prevail.

"I think I'll do that tomorrow. Assuming you don't mind staying with the babies while I drive into Great Falls and back."

"If you're planning to raise the twins, you'd better get used to having to take them with you wherever you go."

His brows slammed down into a straight line, narrowing his eyes. "Now you're telling me I'll be disqualified as a father if I use a baby-sitter?"

Laura was sure Eric knew how to smile, but she had yet to see him accomplish the maneuver. But then, her comment had been unreasonable. "Point taken. I'll stay with the twins while you check with your attorney."

Before her accident, Laura had had adolescent dreams of someday finding a man as protective of her as Eric appeared to be of the twins. But as she'd grown older and finally fallen in love, she'd learned the truth. She was damaged goods, a woman no man would want to marry. She couldn't bear his children.

She swallowed back the bitter memory. A man as macho as Sheriff Oakes would demand nothing less than perfection.

"Come to think of it," Eric said, "who watches the twins when you're at work?"

She cut him a sharp look. Fair was fair, she supposed, and he had a right to know what arrangements she'd made for the twins. "My mother will baby-sit the twins during the school year. She lives only a mile from me and adores Mandy and Becky. She loved Amy like her own, and she's always wanted grandchildren but knew, since my accident—"

"Does that mean in order to get custody I have to come up with a loving grandmother, too, as well as a wife?"

"Well, no, I'd never require that of you." Although Laura's mother would be heartbroken to lose the only grandchildren she was likely to have.

He nodded, but his expression didn't soften much. "Now, you were saying you needed something?"

She forced her thoughts back to practicalities. "A changing table. If you've got a card table or something like that I can use, it will do temporarily."

"I haven't done much decorating of the place, it didn't seem important." Until now, he realized. What did a bachelor need with eight rooms filled with furniture? He only used three or four of the rooms himself. But if this was going to be the twins' home, they needed the right equipment. "Come on, we're going shopping."

"For what?"

"I saw some oak chests of drawers at the general store. Handmade by an old guy east of town. There ought to be one that's the right size. You can help me pick it out. We can put their clothes and stuff inside." He headed for the hallway. He could get another crib, too. At least order one from the catalogs Hetty Moore kept around. And he remembered Susie-Q, Lizzie's little girl, had a jumping swing thing. He'd need two of—

"Eric, the babies are about to wake up. They'll be hungry and need their bottles."

"Oh. Well, okay." So he needed to learn their schedules. No big deal. "We'll feed them and then we'll go."

"What time does the store close?"

He checked his watch. "Six o'clock. It's four now."

"That should give us barely enough time—if the store doesn't have a big selection and you don't linger over your decision."

His jaw went slack. It took that long to get the twins ready to roll? Lord, when he got up in the morning, he shaved, showered, ate breakfast and was on the road in under thirty minutes. How much longer could it take to get two itty-bitty babies organized for a trip of less than a half mile?

It was like preparing for an African safari.

There was a diaper bag, extra bottles, a plastic baggie of pacifiers in case the twins began to fuss. Then Laura had insisted that the infant car seats, which only an hour ago he'd taken into the house, had to be transferred to his vehicle. She was right, of course, that the babies' safety was all-important but the seat belts had tangled. Sorting out the mess had taken Eric a full twenty minutes. She'd suggested, with mock sweetness, that they could take her SUV, which had the seat belts already adjusted to the proper length.

Not a chance! They were *his* kids now.

Still, he had to give her credit. While he had battled frustration, she had remained calm. Cuddling the twins and cooing at them. Checking on his workmanship to be sure the babies would be as safe as possible.

A child could do worse than have her as a mother.

Which didn't mean Eric was going to concede the twins' custody to her, not by a long shot. Blood counted.

By the time they all piled into the police cruiser, a black-and-white SUV with a light bar on top—which he'd been forced to drive because his personal vehicle was a pickup truck that didn't have a place for the twins—Eric was exhausted. He suspected Laura was, too. But she was so tight-lipped, he was afraid to comment.

Hell, they would have been better off to carry the babies down the street to the general store. But then, how would they have gotten a chest of drawers back home if he hadn't driven the SUV?

Not that there was much time left before the store closed to do their shopping by the time they got there.

Laura adjusted Amanda in a cuddly sling across her chest. She had yet to find a sling to handle both babies at once, so Eric carried Rebecca into the general store.

A cheery chime greeted their arrival as he pushed open the door and held it for Laura.

An amazing array of products, from wilted produce to bathroom faucets, cluttered the narrow aisles. Aging Christmas items were still on display on the higher shelves, two-foot-tall aluminum trees, dusty Styrofoam snowmen in jaunty hats and a plastic crèche missing its wise men.

Idly Laura wondered how many years the decorations had been waiting for a frantic last-minute shopper to succumb to desperation.

From the back of the store, a woman appeared. She wore a blue butcher's apron over a print dress and had one of those faces that was best described as having character. Laura guessed a line had been etched for each of the seventy-something years she had lived in Montana.

"Afternoon, Eric. Bet you've run out of frozen dinners again and don't want to eat at—" Her eye caught the baby in his arms, and she halted abruptly. "My sakes, look at what you've got. Isn't she the cutest little thing."

Laura winced as the woman chucked Rebecca under the chin. She'd been told by the doctor that the twins' immune system might not be as strong as those of a higher birth-weight baby, and she hated to take the twins around strangers.

"Excuse me," Laura said. "The babies are—"

"Hetty, I'd like you to meet Laura Cavendish. Hetty Moore and her husband, Joe, own the store."

Laura smiled politely, but before she could prevent it, Hetty had zeroed in on Mandy's rosy cheek, giving the baby a grandmotherly pinch.

"Twins…" she crooned. "You've been keeping secrets from us, Eric. Shame on you. These little bundles are too precious to hide. And their mamma, too. Such a pretty girl."

"I didn't know about them till yesterday, Hetty."

"He's their uncle," Laura tried to explain.

Hetty's eyes widened and she gasped. "You mean Walker has been—surely not Rory. Why, they're only just married, the both of them. I can't think what gets into a man's head these days. My Joe and me—"

"Hetty! It's not what you think. This has nothing to do with my brothers."

She huffed. "I should hope not."

Eric rolled his eyes, and Laura stifled a smile. The good folks of Grass Valley had a tendency to jump to conclusions. Explaining the situation would likely take hours, and there wasn't that much time before the store closed.

"Eric was hoping to buy a small chest of drawers to put the twins' things in," Laura said.

"With two new babies to manage, you'll be needing a lot more than one chest of drawers." On a mission now, Hetty bustled down the aisle toward the back of the store.

"They may not be staying that long," Laura called, hurrying after her.

"Now, honey, you don't have to play coy with me, giving me some wild story about young Eric being the twins' uncle. If he's their daddy, you have to give him a chance to make up for whatever he did that upset you. I'm sure you two can work out your differences."

"We might as well give it up for now," Eric muttered only loud enough for Laura to hear. "Once Hetty gets something in her head, it sticks there like Super Glue, even if it's wrong."

"I don't want people to think you and I—"

"They won't. Not for long."

Just what did that mean? Was he going to take out an ad in the local paper, assuming there was one, to explain the situation? Or was it simply too obvious the handsome town sheriff wouldn't be caught dead with someone like her? Not that she was a dog. But she certainly wasn't model thin. Nor had she ever been considered sexy. Men had never fallen all over themselves to ask her out. And the few who had soon lost interest, either because she knew more about history and government than they did, or because she couldn't give birth to the offspring their egos demanded a woman produce.

"Now here's a nice one." Hetty scooped a display of American flags and red, white and blue bunting off the top of a five-foot high honey-oak chest of drawers. "Conrad Gelb's a true craftsman. I'm sure he'd make up another one just like this if—"

"It's too tall," Laura said. "I'm going to use it for a changing table while I'm here."

"He could make you one of those, too, if you want."

"We aren't a hundred percent sure the babies will be staying—"

"I'm sure." Juggling Rebecca in one arm, Eric lifted the edge of a dust cover from a similar oak piece that was about waist high and had three drawers. "How about this one?"

Laura nodded. "That would work fine."

"Won't hold but a teaspoon's worth of baby clothes," Hetty warned.

"We'll take it." Eric glanced around the store. "How 'bout those swing things babies like?"

To Laura's dismay, and frequently over her objections, Eric went on a shopping spree that would have made most women envious. It made Laura uneasy. She didn't like the thought of anyone wasting money. And she didn't like the idea that Eric was so determined to provide everything possible the twins could want or need. In the long run, that attitude wouldn't be healthy for the twins.

Short term, it would make it all the harder to put the babies back in her car and take them away from Eric.

Finally running out of steam, Eric handed Rebecca off to Hetty, who cuddled, cooed and happily pinched the baby's cheeks.

Joe Moore, Hetty's big, burly husband, who looked nothing like a storekeeper, was called from the back room to help carry the purchases out to the car.

Laura had the distinct feeling she and the babies had been dropped into the middle of a fast-moving stream at flood stage and were being carried along by the current. A helpless feeling and inherently dangerous.

Eric placed the oversize teddy bear near the crib, fluffed its polka-dot bow and stepped back to admire his work. He'd brought everything up from the car. The low chest of drawers was in place across from the windows. The wind-up, jumping-rocking swing was at the closet end of the room right next to an oak rocking chair. Hetty had told him all moms needed a rocking chair.

A dad would, too, he reasoned, smiling. Yep, he'd done all right for his first day as a father.

The cry of a baby preceded Laura's arrival in the nursery, one of the twins in her arms. He couldn't tell them apart yet but he would soon enough.

She handed him the baby. "Mandy needs a change."

"You want me to do it?"

"It comes with the territory, Sheriff. Spending money does not a father make."

"I know that," he mumbled. "It's just that I haven't ever—"

"Changed a diaper. I suspected as much. It's time for your first lesson."

"Maybe I ought to watch first."

"Hands-on is the best way to learn, and Becky dozed off after her bottle, so this is a good time. Unless you'd like to wait until they're both fussing."

"You have a vindictive streak, don't you?" He carried Mandy to the dresser and laid her on the thick pad he'd bought for this very purpose. He should have known Laura would make him initiate the darn thing.

Laura's smile was all too smug. "Possibly."

Almost immediately, Mandy began to fuss and kick her little legs.

"Hold still, Twinkle-Toes." He managed to un-snap the legs on the pink-and-white sleeper but had trouble getting the toes unhooked. "Hey, Sweet Cheeks, how 'bout a little cooperation for your old man?"

Mandy's crying increased in volume.

Eric began to sweat. "Feel free to help out anytime you feel like it."

"You're doing fine."

Like hell! A little more struggling and he got one foot out. The second came easier. He gave Laura a grim smile of accomplishment. "Now what?"

"Take the old diaper off, use a wipe and put on some lotion so she doesn't get a rash."

It all sounded so easy the way she rattled off the instructions.

By bending Mandy's legs over the top of her head, he got the old diaper off. He needed a third hand to reach the new diaper, and by the time he got that more or less in place, he realized he hadn't done the wipe and lotion part. So he started again.

By now Mandy was pretty frantic, little sobs lifting her chest.

He opened the diaper, did a swipe, spread the lotion, reconnected the sides to the front with the sticky tabs and lifted Mandy, smooching her on the forehead, quieting her immediately.

He exhaled in relief, giving Laura a triumphant smile. And the diaper slipped down around Mandy's ankles.

Laura's stern, disapproving expression cracked. He'd thought of her eyes as an ordinary shade of pale blue, and they suddenly sparkled with amusement— at his expense—and he decided they held an amazing depth. Her smile was like a sunrise after a stormy night when the dark clouds had finally lifted. Her laughter reminded him of a lyrical songbird, light and airy. The uncanny transformation flustered and bewildered him. Beneath her tough-as-nails, I'm-the-teacher exterior lurked an entirely different woman.

A woman a man might have trouble resisting—if she were interested.

"I'm sorry." She covered her mouth to silence her laughter, and he was sorry she'd hidden her beautiful smile. "It's just that you looked so—"

"Ridiculous. I know."

"No." Her gaze softened. "Endearing. You were trying so hard, and then—"

"Yeah. I sort of made a mess of things." Except now Mandy had her head buried against his neck, sucking on his collar, and seemed as contented as a baby could be. That part felt good.

"Perhaps we should start again and begin with me showing you the basics."

He met her gaze, nodding. "Starting again sounds like a great idea." He didn't limit his thoughts to simply starting over with basic baby-care lessons.

She should have paid closer attention to Hetty's comment about Eric eating frozen dinners.

Laura gazed into the refrigerator at the meager contents. A gallon of milk, a six-pack of beer, some eggs, two apples—one of which was already half rotten—and an assortment of condiments.

"I'm not much of a cook," he admitted. "Most of the time I grab a burger and fries over at the saloon. Or stick something in the microwave."

She opened the freezer and found the selection pretty much limited to pot pies and lasagna. "You might want to consider adding fresh vegetables to your diet."

One side of his lips kicked up into a half grin. "Guess I'll have to be a good example to the twins, huh?"

Now that he'd stopped glaring at her all the time, he looked less formidable. Which didn't make him any less dangerous. More so, since he was so set on being a good father.

"I'll treat you to chicken pot pies tonight," he said.

"Tomorrow I'll pick up some fresh stuff when I'm in Great Falls. Hetty doesn't have a real good selection."

"I noticed."

While Eric started dinner, Laura surveyed the spacious kitchen. The twins were in their car seats in the middle of a long oak picnic-style table with benches, probably crafted by the same man who had made the chest of drawers upstairs. The cabinets were a darker wood and needed a face-lift as did the tile counters. But there was a big window over the sink that faced west. It was dark now but Laura suspected it would provide a view of some spectacular sunsets.

"How long have you been sheriff?" she asked Eric while she tickled Rebecca's tummy with one finger. Her reward was a wide, gummy smile.

"About five years. Before that I was on the rodeo circuit."

"I noticed the trophies." How could she not when they were on such prominent display?

"I had some Best-All-Around years until I took one too many headers off a bronc named Lucifer. I broke my leg in three places. Now I've got a couple of pins that set off security alarms in airports." Still in his uniform, he stood with his back to the counter, one booted ankle crossed over the other, looking very much at ease. "I had to stay off my feet for six months, so I moved back to the Double O Ranch. About the time I was mobile again the former sheriff announced his retirement. I decided settling down was a good idea."

"But not on the ranch?"

"Walker enjoys punching cows a lot more than I ever did, and he's a good manager. Rory and I still have an interest in the place, though, and help out during roundups, that sort of thing."

"I gather no woman wanted to settle down with you?"

His eyes immediately narrowed, and Laura regretted she'd asked such a personal question. It wasn't that she was prying, exactly. Knowing something of Eric's past, including his recent history, would help her decide if he was suitable to be the twins' father.

"I've never met a woman I wanted to ask." He held her gaze, the microwave humming its monotonous note behind him. "How about you? Have you ever been married?"

She swallowed hard and turned back to the twins. Mandy had spit out her pacifier; Laura plugged it back in. "I came close once. It didn't work out."

"What went wrong?" His voice was a little softer than it had been. Intimate.

Her past was none of his business, except maybe he'd understand better why she was so reluctant to turn over the twins to a stranger. Why she wanted to be their mother.

"He wanted to have a son to carry on the family name." Lifting her head, she looked at him levelly despite the painful knot in her stomach. "I can't have children. I was in an accident and they had to remove my uterus."

His mouth went a little slack. "I'm sorry."

"No more than I am." She forced a shrug she hoped looked casual. "The worst is, they left the rest of my female parts, so I get the joy of PMS without any of the benefits."

The buzzer on the microwave saved him from responding to her revelation. Just as well. Laura didn't want his sympathy.

She wanted a reason, even a small one, to salve her conscience so she could reject him as a suitable father for the twins and raise them herself. After meeting Eric, that had to be the most selfish thing she'd ever wanted in her life.

Dinner didn't go well.

Laura explained to Eric the uncanny knack the twins had for turning fussy the moment anyone sat down to eat a quiet meal. Eric found himself cradling Becky in the crook of his left arm while trying to fork a bite or two of pot pie into his mouth without dribbling the hot gravy on the baby. Not an easy task.

She couldn't have babies of her own. No wonder she was so damn anxious to keep the twins for herself. As much as he might sympathize, that didn't mean he had to hand them over to her. His sister had wanted him to raise her babies. It made sense that they'd live with a blood relative.

As a kid in foster care, Eric had spent hours fantasizing about an uncle or aunt or grandparent who'd show up and give him the home he'd dreamed of having. His *own* family. But nobody came.

He wasn't going to let that happen to Mandy and Becky. It didn't matter how much Laura loved or wanted to raise them. Or that she'd been Amy's *foster* sister.

She wasn't *real* family.

By the time they'd finished eating, the babies

were ready for another bottle. That was followed by a change of diapers and clean sleepers. Tomorrow, Laura warned, she'd give him a lesson in bathing the babies. It was too late now.

"Do you want to do the next feeding on your own?" she asked as she placed Mandy in the crib next to Rebecca. Magically, the pair gravitated toward each other.

"What time does that happen?"

"Usually between one and two. Then they wake again around five."

"How are we supposed to get any sleep?"

She gave him a wry smile that said sleep wasn't a part of the deal.

"I'll handle both feedings," he said generously. "You've been up since early morning." Of course, he hadn't been out to feed his horses yet this evening, and there were still dinner dishes to do. But there weren't many and they could wait until morning. He'd put them in the sink to soak. No big deal.

She arched her brows. "If you're sure."

"I'll have to manage sooner or later. I might as well start now. I'll call you if I run into trouble."

With a shake of her head, Laura told him good-night and headed toward the guest room. He was the most determined man she'd ever met. She suspected, however, it was a case of a fool rushing in when an experienced person would be more wary. Granted, he'd pretty well gotten the hang of changing diapers and could fix a bottle, but in the middle of the night his new skills might not come all that automatically.

The spare bedroom looked as though it had once

belonged to a teenage girl, the white antique furniture and twin bed with a pink flounce likely left behind by the prior owners. It smelled musty, and she opened the window to let in some fresh air. The scent of sage and lush summer grass wafted in the window.

The faint glow of starlight shadowed the rolling landscape and outlined the nearby barn and corral. Unlike her home in Helena, where there was always the sound of neighbors coming or going and the hum of traffic on the boulevard, here silence enveloped the night. It pressed in on her ear drums, sending a message of loneliness that was more easily ignored when drowned out by the presence of others.

The sound of the back door opening broke the quiet, and she caught sight of Eric striding toward the barn. The horses in the corral whickered a soft greeting, moving in the same direction. No matter how tired he might be, caring for his animals came before his own comfort.

She pressed her lips together. Given a chance, he'd do the same for the twins.

Turning away from the window, she opened her suitcase and pulled out her cotton nightgown. She'd been busy all day and was too weary to unpack now. When she'd left home, she had hoped she wouldn't be staying long in Grass Valley, wouldn't need to settle in.

In the face of Eric's determination to be a father, that goal seemed less attainable now.

The next day or two—or maybe one sleepless night up with crying infants—would tell the tale of his resolve.

She'd hope for the best—or perhaps it was the worst she was looking for in the twins' sleeping habits.

Eric went to sleep making plans to hang an old tire as a swing from the cottonwood tree out front when the twins were old enough.

He woke to the wailing sound of the smoke alarm.

He was on his feet, pulling on his pants, before he realized it was the twins crying. How could two tiny sets of lungs make that much noise?

Shaking the fuzziness from his head, he stumbled out of the bedroom into the hallway. He met Laura at the door to the nursery.

"I've got 'em," he mumbled, his voice thick with sleep.

"Becky's been crying for five minutes. She woke up Mandy."

"Sorry. I didn't hear 'em." How could Laura tell which one was crying, for Pete's sake? It just sounded like a racket to him.

They both bent over the crib, each one picking up a baby, which quieted the infants only briefly. Eric followed Laura downstairs, where she retrieved two bottles from the refrigerator, where she'd had him place them earlier, and popped them into the microwave. Jiggling the baby in his arms, he stared stupidly at the glow of the oven until it buzzed.

They each took a bottle and sat down next to each other on the bench at the kitchen table. A moment later the screams were replaced by the sound of eager little sucking noises, not unlike a newborn calf discovering his source of sustenance for the first time.

Eric sighed in relief.

"After a while you get tuned in to their cries and wake up at the first peep. It's better not to let them get too upset."

He grunted noncommittally. That kind of adjustment might take more than a day or two.

Gazing at nothing in particular, his eyes finally focused on Laura's feet. Her *bare* feet. Long, slender toes tipped by polish in a rainbow of bright colors, each toenail a different hue.

He grinned, awake now. "Nice toenail polish."

"Huh? Oh." She folded one foot over the other like a shy little girl. "My neighbors have a nine-year-old daughter who wanted to try out her new fingernail polishing kit."

"And you volunteered?"

"Something like that."

He let his gaze wander higher, surveying the modest nightgown she wore buttoned securely at her throat. He had the oddest urge to slowly undo the gown one button at a time to discover what other surprises were hidden behind her prim exterior.

He'd never had a woman stay overnight in his house. It had never seemed to be the right time. The right woman.

Having Laura here was definitely going to challenge his view of what was "right"…and what was wrong for both him and her.

Chapter 4

Frustration had Eric clenching his teeth by the time he finished his meeting with the attorney the next day. He called his brothers and asked them to meet him at the ranch. Maybe they could help him figure out how to get over or around the custody plan for the twins.

The heart of the Double O had always been the office Oliver Oakes had used. That was the place where he'd designed successful breeding programs, determined how many head of beef cattle had to be culled in the fall so the herd would survive until spring with the available feed…and where his adopted sons were called onto the carpet for their misdeeds.

Walker sat behind the heavy oak desk now, reading Amy Thorne's instructions regarding the future of her children. Rory lounged in the leather chair in the corner, contemplating the problem while Eric paced.

Walker set the papers aside. "That's crazy."

"My thought exactly," Eric said. "Unfortunately, the attorney says it will probably stand up in court. I could appeal, but the twins would be going to their first prom before any higher court heard the case. Meanwhile, Laura would be raising them." He didn't have to explain why the twins were important to him. He and his brothers had all dreamed of having their own families. For Walker and Rory that dream was coming true.

Not so for Eric.

Leaning forward and linking his hands between his knees, Rory said, "I don't suppose it would be a good idea to put a price on Laura's head and let my Indian brothers know about it."

Walker shot Rory a quelling look. "Not funny, Bird Brain," he said, using the nickname he and Eric had chosen for Rory following his Blackfeet naming ceremony when he'd become Swift Eagle. They had decided it was far too classy sounding for their troublesome brother. "Among other things, Lizzie tells me Laura is a nice lady. Very attractive."

"She is," Eric agreed.

"I don't get why she's so damned anxious to raise somebody else's kids, though," Rory commented.

"She has her reasons." Eric didn't feel any need to reveal Laura's personal problems. That was her own private business.

"I've got a gaggle of kids Lizzie and I are raising who weren't born to us," Walker pointed out. "Children have a way of getting under your skin when you're not watching."

At this point, Walker and his wife of a year were

raising six children, four of them teenage boys plus one preschooler and a toddler. Eric expected someday soon they'd get around to having a baby of their own and expand their family again.

He sat on the edge of Walker's desk. "The point is, I want to be a father to Amanda and Rebecca. Raise them. But I don't see how I'm going to do that unless I can magically pull a wife out of a hat somewhere."

His brothers were quiet for a moment, then Rory said, "You aren't bad-looking for a white-eyes. There've got to be a lot of women who'd be willing to marry you."

"Thanks for your vote of confidence," he muttered.

"How much time is Laura Cavendish giving you to come up with a wife?" Walker asked.

Eric shrugged, feeling defeated. "We haven't talked about a deadline."

"Well, that's the answer, then." Rory shoved back from his desk and stood. "While you're learning to be a daddy, Rory and I will help you find a wife."

"We will?" Rory asked.

"Sure. It shouldn't be too hard. Like you say, he's not bad-looking and there are a lot of girls out there wanting to tie the knot. Most of 'em even like babies."

"Now wait a minute," Eric protested. "I don't want to end up with just any woman. I'd like a choice, okay?"

"It all depends on how much you want custody of those babies. If you can drag out your training time and keep Laura around long enough, Rory and I will get you all the candidates you can handle."

"I don't know…"

Walker tucked his fingertips in his hip pockets. "I don't see you have much of a choice, bro. You've got to give it a shot."

* * *

He'd remembered to stop at the grocery store.

Laura watched through the window as he unloaded a couple of sacks from his pickup truck. Knowing what his attorney in Great Falls had no doubt told him, she was surprised he had bothered. But then, she'd already discovered Eric Oakes was a responsible man.

Sighing, she considered how unfortunate it was that Amy and Eric's mother hadn't had the same attribute. Then the siblings might have been raised in an intact family. Which is exactly what Amy had desperately wanted for her babies.

Laura knew she could give them stability, if not a two-parent family. So could Eric, she supposed. But Amy had been leery of all men. She'd never found one she could trust.

Except for her father, neither had Laura. Not when it came down to the nitty-gritty.

Swallowing the familiar sense of grief tinged with guilt for her part in her father's heart attack, she opened the back door and held it for Eric. "Hope you got lots of salad makings."

"Lettuce, tomatoes, cucumbers, onions, baby carrots, croutons, the works, plus enough squash for a night or two. I didn't know what kind of dressing you'd like, so I picked out a couple." He set the sacks on the kitchen table. "Got some fruit, too. Mostly apples and oranges. The apricots looked too green."

She was impressed. Not many men could shop like that, particularly without a list to go by. "Sounds good to me."

"There's some chicken and ground beef, a couple of steaks."

"Wonderful."

He began to pull things out of the bag and stuff them in the refrigerator. She'd have to wash the produce later. For now she'd be happy with the prospect of a balanced diet.

"Did you talk to your attorney?" she asked.

"I did." He put two packages of ground meat in the freezer on top of a frozen lasagna. She noted the meat had been packed in a thermal sack to keep it cold for the trip home.

Laura waited for his concession of defeat. Amy's wishes would prevail in a court of law. The family friend and attorney she'd hired, Bill Williams, had assured Laura there would be no way to challenge Amy's assignment of the twins' guardianship to her. Eric put everything away, folded the sacks and crammed them in with a dozen others under the sink before he turned toward her.

"I agree to Amy's terms."

She blinked, not quite understanding his words. "Her terms?"

Taking his usual pose, he leaned back against the counter and crossed his arms. "Amy wanted me to adopt and raise the twins but only if I had a wife who could be a good mother to them. Right?"

An uncomfortable feeling crept down Laura's spine and she straightened. "That's correct."

"Then I agree to those terms. I'll get married."

She had to swallow a gasp, of surprise or dismay, she wasn't sure which. "You have a woman—"

"I'll find one."

"You think it will be that easy?"

"My brothers are going to help me."

"They're going to help you find a wife?" She gasped. What kind of a crazy scheme had they cooked up? An Internet dating service? A wife-in-name-only until Laura was out of the picture?

"How much time will you allow me to comply with Amy's wishes?"

"Well, I can't—" She faltered. She had come here hoping to find Eric didn't want the babies at all. Or that he was immediately unsuitable. Not for a minute had she expected him to race out and find a wife simply to gain custody of the babies. *Her* babies! "I don't know. I've applied for a curriculum coordinator's job. I expect to hear in a week or two." The job would give her more flexibility than classroom teaching and wouldn't pose the problem of hiring a substitute if she had to stay home with the twins. It would also offer a new set of challenges, creating ways to entice young people to care enough about history so they might not want their country to repeat the mistakes of the past.

"Then I'll find a wife in that amount of time."

"You can't! It would be impossible to—"

"Nothing is impossible if you want it enough."

The way he looked at her, the intensity in his pale-blue eyes, told her he believed just that. Within two weeks he was going to find a wife; one she would find suitable as the mother of the twins. The thought was crazy, entirely irrational.

An irritating voice in her head suggested he was capable of doing anything he set out to do. He was *that* determined.

"I could take the twins back home and let you call me when you found someone."

"*This* is their home, and you believe in fair play. You'll stay."

She licked her lips. Damn him! She did believe in fair play, but she should be able to overcome that dubious personality trait when she loved and wanted the twins so much.

Slowly she nodded. "Until I have to get back to Helena for the new job." Assuming the superintendent picked her. "Then all bets are off."

The grim set of his jaw said that was one bet he intended to win.

Eric's chin dropped to his chest and he jerked himself awake. Three nights of sleep depravation was not a good thing.

He glanced longingly at the hard cot in the jail cell behind him. If he lay down now, he'd conk out until tomorrow morning. He'd never get his month-end paperwork done, and he'd give Laura more ammunition to prove he wasn't a suitable father.

How did single dads manage on their own?

Rubbing his eyes, he stood and walked to the window. The street was pretty quiet. Abe Miller at the garage was pumping gas into Karl Huhn's old station wagon. Down the street, John Jones's pickup was parked in front of the saloon along with a couple of cars he didn't recognize. Out-of-towners, he guessed.

Since the day was pretty well shot, anyway, he decided to go home and start again on the monthly reports tomorrow. If anyone needed him, the office phone rang in the house and he always had his pager turned on.

Locking up, he got into the cruiser to drive the short distance to his house. As a precaution he kept the vehicle secured in his own garage at night, handy if he needed it and not an easy target for kids who had mischief on their minds.

He slipped into the house through the back door, where the scent of cinnamon and apples caught him off guard. A freshly baked pie sat on the counter. Homemade, by the looks of it.

His mouth watering, he went in search of Laura. He found her in the living room.

The twins were asleep on a blanket she'd spread on the floor near the window, a collection of rattles and stuffed animals spread around them. Laura was curled beside the babies, her slender form providing a protective arch as she slept on her side with her head on her outstretched arm.

The length of her delicate neck was exposed in sensual invitation as her hair fell forward. The curve of her hips pulled her jeans snugly across her nicely rounded bottom, a perfect spot for a man to rest his hand and gently flex his fingers. Her brightly painted toenails winked at him with a hint of both humor and passion.

The juxtaposition of a sexy woman in a thoroughly maternal pose plucked at something equally masculine in Eric. A reaction he tried to ignore and failed.

Sitting down on the arm of the couch, he purposefully switched his attention to the babies. They lay on their backs, arms and legs splayed in a relaxed pose, their tiny hands just touching. Two little Cupid's bow mouths worked wordlessly as though they were both dreaming of the perfect bottle.

Hey, kids, I'd like to be your dad. Whadaya think?

The enormity of becoming an instant father weighed down on him. What if he messed up? A thousand things could go wrong when you raised children. Particularly a single man with two little girls.

Maybe Amy had been right to insist he have a wife. Except, his brothers had yet to produce even one candidate. But that didn't mean he'd easily give up on being a dad.

Laura stirred, stretched and blinked her eyes open. She rolled onto her back and started when she saw him.

Eric touched his finger to his lips.

"You're home early." Pushing up to a sitting position, she shook her arm and rubbed at it as though it had gone to sleep.

"I was so tired I wasn't getting any work done at the office."

"The nighttime feedings can really get to you."

"How have you been managing for three months?" For him, it had only been three days. He couldn't imagine being this exhausted for that long.

"Coffee. Black. Gallons of it. And I did take a leave of absence from teaching. Naps are good."

Even so, she was one strong lady. Maybe nature gave women a maternal gene that let them survive for months at a time with little or no sleep. Next time he'd stand in that line, too.

"You baked a pie," he commented. "Smelled good when I came in."

She levered herself up to sit on the edge of the

couch. "The twins and I went to visit Hetty this morning. She had some apples on sale. Couldn't pass them up. Besides, I like to bake."

"That's a nice coincidence because I like to eat home-baked pies. Home-baked anything, for that matter."

"I thought you might."

They shared a companionable smile that went a little deeper than friendship and held no trace of the battle they were waging for custody of the twins.

His gaze shifted to the sleeping babies. "What was my sister like?"

She hesitated, her attention following his to the infants. "She was almost painfully shy when she came to us. Afraid of what was happening, afraid she'd be sent back where she came from, I suppose."

He remained silent, hating that his mother had treated his sister so poorly. Hating that he hadn't been there to help Amy.

"I think Amy warmed up to me sooner than to my mother," Laura said. "She used to love fussing with my makeup. Sometimes I'd do her hair up on top of her head, princess-style. We'd all go to movies together. She liked that."

"She was lucky she found a good home." Just as he'd finally landed with Oliver Oakes.

"I was getting older and my mother needed someone to mother. Amy gave her that opportunity."

"Was she smart? You know, a good student?"

"She was smarter than her grades reflected, I suspect. Her favorite class in high school was choir. She was a lovely, clear soprano. Not a big voice, but she did get to sing a couple of solos. She was thrilled—and terrified."

He chuckled. "That must not be genetic. Growing up, if I sang in the shower, my devoted brothers turned off the hot water to get me out of there."

She looked at him, surprised. "You have a very nice speaking voice. I would have thought—"

The shrill sound of the phone ringing shattered the moment. Eric bolted toward the kitchen in the hope he'd get there before the jarring noise woke the babies.

Laura fell to her knees as Rebecca's eyes flew open. So did her mouth. Laura stuck a pacifier in. The twins had only been sleeping for a half hour or so. If they woke up now, they'd be even fussier than usual during dinner. And Becky had an uncanny way of insisting if she was going to be awake and miserable, her sister should be, too.

Laura rubbed the baby's tummy, watching in relief as Becky's eyes fluttered closed again.

In the background, she could hear Eric talking on the phone. When she'd awakened and rolled over, finding Eric staring down at her and the twins, her heart had lodged in her throat. There'd been a softness in his gaze that had both startled her and sent a low, curling heat through her midsection.

She rarely experienced a sensation like that. In recent years, since her breakup with Gary Swanson, she'd avoided any thought of wanting a man. She didn't want to be hurt again. Couldn't bear the possibility of a man telling her she was damaged goods.

But Eric had sneaked up on her when her guard was down. And he did have the nicest baritone voice that could lull a woman into thinking about things she shouldn't.

Living together carried with it a false sense of intimacy, particularly the late-night feedings they shared, the house quiet, Eric bare-chested. Her imagination far too active.

She was trying—no doubt foolishly—to give him a chance to prove he was a fit father for the twins. She couldn't confuse their unusual situation with anything resembling a personal relationship. They were still vying for opposite goals. Her own personal reactions were irrelevant under the current conditions.

He returned to the living room, walking softly. He spoke the same way.

"That was Kristi on the phone. She and Lizzie want to throw us a baby shower on Sunday, after church. The congregation will put together a pot-luck."

"Are you sure you want to involve that many people? When I take the twins back to Helena—"

"I'm going to find a wife, remember?"

"Are there prospects at church?"

"Maybe," he said grimly. "If nothing else, there are a whole lot of folks in this town who'll help me out with the twins if I need them."

Laura suspected that was true. But it wasn't the same as having two parents.

The phone rang again, and she grimaced as Mandy woke this time. The nap was pretty much over, she guessed.

A minute later she had Mandy in her lap when Eric reappeared.

"We've got some vandals knocking over mail boxes out on Settlers Road. I've got to go check it out."

"When do you think you'll be back?"

He shrugged noncommittally. "I don't know. Save some pie for me."

"I will." She remembered her father being called back to work to handle a crisis or having to work overtime. He'd been a city cop, but the job was the same. You went when you were called.

Which was another reason Eric wouldn't be a good choice as a parent if he didn't have a wife. With his unpredictable schedule, he'd have to hire full-time, live-in help to care for the twins. He couldn't rely solely on his friends and relatives. And child-care workers were notoriously unreliable, often changing jobs or moving away on a whim. The twins would be in the hands of a continually changing series of housekeepers or nannies.

That wasn't what Amy had wanted for her children. No matter how wonderful Eric was with the babies, what a great father he might be, Laura could never approve an arrangement like that.

A half hour later, the twins were in full-throated complaint when the doorbell rang. With Becky taking her turn in the portable swing, Laura carried Mandy to the door. The movement caused Mandy to burp, sending a rivulet of milky spit-up down Laura's shirt. She wiped at it halfheartedly and opened the door.

A perky young blonde in low-riding, skin-tight jeans, a tank top that left her stud-pierced belly button bare and a Stetson with a rhinestone band stood on the porch. "Hi, is Eric around?" she chirped.

"He got called out to investigate some vandalism."

"Oh, well, you know, Rory sent me." She made it

sound like a secret password to get into a Depression-era speakeasy. "I'm Crystal, Crystal Lereaux—with an *x,* you know—but everybody calls me Crystal."

"Is there something I can do for you, Crystal?"

The girl looked past her into the house. "Well, like, is he going to be gone long?"

"He wasn't sure."

"Well, like, I mean, maybe I can wait for him?"

By now, Mandy was quiet but Becky was fussing again, so Laura opened the door wider. "Come in, please. As you can see, I'm a little harried at the moment."

"Sure. Whatever."

She walked in, and Laura had to wonder how anyone could walk and wiggle their butt in quite that way. She must not have bones in the same places Laura did.

"You're a friend of Rory's?" Laura managed to switch the twins so Mandy was in the swing, Becky in her arms and quiet again.

"Sort of, you know. I mean, I've seen him around the rodeo sometimes."

Her *you know*s set Laura's teeth on edge. Not that the students in her classes didn't speak the same way. But it wasn't one of their most endearing traits, from Laura's perspective. "Rory wanted you to see Eric?"

"Yeah, like he said Eric was a cool dude, a champion bronc rider and was thinking of getting married."

Laura drew in a sharp breath just as Crystal noticed the trophies on the mantel. Was this woman Rory's idea of a perfect wife for Eric?

"Oh, wow, man, would you look at those chunks of silver! He must'a hit the mother lode!" Crystal wiggled across the room to examine the trophies, stepping right in the middle of the babies' blanket Laura had spread on the floor. She barely avoided trampling a plastic rattle in the shape of a spoon with her hand-carved, high-heeled leather boots.

Laura barely held her tongue at the girl's thoughtless behavior. Eric was thinking of *marrying* this…this little *twit?* Not for all the silver in the world would she hand over the twins to a woman like Crystal.

"So, hey, I mean, does he have any new ones?"

"New ones, like what?" Laura grimaced, her jaw hurting from clenching her teeth so tightly together.

"Like these trophies are ancient history. Isn't he on the circuit anymore?"

"I don't think so." The most recent was only five years old. In Laura's book, that was darn recent. Besides, from what Eric had told her, he'd been seriously injured riding a bronc. Thank goodness he'd had enough sense not to go back on the circuit.

Disappointment melted the girl's chipper expression like a flame melts wax. "Bummer."

With superb timing, Eric chose that moment to appear, coming in the back from the kitchen.

"Hello. I didn't know we had company."

"This young lady is Crystal Lereaux—with an *x*. It seems Rory mentioned to her you were looking for a wife. She was very impressed with your trophies until she realized how *old* they are."

In a quick, sweeping gaze, Eric took in the young woman by the fireplace, probably half his age, and Laura's disapproving expression as well as her protective hold on one of the twins. What the hell had Rory been thinking?

"Nice to meet you, Crystal. I'm Eric Oakes."

Her eyes widened. "You the law?"

"County sheriff."

"Oh, that's heavy, man. I mean, Rory only said, you know, like you were his little brother."

Eric winced. His brother was going to have a lot of explaining to do next time Eric saw him.

"Crystal, why don't you and I walk over to the saloon? I'll buy you a drink and we can get acquainted."

"You better check her ID first," Laura muttered. She bent down and scooped up the babies' blanket, tossing it onto the back of the couch.

He gestured for Crystal to join him. He was sure she had a false ID, which wasn't going to be necessary. "We won't be long," he said to Laura.

"Don't rush on my account. I'm sure she'll be delighted to hear your *old* rodeo war stories." Her sweet, syrupy voice stung like acid on a reopened wound. It wasn't his fault his brother had picked out a rodeo groupie who was used to riding cowboys with their spurs on. He'd given up that gambit a long time ago.

He ushered Crystal out the door and down the porch steps. She was one hot package, all right, with her tight little rear end, minuscule waist and unrestrained breasts that threatened to fall out of her tank top. But no longer his style, if she had ever been.

Now he was settled, moving all too rapidly toward middle age. He needed a woman with a certain maturity. One who knew how to handle kids, that was for sure.

He definitely didn't want a near juvenile—a rodeo groupie—for a wife.

Coming to a halt beside Crystal's pickup, an extended-cab version with long horns mounted on the hood, he said, "You know, if we have a drink together it may be too late for the long drive you'll have later. Maybe we ought to skip it."

"You're brushing me off?"

"Isn't that what you'd like?"

She looked embarrassed. "I guess. You are a little old for me."

Tell me about it. "I really appreciate you driving all this way, and I'm sure Rory will, too." *Particularly after I plant his head on top of the flagpole in front of the sheriff's office.*

"That's okay. He's a pretty cool dude—for an old guy."

"I'll let him know." He opened the truck door for her, and she climbed into the cab. "Drive carefully."

"I always do." She slipped the key into the ignition and closed the door. "You might want to watch out for the housekeeper you've got, know what I mean? She is like, you know, so not cool."

"I'll be careful." He stepped back from the truck.

Crystal whipped the truck into a U-turn and sped out his drive toward Main Street. Before she was a block away, she'd broken a half-dozen traffic laws. Eric had no interest in pursuing her in order to give her a citation. Or for any other reason.

He went back into the house. Laura was sitting on the couch with the twins.

"That was a quick drink," she said.

"I plan to have a chat with Rory about robbing the cradle. Crystal agreed we wouldn't be a good match."

A faint smile teased at the corners of her lips. "Did you catch your vandals?"

"Couple of boys from Hill County decided to take a joyride in their dad's pickup after a few too many beers. The sheriff over there locked them up and called their folks."

"Lucky they weren't hurt." She lifted a sleepy baby to her shoulder. "I saved a dinner plate warming for you in the oven."

"And the pie, I hope."

"Help yourself. I think these little ones have finally worn themselves out. At least temporarily. I'm going to put them down for the night."

He hesitated, but only for a moment. "I'll give you a hand." With the same care Laura had shown, he lifted the second twin—Mandy, he thought.

"It's so late, you must be starved."

His stomach rumbled right on cue. "Waiting a few minutes longer won't hurt me, and you've had the kids all day." Besides, he'd kind of missed being with the babies when he was out on the road. They were nice to come home to.

So was Laura, he realized with a start.

For now he didn't want to analyze that thought too closely. It was enough to recognize the merit of a woman who wasn't half his age, had a vocabulary that included multisyllable words and knew her way around a kitchen.

He didn't need to consider the unguarded moments when his thoughts about her turned to the woman beneath her chaste exterior. The way he wondered how and where she liked to be kissed. And stroked. Or what it would take to arouse the passionate woman he was sure she'd hidden away even from herself.

Chapter 5

She hadn't seen this many vehicles in one place since she left Helena.

The church's parking lot was awash with pickup trucks and SUVs, all of them muddy and many of them sporting fender dings and signs of rust. In comparison, her SUV appeared pristine even though it was three years old and had close to fifty-thousand miles on it.

A bell tower with a lightning rod topped the small whitewashed church, and there were flourishing beds of forget-me-nots, marigolds, snapdragons and baby's breath across the front of the building. There were also lots of people in their Sunday best visiting with friends and neighbors as they waited for the morning service to begin.

Laura managed to get out of the truck and lift Rebecca out of her car seat before Lizzie and Kristi descended on them.

"Hmm, let me get my hands on that precious baby," Kristi said, taking Becky from her.

On the far side of the truck, Lizzie was doing the same with Mandy, Eric standing out of the way with an amused smile on his face.

Laura picked up the diaper bag from the floor of the back seat. "I brought some double-chocolate brownies for the potluck."

Kristi nuzzled Becky's neck, eliciting an openmouthed smile in return. "You didn't have to go to all that trouble. You're the guest of honor. Well, the babies are, actually, but you're our guest, too."

"It wasn't any trouble. I like to bake."

"I bet Eric loves that!" Her blue eyes sparkled with delight.

"Well, between the twins' feedings and baths and whatnot, there isn't all that much spare time to make anything fancy. But brownies are easy. I confess I used a boxed mix."

"Bring them along. I'll have someone put them in the rec room. That's where the party will be after the service. For now, we want you to meet the rest of the family." Kristi took off walking with Rebecca propped on her shoulder.

Laura followed, keeping a spare eye on Lizzie, who had a firm hold on Mandy. "I'm not sure how the babies will do in church. They may start crying."

"If they do, one of us will take them outside."

"They should be kept out of drafts." She turned

back to Eric. "Can you get the car seats? The babies might be more comfortable if—"

He waved. "I'll get 'em."

Kristi made a beeline for two men in Stetsons, fancy, Western-cut shirts and new jeans who were standing off to the side of the crowd. A toddler circled one of them as though she were on a merry-go-round.

"Honey, didn't I tell you the twins were adorable?"

The taller of the two men, who was clearly of Native American descent, put a possessive arm around Kristi. "If you say so, hon."

Kristi asked Laura, "Which one is this?"

"That's Rebecca," she answered.

Kristi gave the twin a quick kiss. "Laura, I'd like you to meet my husband, Rory. And this is Walker, Lizzie's husband." She nodded toward the second man. "They're Eric's brothers."

Both men politely tipped their hats.

"Yes, I can see the family resemblance," Laura said, straight-faced.

Their smiles froze for a moment, then Walker grinned. "Rory and Eric got all the ugly genes. I got the handsome ones."

"Now, wait a minute," Rory protested. "How 'bout we take a vote on that. Kristi, you go first."

"That's okay," Walker agreed, reaching out for his wife and drawing her closer, along with Becky. "Slick, here, will have the last word, and she'll agree with me." He bent down to pick up the toddler, who had begun tugging on Lizzie's skirt.

"I wouldn't think of interjecting myself into any argument you're having with your brother," Lizzie said. "You're on your own."

Laura, however, wasn't averse to a little screw tightening. "Evidently Rory is the one who thought a rodeo groupie under the age of consent would be a perfect bride for Eric."

"You did?" Kristi looked at her husband accusingly. "Why would you think a thing like that?"

He flushed. "Well, I—"

Eric arrived. "Where do you want the car seats?"

"Put them in the rec room," Kristi said. "And could you get one of the boys to take Laura's brownies in there, too?"

"Not Fridge!" Walker and Lizzie said in unison.

Everyone laughed as Eric walked off, and then Lizzie explained the joke. "We have four teenage sons, whom we've adopted. I'm afraid Fridge has a hollow leg."

"Two of them," Walker added.

Lizzie finished her thought. "It's unlikely he would have enough self-control to avoid finishing off the brownies by himself."

"He's a really sweet boy," Kristi said, defending the youngster. "He came over to fix the autoclave at the clinic the other day."

"And raid the refrigerator?" Walker asked.

It was Kristi's turn to blush, and she shrugged. "I gave him some money for an ice-cream cone at the drugstore. He said he was hungry."

They all had another laugh, but their laughter was so filled with love, Laura couldn't help but think that Fridge had found himself a wonderful home and family.

By now people were moving into the church. A red-headed teenager named Scotty showed up to deliver the brownies to the rec room, and everyone else filed in for the service.

Laura found herself squeezed into a whole pew filled with members of the Oakes family—teenage boys, a little girl who had to be biologically related to Scotty, their hair the exact same shade of carrot red, and Susie, who was the toddler in her father's arms. A five-year-old, who was obviously Rory's son, popped up from somewhere to sit next to his father. Eric eased his way into the pew, taking his place beside Laura. His sisters-in-law continued to claim possession of the twins, which made Laura slightly anxious in spite of knowing the babies were in good hands.

Before the minister appeared, Laura whispered, "You have a very nice family."

"Yeah, I like 'em. Most days." He leaned forward to pick up a hymnal, opening it to the first song.

Laura suspected Eric more than liked his siblings and his extended family. As an only child with a limited number of aunts and uncles, none of whom lived in Helena where she'd grown up, she'd always envied families like his. They seemed to make their own fun. That was probably why both Laura and her mother had been so welcoming of Amy.

Not that her far smaller family unit hadn't had fun, too. Sunday mornings roughhousing with her dad and reading the comics together were memories she'd always cherish. There simply weren't as many people in her family as other folks had.

Reverend McDuffy, with his white hair and folksy

way, provided his congregation with a blessedly short sermon, perhaps because of the shrill duet Rebecca and Amanda began shortly after he started to speak.

As the congregation stood, Laura plucked Becky from Kristi's arms. Eric claimed Mandy. Together they slipped out a side door and found a quiet bench behind the church where they could feed the babies.

"For such tiny things, they sure have big lungs," Eric commented.

"Future opera stars," Laura suggested. "Although their harmony is a bit jarring."

He grinned and plugged a bottle into Mandy's mouth.

Sitting companionably on the bench, the babies sucking on their bottles as though they hadn't eaten in days, Laura leaned back and relaxed. Big Sky Country was putting on a show today. In the distance, a line of dark, black clouds bisected the wide swath of cerulean sky, and the hazy outline of the Glacier Park mountains was barely visible. Closer at hand, redtail hawks spiraled upward, catching the lift from the warming earth. In between, prairie grass shimmered silver and green in an almost imperceptible breeze.

"This is nice," she said on a sigh.

"Yeah."

"Can't think why Grass Valley doesn't get more tourists."

"Maybe because we don't want them."

She cocked an eyebrow. "Good point."

The hum of a dragonfly's wings and the call of a mockingbird filled the silence. It was all Laura could do to remember that this peaceful interlude only masked reality. This moment wasn't hers to keep. Just as the twins weren't Eric's to keep, unless she said so.

Odd how that one thought carried with it so much regret.

A few minutes later, Lizzie found them, announcing that the potluck and baby shower were about to get underway.

Virtually the entire congregation stayed for the potluck, and most of them brought at least a small present for the twins. The adults sat in a circle on folding chairs, the more agile ones on the floor, during the gift-opening process, while the younger children played outside under the supervision of a mother or two. The teenagers lounged around outside, too, ogling each other, giggling and generally acting like adolescents do everywhere in the world.

Not that it was any of her business, but Laura surreptitiously glanced around the room. There seemed to be no single women between the ages of twenty and thirty, no marital prospects for Eric. To her dismay, she was pleased with that observation, and her reaction wasn't entirely due to the threat that his finding a bride would mean she might have to give up the twins.

It had far more to do with her own totally inappropriate, no doubt unwelcome attraction to the man.

Shaking away that errant thought, Laura opened the first package, a small box with a big, pink bow from Marlene Huhn. Inside she found two bibs with the twins' names beautifully hand embroidered on them, making the bibs almost too nice to use.

"These are exquisite. Thank you," Laura said.

One gift led to another and then another. There were crib sheets and blankets, dolls and rattles, hand-made wooden pull toys the twins wouldn't be able to use for ages, but still much appreciated.

Doc Justine gave her a book on what to expect in a baby's first year of life. "Most babies come up with something those authors didn't think about, so you give me a call when they do. We'll take a look."

"Thank you. I will." She flipped through the pages, a little overwhelmed by it all. She had a similar book at home but hadn't thought to bring it. She passed this one to Eric. If the babies stayed with him, he'd need it.

Trying not to think about that possibility, she continued unwrapping presents.

Valery Haywood had crocheted two sweet little sweaters, one with a fuzzy poodle and the other with a kitty on it.

The gift from Hetty Moore was even more welcome.

"A double Snugli carrier," Laura exclaimed as she opened the box. "Wherever did you find it?"

"We get enough catalogs at the store every day to fill a barn. Took me a while to find what I was looking for, but there you are." Hetty beamed with pleasure.

"Thank you so much. It's…everything is so wonderful. And thoughtful."

Laura was touched that these men and women, who were strangers to her and the twins, would go to so much effort for them. But perhaps the gifts were just another example of the love and support Eric had in the community. They wanted him to keep the babies, not Laura.

She wasn't quite that quick to be persuaded, however. In this case, it took more than a village to raise a child.

As the grand finale, Kristi rolled out a tandem stroller, and everyone oohed and aahed.

"The family went in together on this one," she said. "Granted, we don't have a whole lot of sidewalks in Grass Valley but we got the model with the bigger wheels so it would go better on gravel and dirt."

"It's wonderful," Laura said. There were miles of paved walking paths in her townhouse complex and around the neighborhood. Eric's family hadn't thought about that.

Eric plucked Rebecca from Valery's arms—she was about the tenth woman who had cuddled her in the past hour—and put the baby in the stroller. "Whadaya think, Tinkerbell? Shall we let your sister try out her seat, too?"

With a happy squeal, Becky let her approval be known.

By the time the shower was over, and everyone had had their fill of potluck, the twins were exhausted from overstimulation and Eric needed help carrying all the gifts to the truck.

When Laura put Mandy into her car seat, she was crying hard and wouldn't take her pacifier. "It's all right, sweetie, you're just tired. Mommy will have you home in a few minutes and in your own bed so you can have a nice, long nap."

Eric's hands froze on the stroller he was folding to put in the back of the SUV. He hadn't heard Laura call herself Mommy before, but the word had sounded as natural as putting thick cream on strawberries.

She wanted to be the twins' mother. She'd made no secret of that. And maybe she even deserved it, since she and her mother had given Amy a home when his sister had needed a safe place to be. Laura would probably be a damn good mother, too.

But the twins belonged with family. That meant him. For the life of him, he didn't see any room for compromise on that issue.

Besides, it had been less than a week and he'd already bonded—if that's what you call it—with the twins. He loved them. Even in the middle of the night when their cries dragged him out of bed, he loved the way they snuggled into his arms and looked up at him with complete trust. He'd never be able to walk away from them. Or let them be taken from him.

As he finished folding the stroller, stuffed it inside and lowered the SUV's hatch, he wondered how any parent could.

He also knew it wouldn't be easy for Laura to give them up.

Since he hadn't been paged all day while at the church, Eric assumed law and order prevailed in Grass Valley. Therefore, discovering that the three messages on his answering machine at home had nothing to do with breaking the law didn't surprise him. Which didn't make him all that thrilled with the messages.

He found Laura collapsed on the couch after putting the twins down for their nap. Her head was tipped back, her eyes closed, and there were dozens of unwrapped presents piled on the floor they hadn't had a chance to put away. A tiny frown marred her smooth forehead, and he had an almost irresistible urge to kiss that frown away.

Instead, he shoved his hands in jean pockets and cleared his throat.

She opened her eyes, as blue as a Montana sky, and Eric got another jolt. Clearly he'd been celibate too long.

"I had some phone messages while we were gone," he said. "It seems one of my brothers placed a personal ad in a couple of newspapers."

Her brows arched. "A couple?"

"Two or three." Helena. Great Falls. Boise, Idaho. God, what had they been thinking?

"Impressive."

"The newspapers printed some pretty flattering things about me." Mostly lies, Eric decided. Certainly exaggerations. "We may get a few women dropping by in the next few days. To meet me."

"I see."

Well, hell! She could at least react to the possibility he'd actually find a wife. He wasn't all that bad a catch. He had a good job, a house. Money in the bank.

"I just wanted you to know," he said.

"I'll try to stay out of your way."

"I'll make sure, if I pick one of them, that they'll be a good mother for the twins."

"And I promise to represent Amy's wishes as best I can."

He heard her unstated threat. *It's in my hands!*

The phone rang.

When he didn't move, Laura cocked her head toward the kitchen. "You'd better answer that. She could be the one."

Eric scowled and stalked toward the kitchen. This whole deal of needing a wife was totally unreasonable. Laura ought to see that. He was capable of raising the twins on his own. In Grass Valley, he'd have plenty of help. Besides, he didn't want to be forced into marriage to anyone.

He snatched up the phone. "Eric Oakes."

"Is, uh, Laura Cavendish there?" a male voice asked.

Well, if that didn't just beat all! "I'll get her."

He marched back into the living room. "It's for you."

She looked up in surprise. "My mother?"

"Not unless she has a bad case of laryngitis. I'd say it was a guy."

"Oh." With a little shake of her head, which shifted her hair across the delicate line of her jaw, she pushed up to her feet. "I can't imagine…"

Yeah, sure, like she was pulling one over on Eric. She had a boyfriend. So what? It didn't mean the guy would end up Becky and Mandy's dad. Eric was first in line for that job.

He paced around the living room until Laura returned.

"That was the superintendent of my school district, Alex Thurman," she said.

All the steam Eric had built up over the unfairness of his situation with the twins blew away. "On Sunday night? He wields a mean whip."

"Not really." She seemed agitated, picking up one of the gift boxes they hadn't yet put away, looking at the contents, then setting it aside. "I mentioned to you the curriculum coordinator's job I applied for. He just offered it to me."

"Congratulations."

"The problem is he wants me back in town by the first of the month."

"That's only a week away."

"I'll need to get things set up before classes start in late August, so the teachers can prepare."

Eric could understand that. But what about the twins' future? Where did they fit in?

He still needed a chance to prove he was the father they needed.

And find a wife.

A week didn't give him much time.

Chapter 6

The first of Eric's wannabe brides from the personal ads showed up early the next morning.

"Bernice Zeidlitz here," she said, extending her hand when he opened the front door. "My friends call me Bernie. You must be Eric Oakes."

"Uh, yes." She pumped his arm as he tried to blink the sleep from his eyes. It was a little after eight, and the twins had alternated being awake last night, which meant Eric had gotten little sleep himself.

Scanning him up and down like a piece of meat hanging in a cold-storage locker room, she said, "You'll do, I suppose. Reasonable physique for a civilian, but I don't like seeing men half-naked. Proper attire is important for morale."

His or hers? Rubbing his hand across his bare chest, he figured she was lucky he'd bothered to pull on his pants. The woman was on the stocky side, closer to forty than thirty and wore her blond hair in a short, no-nonsense style. But Eric wasn't in a position to be picky about who he married. He wasn't looking for a lovefest, just somebody who was good with babies. "I was sleeping. We had a hard night with the—"

She marched past him into the living room. "Sounds like we'll have some trouble adjusting to each other's biorhythms. I'm a morning person. Up with the dawn, that's my motto. 'Reveille' was my favorite time of the day at boot camp."

"Boot camp?"

"Right." She did a smart about-face and stood at parade rest. "Marine drill sergeant, recently retired. I'm ready to settle down to a home and family now. This seems like as good a place as any."

Good God! "There are a few things we need to discuss before—"

"Where are these new recruits you've got? The twins?"

"They're upstairs sleeping. As I said, it was a long—"

"Sleeping? At this hour? We can't have that. Need to get them on a proper schedule." She headed for the stairs. "Up at six. Breakfast from six to six forty-five. Then playtime."

"Now, wait a minute." He took off after her, but she was quick, apparently in great physical shape, and got to the second floor before he did.

"Which way?" she asked.

"Let's wait until they wake up, then you can meet them when they're at their best." Unless he could get rid of her first.

"I always say, begin as you plan to continue. Might

as well get the little darlings started on their schedule now."

Laura appeared in her doorway, pulling on her robe and looking suitably rumpled from their exhausting night.

Bernice halted abruptly.

"Who are you going to put on a schedule?" Laura asked, running her fingers through her sleep-mussed hair.

"More to the point, who are you?" Bernice wanted to know. She shot an accusing glance toward Eric. "I have no interest in being a part of a ménage à trois."

Nor did Eric. "Laura Cavendish meet Bernice Zeidlitz, marine drill sergeant, retired. She came in response to the personal ad in the paper."

Laura's lips tightened, her eyes narrowed. "I see."

"Drove most of the night to get here," Bernice announced. "Wanted to be first in line, so to speak. Don't believe in that old military saw of not volunteering for anything. But it looks like you outmaneuvered me and hit the beach first."

"No, that's not—"

Eric took Bernice's arm, trying to ease her back downstairs. From the feel of her biceps, short of tossing her over his shoulder, he suspected she'd budge only if she wanted to.

"How about I fix you a cup of coffee?" he offered in lieu of a wrestling match, which he wasn't all that sure he'd win. "You've had a long drive. It's the least I can do."

She hesitated long enough that Eric wondered if she were planning to overwhelm Laura and establish her own beachhead right here in the upstairs hallway.

"How 'bout you point me in the direction of the

kitchen? I'll get the coffee started while you finish putting on the uniform of the day."

"Perfect. Downstairs and around to your right."

"Hope you like your coffee high-octane. That's not an area where I'm willing to compromise." With a quick nod as her salute, she paraded past him to the stairway, head held high, back ramrod straight.

She was barely out of sight when Laura said a sharp, "No."

"That makes it unanimous." He gave her a weary smile. "I'll get rid of her as soon as I can."

"Thank you." Anger laced her taut response, which was in direct contrast to her sleep-rumpled appearance.

Eric liked her softer side, the way she looked in the night holding one of the twins, her drowsy smile when the baby went back to sleep. It was the kind of smile that made him want to cuddle her in his arms, hold her spooned against his body as they lay in bed waiting for sleep to come. Except he figured he'd want to do more than just snuggle together.

Which wasn't on the agenda for either of them. She had a job to go back to, a boss who wanted her there in a hurry. Eric was fighting her for custody of the twins. Hopping into bed together didn't seem like a good plan. Not that his libido was in full agreement with that decision, particularly at a moment like this when both of them were only half-dressed. And the alternative of sleeping with Sergeant Zeidlitz gave him the chills.

As though reading his thoughts, she tugged her robe more securely around her. "Instead of giving your address to every woman who calls, maybe you ought to do a little prescreening on the phone."

"Good idea. I'll be sure to check if they have any objections to seeing a man's bare chest."

Laura's brows shot up. "She doesn't like your chest?"

"Apparently half-naked men offend her sensibilities."

She sputtered a laugh. "And here I was thinking what a really nice chest you have."

"You were?"

"Muscled but not too hairy." The hint of a blush colored her cheeks, and she glanced away, shrugging. "I'm not fond of hairy."

"I didn't know women noticed one way or the other."

"Oh, yes, they do." A tiny smile teased at the corners of her lips. "Men's chests provide endless hours of conversation in college dorm rooms, for instance."

"I thought it was only guys who talked about—"

"Oakes!" Bernice bellowed from downstairs. "Where do you keep your coffee?"

Eric held up his hand to Laura. "I'll get back to you on that list after I get rid of Sergeant Zeidlitz." He ducked into his room to grab a shirt, and as he did he heard Laura's soft chuckle behind him.

In spite of himself, he smiled in response. *She likes my chest.*

Laura hurried to take a quick shower while the babies were still sleeping and Eric was dealing with the latest would-be bride. At least this woman hadn't raised an iota of jealousy on Laura's part. Her reaction was closer to anger that someone would try to take over the entire household, including *her* babies, without so much as a by-your-leave.

Good grief, somebody should have made that woman a general!

Besides, how on earth could any woman not like looking at Eric's chest? Or anything else about him, for that matter. His reluctant smile—when he deigned to use it—brought a twinkle to his clear blue eyes. His broad shoulders looked capable enough to take on a world of burdens. Even from the rear view, his buns in tight jeans were worth admiring.

And Bernice didn't like his bare chest? Unbelievable.

Laura sighed as the water pelted her body, and wished she could linger in the caressing warmth. She hadn't had a chance to indulge in a long, leisurely shower in months. Not since the birth of the twins. If she retained custody it would probably be years before she had that opportunity again.

A price she was more than willing to pay, she reminded herself.

Stepping out of the shower, she toweled off and ran a quick comb through her hair. One of the advantages of a two-parent family was the chance to take turns caring for their babies. A nice arrangement for those who could work it out, and exactly what Amy had wanted for her twins.

Which meant if Eric found a suitable wife, Laura would have to relinquish the twins to him…and a stranger.

A sharp pain sliced close to her heart. Tears stung her eyes.

If she were *whole,* capable of producing children of her own, she might have found a man to love years ago, one who could love her in return. But life had dealt her a hand that was one card short of a full house. Since her accident she had felt the emptiness in her womb as though it were a cavernous pit devoid of hope.

Becky and Mandy had filled that hole in her life. To give them away would break her heart.

By the time she'd dressed, the twins were cooing in their crib, conversing in a language only they could understand. Laura imagined the two of them would always share a special link that would grow stronger over the years. She desperately hoped she'd be there to see it.

She changed their diapers, adding her own nonsense syllables to the conversation, and carried them both downstairs. The aroma of black coffee was so strong it gave her a caffeine jolt simply by inhaling the scent.

She peered cautiously into the kitchen. Eric was sitting alone at the table, a coffee mug in front of him.

"Is she gone?"

He glanced up and smiled. "Marched off into the sunrise whistling the theme from *Bridge over the River Kwai.*"

"Oh, dear." She laughed.

"Yeah." Holding out his hands, he said, "Let me have one."

"You can have both. I'll fix their bottles."

"Watch out for the coffee. It'll grow hair where you really don't want it growing."

"Thanks for the warning."

He took the babies, adjusting one in each arm as she went to the refrigerator to get the bottles she'd mixed last night. Over the past few days she'd grown comfortable in Eric's kitchen. The appliances might not be the newest, the counter was tile rather than a more modern

granite, but it had a workable layout. A family kitchen
that only needed a woman's touch to make it a home.

"In a way I feel sorry for her," Laura said. She put
the bottles in the microwave and punched in the time.

"For the sergeant? I don't think she's looking for
sympathy."

"Hmm, maybe not. But every woman deserves to
find love somewhere." With the microwave humming,
she leaned back against the counter. The twins were
completely content in Eric's arms, looking up at him
as though he'd painted the moon especially for them.

"I doubt the recruits she trained had a lot of love
for her. She is one tough lady."

"All the more reason why she's looking for love
now." Which made her and Bernice sisters of the heart,
even if Laura wouldn't trust the woman to raise the
twins. Raising children required far more flexibility
than molding marines into a fighting force.

The microwave dinged. She retrieved the bottles,
screwed on the tops, gave them each a good shake,
then tested them for temperature with a few drops of
formula on her wrist.

"I think you're right about making a list," Eric said.

"Oh?"

"Bring me a pad of paper and a pencil from the
drawer over there." He gestured with a nod of his head.
"We'll do it together."

Great. She was going to tell him exactly who he
needed to marry so he could get custody of the twins.
Talk about being her own worst enemy!

Between them they got everything arranged, each
with a baby and bottle, the pad and pencil in front of

Eric, Laura sitting opposite him at the table. The twins latched on to their respective bottles; Laura and Eric got to work.

"She has to be good with babies," Eric said. He had Becky's bottle propped under his chin while he wrote that down on the paper. "How about being experienced with babies?"

"That would be a plus," Laura conceded. "But remember, most new parents aren't experienced. I certainly wasn't but I've managed pretty well."

"Yeah, you have. We'll give experience bonus points. What else?"

"After Bernice, maybe we ought to say flexible."

He grinned at Laura and wrote that down. "Got it."

She was at a loss what else a mother needed to be successful. "Love of the twins seems like it ought to be the primary ingredient."

"That's a given."

"She's going to be your wife. Don't you have any ideas?"

He pondered that for a moment. "Good-looking?"

"It figures a man would think of that first."

"I don't mean she has to look like a fashion model. But if we're going to…you know… If you were planning to get married, wouldn't you want your husband to be decent-looking?"

"If he loved me and was good to the twins, I wouldn't care what he looked like."

"Except for the hairy-chest part."

Her sharp laughter startled Becky, and the infant's eyes flew open. Laura brushed a quick kiss to the baby's forehead to soothe her.

"Sense of humor." Eric wrote it on the list. "That's important in a wife."

"In a husband, too."

Their eyes met and held, sending a warm quiver of awareness burrowing into Laura's midsection. The air in the kitchen grew heated, as though the oven had been switched on or the day had turned excessively warm.

"Intelligent," he said softly, his gaze still focused on her.

"You like intelligent women?"

"You can't spend all your time, uh, in bed. I like a good conversationalist. Besides, when the twins are older, she'll have to help them with their homework and stuff."

"You won't?"

"Sure, but I wasn't all that good at English and history. Math was easier."

"History is my specialty. When I was young, I spent so much time at the library reading musty old books, they threatened to charge my parents rent. Now I try to teach kids what's happening today is tomorrow's history."

His lips twitched with a smile. "There was a girl in high school—Emily Trudough. She let me read over her shoulder during history tests. Without her, I never would have gotten through the French Revolution."

"Tony Eaton got me through geometry."

"Guess that means we don't have to put down honesty as a criteria."

She laughed again. "Juvenile crimes of the minor sort can be excused, I suppose."

They discussed a dozen other issues. Since he lived

in a small town, the would-be bride had to be comfortable with that. Liking the outdoors was important, too. Montana had more of that than anything else.

Hobbies were considered but they didn't seem to matter to Eric as long as they didn't include skin piercing or yodeling.

There was one question she didn't want to ask. The answer seemed all to obvious. But a man ought to give some thought to his answer before choosing a wife, as she knew all too well.

"What about more children?" she asked, her throat tightening in anticipation of his answer.

He wiped some dribble from Mandy's lips with the corner of clean cloth diaper and glanced up. "Sure. I've always wanted a big family. Maybe not four adolescent boys at once like Walker has but big enough for some roughhousing. When you're dumped like I was as a kid, you think a lot about family. How important it is. From what you've said, Amy was probably the same way."

"Yes, she was." Which is why Laura had been sent off on this fool's errand, risking the chance she wouldn't be able to keep the twins for herself.

But giving Eric—or any other man—the family he longed for wasn't in the cards for her.

In that regard, she'd never measure up.

After a simple breakfast, Eric went to the office, and Laura tried to do some laundry. Not only had a load of dirty baby clothes piled up, she had all of the shower gifts to take care of before the twins could use them.

Apparently the twins had a different idea about how she would spend her day.

They wouldn't nap for more than twenty minutes at a time. They woke crying as though the end of the world were about to arrive. They weren't hungry and wouldn't take their pacifiers.

Laura was at her wits' end and frantic with worry. Eric had been called out somewhere. He probably wouldn't have known what to do any more than she did, and she'd read through the entire baby-care book without finding a solution to their crying.

Out of desperation, she called Doc Justine at the medical clinic across the road, about a block away.

Kristi answered and listened to Laura's concerns.

"Bring them right over. It may be nothing to worry about but we'll take a look at them."

Rather than take the time to put the car seats back into her car, Laura used the new dual Snugli carrier for the twins and walked the short distance to the clinic. Normally she would have enjoyed the brisk walk. The day was gloriously sunny, the temperature in the seventies. Wildflowers dotted the open fields. But she was simply too distraught and harried for this to be a pleasurable stroll.

Naturally the twins thought it was a wonderful outing. They both dozed right off to sleep, the rocking motion as she walked—and their obvious fatigue—lulling them into giving up the battle to stay awake.

The clinic was in an old Victorian house with dormer windows and a wide front porch. A little bell jingled as Laura opened the door and stepped inside. Glass-topped display cases filled with antique medical equipment lined the entry hall, and the faint scent of antiseptic laced the air.

Kristi appeared from a room on the left, looking crisp and professional in her turquoise medical jacket. "Hi, Laura. Your little bundles not bringing much joy today, huh?" She brushed her palm over Mandy's head in a quick caress that probably gave her an instant gage of the infant's temperature.

"Right now they're being angels. But they were awake half the night, and they've been fretful all afternoon. I couldn't get them to sleep—until now."

Doc Justine arrived from the opposite side of the house. "Let's get double-trouble into an exam room where we can take a look." Barely pausing beside Laura and the babies, the doctor strode across the hall and toward the examination rooms.

Laura followed. "Now that they're finally asleep, I hate to wake them up."

"Unless you want to learn how to sleep standing up yourself," Doc Justine said, "we'd better find out what's wrong and fix it."

Laura shot a troubled glance at Kristi.

"Don't mind my grandmother," she said. "Med schools didn't teach bedside manner when she attended, but she knows what she's doing."

"Humph! Never cured anybody of anything with sweet talk." Despite her crusty bearing, the doctor lifted Becky from the Snugli carrier as gently as a light breeze would lift a feather.

Kristi did the same with Mandy.

Both babies began to squirm as their temperatures

were taken, hearts listened to, ears and bottoms examined, all with a minimum of wasted motion.

Finally the doctor announced, "Fine, healthy babies, both of them."

"Then why are they so fussy?" Laura asked, a new wave of desperation washing over her. She dreaded the thought of another sleepless night.

"Go ahead and tell her, Kristi," the doctor ordered.

"It looks like teething to me."

Astonished, Laura looked back to the doctor for confirmation. "Teething? They're only three months old."

"More like sore gums, actually. Nothing to worry about." Doc Justine unhooked her stethoscope from around her neck and draped it over a wall peg. "Used to be we'd say a baby that teethed early was extrasmart. Course that isn't true, but it gave the mothers some comfort."

"But what do I do?" Suddenly Laura felt helpless, ill prepared for motherhood. She'd never considered teething or sore gums to be the problem, though perhaps she should have.

"Used to be we'd have the mother rub a little whiskey on the baby's gums to ease the pain."

"Whiskey?" Laura gasped.

"Near as I can recall, the whiskey was more a comfort to the mother when she took a nip or two off the bottle herself."

Laura sputtered an objection.

"Grandma, will you stop baiting her." Shaking her head, Kristi finished dressing Becky. "I'll call Harold over at the pharmacy and have him pull some numbing gel off the shelves. Just rub a little on their gums every few hours as needed. They'll sleep better, and in a day or two the gums will stop hurting."

"I certainly hope so." Laura tugged Mandy's shirt back on and hooked her tiny overall straps in place. The baby was crying so hard now, tears welled in her eyes. "Oh, sweetie, I'm so sorry your mommy didn't know what to do."

Doc Justine's hand closed over Laura's shoulder, squeezing gently. "You and Eric are doing a fine job with these babies. They're as healthy as can be. They're lucky to have parents like the two of you."

Tears stung Laura's eyes, too. She and Eric *couldn't* be the twins' parents, not at the same time, at any rate. And not for the long haul. One of them was going to lose custody. Laura was desperately afraid she'd be the one, and the strain was beginning to tell.

Eric returned home about dinnertime. He found the twins sleeping peacefully in the playpen near the window in the living room, Laura curled up on the couch equally out of it, her hands pillowing her head. A huge pile of unfolded laundry filled the overstuffed chair by the fireplace. There had been no sign of dinner preparations in the kitchen as he passed through.

Given everyone's sleepless night, he suspected Laura had collapsed from exhaustion. He didn't blame her in the least.

She stirred, stretching her legs. Her mouth worked but she didn't speak. During the course of the day, she'd worn off her lipstick, leaving her lips a natural shade of rose and all the more inviting because she was so guileless.

Eric wondered how she would react if he kissed her the rest of the way awake.

He hunkered down beside her. Tempted, he teased the tips of her ginger-blond hair with his fingertips. Silky. Lush and thick. The kind of hair a man wanted to thread his fingers through as he kissed a woman senseless.

Her eyes blinked open, sky blue and filled with surprise. Or maybe it was pleasure.

"Hey, Sleeping Beauty." His voice was hushed, his throat tight. "You have a hard day?"

"Mmm, you could say that."

He focused on her mouth. If he leaned forward a few inches, his lips would be on hers. "You want to tell me about it?"

She studied him with quiet intensity. "The twins were so fussy I finally took them to see Doc Justine. It's nothing serious," she hastened to add. "Sore gums. She had me get some numbing gel at the pharmacy."

Relieved the babies were okay, Eric relaxed from his momentary fright. "You did the right thing, taking them to see the doc, I mean."

"When I went to get the gel, the pharmacist practically forced a two-scoop chocolate ice-cream cone on me." A tiny furrow formed between her brows. "He didn't let me pay for it, either."

"Harold's quite a character. He rarely lets his customers decide what kind of ice cream they'd like. He makes the decision for them, and he must have thought you needed an extra pick-me-up."

Her lazy, contented smile agreed with Eric's assessment. "Nothing has ever tasted so good."

"I'm glad." Unable to help himself, he brushed a few strands of hair back from her face, then rested his hand on her downy-soft cheek.

A sigh shuddered through her. "How was your day?"

"Routine." There'd been a gas station robbery in a neighboring town, and he'd been alerted. But it wasn't his jurisdiction so he wasn't the primary investigator. Just back-up this time. In rural counties, they helped each other.

"You must be tired, too. You didn't get any more sleep last night than I did."

"I'm okay." He liked being right where he was. Close to her where he could catch her feminine scent, a combination of baby powder and the sweet perfume of a woman.

Her eyes opened wider. "Oh, my gosh! I haven't even started dinner."

"There's no rush. In fact, why don't I take you out to dinner?"

"Out?" She echoed the word as though he'd spoken in a foreign language.

"Yeah. We can go to the saloon in town. They've got pretty good burgers and sandwiches. A couple of decent salads, if you'd rather eat light. Nothing fancy, of course."

"You don't know how tempting that sounds."

She was tempting, too. The vee of her blouse collar opened just enough to reveal the swell of her breast as she took each breath. The smooth curve of her hip was within his reach. Her soft, sensual lips…

"But what about the twins?" she asked, her voice still rusty with sleep, her eyes as deep as velvet. "Do you think it would be all right to take them?"

"Sure. We could put them in their car seats right in one of the booths with us. They'd probably love all the activity." He would enjoy a different kind of action, one of a far more intimate nature.

"All right. Let's do it."

For a moment he thought she'd agreed to do what he'd been so vividly imagining, and his body reacted with a powerful ache. The two of them together, right there on the couch, caressing, stroking, exploring with hands and lips and tongue.

And then one of the twins awoke, babbling little cooing sounds. Laura levered herself to a sitting position, gave Eric a wistful smile, and the moment passed.

He sat back on his haunches. He didn't know whether to thank little Becky or curse the infant's bad timing because he wasn't quite sure what was happening between him and Laura.

Or what would happen if he pursued the matter.

Would she just be another woman who walked away from him?

Chapter 7

The jukebox blared a hard rock number, a twirling spotlight spun overhead, and the saloon smelled of stale beer. The floors were darkly stained and worn from years of use. The vinyl seats in the booth had long since lost their spring.

The twins loved the place.

So did Laura, more because she was sitting across the table from Eric than because of the ambience.

He'd almost kissed her. She could hardly believe it was true.

She'd felt his warm breath on her lips, sensed his desire. In response, heat had gathered in her midsection, stealing her breath. Her nipples tightened and a heaviness weighted her limbs that she hadn't experienced in years. All because he had looked at her that way.

And then Becky had done her thing. Darn it all!

She reached for the menu, her hand trembling with residual frustration.

Eric leaned forward across the table. "Take a look at the two guys at the bar and tell me what you think."

"What?"

"What do you think they're doing here?"

Trying not to be conspicuous, she glanced over her shoulder.

Dressed in khaki pants and sports shirts, the two men were drinking beer, and it looked like they'd each had a hamburger and fries. Both in their late twenties, one man was a good fifty pounds over-weight, and he straddled his bar stool as though it were a horse. The other guy was lean, with stringy brown hair that hadn't been cut in a year. Neither wore cowboy boots like every other male in the saloon, Eric included. He'd changed into jeans and a denim shirt, rolled the cuffs up and looked like he was a working ranch hand come into town for a bite to eat. Not a cop.

She turned back to him. "Not locals."

"Tourists?"

"I wouldn't think so. More like hunters taking some time off from their wives, but it's not hunting season."

"Then why are they in Grass Valley?"

She frowned and decided to reverse the tables on him. "Why are you so curious about them?"

"Well, for one thing there was a gas station robbery in the next county this afternoon. For another, I spotted an unfamiliar pickup with a shell in front of the saloon. We don't get much out-of-town traffic. Makes me wonder."

She loved the way a police officer's mind worked,

filled with curiosity and always asking questions. They noticed things no one else would. Her father had been like that until he died—a heart attack at far too young an age. She'd always felt she'd been at fault for his premature death. If she hadn't insisted on that wild joyride in the back of the pickup.

"So what do you think?" she asked, pressing away the memory along with the guilt. "Robbery suspects?"

"Neither one fits the description of the perp. But eyewitnesses can be pretty far off the mark."

"I suppose." She glanced at Becky, gave her a smile and tickled her tummy. That circling light overhead had her enthralled.

The bartender finally showed up to take their order.

"Hey, Sheriff. How's it going?"

"Can't complain or you won't vote for me next time."

The young man grinned, barely old enough to vote, Laura suspected.

"Laura, meet Stitch Overholt. He's got a spread out east of town and is moonlighting here 'cuz his wife's expecting their first."

The young man glanced at the babies in their car seats. "Sure hope we only get one at a time. I don't know what I'd do with two."

"I'm sure you and your wife would manage," Laura told him.

"Yes, ma'am." He flushed a beautiful shade of pink. "What can I get you two?"

"First, what can you tell me about those two at the bar?" Eric asked. "Have they been in before?"

The kid thought a minute. "I seen the heavy-set guy a couple of weeks ago."

"Either of them say what brought them to town?"

"Nope. Not that I can recall. Probably just passing through."

Nodding, Eric glanced at Laura. "What did you decide to have?"

She recognized the signal to not ask any more questions, and looked up at the young man. "The Cobb salad and whatever you have on draft."

Eric's head snapped up. "A beer?"

"I had a hard day, remember?"

He grinned at her. "Since I'm not in uniform, I'll have a double burger, fries and the same as the lady to drink."

"Yes, sir. If it's okay to say so, Sheriff, your wife's real pretty."

Heat scalded Laura's cheeks. "I'm not—"

"You've got a good eye, Stitch. But you'd better get back to work before I decide you're hitting on the wrong woman."

"Yes, sir." He backed away from the table and all but ran back to the kitchen to place their order.

"I'm sorry," Laura said. "I thought we'd stopped people from thinking—"

"Don't worry about it. Stitch just hasn't gotten the word yet." His thoughts had clearly shifted back to the two men at the bar. Not tourists, yet passing through, one of them for the second time.

Obviously Laura and the twins took a back seat when he had law enforcement on his mind.

So much for their almost kiss.

They were putting the twins down for the night when Eric's office line rang. He hurried across the hall from the nursery and answered the phone in his bedroom.

Minutes later he reappeared, dressed in his uniform and wearing his gun on his hip.

"I've got to go out," he announced.

Disappointment shot through Laura. "Now?" What a ridiculous question. Of course he had to go. He was the local sheriff. He gets a call and he has to respond. Whatever had she been thinking...or hoping for?

"Another gas station robbery. They appear to be moving west."

"The same perp?"

"Same MO."

"Our guys from the saloon?"

"It's possible. This time the attendant spotted a pickup with a shell on the back when the perp fled. He had an accomplice." He bent over the crib to kiss the twins good-night. "I passed on the license number of the pair that was at the saloon."

He stood up just as she was bending over to straighten the crib sheet, and they collided. He grabbed her by the shoulders to steady her, which brought their bodies in contact from shoulders to hips, her breasts brushing against his chest.

For a breathless moment they stood there, uncertainty and desire mixing in the air, overwhelming the scent of baby powder. Laura's heart pumped hard, as though she'd run up a dozen flights of stairs. She was trapped. A part of her wanted to run, to avoid the heartbreak that even a single kiss would lead to. Another part of her demanded that she take what she could. Drawn like a hummingbird to the promise of sweet nectar, she leaned forward.

Instead of meeting her mouth with his, Eric's hands slid down her arms in a slow caress until he was holding both of her hands. "Sorry," he whispered.

Sorry? That he didn't want to kiss her? Dear God! Was there anything more foolish than an overeager woman?

"I really have to go."

"I understand." In her self-delusion, she'd read the signs all wrong.

"I don't know how late I'll be."

With what was left of her pride, she lifted her chin. "That's all right. The twins and I will be fine."

A slight frown furrowed his forehead, and he released her hands. "I'll see you in the morning, then."

Unable to speak past the lump in her throat, she nodded.

"There's a woman planning to stop by tomorrow. Delores Haghan. She called about the ad. Sounded like a possible over the phone."

Disappointment, sharp and painful, left her standing in the nursery as Eric walked out. She heard his footsteps descending the stairs, then the back door open and close. Only then did she let the tears come.

How many times did she have to learn the same lesson? She wasn't worthy of a man's love.

By morning Laura had her emotions back under control, blaming the whole incident on what turned out to be PMS. That was the cruelest joke of all. Her hormones could go on a rampage like any other woman's but she'd never be able to deliver the goods—a baby of her own.

When one door closed, she reminded herself, another one opened. The twins were her solace, her joy. A consolation prize she intended to cherish. Eric Oakes would have to come up with a whale of a good prospect for a wife before she would even consider relinquishing the babies to him.

And he'd need to do it in a hurry. Both for the sake of her heart and her career, Laura couldn't remain in Grass Valley much longer. She needed to accept that job Alex Thurman had offered her and get on with her life.

With Becky in her arms and Mandy in her car seat, Laura was feeding the twins when Eric came into the kitchen for breakfast.

"Good morning." He went to the bread box, took a couple of slices and dropped them in the toaster before pouring himself a mug of the coffee she'd fixed. "Once I got home last night, I must have crashed pretty hard. I didn't hear the babies at all."

"I thought you'd be tired, so I let you sleep. The twins were good, though." She kissed Becky's forehead. "They slept four hours straight and only woke up once, at three. And went right back down again after I put some of that gel on their gums."

"Boy, that sounds like progress, doesn't it?"

She stiffened her resolve. "Yes. But last night does illustrate the problem of my even considering giving custody of the twins to you."

"How so?"

"Eric, you get called out to work at irregular hours. Unless you have a wife—"

"I'm working on it."

"I'm aware of that. Under some circumstances a live-in housekeeper might do. But I'm not willing to agree to an arrangement like that. A housekeeper is too likely to move away or want to get a better job."

The toast popped up but he ignored it. "In a pinch I could take the twins to Rory's place. Nobody's more qualified to take care of babies than Kristi is."

"The point I'm trying to make is that the twins deserve a consistent caregiver. A real *mother* figure. It's what Amy specifically wanted, and I'm not convinced you can provide that."

"You promised to give me some time."

"Time's running out, Eric. I've got to get back to Helena. I have my own life to think about."

"So you're saying you'll never have an emergency? Not even a late-night meeting you have to attend?"

"Not on my new job. And if I do, my mother lives only ten minutes away. She won't be a stranger to the twins but someone they are familiar with and already love."

He yanked the toast from the toaster and spread butter on the cold bread. "Sounds like you've already made up your mind what you're going to do."

"Not entirely. You said there's a woman coming today."

"Great. If she's not satisfactory in your view, I lose, huh?"

She hated herself for agreeing with his assessment, but that was about the size of things. "I'll be happy for you to be a part of the twins' life. You're their uncle. We can keep in touch. You can come visit."

"Forget it, Cavendish. I plan to fight you for the twins. In court, if I have to. Family counts."

She opened her mouth to speak but snapped it shut when the doorbell rang. The next wannabe bride applicant? Her stomach did a tumble.

Before he turned to leave the kitchen, Eric sent her a look that said he'd never give up.

Stubborn man! Why couldn't he have been content with being a loving uncle? In a child's world, that was an important role. Why did he insist on being their father when Laura wanted so much to be their mother?

She lifted Becky to her shoulder, gave her a little pat on the back, eliciting an unladylike burp. Then she switched the babies around, holding Mandy as she finished her bottle.

From the living room, she heard feminine laughter and Eric's deeper response. She grimaced at the good time they seemed to be having. Dear heaven, they'd only just met. What could they be laughing about?

Holding the woman by the hand, Eric brought her into the kitchen. She appeared to be about thirty with long, brunette hair and wide brown eyes that were striking in their intelligence and good humor. Her figure was equally well endowed.

Eric introduced them. "Delores, meet Laura Cavendish. She was a good friend to my sister."

Very poised, Delores crossed the room and extended her hand. "Call me DeeDee, please. And I'm honored to meet you. From what Eric told me yesterday on the phone, I can't imagine having a better friend than you were to his sister." Her eyes strayed to Mandy, and she smiled without a hint of guile.

"Nice to meet you, too," Laura said, straining to be polite. "Amy and I were more than friends. We were like sisters."

Sitting down at the table, DeeDee gazed with obvious longing at the twins. "What about the biological father? He'd have rights—"

"He's never been in the picture," Eric stated unequivocally. "From what Laura has told me about the way he treated Amy, he wouldn't get a warm reception if he showed up around here."

DeeDee glanced up at him, smiled, and looked back at the twins. "They're three months old?"

"A little more than that now," Laura said.

"This next year is going to be so exciting. They'll grow so fast and learn so much."

"You know about raising babies?"

Her bright, happy expression filled with sorrow. "I lost my husband and our two-year-old son five years ago in an accident. I never read the personals, really I don't. But for some reason I spotted Eric's ad." As though she couldn't help herself, she trailed a loving finger along Becky's cheek. "It seemed to reach out, as though it was written just for me."

Laura swallowed hard. She had no idea how any woman could recover from the loss of both a child and her husband. "I'm sorry."

"I checked out the accident," Eric said. "A multicar crash on Interstate 90. A big rig jackknifed. More than a dozen vehicles were involved, five deaths including DeeDee's husband and son."

Laura's stomach knotted.

DeeDee glanced toward Eric and then included Laura. "Please don't think I'm trying to duplicate the family I had. I know I can't do that. But it's time I moved on with my life and well..." Very gently, as if she were testing the water in an unfamiliar swimming pool, she lifted Becky from the car seat. "If I had a chance to love these two precious babies, I'd feel like I'd fulfilled my life." She glanced over her shoulder, her smile hopeful. "I'd be a good wife, too, Eric. I promise."

For a moment Laura wanted to snatch the baby back from DeeDee. The woman had no right to hold *her* child—the baby she loved. But that wasn't true. If Eric had found an appropriate wife for him and a good mother for the twins, Laura had to accept that. It's what Amy had wanted.

Her lungs nearly closed down tight. Who in their right mind would expect her to give up the twins to someone else when she had the power to say no?

Except the nagging voice of her conscience told her she wouldn't have any other choice. Not if it was the right thing to do.

They'd all visited for a while in the kitchen, DeeDee getting acquainted with the twins. Eric had to admit it was damn uncomfortable, DeeDee talking like the babies were already hers to raise and Laura barely able to string two words together, she'd been so tense.

Not that he blamed her. She loved the twins, and DeeDee looked to be a serious contender to replace her as their mother.

Once they managed to get the babies down for their nap—sort of fumbling all over each other in the process, Eric decided to take DeeDee on a tour of the place. At least that would give Laura a few minutes of peace.

He walked DeeDee out to the corral. Both of his sorrel geldings trotted over to the fence to greet them.

"I only keep a couple of horses here," he said. "Mostly for recreation or if someone gets lost and we have to do a ground search."

"Oh, they're a handsome pair," DeeDee said. She stroked the muzzle of the first one who'd hung his head over the fence.

"That's Archy and the other one is Bashful."

She laughed. "I'm sorry I didn't think to bring apples or carrots for them."

"They're really looking for sugar cubes, but that's bad for them." Resting his arm on the top rail of the corral, he studied her while she petted the horses. Attractive. Certainly friendly. Nice figure. Laughs easily, which was saying something for a woman who'd lost her entire family not that many years ago. "Do you ride?"

"I haven't in years. My grandparents used to have a ranch not far from Jordan, which isn't actually close to anywhere. I spent some summers there as a kid."

"So you like small towns?"

"Absolutely. I loved being at Grandma's house and taking the big trip into Jordan on Saturday to do the shopping." Her smile was warm and engaging, filled with happy memories. "Great Falls is fine. And I have lots of friends there. But moving here wouldn't be a problem. Grass Valley looked quaint as I drove through."

Quaint wasn't exactly how Rory would describe the town—that sounded a little too high class, he thought. Like Swift Eagle was too ritzy sounding for Rory. He was just a guy. Eric's brother. Like Grass Valley was just a town.

"The one thing that does bother me," she confided, "is guns. Particularly around children."

He could understand that and echoed her concern. "At home I keep my weapon in a locked safe in the kitchen right by the back door. I never wear it inside the house. And my bigger artillery I keep at the office, also under lock and key."

She smiled at him softly. "You're a good man, Sheriff Oakes."

He sensed she was a good woman, too, and damned if he wasn't sorry there weren't any sexual sparks flying. He ought to be attracted to her. Everything about her seemed *right*.

Maybe when they got better acquainted...

He showed her his small barn, not that it was worth writing home about, but it served his purposes, and the detached garage where he housed his police vehicle at night. His tools were stashed there, too.

"I've got two acres here plus the house. I also have an interest in the Double O Ranch out east of town, but my brother runs that."

"A brother?" She cocked a brow in wry amusement. "You mean there are more like you somewhere?"

He felt heat color his cheeks. "Naw, I'm unique."

"I can see that, Eric. I really can."

Well, hell! He'd finally found a woman who thought he walked on water and he didn't get the charge he'd hoped for. He kept thinking about Laura inside the house, worried about what was happening, terrified she'd lose the twins.

Damn, life wasn't fair.

The day seemed to drag. He took DeeDee to the office. She seemed dutifully impressed with his job and the jail cells, and gratified they were unoccupied.

He took her to lunch at the saloon. Nobody commented, but he got an odd look from Joe Moore, who was sitting at the bar having a hamburger and a beer.

When they got back to Eric's house, DeeDee gave Becky her afternoon bottle and seemed to relish the experience. *Poignant* came to mind.

Distress registered in Laura's expression. But to her credit, she didn't say a word. She was one courageous lady because Eric knew how much she was hurting.

In Eric's head, a clock as giant as London's Big Ben kept ticking. He didn't have much time to choose a wife. Laura was planning to leave soon. She'd take the twins with her unless he could find a way to stop her.

After the twins went down for their nap, Laura stayed upstairs, claiming she had some paperwork to do for school.

Downstairs DeeDee stood in the middle of the living room, glancing around as though studying every angle, every nuance, branding them into her memory.

She exhaled deeply. "I think both of us have a great deal to think about."

"Yeah. That's true."

"I'm going to go back home now—"

"You could stay the night. The accommodations wouldn't be great but—"

"No. I'm going back to Great Falls." Slowly she walked toward him, then stood on tiptoe, pressing a kiss to his lips. "You call me about your decision, okay?"

"Yeah, I will." He wanted to feel something. Anything! But the warmth of her lips didn't do squat for him. Or his libido. Why the hell not? She'd make a great mother for the twins but—

Palming his cheek, she smiled. "It's not there, is it?"

"I don't know. I mean—"

"It's okay. I loved my husband desperately. It was probably foolish of me to even think of this kind of marriage of convenience. But you have taught me something."

He frowned. "What's that?"

"That I am capable of caring about another man. I needed that lesson." Her smile was both sad and hopeful. "I'm going to use that lesson and move on with my life. Thanks."

"DeeDee, I—"

"No. From what I've seen, you ought to be taking a serious look at Laura."

"She loves the twins, but I'm not part of the package."

Cocking her head, she studied him a moment, then smiled. "Well, thanks for the grand tour. Keep me posted, huh?"

"Sure, I—"

She was out the front door before he had a chance to say anything else. Slipping into her two-door sedan, she gave a friendly wave as he stood rooted to the front porch. And then she was gone.

Desperation gnawing at his gut, Eric wondered what to do next. He'd pretty well eliminated all the women who had called, and he hadn't had the courage to propose to the one applicant who had pretty well fit the bill. Laura had a job to go back to in Helena.

Behind him, he heard the screen door open and her footsteps on the porch.

"I thought DeeDee might stay for dinner. I was going to do a chicken casserole."

He didn't turn, couldn't bring himself to look at her. "She needed to get back home, to Great Falls."

"I see."

He whirled around. "No, you don't. She knew, dammit, that I wasn't going to propose to her. She matched every damn item on the list we made, but I wasn't going to pop the question." His breath drove hard and painful through his lungs.

Her frown lowered her brows. "Why not?"

"Because it wasn't fair to you, that's why not."

She shook her head. "I don't understand."

"You love the twins. So do I. Amy wanted them raised by both a mom and a dad." He didn't know why he hadn't throught of this before. Maybe DeeDee's comment had triggered the idea.

Maybe he should have considered the possibility earlier.

Shoving his fingers through his hair, he took a deep breath, almost as if he were planning to jump off a cliff into a deep pool of icy-cold water. "The only thing that makes sense here is if you and I raise them together. That the two of us get married."

Chapter 8

Laura gaped at him, dumbfounded. Her heart was in her throat, her stomach had plummeted clear to her toes. Knees suddenly weak, she reached for the porch railing to steady herself.

"What are you saying?" Her voice was barely more than a whisper. Was he really proposing marriage? Or had her hearing been affected by too many sleepless nights? Or too many fantasies?

Folding his arms across his chest, he leaned back against the porch post. "It's the logical thing to do. Amy will get what she wanted, and we'll both get to raise the twins. We'll adopt them together."

Whatever was happening, this wasn't like any proposal Laura had dreamed of receiving. "Logical? For two people to marry who barely know each other?" Forget she was falling in love with Eric. That wasn't the issue. "You can't get married just for the sake of the children. That isn't at all logical."

"Why not? Couples stay married for their kids all the time. You wanted me to find a wife out of the blue. At least you and I have been living together for more than a week. We haven't come to blows yet."

"That's hardly the same thing as being married." Separate bedrooms. They hadn't even kissed, not once, assuming close didn't count. Their most intimate moments had been during the middle of the night when they each had a lapful of baby.

Trying to regain her equilibrium, Laura sat down on one of the two wicker chairs on the porch. She couldn't agree to a marriage without love. The pain of living with Eric, being his wife, and knowing he didn't love her would be too much to bear. Eventually it would wear away at her self-respect and her patience. Her libido would either shrivel to nothing or spin helplessly out of control from overstimulation because Eric didn't desire her in the way she wanted him.

It wouldn't take long for others to realize their marriage was a farce. Even the twins, as they grew older, would recognize the absence of love.

She blinked back the tears of regret that flooded her eyes. "No. I can't do that."

Straightening, Eric jammed his hands in his pockets. She'd let him know exactly where he stood: at the end of the line in terms of a marriage prospect. DeeDee had been way off base about Laura wanting to give him the time of day. He tried not to feel disappointed. She hadn't come to Grass Valley looking for romance.

But he wasn't a man who gave up easily. And he wasn't going to lose the twins if he could help it.

"Okay, here's another idea," he said. When a rodeo bronc threw you, you tried again. Winners didn't quit. "A compromise. We can keep on as we are, you living here, taking care of the twins. A housekeeper-nanny arrangement."

Her eyes widened, then narrowed. "Eric, I have a job. A career. I'm about to be promoted. You can't expect me to simply give up—"

"We've got a school right here in town. Maybe not as big as the one you're used to or as fancy. It's a K-through-12 with about four hundred students. Small classes. Good academics. They're on summer break right now but I could take you over there. Let you take a look."

"You're suggesting I could teach, and in my spare time I can be your housekeeper and the twins' nanny? Do you have any idea how many hours a teacher works beyond the hours they spend in the classroom? It's a sixty-hour week."

Mentally throwing up his hands, he paced around the porch, his booted feet heavy on the old wooden planks. "You don't have to work at all. I'll pay you, whatever you want. I've got plenty of income to support you and the twins." He was getting desperate now, his options shrinking to none. "For God's sake, I don't know what else to suggest. I'm running out of ideas. You could give me some help here, okay? I'm trying to make this work for both of us."

She dipped her head, her blond hair sliding across her chin, forming an impenetrable veil of gold. "I know. But I don't think it's possible. Not the way you're proposing we do it."

His jaw clenched on a curse. "Makes me wonder if you ever intended to give me a chance with the twins. Maybe you planned all along to show up, tell me I didn't fit the bill and then scurry back to your own life."

"That's not true. At least, not entirely."

"Yeah, sure." He walked off the porch steps. Behind him the sun was lowering in the sky, casting long shadows, and the summer air was beginning to cool. In the distance the plains stretched out to the horizon, broken only by an occasional rise in the ground that could barely be called a hill.

He loved this country. It was his home, tough winters and blistering summers alike. Oliver Oakes had brought him here almost twenty years ago, and Eric had put his roots into the soil. He didn't want to move to Helena. He doubted, with the metal pin in his leg leftover from his rodeo days, the police force would hire him. So what kind of job could he get? Night security? Hell, that was no kind of job at all.

If it made any sense for him to go with her to Helena, he'd give it a shot. But it didn't.

On the porch, he heard the creak of the wicker chair as Laura stood. "I'm sorry, Eric. I'm not sure what I expected when I came here, but I… I have to go home."

"You're taking the twins?"

"I can't leave them. Not under the circumstances."

He swore low and succinctly.

"If you don't mind," she said, "I'll stay the night, do

some packing and leave in the morning. I don't want to disrupt the twins' schedule too much."

"Whatever." He shrugged, though it pulled shoulder muscles that were way too tense. She'd been perfectly willing to disrupt not only his schedule but his life. He almost…almost wished he hadn't learned about the twins. That he had a sister. That he was an uncle to his own flesh and blood.

It would be easier if he hadn't known.

For the first time since the twins were born, Laura was grateful for their penchant for being fussy during dinner. Between the racket and juggling babies from car seat to wind-up swing to someone's arms, conversation was impossible. She didn't know what to say to Eric, anyway.

Apparently he didn't, either. He looked so glum, he might well have just lost his best friend. In a way, she supposed that's what he was feeling. She was taking the twins away from him.

It was as though she were killing his sister—for a second time. And he'd only just learned that she had existed.

But what was she supposed to do? Of course men did raise babies on their own. Even adopt babies themselves. But that wasn't what Amy had wanted for the twins. And with the irregular hours that came with Eric's job, the logistics seemed insurmountable.

Even so, her conscience kept sitting on her shoulder, jabbering at her that there had to be another way. She hated to hurt anyone. Eric was a good man. He'd make a wonderful father.

But she'd make a good mother, too. The twins were her only chance to prove that.

In her effort to do the right thing, she'd put both herself and Eric in an untenable position.

Getting up from the table, she cleared their plates. She noted Eric hadn't eaten much more than she had. Their respective appetites had apparently fled together.

"Why don't you leave all that?" he said, holding Becky to his shoulder and patting her back. "I'll get it done while you start your, uh, packing."

She swallowed hard. "Are you sure?"

Nodding, he shifted Becky to the other shoulder and reached over to give the swing another crank, setting Mandy in motion again. "I've got it covered."

"All right." The tension in the room was too thick, her conscience too prickly for her to want to linger.

Upstairs, she gazed around the nursery, not knowing quite where to begin. The twins had received so many gifts she'd need more than the one suitcase she'd brought to pack their things in now. And what should she do about the dual stroller? Eric's family had given them that. It didn't seem fair to haul that off to Helena.

Or the infant swing, which Eric had bought himself. And the oak dresser.

Maybe he could get his money back. The dresser, at least, he could use for other things.

She set out a couple of clean outfits for the twins to wear in the morning. The bibs Marlene Huhn had hand embroidered were in the same drawer. Laura ran her fingertips over the carefully scripted names. She'd like to take the bibs with her—for the twins.

They needed to have tangible evidence of their short stay with their uncle Eric.

Regret thickened in her throat as she placed the infant garments in the suitcase. If Eric had expressed any affection for her, she might have stayed with him. Agreed to be his wife and hope that someday his feelings for her would deepen.

Very likely that would have been a foolish dream. One that would hurt more acutely with each passing year.

Finally she'd squeezed everything she could into the twins' suitcase. She'd need a cardboard box or some grocery sacks in order to pack the rest of the toys and clothing. Eric would have to decide what he wanted to do with the larger gifts.

As she walked down the stairs, she heard Eric singing softly, his voice a mellow baritone. Her heart hitched when she realized it was a lullaby. He, or more likely his brothers, had been wrong about Eric not being able to carry a tune. He and Amy shared the same musical talent.

Tiptoeing into the living room, she found him with Mandy settled in the crook of his arm and Becky propped on his crossed knees. The sweet, haunting sound of his voice reached out to her even as it soothed the babies. The pain and desolation she heard tore at her heart.

Dear God! How could she do this to him? The elemental unfairness of their situation shattered what little self-control she'd been clinging to, and tears edged down her cheeks. Whatever was best for the twins had to be the right thing to do for all of them. If she suffered in some small measure as a result, it was a minor sacrifice to make for their happiness.

"I'll stay," she whispered.

Slowly Eric lifted his head, his eyes red-rimmed, questioning her.

"I've changed my mind," she said with a little more force. "I'll stay with you and the twins, if you still want me to."

He seemed to struggle to regain his composure. "Yeah. That would be fine. Good."

Impressing her with his enthusiasm didn't appear to be on his mind. "Not as your housekeeper, though. This is a pretty small town. If you and I live together, no matter what we said about our relationship, people will think that—"

"We're having sex."

"Yes." Her lips had gone as rough as toast, and she licked them. Not that it helped much. Her mouth was almost as parched as her lips. "I don't want the girls growing up thinking that we're doing anything...illicit."

"Then you're thinking we ought to get married?"

Actually, she was thinking she'd lost her mind. She'd turned down his proposal only hours ago and now she was asking him. In both cases, they were acting as though they were negotiating a contract that would barely change their lives. Like buying a car. Or taking out a loan for a vacation trip.

"I assume we're talking about a marriage-in-name-only," she said.

He eyed her a moment before speaking. "If that's what you'd like."

Love would be so much nicer. That wasn't one of the choices. "I think it's wiser that way, don't you? No emotional baggage. Just an arrangement."

Mandy had dozed off, and he tried to adjust her position. Laura hurried to pick her up. Her hand brushed against Eric's, warm masculine flesh against her cooler skin. A sensual current shot up her arm, speeding on its way to her midsection, and she nearly wept because that was all she'd ever experience with Eric—unfulfilled desire.

How in heaven's name would she avoid making a fool of herself for the rest of their married life when he affected her so strongly after only a week?

An easy trick to accomplish, she reminded herself, since he didn't appear to want her in the same way she'd begun to want him.

She slipped Mandy into her car seat on the floor as gently as possible so she wouldn't awaken.

"You do understand," she said, "that by marrying me—even if it weren't just an arrangement—that I'd never be able to give you the family you wanted. More children."

He glanced at Becky, asleep in his arms. "That won't be a problem."

"Fine, then." Contract agreed to. Shouldn't they at least shake hands, she thought on the edge of hysteria. Fix their signatures to some multipage form? "I'll have to call my boss, let him know I can't accept the coordinator's job. Or even teach in the fall." She'd miss that. She truly loved cramming history into those rebellious teenage brains when they were barely aware it was happening. Or helping other teachers to do the same with their students.

"You want to teach here?" Eric asked. "I could talk to the principal, see if there are any openings."

"To tell you the truth, for the next year or so, maybe until they're in school, I think it would be better if I stayed home with the twins."

His lips twitched ever so slightly. "A full-time, stay-at-home mom?"

"Their first few years are crucial. If you can afford—"

"I can. And I like the idea." As gently as if he were handling a porcelain doll, he laid Becky on the couch beside him. "What do you want to do about the wedding?"

"Well, I…" She hadn't been thinking that far ahead. How should she act, what should she wear for a marriage ceremony that was no marriage at all? "Let's keep it small. Very low-key."

"I could arrange for a judge in Great Falls to marry us in his chambers."

"That will be fine," she agreed. She refused to mourn the loss of a church wedding in a white gown with friends and family hovering around her. Her marriage to Eric would not be a celebration.

"We'll need a license. And it may take a few days for the judge to clear his calendar."

"No problem. When we get the license, we can begin formalizing the adoption."

"Sounds reasonable. I'd like to have my brothers attend the wedding, if you don't mind. You could invite your mother."

Sitting on the floor beside Mandy, she fiddled with the pad in the car seat, straightening it. Trying to breathe past the pain in her chest.

"Since it's the only wedding I'm likely to have, I imagine inviting my mother would be a good idea. It's going to be hard enough on her as it is, moving the twins up here permanently. She'll miss them terribly."

"She can visit whenever she wants. Kids need a grandma, and I've got lots of room for her to stay here."

"I'll tell her. Thanks."

"It'll be your home, too. You can have anyone visit that you want to. You'll probably want to do some redecorating, too. As long as you don't go hog wild, anything you want is fine with me."

"There's the furniture at my condo." She glanced around, trying to imagine her lighter, more feminine taste contrasting with his masculine choice of leather and dark wood. "I'm afraid it won't go well with what you already have."

"Then we'll toss my stuff. Or move it into the den. I want you to feel comfortable here."

He was being so damn generous it hurt. But most of all, it hurt because he didn't love her.

What else could she expect? Gary Swanson, the one man she had been foolish enough to believe *could* love her, had made it clear she was less than the ideal mate. So be it. She'd devote her life instead to being the best mom possible.

With luck, she and Eric would become friends. Companions who put the best interests of the twins first. She didn't dare hope for more.

Glancing out the living room window, she noted twilight was beginning to settle in, leaving the cottonwood tree in the front yard in shadows. When they were old enough, the girls would love having a swing hanging from one of the big branches.

Her chin quivered. She'd look forward to giving them their first push.

After spending the next morning making arrangements for the wedding and starting the adoption ball rolling, Eric headed across the road to Rory's place. He was going to tell his brother about the upcoming nuptials and wished he felt better about the situation.

He'd practically forced Laura into agreeing to marry him. Backed her into a corner. She was so damn softhearted she hadn't been able to take the twins away from him. She'd sacrificed her home and her career for his sake and her own desire to be a mother. Not many women had that kind of courage or were that generous.

He wasn't sure what he could give her in return. But he'd do his darnedest to make sure she was never sorry about her decision.

Five-year-old Adam was riding his two-wheeler in circles on the clinic driveway, his dog, Ruff, chasing him around and around. The dog peeled off from the game to greet Eric, his shaggy tail wagging like a semaphore flag. Of indiscriminate breeding, Ruff appeared to be mostly sheep dog, his eyes hidden behind long, uneven bangs.

"Hi, fella." He scratched Ruff behind his ears and patted his side, so thick with fur it was hard to tell where the dog ended and the fur began.

"Hi, Uncle Eric." Adam wheeled around and slid to a stop in front of Eric, sending gravel sailing from the ten-inch wheels.

"Hey, there, kid. I'm gonna have to ticket you for reckless driving if you keep this up." He knocked his knuckles on top of the boy's safety helmet.

"Uh-uh. I'm too little to get a ticket."

"Don't count on it, Little Gray Puppy. I'm a pretty tough cop, you know."

"Little Gray *Wolf!*" The youngster giggled, laughing at Eric's incorrect use of his Indian name, his dark eyes flashing. "You're not tough. You're my *uncle.*"

He gave the boy's shoulder a squeeze. The twins would grow up knowing Adam and any of the boy's siblings who might come along. Walker's kids, too. They'd have lots of cousins to play with and watch out for them. They were lucky little girls—all because Laura had such an unselfish heart.

A stab of guilt reminded him that he'd taken advantage of that admirable trait. Somehow he had to make it up to her.

"Where's your dad?" he asked.

"He and mom are inside fixing up a raccoon with a hurt foot. Want me to show you how I can do a wheelie?"

"Maybe later, okay?"

Ruff followed Eric as far as the clinic door, then dashed back to rejoin his playmate. The circling began again.

Inside the clinic, stainless steel glistened in the examining room where Rory and Kristi were bending over a sleeping raccoon working their medical magic.

"I sure hope you got paid before you started that

procedure," Eric commented. "Last I heard, insurance benefits for raccoons didn't pay real well."

Kristi smiled at him from the end of the table.

Without looking up, Rory said, "He's kind of an old guy. We figure if we fill out the forms right Medicare will pick up the tab."

"Great. My brother's committing a federal offense, probably a felony, right under my nose."

Kristi shook her head in amusement, and Eric's lips twitched. She was used to their bantering by now—even when it revolved around an anesthetized raccoon.

"I figure I'm safe from the long arm of the law. It's not your jurisdiction so you won't bother to lock me up. Besides, if you did, you'd have to feed me, and you can't afford my gourmet tastes." Rory finished stitching the injury, clipped the thread and glanced over his shoulder. "What's up?"

"Laura and I are going to get married."

"Eric!" Kristi shrieked. "That's wonderful! She seems like such a nice woman, and the twins are so beautiful."

"Yeah, well, it's not exactly—"

Rory said, "I thought you were going to pick one of the women who answered the newspaper ad."

"They didn't work out."

"When? When?" Kristi wanted to know. "Lizzie and I will have to have a shower for her. Oh, this is so exciting."

"We're getting married next Tuesday. Judge Cole's office in Great Falls."

Kristi's eyes widened, and she gaped at Eric.

"Wow," Rory muttered. "That's pretty quick."

"You can't possibly get married that soon," Kristi gasped. "Or in a *judge's* office, for heaven's sake. That wouldn't be fair to Laura. Whatever are you thinking?"

"It's what we decided," Eric insisted, frowning.

"If that's what they want, honey—"

"Nonsense." Kristi yanked off her latex gloves and dropped them into the trash can, then nailed Rory with a wifely look. "I remind you, Rory Oakes, that both you and Walker were married right here in the Grass Valley Church with Reverend McDuffy performing the ceremony. Eric and his bride deserve just as much. And I'll tell you, as a recent bride, that as terrified as I was that day, I wouldn't have traded that ceremony for all the tea in China. I'll hold those memories close to my heart for the rest of my life."

A blush appeared beneath Rory's olive complexion. "Me, too, I guess. Though the honeymoon is what I remember best."

Rolling her eyes, Kristi hooked her wrist on her waist and glared at Eric. "So that's settled. You're going to be married at the church."

"I don't even know if McDuffy would be available next Tuesday. He might have something else on his schedule."

"Fine. Pick another time when he is available and ask the reverend to perform the ceremony. Tuesday is way too soon, anyway. Laura is going to have to find a dress, probably have it altered. She'll need to order flowers and let her friends know about—"

"Laura doesn't want to make a big deal out of the wedding," Eric insisted, his temper rising. This whole arrangement was hard enough on both him and Laura as it was. He didn't want his sister-in-law sticking her nose into his business. "Neither of us wants to make a fuss."

Kristi's eyes narrowed and she shook her head. "Maybe you don't want a big production, but I'm telling you every woman dreams about her wedding from the time she's old enough to know what a wedding is. Nowhere in that dream is she standing in front of a judge who is wearing a black robe. Trust me on this, Eric."

"She's probably right, White Eyes," Rory said with a shrug. "Unless there's some big crisis, waiting another week or so wouldn't hurt, would it?"

"I guess not. But the fact is, she seems happy enough with the judge thing. She may not want to drag out this whole ordeal."

"Men!" Kristi huffed. "You leave Laura to me and Lizzie." Standing on tiptoe, she brushed a sisterly kiss to Eric's cheek. "Congratulations, Eric. I'm sure you and Laura will be very happy together."

Left standing alone with Rory in the examining room after Kristi whizzed out the door, Eric shook his head. "Is she always like that?"

"You mean stubborn and willful?"

"Yeah. Something like that."

Rory grinned. "She's great, isn't she? A take-charge kind of gal."

Eric mentally groaned. Already this marriage business wasn't working out exactly as he had anticipated. He had the terrible feeling a woman who became a wife metamorphosed into someone quite different.

He didn't want that to happen to Laura. He liked her just fine the way she was.

Chapter 9

"Yes, Mother, I know it's sudden." Twisting the long, curling phone cord around her finger, Laura paced across the kitchen. The twins were down for their afternoon nap. It had seemed like a good time to break the news of the wedding plans to her mother. Or rather, Laura had decided there was no sense in putting off the inevitable.

"You barely know the man, dear." A rare hint of censure slipped into Barbara Cavendish's voice. "I think you ought to take some time—"

"He's as fine a man as I've ever met, Mother. And he loves the twins as much as I do." Only one small element was missing that would make theirs a match made in heaven—Eric didn't love her.

"But what about the wedding itself? I'd always

hoped we could have a nice affair, nothing lavish, of course, but something where we could invite—"

"I'll be just as married this way. Eric and I have discussed—"

There was a knock on the back door and it opened. "Hello? Anybody here?" Kristi poked her head inside, grinning like a schoolgirl who had just learned the biggest secret in town. "Oh, there you are."

"Mom, I've got company. I'll call you back, okay?"

"I just wish—" Barbara sighed. "All right, honey. I'll talk to you later."

Lizzie followed Kristi into the kitchen. "Sorry if we interrupted you," Lizzie said with her usual gracious manner.

"I was talking to my mother."

Exuberantly Lizzie wrapped her arms around Laura, hugging her. "I hope your mom is as excited as we are. Eric just told us that you're getting married. Welcome to the family."

"We all wish you both the very best," Lizzie said.

"Thank you. I know it's a little sudden—"

"You've got that darn straight, sister." Laughing, Kristi led Laura to the table and sat her down. "There is no possible way we can get everything done by next week."

"Done? There's really nothing to—"

"You have to buy a gown. Even the fastest alterations take a week or more."

"I have a nice summer suit at home," Laura protested. "I thought I'd wear that." She'd ask her mother to bring it to the courthouse. Which meant she'd have to change in a stark public restroom, she realized with a shudder of dismay.

Lizzie sat opposite Laura at the table. "I think Kristi has something else in mind."

"In addition to getting you a gown, we need enough time to pull together a shower for you."

"Absolutely not. You've already given the twins—"

Kristi waved off her objection. "Furthermore, there's no way you want to be in a position that Lizzie and I can lord it over you twenty years from now that we were married in a church and you were married in some blah judge's chambers, for heaven's sake. So the judge thing is out."

Beyond confused, Laura stared at her future sisters-in-law. "You're not the kind of people who would—"

"Of course we're not now. But who knows what we'll be like when we hit menopause. You need to protect yourself."

Lizzie made a choking sound that was somewhere between a cough and a laugh, quite indelicate for her usually sophisticated manners.

"Now, as I see it," Kristi explained, "a trip to Great Falls is in order for the three of us. We'll help you pick out a gown—"

"She may not want to spend the money," Lizzie warned. "A formal gown can be pretty expensive for something you only wear once."

"Well, that's easy. She can borrow mine," Kristi volunteered. "Or yours," she suggested to Lizzie. "All three of us are about the same size."

"I didn't actually wear a gown when I married Walker—though I admit I arrived in Grass Valley with a gown in the trunk of my car that was suitable for a cathedral wedding." She smiled at the memory. "I decided on something a little less ostentatious when the time came."

Laura spoke up. "I appreciate you're both trying to help—"

"Whatever you decide," Kristi insisted, "you've got to have your own veil. I mean, the twins will want to wear that when they get married, don't you think?"

Tears suddenly welled up in Laura's eyes. She'd never been a weepy person, but the strain of the past ten days plus the approach of a loveless marriage had sent her emotions over the brink. Picturing Becky or Mandy at their own wedding coming down the aisle wearing the same veil she had worn to marry Eric was more than she could handle.

She covered her mouth with her hand as the tears crept down her cheeks.

Kristi patted her hand. "There, you see? You'll need your own veil. We'll fix you up with tons of borrowed stuff, won't we Lizzie?"

"I have a pearl necklace my grandmother passed down to me that you're welcome to borrow. I did wear that for my wedding."

"I'm sure Eric would want you to wear one of those frilly blue garters…so he can remove it," Lizzie finished with a grin.

"No, I really don't think—"

"Now, the reception." Kristi hopped up, found a notepad by the telephone and a pencil. "Obviously there's nowhere decent in Grass Valley to hold a sit-down dinner, and I'm not fond of a potluck for a wedding reception. But I had a cake and punch reception, and Harold at the pharmacy furnished ice cream."

"Which Fridge consumed in copious quantities," Lizzie added.

"Yes, well…"

Kristi was writing everything down. "Do you want to do printed invitations or drop notes to your friends? I could do up something simple on the computer, unless you'd rather go a little more formal."

"Formal won't be necessary."

"Lizzie, would you check with the minister about his calendar? See if he's got a Saturday open early next month. I get the feeling Laura and Eric are eager to get things going here."

Her head spinning, Laura said, "I really need to talk with Eric about this. We'd agreed—"

"I've already talked with that brother-in-law of ours. He'll agree to whatever we decide."

"Have you and Eric discussed a honeymoon?" Lizzie asked.

Laura flushed. In their case there wouldn't be a need for a honeymoon because they wouldn't be indulging in the intimacies that were usually involved. "No honeymoon." When both women looked at her in astonishment, she quickly added, "We can't leave the twins."

"Oh, we absolutely insist that you do leave the twins. A husband and wife need at least one night without interruption."

Lizzie nodded vigorously. "I'll second that. In fact, I'd recommend a week or more."

"Rory and I will baby-sit the twins," Kristi volunteered. "He needs to practice being around babies just in case, huh?" Her Cheshire grin suggested an ulterior motive behind her offer.

Laura made an attempt to gain some control over the wedding plans. But dealing with Kristi was like being caught up in a tornado; the wind took everything in its path.

She turned to Lizzie. "Is she always like this?"

"I think it comes from years of ordering people to use a bedpan."

Laura choked on a laugh. This whole wedding business was too much for her to deal with. If Eric wanted to object to Kristi's plans, he'd have to do it himself. She simply didn't have the strength to argue in the face of her own precarious emotions. Tears were far too close to the surface whenever she thought of the future and how she would survive a loveless marriage.

And the fact was, she would like something nicer than a simple ceremony in a judge's chambers. This was an event she didn't plan to repeat.

"You're right, ladies." Her quiet, determined voice halted their steamroller of ideas, much like a teacher silencing a classroom of rowdy youngsters. "Eric and I will be married in the church, and I'm going to wear a dress and a veil, just like I've always dreamed of doing. Eric will simply have to get used to it."

Kristi's gentle smile and her touch on Laura's hand told her that she'd made the right decision.

Eric scooped up some oats for his horses, handed a bucket to Laura and carried his to Bashful's stall while she fed Archy. It was well after dinnertime and the twins were down for the night, or at least for a few hours. Somehow in the past couple of weeks, chores had slipped to the end of his list of things to do.

"I'm going to have to get a couple of Walker's boys over here to exercise my horses," he said, giving Bashful an affectionate slap on his haunches. "I haven't had a chance to ride them since you and the twins have been here."

"The twins do consume a lot of time."

"Twice as much as one baby, I imagine."

"I don't know. I suspect babies simply fill up all the available time no matter how many there are. It's their nature."

"Yeah." For a woman mostly raised in the city, she looked comfortable around a horse, running her hand over Archy's mane, scratching behind his ears. Funny, he'd asked DeeDee right off if she liked to ride. He'd never bothered to ask Laura. Now it didn't matter. Either way, they were getting married.

God, he hoped this marriage was the right thing to do, not only for him and the twins but for Laura, too. She was giving up her home, her life, a career she was good at. He didn't want her to suffer for her sacrifice.

"Kristi and Lizzie came by this afternoon while you were out," she said.

"I thought they might. When Kristi gets a bit in her mouth, there's no stopping her."

Laura stepped out of Archy's stall, latching the door behind her. "They think we ought to get married at the church here in town."

"I already arranged things with Judge Cole."

"I know. And it's up to you, really."

He heard the hesitation in her voice and a hint of longing. "Is that what you'd like to do? Get married here?"

"It still wouldn't be anything fancy. Just family. But a judge's chambers seems so—"

"Cold. I know."

"It's the only wedding I'll ever have."

He swallowed hard. "Then we'll do it in the church." She deserved that and more for giving up so much. "You pick the date."

"I suspect by now Kristi already has." Laura's amused smile spoke volumes about what a good person she was. "I doubt I'll have to plan a thing. Including the honeymoon, if we let her have her way."

"Uh, honeymoon?" He hadn't thought that far ahead and wasn't sure he ought to, considering what a honeymoon usually entailed. Their in-name-only marriage wouldn't last long if he did.

"I told Kristi we couldn't leave because of the twins."

"That's true. It wouldn't be much of a honeymoon with a couple of babies along."

"She said she and Rory would baby-sit."

"Oh." He shoved his hands into his hip pockets as the image of Laura naked and beneath him popped into his head. His jeans grew snug at the thought, and he dropped his hands to his side, fisting his fingers.

"Under the circumstances we don't have to go anywhere. But people might think it's a little odd if we don't take at least one day."

The *night* was what he was thinking about. "Sure. We can do that. For appearances' sake, I mean."

"All right. You can make whatever arrangements you think will be suitable." Her gaze darted around the barn as though she was unable to look at him. "I'd better go back inside. I don't like to leave the twins alone too long."

"Fine. I'll be along in a few minutes." As soon as his libido cooled down a little. Maybe after a quick dip in the water trough.

After she left the barn, Eric leaned against Bashful's stall, exhaling slowly. How the hell was he going to keep his hands off Laura during their *honeymoon*, for God's sake?

He gritted his teeth. One night was going to seem like an eternity.

The following day they drove into Great Falls to get the marriage license and sign the formal papers to jointly adopt the twins. Two days after that Laura opened the front door to a tall, slender woman with salt-and-pepper hair who appeared to be in her sixties. She carried a briefcase in her hand.

"Hello, I'm Mabel Cannery from Children's Services."

"Oh?" Laura felt a moment of panic. Why would Children's Services come to see her?

The woman's smile was reassuring. "You must be Ms. Cavendish. You and Eric Oakes filed to adopt Amanda and Rebecca Thorne."

"Yes, come in. Please." Assuming this was a routine follow-up to the papers she and Eric had filed, Laura opened the door wider and stepped back out of the way. Glancing around, she mentally groaned at the toys and blankets scattered across the living room. If only she'd had a little warning. She hurried to pick up some of the debris.

"Please don't worry about the mess," Mabel said. "If there weren't some clutter around, then I'd worry." She headed directly for the twins, who were in their playpen by the window. "What beautiful little girls."

"Yes, they are."

"Is Eric around?"

"He's at his office. I can call—"

"No, that's all right. I'll stop by to see him. This is only a preliminary home visit, and he and I are old friends."

"You are?"

"Between his father, Oliver Oakes, and more recently Walker, the Oakes family has pretty well kept me employed for the past twenty-some years."

"You were involved with Eric's adoption?"

"I was. And Walker and Rory." She glanced down at the babies again. "They seem to have established a family tradition, adopting children."

"Eric is actually the twins' uncle."

"Yes, that was indicated in the adoption papers." She placed her briefcase on the coffee table and popped it open, removing a file folder. "I was wondering about the twins' biological father."

"I have no idea who he is."

"Generally speaking, a good-faith effort to locate the father is required in situations like this."

"I don't think he'd be at all interested in exerting his parental rights. He made no effort to contact Amy, their mother, at any time during her pregnancy or in the months since."

"I understand. The birth certificates indicate father unknown. Did Ms. Thorne know the father?"

Laura bristled slightly. "She didn't reveal that information to me. Her specific wishes were—"

"Yes, I have a copy of her request. And I understand you are currently the twins' legal guardian."

"Is there going to be a problem?"

"I wouldn't think so. I'm confident Eric will be a fine father, and you certainly appear well qualified. I simply wanted to clarify the situation."

"Of course." Becky was starting to squirm and fuss, so Laura picked her up. "Eric and I plan to marry soon. We'll provide the best home possible for the twins." Certainly better than their abusive father could, even if he were interested.

"I'm sure you will." She made a few notes in the file, then put it back in the briefcase. "I'll stop by to see Eric. I have to take some papers out to the Double O for Walker and Elizabeth to sign, so I'm actually killing two birds with one stone on this trip." She smiled and chuckled softly. "Not that the county will appreciate how efficient I'm being by saving the mileage expense for a second trip."

"I'm sure the taxpayers, at least, will appreciate your efforts, Ms. Cannery."

She brushed a hand over the back of Becky's head and glanced again at Mandy in the playpen. "I'd say these two are very lucky little girls. Thank you for seeing me, Ms. Cavendish. I wish you all happiness."

Laura saw the social worker out as far as the porch,

exhaling as the woman drove toward Eric's office. She didn't even like to think of the twins' biological father, much less consider he'd want to be involved in raising them.

Surely the issue would never arise.

Most women had months to plan a wedding. Laura had had less than two weeks. Although Kristi had been such a whirlwind, there'd been little left for Laura to do.

She'd taken a day to meet her mother in Great Falls to shop for a dress—an ankle-length white dress that was a little too formal for Grass Valley but she hadn't been able to resist the scalloped lace neckline and empire waist that emphasized her bust. Deep in her heart, she knew the reason she'd succumbed to the temptation of the dress. She wanted to impress Eric.

She sighed at her foolish impulse.

"Are you all right, dear?" her mother asked.

They were in Reverend McDuffy's office waiting for the ceremony to begin. The groom was somewhere in the building, but Laura hadn't seen him since last night when his brothers had dragged him off for one last bachelor's fling.

"All brides are a little nervous, aren't they, Mother?" Though Laura had more reason than most to feel anxious. She'd actually been so afraid Eric would change his mind at the last minute that she hadn't finished dressing until he arrived at the church.

"I suppose. But this has all been so rushed." Looking worried, Barbara Cavendish fussed with Laura's veil, adjusting it at her shoulders. "Did you really fall in love with Eric in such a short time?"

The lump in Laura's throat was so painful, she could barely swallow. Tears stung her eyes. "Yes," she whispered, unable to find her voice.

"Then everything will be fine. And you know..." Her mother's eyes glistened, too. "I think Amy would be very happy that she had a part in bringing you and her brother together."

"I hope so. I really do."

"Your father would be so pleased, too. He wanted so much for—"

"Oh, Mom." Unconcerned about mussing her dress, she embraced her mother, holding her tight. "I've always felt guilty about Dad dying like that. If he hadn't been on duty and the one to respond to that stupid accident I was in and find me all mangled—"

"Laura Cavendish, don't you think for a minute that your father's heart attack was your fault. I had no idea that for all these years—" Barbara stroked her daughter's cheek, brushing away a tear. "Don't you remember that Grandpa Cavendish died at an even younger age than your father did. Whatever was wrong with your father's heart, it was genetic. You had no part in his death."

"But if he hadn't been the one to—"

"Hush. Today is *your* day. Donald wouldn't want you shedding tears over him today. More than anything else in the world, he wanted you to be happy."

"I know, Mom."

She sniffed. "Then do exactly as your father would want. Enjoy every moment of your wedding."

"I'll try." Although if her marriage to Eric had been based on love, not the desire to provide a home for Amy's twins, Laura would be much happier. "Mother, would you walk me down the aisle? That way, Dad will be with us both."

Her mother looked shaken by the suggestion but nodded. "I think he'd like that idea."

The office door opened, and Kristi poked her head inside. "Everything's ready for you."

Laura drew a deep breath and picked up the spray of cut flowers she would carry down the aisle. This is what she wanted—for herself and for the twins. Eric would be a wonderful father. A good many women would have settled for less.

Her courage almost faltered at the entrance to the small church. The small gathering of close friends and family members she'd hoped for nearly filled the chapel. The townspeople were present to add their blessings to the ceremony.

She took Barbara's arm, as much to steady herself as to honor both her mother and her father. The organist switched songs, and together they stepped forward. In a way, she felt her father's presence, too, and tried to force a smile. For him. For the love they had shared and the guilt she'd carried for so long about his death.

Her heart thundered in her ears so loudly she could barely hear the music as she walked down the aisle. Her mouth was dry and the flowers she carried shook as though caught by a sudden draft coming through the open doors.

Concentrating on taking one step at a time, she finally looked up and saw Eric waiting for her, handsome and elegant in a Western-cut pale-blue suit and bolo tie. Her breath snagged in her lungs at the smile on his face, the admiring look in his eyes. Hope surged through her as she walked toward him. For whatever reasons they'd been brought together, their marriage *could* work.

She vowed to do her part—from this day forward.

With a nod of acknowledgement to Eric, her mother left her side to take her place in the front row of pews, and the marriage service began.

The preacher's words were a blur as she clandestinely watched Eric from the corner of her eye. What was he thinking? That he'd been forced by her into this marriage in order to raise the twins he'd come to love? Despite the hope she harbored for their future, would he come to hate her for what she'd done? Granted, he'd been the one to first suggest marriage. But that didn't mean he might have preferred some other choice which included the twins but not her.

He was an honorable man. She knew that was true. He'd respect their vows but at what cost to him? He'd never find the perfect woman, his own true love, as his brothers had. It all seemed so unfair, what she'd done to him. Or perhaps what they'd done to each other.

Suddenly she felt Eric slip a gold band over her finger. She had a moment of regret that she hadn't gotten Eric a ring, too, just before Reverend McDuffy said, "I now pronounce you husband and wife. You may kiss the bride."

Startled from her musings, she looked up at Eric. They'd never kissed before. Not once. They'd come close. She'd certainly thought about kissing him. But never once had that fantasy come true.

One corner of his lips hitched into a half smile. "Maybe we should have practiced this part before we had an audience," he said softly for her ears only.

Before she could respond, he bent his head and captured her lips with his. Tentatively. Asking permission. His fingers lightly caressing her cheek.

A sigh of welcome, of recognition, trembled across her lips. Her heart wanted to believe this was right. That marriage was meant to be. The feel of him, the shape of his lips, their warmth, was familiar to her, as though in some other life they had been lovers. The scent of his spicy aftershave was twenty-first century but her response was as ancient as time itself.

For a fanciful moment she thought of all the famous lovers who had filled the books she so loved to read—Romeo and Juliet, Antony and Cleopatra, Eliza Doolittle and Henry Higgins. She and Eric were none of those and yet they were the same.

Her heart was pounding hard when he broke the kiss, and she had no idea how long they'd been standing there in front of the congregation as husband and wife. Seconds or hours, it was as though time had stood still.

A ripple of applause circled the audience. One of his brothers said, "Way to go, White Eyes!" And Laura felt heat race to her cheeks.

Eric winked at her, turned them to face the crowd and they walked down the aisle together, her hand tucked in his arm.

Sometime later, while everyone was enjoying their

fill of cake and ice cream, Rory came over, nudging her with his elbow and giving Eric a knowing look.

"You gotta watch out for this guy tonight," Rory said, nodding toward his brother. "I'm told our sheriff likes to play with handcuffs."

She sputtered, almost spilling her punch. "Thanks for the warning. I'll keep that in mind."

Indeed, after their kiss at the altar, their one allotted night for a honeymoon was very much on her mind. Handcuffs, however, had not been part of the image.

And then she recalled all too clearly that she'd been the one to insist on a marriage-in-name-only.

Eric was a man who played by the rules. Unless she did something drastic, he wasn't likely to change her decree.

Worse, despite the warmth of his kiss, he might not want to.

Chapter 10

Laura got out of the SUV and stood beneath the pines, inhaling the sweet scent of the forest southeast of Great Falls. In front of her was a rustic ski lodge constructed of the same pines, a long porch stretching across the front of the building. In late August, no snow had fallen yet. Few cars were in the parking lot.

"This is lovely," she said. An idyllic spot for a honeymoon, remote and peaceful. Romantic. But perfect only if the marriage was to be a real one.

"Rory told me about the place. He and Kristi spent a few days here in June after they got married." Walking to the back of the truck, he lifted the hatch and hefted their two small suitcases out. He'd changed into jeans and a polo shirt at the church; she'd switched from her wedding gown to slacks and a blouse.

He stopped beside the truck, studying her and she

felt her forehead furrow. "You were pretty quiet the whole drive. Are you okay?"

Not really. "I miss the twins," she said, hedging. "I haven't been away from them for a whole night since I brought them home from the hospital." While that was true, being away from the twins wasn't Laura's biggest concern at the moment. Her honeymoon was.

"Then you deserve a night off. All mothers do now and then. Kristi and Rory will take good care of them." He cocked his head toward the lodge.

The nervous flutter in Laura's stomach that had plagued her since their kiss at the altar picked up velocity as she walked up the porch steps beside him. They'd left the reception early and made the trip here in little more than four hours. Now, as the sun dipped behind the mountain ridge, waning columns of sunlight danced through the tops of the trees, turning the pine needles to silver.

At the knotty-pine registration desk, a bright young woman wearing a white shirt with the lodge's logo on the pocket greeted them with a warm smile.

"Good evening. You must be Mr. and Mrs. Oakes."

Laura's stomach took another dip. Mrs. Oakes. How long would it take her to get used to her new name?

As though he did this sort of thing every day, Eric signed the register for them both while she fidgeted with the shiny gold band on her finger. A sure giveaway that they were newlyweds.

The young woman passed him the key. "The honeymoon suite is through those doors and to the left. Room five. Dinner is served until nine o'clock, and breakfast is available starting at six. The suite has a hot tub. It's very private," she emphasized with a knowing smile.

"Thanks."

"I didn't bring a swimsuit," Laura whispered as they walked away from the front desk.

He canted her a wicked smile. "I think the young lady was making the point that we won't need a swimsuit."

"Apparently I forgot to mention that I'm the modest type."

"I'm not."

They went out the back and followed the decking around to room five. He slipped the key into the lock and pushed open the door, holding it for her.

She hesitated at the threshold. "Maybe we should have gotten separate rooms." At opposite ends of the lodge, she thought a little hysterically.

"We'll manage with one."

Having a good many second thoughts about their arrangement, she took a shaky breath and stepped inside.

There was nothing rustic about the huge bed that filled one end of the room or the cozy love seat in front of a native rock fireplace. A sliding glass door beside the fireplace led onto a small porch and provided a view of the grassy ski slopes beyond the lodge. On the opposite side of the room the enclosed hot tub was clearly visible through another glass door.

Thus far she'd only seen Eric naked from the waist up. But it didn't take much imagination to picture the rest of him—narrow hips and long, muscular legs lightly covered with sandy-brown hair. His manhood nestled in a thatch of the same color hair.

She blinked, trying to rid herself of that image but to no avail.

"This is great." he said, placing her suitcase on a

stand in the walk-in closet. "No wonder Rory has such fond memories of his honeymoon."

"It's possible he was remembering Kristi more than the accommodations."

"Yeah, I guess he would." He strolled around the room, testing the bed, opening drawers in the low dresser, peering outside. "Well, what do you want to do? Eat dinner or take a dip in the hot tub first?"

"Dinner," she blurted out, though she wasn't in the least hungry. Her nerves were too on edge to eat a bite. But that was better than the alternative of getting naked in a hot tub with Eric.

Her gaze slipped to the bed. No matter how large it was, sleeping with him wasn't a good plan, either. And she doubted either of them would be comfortable on the love seat. The floor would be a better choice.

"Okay," he said. "You need to freshen up or anything?"

What she needed was a fairy godmother who could either turn her into a woman Eric could love or a robot who wouldn't care one way or the other.

"It will take me just a minute to get ready." She unzipped her suitcase, snatched her makeup kit and fled into the bathroom. One night. That's all she had to survive of this farce of a honeymoon. Then they could both go back to being parents to the twins. Friends. They wouldn't have to pretend to be anything more.

The realization did nothing to calm her nerves.

While Laura was doing whatever women did to get ready for dinner, Eric slipped out onto the porch overlooking the ski slopes. He needed some fresh air. Lots of it. The colder the better.

Coming here had been a bad plan.

He'd taken one look at that king-size bed and knew he wanted Laura there with him. Sleep wasn't part of the equation he had in mind.

He'd known for a long time that committing to a woman wasn't in him. He was too damn afraid she'd walk out on him like his mother had. He'd convinced himself no woman would stick with him. So he'd indulged in short-term relationships. When things got too hot, he bailed out.

Mostly, he'd kept himself at arm's length from any woman who even hinted at permanence.

Now he was married. He wanted to make love with Laura.

Unless he screwed up royally, she wasn't likely to leave. Because of the twins. Not because of him.

He wished to God things were different. That he was capable of giving her all she deserved.

He jammed his hands in his pockets and watched the soaring flight of a bald eagle in search of his evening meal, envying the fact that eagles mated for life.

All Eric could do was give Laura the best he had to offer and hope that was enough. His genes didn't come with a how-to book on commitment to a woman. Or vice versa, as nearly as he could tell. No woman had ever committed to him, either.

Only a few families were eating in the high ceilinged dining room, although it was easy to imagine the place packed during the ski season.

Laura nibbled at the chicken salad she'd ordered.

"You don't act like you're very hungry," Eric commented. He'd consumed the better part of a T-bone steak smothered in mushrooms plus a baked potato and green salad.

"I guess I ate too much of Harold's ice cream."

He cocked a skeptical brow. "Really? I didn't see you eat any."

"I'm sorry. Weddings can be pretty nerve-racking."

"Then I've got the perfect antidote. A long soak in the hot tub."

"Eric, I don't think—"

"I won't even peek. I promise."

In truth, the heat of the hot tub might relax her enough so that she could sleep. Even on the floor, if need be.

She pushed her plate away. "I'll take you at your word, Sheriff Oakes."

An obliging grin tilted his lips. "You've got it, Mrs. Oakes."

Her heart pulsed a little harder at his easy use of *Mrs. Oakes.*

Even as they walked back to their room, Laura wasn't all that sure she could trust Eric's word. Why shouldn't he look? And if he did, would he be disappointed?

She didn't have a great figure. Adequate, she supposed. But hardly model thin. She had no idea what appealed to Eric in a woman physically, or if she had any of the attributes he'd be looking for if their circumstances had been different. On a night like this—

in a hot tub—he surely wouldn't be focusing on wit and intelligence.

And she was driving herself crazy over nothing!

She'd get naked, get in the tub and relax. It was no big deal. Eric was in charge of his own thoughts; she wasn't about to change them.

She undressed to her bra and panties in the bathroom, wrapped a big, fluffy towel around her and walked out onto the enclosed porch. Eric was already there, up to his chin in steamy water.

"Remember, no peeking." She slipped off the towel and slid into the water all in one motion. If he'd gotten a glimpse, it was a brief one.

"You cheated," he accused her. "What's with the bra and panties?"

"You *peeked,* so we're even." She shot him an I-knew-you-would grin.

Slowly the heat seeped into her muscles. She leaned back, looking up at the stars sparkling in the black velvet sky. Fancifully, she thought they were winking at her. Wishing her well.

This was the start of her new life. Some things from the past she'd miss—her teaching job, her close relationship with her mother. And she'd continue to grieve the loss of Amy, her little sister.

But she'd managed to keep the twins to raise as her own and find a good man to spend her days with. When one door closed…she thought with a sigh. Today she'd opened a new door.

"This is really nice," she murmured. "Maybe we should put in a hot tub at your place."

"*Our* place, and I'd be willing to consider it." His

voice was low and husky, rough with an emotion she couldn't identify.

"Actually, I was kidding."

"I wasn't."

She looked into his pale-blue eyes and found them dark with what could only be sexual desire. Despite the heated water, an even hotter river of response ran through her.

"I know what we said, the rules you wanted," he said. "But I'm only human, Laura. You're a beautiful woman. You have to know what you do to me."

She didn't. Not really. But she did know what he did to her, the thrumming need that had been building in her almost from the first moment they met. If she didn't act now on that need, take advantage of the moment—her honeymoon—when would she?

She stood in the tub. Water sluiced off her body, making her bra and panties transparent, and the cool mountain air struck her, causing her to shiver with both need and desire as she extended her hand. "I'm human, too, Eric."

He was quiet for so long she was afraid she'd made a dreadful mistake. Read him wrong. As he slowly perused her, she flushed in both mortification and embarrassment, aware her nipples were visible as brown circles beneath her suddenly see-through bra. Instinctively she crossed her arms over herself.

"Don't do that." Standing, he took her hands, gently uncrossing her arms. "I just wanted to look."

His jutting arousal reassured her that he wanted more than a look, and she drew a quick breath. In her imagination she hadn't fully appreciated what a big man he was, hadn't comprehended the strength of his masculinity. Or how feminine he would make her feel.

He slid his hands up her arms, cupping her shoulders in a tender caress. "Are you sure this is what you want?"

She licked her lips and swallowed hard. The heat of the hot tub combined with desire, clashing with the cool air, and she trembled. She was allowing herself the honeymoon she'd always dreamed about. For the moment, she wouldn't allow herself to admit this one night wasn't real. She'd act out the fantasy. Relish the moment. Tomorrow would be time enough to return to reality, to the knowledge that their marriage was based only on their mutual desire to raise the twins.

Her voice shook. "Yes. This is want I want." And more, though she wouldn't allow herself to voice that desire.

Slipping a hand behind her neck, he held her as he lowered his head to touch her lips in a chaste kiss that held both question and the promise of more to come.

"Yes… Eric… Please."

He didn't ask again as he eased her up out of the hot tub and wrapped her in the thick towel, rubbing away the chill. His kisses followed the path of the towel, first tasting her flesh at the juncture of her throat. Dipping lower to the crest of her breasts, his lips teased near her puckered nipples before he discarded her bra and moved on to her belly.

She groaned at the omission, the ache of wanting to be kissed in exactly the spot he'd missed.

"I'll attend to that detail in a minute or two," he promised, reading her frustration.

She speared her fingers through his neatly trimmed hair and held his head to her as he knelt in front of her, slipping her panties down her legs and worshiping her as she had never before been revered. Her heart soared even as her body pulsed in response to his intimate touch.

The light from inside the room cast a golden reflection across the still water in the hot tub. Steam continued to drift upward. It seemed to catch the scent of the forest, basic and elemental, and bring it back to her. She dragged the fragrance in on quick, excited breaths even as she wanted to fully experience her body joining with Eric's.

"Please…could we…" Go inside, she meant to say but his tongue was doing wonderful, impossible things to her and she couldn't think…couldn't speak coherently.

Her explosive release caught her off guard, so sudden and powerful. She cried out. Her legs wobbled, weak as rubber.

He stood, drawing his work-roughened palms up over her hips and midriff until his thumbs slicked over her nipples. His intense, glittering gaze locked on hers and he smiled triumphantly. He pulled her close, letting her feel his arousal pressed against her belly.

"I think it's time to go inside now," he said.

Steadying herself with her hands on his chest, she nodded. "Good plan."

To her surprise, he scooped her into his arms, carrying her over the threshold into their room. She'd never felt so cherished, so at the mercy of her own desire and that of a man. If this was the only night she'd experience this total immersion in Eric's searing sensuality, then so be it. She'd have this memory to last her a lifetime. Tomorrow would be time enough for the marriage of convenience she'd been so determined to insist upon.

The mattress was firm, the sheet cool on her back as he laid her down. He stretched out beside her and looked into her eyes, smiling slightly.

"Rory was right," he said, his voice husky.

She arched her brows.

"Honeymoons are worth doing."

He captured her mouth in the kind of kiss she'd longed to share with Eric. Hot, moist and deep. His avid exploration with his tongue stole her breath. She responded with matching abandon.

She clutched his shoulders as his hand kneaded her breast. Her nipple hardened and beaded beneath his palm. Between her thighs where she was still sensitive from her earlier climax, moisture flowed again at his slightest touch.

She moaned. "I want you."

"There's one more thing I want to do first. I promised."

His mouth covered her breast. He laved and suckled, driving her wild. She sobbed, trying to get closer to him, struggling to become one with him. To her amazement, another climax burst through her.

"Oh, my!" she gasped. "I never thought I'd—"

"You're going to do it again, too."

She didn't have time to think, to recover, before he spread her legs. He took his time easing into her, moving with an erotic slowness that aroused her again simply because of his caution. His caring ways brought tears of gratitude to her eyes.

"Wrap your legs around me, Blue Eyes."

Smiling at the nickname he'd given her, she did as he asked, and he thrust into her, stretching her. She clenched around the hard, pulsing length of him, accepting him, and she wanted to cry out in celebration that they were a perfect match. She rode a glorious edge between victory and surrender as he pumped into her. Muffling her cries against his throat, she tasted the salty flavor of his skin, inhaled his scent, as rich and elemental as the forest outside their door.

Her heart took one final leap to a place from which there was no return. Light splintered into a million shards and she was lost in another world.

Eric gathered her into his arms as his body jerked with his final release, pulsing deeply within her. Had he ever known a more responsive woman? One who gave so much of herself? Not in this lifetime.

Her taste was still in his mouth, on his lips, as he rolled to his side, bringing her with him. He kissed the damp hair at her temple as she curled against him. Kissed her lips. Felt his body go weak.

With what little energy he still retained, he asked, "You okay?"

Her cheek moved against his chest, and he sensed she was smiling. "What happened to the handcuffs?"

"Darn. Must have left 'em in the truck."

She cuddled closer.

That was the last awareness he had before dawn eased its way through the open window.

Disoriented by the unfamiliar surroundings, he

rolled over. Immediately the memory of the night returned to him along with a sense of regret that the other side of the bed was empty. Only Laura's feminine scent remained on the pillow, and the sight of rumpled sheets gave evidence of the night they'd shared.

He spotted her standing on the deck outside watching the morning light turn the sky from pale rose to a crystalline blue. Her nightgown and sheer robe allowed him to see only the shadow of her silhouette. That was enough to cause a low, harsh groan to escape as he realized how much he wanted her back in bed again.

So much for their in-name-only agreement.

Unless Laura regretted last night.

Swinging his legs over the side of the bed, he found his shorts and tugged them on. He pulled the sliding door open but she didn't turn around.

"What's up, Blue Eyes?"

"I was just thinking how nice it would be to stay here longer."

"Uh, we could do that." He'd be happy to play hot tub tag all day long, if she was willing.

Turning, she smiled, and he didn't see any regret in her eyes, but there were questions.

"That wouldn't be fair to Kristi and Rory. They only volunteered to baby-sit the twins for one night."

"I could call. See if they could manage another day or two."

She rubbed her bare arms against the cool of the morning air, her skin as soft as silk, he remembered, and she seemed to consider the possibility.

Slowly she shook her head. "No, I think we'd better go home."

"If that's what you'd like." He didn't want to press the issue. It was her decision to make. She'd set the ground rules initially.

After last night he had a pretty good idea those rules could be modified.

If he played his cards right.

"Eric?" She turned away as though she couldn't quite bring herself to face him. "When we get home—"

"Yeah?" He cringed at the question he knew she was asking. Not about having more sex. He could handle that, big-time. But about what their relationship would be. A question about love.

"After last night, I was wondering—"

"Laura, honey, you gotta remember who I am. Last night was terrific—more than terrific." He stepped forward, touched his hand to her shoulder but she moved away, no doubt guessing what he was about to say. "But I'm not sure I know how to love a woman. I've given my vow I'll be faithful to you, and that won't be a problem. But I'm not sure I can ever give you anything more than that." He dropped his hand to his side. "I'm sorry."

Her head lowered, as though she had suddenly discovered some new fascination with her toes. "Why don't we pack up and get home. The twins probably miss us."

Eric cursed himself for being less than the man he should be. But hey, life sucked sometimes. He'd do the very best he could for Laura...and the twins.

That, at least, was something she could take to the bank.

They returned home by early afternoon, and Laura carried her suitcase upstairs to her room, dropping it

on her bed. There was so much she had to do—arrange
to have her furniture and personal possessions packed
and shipped to Grass Valley, sell her condo, change
her name on her driver's license and social security,
myriad tasks that would take weeks to accomplish.

She turned, surprised to find Eric had followed her
and was leaning against the doorjamb.

"I thought I'd clean the stuff out of my closet, make
room for your things."

She hesitated for a moment. If only he'd spoken
words of love to her last night, she would leap at the
chance to move in with him. But that hadn't happen.
To the contrary, he'd denied any feelings for her.

"I thought we'd go back to the way we were." The
absence of those all-important words, his love, created
a dissonant chord in her conscience.

He lifted his shoulders in a lazy shrug. "Seems to
me that we've already let the horse out of the barn,
as it were. And we do have to keep up our image that
we're married. For the sake of the twins."

When she didn't immediately respond, he said, "If
it'll help, I'll let you use the handcuffs next time."

She stifled a laugh as the thought of him bound to
the headboard became an intriguingly vivid picture in
her mind. It wasn't an offer of commitment by a long
shot but it was intriguing. "If you're sure."

"About the handcuffs? We'll see about that. But you
sharing my room and my bed? Yeah, I'm sure." He
nodded. "Let's go get the twins, and I'll start cleaning out my closet."

She didn't know how to react to her changing circumstances. She'd never believed in sex simply for the

sake of sex. Her emotions had to be involved. With Eric, they certainly were.

Did sleeping with him mean she'd compromised her principles?

Yet if he still wanted her, how could she say no now that she had once experienced the passion he offered?

"Isn't that hot tub the greatest?" Kristi asked.

The twins were sleeping, and she'd trapped Laura in the kitchen while the men were outside discussing important things, like which football team would make it to the Super Bowl this year. Out the window, Laura could see Adam circling the driveway on his bike, Ruff close on the boy's heels.

She felt her cheeks warm at the memory of her honeymoon. "Yes, the hot tub was very nice. Eric's thinking about putting in one at the house."

"Oh, a man after my own heart. I'll have to mention that to Rory." She rinsed the last of what appeared to be lunch dishes and set them on the rack to dry. "So tell me everything that happened. How did it go with you two?"

"You want every intimate detail? Or just the highlights?"

"Well, I am a trained medical professional," she said with mock seriousness, her eyes sparkling. "You're welcome to tell me anything you'd like, confident my lips are forever sealed."

Laura laughed. "I'd rather hear how you got along with the twins."

"They were wonderful." Sighing, she looked dreamy. "I can hardly wait to have another baby. Rory, on the other hand, was something less than enthusiastic at three in the morning."

"I know the feeling." Although, that quiet hour in the dark of night was precious to Laura, most especially when she shared those moments with Eric.

She heard a baby waking in the other room. Love welled up in her chest and she hurried toward the cry. "Mommy's coming, honey."

Whatever else might happen in the weeks and years ahead, she would always be Becky's and Mandy's mother. By marrying Eric, she had solidified her position. And she loved him for it.

Chapter 11

"Maybe that chair would look better next to the window."

Eric leaned on the wing chair that the movers had brought from Laura's condo, exhaling a weary breath. "That's where it was a half hour ago. Before you had me put it next to the fireplace, which was after you wanted it over by the stairs."

Laura winced. "I know. It's just so hard to mix and match our furniture together." His was dark wood and leather, hers was blond wood and pastels. They might not clash, exactly, but they didn't blend, either.

"I've got a really great idea." He plopped down in the chair, extending his legs. A sheen of sweat dampened his forehead. "Why don't I call a thrift shop in Great Falls, have them pick up the whole kit and caboodle, and we'll start over from scratch."

"No," she gasped. Her hand trembled as she shoved back her hair from her face. "All this furniture is perfectly fine. I just need to figure out—"

He propelled himself out of the chair, and the next thing she knew his arms were wrapped around her. They'd been married ten whole days—and nights. From their wedding night, he'd maintained he wasn't capable of love. Despite that, she wouldn't have given up a moment of the nights she'd spent in his arms.

She'd learned Eric's body as intimately as a woman could—the feel of his flat belly beneath her palm, the ripple of muscles across his shoulders as he entered her, the light furring of hair on his legs and the dreadful scar left by his rodeo accident.

In return, he'd learned every inch of her body, kissed every centimeter and found erogenous zones she hadn't known existed.

Despite all of that, she would have happily sacrificed dealing with the mess the arrival of her things from Helena had caused. Even though she had given her dining room set to a neighbor, plus a few odds and ends, there were boxes stacked everywhere. The thought of unpacking it all while trying to care for the twins was nearly overwhelming. She still had to list her condo with a real estate agent, arrange to have the carpets cleaned. The tasks seemed endless.

In spite of all the pressure, perhaps her tension was in large measure due to her own ambivalent feelings. Only time would tell if she'd done the right thing by choosing to marry Eric without his love.

"If I'd realized how hard this would be, I could have given the rest of my things to charity in Helena and saved the price of moving it here." She rested her head on his shoulder. He was so sturdy, such a rock. At least, he had been through the first three hours of rearranging furniture after the movers had left. Now he appeared to be faltering. Who could blame him?

"We'll work it out. You could use a sitting room upstairs. You know, somewhere to get away from the twins."

She eyed him skeptically. "Which of these pieces of furniture would you like to carry upstairs?"

He groaned. "Good point. Maybe I'd better put in an emergency call to my brothers, round up some strong backs."

Her laugh was cut off by the doorbell ringing. Almost no one in Grass Valley did anything but knock. And then they were as likely as not to go to the back door and let themselves in.

Eric planted a quick kiss on her lips. "I'll see who that is. With any luck it will be some weight lifter who's looking for a good workout."

While he went to answer the door, Laura scanned the room. There had to be some way for all of this mismatched furniture to work together. A blending of tastes. But for the life of her, she couldn't see how. Clearly she'd spent too much time reading about history and not enough learning the ins and outs of home decoration.

Perhaps Eric's idea of an upstairs sitting room would be the best use of the furniture.

As she considered the possibility, Laura became aware Eric hadn't returned from answering the door, and she could now hear masculine voices. Voices that were less than friendly.

She stepped to the door, opening it to find Eric

talking to a tall man with stringy blond hair and tattoos on his forearms. Eric's wide-legged stance was
aggressive; the stranger appeared to be mocking him.

"Eric?"

He turned, his expression strained. "This is Russ
Ungar. He claims he's the father of the twins."

For a moment Eric's words didn't register. Then
all of the blood drained from Laura's head, and she
thought she was going to faint. Her stomach knotted on
a wave of nausea. This wasn't happening. It couldn't.
A biological father had rights that no one could counter—not a foster sibling, as she had been to Amy. Or
a half brother, as Eric was to Amy. The fact that they
both loved the twins beyond reason wouldn't matter
in the face of his paternal rights.

But he was an abuser. Amy had worn the bruises
he'd inflicted the day she moved into Laura's condo.
The man didn't deserve to walk the face of the earth,
much less be a father to his children. Assuming he
was their father.

"How do we know you're who you say you are?"
she asked.

"I've been asking the same question," Eric said.

"For now, you'll just have to trust me, sweet cheeks."
He glanced around the porch and to the outbuildings.
"Looks like you landed yourself some nice digs."

She straightened her spine, prepared to block him
from the house and access to the twins, if need be.
"What do you want?"

He leaned back against the porch railing as though
he were a neighbor dropping by for a friendly visit. "I
went looking for Amy at your condo, honey bunch,"

he said to Laura. "She talked a lot about you. Loving sister and all that."

"You're a little late to express your condolences, if that's what you're after."

Ignoring her comment, he said, "The neighbors told me what happened. That's real sad, her passing and all." He didn't look at all remorseful. Bored was closer to the truth.

"How about getting to the point, Mr. Ungar," Eric said. "My wife asked you what you wanted."

"The neighbors also told me you and this cowboy got married—and kidnapped my sweet little babies."

Laura gasped. "We did no such thing!"

"It's time for you leave, Mr. Ungar." Eric stepped between Laura and the stranger, giving him little room to maneuver. "You're trespassing on private property."

Alarmed, Laura realized Russ Ungar was an inch or two taller than Eric and lean as a whip. She knew Eric was strong and quick, but doubted the man cared about fighting fair, which gave Russ Ungar the advantage over an honest man. And Eric's gun was locked away in the safe in the kitchen where he always kept it when he was at home, for safety's sake.

Laura wished he had it strapped to his hip.

"Don't get your shorts in a knot, cowboy."

"Sheriff Oakes to you, Mr. Ungar. Now, let's move it off the porch."

The man didn't budge. "Well now, since you're the law around here, you must know all about parental rights. Seems to me I've got plenty. Don't you agree?"

"You're not going to take the twins," Laura stated

emphatically. She'd give her own life first before allowing the man who had abused Amy to have them.

Eric stood his ground, as determined as Laura. "You'll have to prove whatever rights you've got in a court of law. I suggest you get yourself a very good attorney because we'll fight you every inch of the way. From what Laura has told me, assuming you are who you say you are, you'd have a lot to answer for in front of a judge."

His lips twitched into a smirk again. "You're scaring me, Sheriff," he said sarcastically. "Amy's dead. All you've got is hearsay, and that's not gonna cut it in a courtroom."

"I find it interesting you didn't deny my accusation. The sign of a guilty man, I'd say."

Eric gestured toward the man's car just as Laura heard Becky's wake-up cry over the baby monitor in the living room.

Ungar shot a glance in that direction, then raised his eyes toward the second floor. "Ain't that the purdiest sound you ever heard? I think I'll go on upstairs and say howdy to my little darlings."

"No!" Laura cried.

He managed one step toward the door before Eric had him in an arm lock.

Ungar struggled against Eric's forceful grip. "Hey! You're hurting me, dammit! I'll have you charged with assault."

"Walk, Ungar, or I'll break your damn arm."

Continuing to manhandle him, Eric marched him to his car, which was parked out front. He slammed Ungar against the side of the vehicle. Holding him there, he used his free hand to open the driver's door.

"You got any weapons in there, Ungar?"

"None of your damn business."

Cursing himself because his own weapon was safely locked away, Eric called to Laura. "Get back inside and lock the doors. Call Rory and tell him what's going on. Tell him I need backup. Then stay with the twins."

He glanced around under the driver's seat as best he could. Except for an empty cigarette pack, it looked clean. But that didn't mean the guy didn't have a weapon stashed in the glove box or trunk. He wasn't going to take the risk that Ungar could get to his gun before Eric could get to his revolver inside the house.

He'd wait for backup.

"Let me go, man," Ungar complained. "You're busting my shoulder."

"Gee, I feel real sorry about that." He yanked Ungar's arm a little higher.

"You can't keep me away from my own kids if I want to see them."

"You aren't going anywhere near the twins without proof of who you are and a court order." Which he just might be able to get, damn it to hell. If he was their father.

A minute later, Rory trotted up, shotgun cradled in his arm. "Whatcha got?"

"A sleazebag." Eric wrestled Ungar to the front of the car. "Nice and easy now. I'm going to let you go and I want you spread-eagled on the hood. You know the drill." From the looks of Ungar's tattoos, which were pretty rough, they'd been done by a prison artist. All the more reason to keep him away from the twins.

Once Ungar was in position, his feet and arms

spread wide, Rory pressed the shotgun to the small of his back. "Keep in mind I've got a real itchy finger when it comes to guys who abuse women," he said.

Eric didn't doubt his brother would pull the trigger if he had to. His sympathy toward dumb animals didn't stretch to punks like Ungar.

A quick search of the car didn't turn up any guns. Eric wished it had. He'd bet his badge the guy was on parole. A weapons violation would send him back to prison. Which would be fine with Eric.

He backed away from the car. "He's clean," he told Rory.

His brother lifted his shotgun. "No quick moves. I'm still feeling real twitchy."

Straightening, Ungar gave Eric a malevolent glare. "Don't get cocky, Sheriff. I'll be back."

"You'd be smarter not to bother."

He sneered and got into his car. The engine cranked over. He shifted into reverse, hit the gas and kicked up gravel as he backed away.

Eric and Rory watched as the car peeled out onto the main street.

"I didn't like the sound of any of that." Rory popped the shells from the shotgun. "Laura says he's the twins' father?"

"That's what he claims." The adrenaline that had flooded his system slowly ebbed away, leaving Eric more worried about the threat Ungar presented than he'd care to admit. "Thanks for backing me up."

"No problem."

"I've gotta check on Laura and the twins." He also intended to give Laura the combination to his gun safe and teach her how to use a weapon. He didn't want to leave his wife unprotected. Or the twins.

And as soon as he was sure Laura was okay, he was going to do a computer check on that Ungar character. He was hoping there was a warrant out on the guy. That would take care of the problem. Temporarily.

Inside, he took the stairs two at a time. The door to the nursery was closed.

He rapped his knuckles lightly on the door. "Laura, it's me." He eased the door open.

Her eyes were wide, her fair complexion pale as she looked up at him. While she was feeding a bottle to Becky, the most telling thing was the carving knife on the table beside the rocking chair.

"He's gone," Eric said.

"He'll be back, won't he?"

"Probably."

Silent tears flooded her eyes and spilled down her cheeks. "Why would a man like that want our babies?"

Our babies. His throat tightened on the impact of her words.

"I don't know." In fact, it seemed odd. It would be more reasonable for him to be grateful not to be stuck with child-support payments—assuming he even had a job.

"I won't let him take my babies." She swallowed a sob and tilted her chin at a stubborn angle. "If I have to, I'll take them away. Start a new life in a place where no one will find me."

Her words cut through his gut as painfully as though she'd used the carving knife on him. She hadn't meant the twins were as much his as hers. She would leave him in a heartbeat—for the sake of the twins.

He knelt beside her, stroking Becky's head. "He won't get the twins. I swear it on my word of honor."

She touched him then, the trembling brush of her fingertips across his hair. "Thank you."

He chided himself for wanting more than her gratitude.

Fear twisted through his gut. What if he couldn't keep his vow? What if they did lose the twins to Russ Ungar? Would Laura want to stay with him?

"Can you find out something about that man? Maybe you can arrest him for something if he comes back."

"I plan to do exactly that—check wants and warrants—as soon as I can get to the computer in my office. He's sure to be in the system somewhere. I'd bet my Stetson he picked up those tattoos in prison."

"He's an ex-convict?"

"That would be my surmise."

She grabbed her lip between her teeth, and her chin trembled. "Do you think he really was Amy's boyfriend? Why would she pick a man like—"

"I don't know." He couldn't imagine any woman wanting to be with Russ Ungar, but he'd seen women make some dumb choices—and pay for it with broken bones and sometimes their lives. "I'm going to try to find out."

Taking her hand, he pressed a kiss to her palm. Laura and the twins were his family now. He wasn't going to let anything happen to them.

To his dismay, a few minutes later at his office, he discovered the state computer system was down— again. His background search on Ungar would have to wait until the morning.

* * *

After the twins had their nighttime bottles, Eric went to take a shower. Laura promised she'd be along in a minute. But when he returned to the bedroom, she wasn't there.

Troubled, he walked down the hall to the nursery. He found Laura rocking Mandy, who was asleep. Becky was in the crib right next to them, her eyes closed, her little arms and legs as relaxed as only a baby could be.

Their mother appeared considerably more tense.

"I thought you were coming to bed when the twins were settled," he whispered. Holding Laura at night, loving her, he was able to think of Laura as his. Not his wife because of her love for the twins. But *his*— her soft skin that smelled of baby powder, her hair that carried the scent of lemon shampoo, the open response she gave him. All his to explore, to possess. Not an illusion that could easily vanish under the harsh light of day or the threat of a paternity claim.

"I can't seem to leave them." Her chair moved back and forth in a hypnotizing rhythm. "I keep thinking that man will show up and snatch them away from us."

"He's not coming back tonight. I promise." Gently he lifted Mandy from her arms and placed the baby in the second crib, the one the movers had brought from Laura's condo this morning. Little Bo Peep and her sheep were scattered across the sheet and bumper pads.

"I don't think I'll be able to sleep," Laura protested when he took her hand.

"Then just let me hold you." He needed the reassurance as much as she did. Sleep wouldn't come easily to either of them tonight.

Laura allowed him to guide her to their bedroom. If anyone could drive her fears away, lift the encroaching shadows that plagued her, it would be Eric. She trusted him in ways she'd never trusted another man. Her heart demanded that of her even while her intellect warned her to be cautious, that she was risking heartbreak.

She ignored the niggling voice of reason. For better or worse, she'd married Eric Oakes. She intended to stay that way unless and until he made it clear he no longer wanted her.

A shudder of apprehension went through her as she realized that might happen if their chance to raise the twins together evaporated because of Russ Ungar.

These were the only children she'd ever be able to offer him.

"Don't think about it," Eric urged. He tugged her knit top off over her head. "He's not going to bother us tonight."

"I know. It's silly of me." She toed off her shoes, all too aware that Eric was wearing only his briefs, his arousal evident. His physical presence had become familiar to her. The breadth of his chest, his muscular legs and the jagged scar on his thigh from surgery following his rodeo injury. Everything about him was so beautifully masculine, she could imagine him as a Greek god come alive from the pages of one of her history books. Surely he had the power to protect her…and the twins.

"Nothing you do is silly."

Her gaze dropped below his waist. Despite his appeal, her own pang of loneliness and need, she turned away from him. "I'm sorry. I don't think I can do it tonight. I'm so stressed—"

"We're just going to hold each other, Laura. That's all. Because my body responds to you doesn't mean I have to act on it."

Reaching for her nightgown, she slipped it on. "It doesn't seem fair to you."

"I promise I'll survive." He pulled back the covers for her.

Gratefully she eased down onto the bed, snuggling as he tucked her in. The ache of fatigue and tension tugged at her, and she curled onto her side.

The light clicked off. Behind her the mattress dipped as he crawled into bed, too. He wrapped his arm around her, spooning her against the warmth of his body. The weight of his arm, locked around her midsection, protected her. His breath across her cheek was a gentle caress. This is what she needed. To be guarded, her fears eased while she slept.

Except, the press of his arousal against her buttocks awakened another need she had—not to be protected but to be loved. Desire stirred within her.

The sensation, the urge, rose slowly, and she turned in his arms, placing a kiss on his lips. "Does a woman have a right to change her mind?"

"I'd say that right is probably in the constitution someplace. And I'm sworn to uphold the laws of the state and the constitution."

"I'm glad."

She claimed his mouth and that was all the encouragement he needed. His loving was gentle, as familiar as breathing, as hopeful as the sun after a stormy day.

Except for their rasping breaths, the house was silent. The stillness blanketed them like a velvet shield. No one could enter, no one could bring them harm.

Their hands caressed, soothed and explored. Aroused. Their lips and tongues did the same across plains and valleys that they had each intimately learned about the other.

When he slipped into her, she arched up in welcome. In return, he drove away the darkness that had entered her soul. Together they soared into a light that was brighter than dawn and more enduring, if only they could cling to each other.

At breakfast the next morning, Eric sipped his coffee thoughtfully. He'd dressed for work. In contrast, Laura was wearing a cozy flannel robe against the cool fall-like air. She'd brushed her hair into place but hadn't yet applied her makeup. He liked her that way, her cheeks a natural rosy color, her complexion as fair as sweet cream. Heck, he liked seeing her across the table from him morning, noon and night, dressed any way she chose.

He cleared his throat. "How'd you sleep last night?"

"Better than I thought I would." She smiled wryly. "You're a good antidote for my stress."

"Glad I could oblige."

Unfortunately, he hadn't slept as well. His brain had kept turning over ideas, searching for ways to block Russ Ungar's next move, if he intended to make one.

"I've got to get to the office, see if the state computer system is back in service."

"I'm not sure what I hope you'll find." She spread butter on her toast and took a dainty bite. "If he has a criminal record, which you think he does, that could make him all the more dangerous. But if he's wanted for something now, you could send him to prison for the next hundred years or so. That would keep him occupied long enough for the twins to grow up."

"Frankly I'm hoping to discover he couldn't possibly be the twins' father. That would solve the problem."

Thoughtful creases bisected her forehead. "You mean, if he had been in prison at the time Amy got pregnant?"

"Something like that. Assuming no conjugal visits, of course."

"That would be perfect. Even if Ungar decided not to exert his so-called paternity rights, I'd hate to have to tell the twins someday that the man we met yesterday was their biological father." She visibly shuddered. "I'd rather not have them know."

"I'm not so sure about that." Shoving back his chair, he stood and carried his mug to the coffeepot for a refill. "My father is named on my birth certificate, but I don't have any memory of him. I always wondered if I was like him. Or if I'd want to be."

"Pray the girls never want to be like Russ Ungar."

"Yeah, I know. You sure Amy never said anything about her boyfriend? Let his name slip, even once? Or mentioned what he looked like or did for a living? Any hint?"

"Not that I can recall. I think she was embarrassed she'd gone off with him and then stayed as long as she did. It wasn't until she knew she was pregnant and decided not to put her baby at risk that she finally ran away."

"Abusers have a knack for convincing a woman he's going to reform. Or that getting knocked around is somehow her fault." He leaned back against the counter, his fingers wrapped around the mug. "Whatever happens, someday the twins will want to know about their father. What kind of a man he was."

"They'll have you as a role model." A smile softened her worry lines. "You'll be the one to teach them what a good man is like."

"You think?"

She nodded. "I know. Assuming we can ward off the threat Ungar represents. You promised we could."

He downed another slug of coffee and set the mug on the counter. "Guess I'd better get busy, then. I'll give Rory a call, see if he can come over to stay with you."

"Why?" She looked surprised by his suggestion.

"I don't like the idea of you and the twins being alone. Ungar's a wild card—"

"I'll be fine, Eric. Your office is less than the length of a football field away. For that matter, if he shows up while you're there, you'd see his car going by."

He weighed his concern for Laura's safety against the risk of leaving her alone. "All right," he said cautiously. "But I want you to lock the doors after I'm gone and stay inside."

Never in the time he'd lived in Grass Valley had he locked his doors. It hadn't been necessary.

For the safety of Laura and the twins, today it was.

Chapter 12

Picnic tables with colorful paper tablecloths and plates were set up near the ranch house at the Double O to celebrate little Nancy's third birthday. Balloons tied to the tables tugged at their strings in a light breeze. Her first-ever birthday cake had Nancy dancing around, as excited as a butterfly just emerged from its cocoon.

For Laura the party provided a respite from worries about Russ Ungar. They hadn't heard a word directly from him in three days, although Eric was still checking his sources to get more information about the man beyond his prison record.

She fervently hoped Ungar had decided not to make trouble over the twins.

Once the cake and ice cream had been demolished, the teenage cadre of Oakes boys rounded up the younger guests to give them horseback rides in the corral.

Laura smiled at the thought of the twins' first birthday and what she would do to celebrate that milestone event. She glanced at the babies napping in their playpen in a shady spot on the porch. Please, God, let them still be hers to raise when they turned one year old. And twenty-one, for that matter, although they might not appreciate motherly interference at that age.

Kristi, looking a little haggard, joined her at the edge of the porch. "I don't know how Lizzie does it. A gazillion kids of all ages, noisy as all get-out, screaming and shouting, and she looks as cool as though she'd just stepped off the pages of Glamour."

Laughing, Laura said, "I suspect she's pleased we didn't get an afternoon thundershower to drive the party indoors. That might have been a bit much even for her."

"I don't know. She's one of those people you want to have around in a disaster. Never seems to lose her head. My guess is that she had a contingency plan all worked out."

She boosted herself up onto the porch railing, a woman comfortable in her own skin. Although both of Laura's sisters-in-law were a few years younger than she was, they appeared to have their acts very much together. They were also smart and fun to be around. Laura didn't feel nearly as confident of herself since her marriage as she had before. Then, although she'd often been lonely and heartsick at the knowledge she'd never have children of her own, she'd worked her way into a comfortable niche teaching history to adolescents. Cramming it down their respective craws, if need be.

Now the rules had changed. Her whole life had changed, and sometimes she felt as though she was walking a tightrope. Maybe if Eric loved her, she wouldn't feel like an imposter, that she belonged here as a member of the Oakes family. But Eric didn't believe he was capable of the love she so desperately wanted, which made her feel vulnerable. Someday he might meet a woman he could love, and she would have to give him up.

"Have you heard anything more from that guy Rory helped Eric run off?" Kristi asked.

Mentally, Laura shook away her troubling thoughts. "Not a word, thank goodness. Eric checked him out. Russ Ungar not only has a record for petty crimes, he spent almost a year in the Montana State Prison in Deer Lodge."

"Well then, he couldn't be the twins' father, right?"

"Unfortunately, he'd been arrested but was out on bail about the time my foster sister, the twins' mother, must have gotten pregnant."

"So this Ungar character could be the girls' biological father?"

"Just because he wasn't in jail doesn't prove anything about paternity." She'd been telling herself that for the past two days, since Eric did the data search. Somehow it wasn't all that reassuring.

Carrying baby Susie on her hip, Lizzie strolled over to them, her blond hair still neatly held in place by a gold clip at the back of her neck. She lowered Susie to the ground, and the toddler took off for the porch steps to visit the twins.

"Don't wake the babies," Lizzie admonished.

She gave Kristi and Laura a weary smile. "I swear, I've managed parties for three hundred guests at the fanciest country club in Marin County that weren't as exhausting as this."

Kristi clapped her hands. "Heaven be praised! She's human."

Lizzie looked at Laura, puzzled.

"I think she's pleased you're as exhausted as she is," Laura explained, "what with all the commotion. It's been a wonderful party. All the children have enjoyed themselves."

"Thank you. But the truth is, I do have another reason to feel so tired."

"Oh?" Laura and Kristi said in unison.

Lizzie's smile was just this side of smug. "I'm pregnant."

"Oh my God!" Kristi wailed. "That's wonderful!"

"Congratulations. I'm happy for you," Laura said. She was pleased, even though the familiar pang of regret that she'd never have her own child caught her off guard for a moment. She had the twins. An enormous blessing she'd never anticipated. "Walker, in particular, must be thrilled."

"We both are." Lizzie grinned. "Although I don't think either of us had ever imagined we'd have seven children."

"Mercy, no," Laura said with a laugh. She'd be content with two.

Kristi hopped down from her perch. "Guess what?

I'm pregnant, too. We'll be able to raise our babies together."

Lizzie opened her mouth and let out an unladylike scream. "That's wonderful!" She wrapped her arms around Kristi, and the two women hugged each other, laughing and crying at the same time.

Susie toddled to the porch railing, extending her arms. "Mamamama," she babbled.

Pressing her lips together, Laura couldn't recall a time when she'd felt so left out. It wasn't the fault of these two women who had so recently become her friends. She'd simply never be able to join the sorority of women who had given birth to a child.

If Russ Ungar had his way, she might not be able to lay claim to her one chance at motherhood.

Kristi and Lizzie were each feeding a twin in the ranch house living room when Eric strolled inside.

He tipped his Stetson to the back of his head. "Now that's quite a sight."

"Your sisters-in-law are getting in practice for their own little bundles of joy," Laura said. "They're both expecting."

"Really?" He grinned. "Son of a gun. Sounds like my brothers have been busy."

"If you're like the rest of the Oakes boys," Kristi said, "I'll wager Laura will be joining us in maternity clothes not too long from now."

Eric snapped his head toward Laura, and she looked away, making a concerted effort not to let the pain show on her face.

"Sorry, ladies, I'm afraid that's not possible." Picking up a receiving blanket, she folded it carefully in her lap. "I'm not physically able to have a baby."

Kristi gasped, and Lizzie eyes widened in surprise.

"There's a lot being done in the fertility arena these days," Kristi said. "It's possible that whatever the problem is, there could be a way—"

"Not in my case. My uterus was removed when I was sixteen." Uncomfortable with the conversation, Laura stood, though she didn't quite know where to go or how to hide from her greatest flaw.

Eric rescued her by taking her hand and tugging her close to him. "I had this great idea, which is why I came looking for you. Since we've got a whole cadre of baby-sitters available, how 'bout I take you riding? I'll give you a minitour of the ranch."

However grateful Laura was for the change of subject, she didn't think it was right for her to take advantage of the two women who'd been so kind to her since she arrived in Grass Valley. "They've both been working hard all day. It wouldn't be fair to dump the twins on—"

"Don't be silly." Lifting Becky to her shoulder, Lizzie patted the baby's back. "The twins aren't any trouble, Susie will be down with her nap for another hour or two, and you don't get many chances to get away from the babies. Besides, Walker has everything under control outside. Go on while you can."

Laura glanced at Kristi.

"We'll be fine here." Her smile held a wealth of both understanding and sympathy, an ability which no doubt served her well in her role as a nurse. "Enjoy yourself."

Not allowing Laura to object further, Eric led her out of the house through the back door, grabbing a spare hat for her from the mud room as they went.

"We'll commandeer one of the mares for you that the kids have been riding, and I'll saddle up a gelding."

"You sure you won't get an argument from Nancy or one of her friends?" she asked.

"Last time I looked, the three-year-old set was feeding carrots to a couple of rabbits Walker got her for her birthday."

"I hope he has them in separate cages or he'll have more bunnies than he counted on."

The family's black-and-white Border collie followed them into the barn, where Eric hefted a saddle from a rack in the tack room, carrying it to the stall of an Appaloosa. The air was cool and rich with the aroma of hay and horses. Dust motes twisted in a column of sunlight that slanted through the open doorway.

"Sorry Kristi and Lizzie made you feel uncomfortable back there," he said.

"They're not the problem." She was, or rather her reproductive system was. "It's just as well they know the truth so they won't start wondering what's wrong with you when I don't get pregnant."

"Nothing's wrong with either of us." Canting his head, he slipped beneath the brim of her hat to give her a quick kiss.

A shimmer of pleasure slid through Laura's midsection. She marveled that a simple kiss could erase the bitter sense of failure that plagued her whenever she thought about being barren. His touch was like a healing balm on her soul.

With practiced hands, he saddled the gelding. Every movement had its own beauty, a masculine dance that was both graceful and a communion between the man and the animal.

He led the horse outside and looped the reins over the corral fence next to the mare he'd chosen for Laura to ride.

He glanced down at her casual running shoes. "Looks like we're going to have to get you some riding boots."

"These will be fine as long as you don't expect me to leap six-foot fences."

"This is cow country, Blue Eyes. The sheriff's best girl ought to have proper riding equipment."

"The next time we go to Great Falls," she promised with a smile. In her old life, she'd never imagined needing riding boots except for doing a Texas two-step on a Saturday night. In Grass Valley, they were de rigueur every day of the week.

He cupped his hands near the stirrup. "Up you go."

Mounting, she drew a quick breath. "Oh my, I don't think I've been on a horse since high school. I'd forgotten how high you are up here."

"You okay?"

If Eric could find it in his heart to love her, she'd be terrific. "I'm fine. Fortunately, altitude doesn't give me a nosebleed."

He chuckled as he adjusted her stirrups, from time to time grasping her calves or running his palm along her thigh with casual intimacy. Whether she was fully dressed or stark naked, his lightest caress aroused a deep passion within her. Since their wedding night, she'd developed a serious addiction to making love with Eric. Never with any other man had she been so sexually ravenous.

With a sigh, she realized she might never get enough of the man to satisfy her cravings.

He gave one last tug to the stirrup. "Something wrong?"

"Not at the moment."

He mounted his gelding, and they rode away from the corral, the Border collie trotting along behind them.

"Is it all right that the dog's coming, too?" she asked.

"Bandit likes to hunt rabbits and prairie dogs when he gets a chance."

"I hope he doesn't catch one while I'm around." She had a soft heart for little creatures.

"I don't think we have to worry about that. He's not as fast as he used to be."

"For which I'll count my blessings."

After the heat of summer, the prairie grass had turned golden brown, and stretched out across the land like ocean waves shifting in the light breeze. Bandit's zigzag course roused a quail into flight. With a bark, he leaped into the air, jaws snapping, but the bird was long gone.

"That dog must have tried to catch a thousand quail over the years and hasn't caught one yet," Eric commented. "You'd think he'd learn."

"He probably thinks it's a game and he's winning."

"Yeah. You ever have a dog when you were a kid?"

"We had a wirehaired terrier when I was about five.

His name was Spiffy and he loved to lick my ice-cream cone, which mother abhorred, of course."

"Understandably. Germs and all." He quirked a grin.

"Mmm. Unfortunately, he also liked to hop over our backyard fence and dig up the neighbor's flower beds."

"I bet that made him popular around the neighborhood."

"We added about three more feet to the fence, but Spiffy still made it over the top. Or dug underneath it. Finally Dad gave the dog to a friend who had some acreage outside of town and a fenced doggy run. But my ice cream never tasted quite the same after that."

"Maybe we can talk to Harold at the pharmacy about a new flavor of the month."

"Why don't we keep that idea to ourselves for now?" She shuddered daintily. "Mother got a poodle a couple of years ago for company."

"Out here a poodle wouldn't last long. Too many predators."

Laura adjusted easily to the motion of the horse, and they rode along in comfortable silence. Once Bandit spotted something in the grass and raced off out of sight only to trot back minutes later, rejoining them with no sign that he'd caught anything.

In the distance the mountains were purple shadowed as the sun drifted toward the west. It wouldn't be long before the days grew significantly shorter—and colder. Snow often fell at this latitude by mid-September. Sometimes sooner. But Eric's home was warm and cozy, and Laura pictured them curled up on the couch in front of the fireplace, protected and safe, while storms whipped around outside.

"You think we ought to get the twins a puppy?" he asked.

She slid him a surprised look. "Why don't we wait for a while? They'll appreciate a dog more when they're older, and I won't have to deal with diapers and housebreaking a puppy at the same time."

"Sounds reasonable. But they ought to have a big dog, not a poodle. You know, one of those breeds who have to grow into their feet."

"I assume that translates into you've always wanted a big dog for yourself?"

He shrugged sheepishly. "Blame it on a deprived childhood—at least until Oliver Oakes brought me here to the ranch. We always had a dog around then."

Her heart went out to him. His early childhood had been terrible, and she was sure he'd take care to see that the twins would have a better one. She vowed to do her part, too.

When they returned to the corral an hour or so later, Laura felt as though she'd been granted a special interlude that had brought her and Eric closer together. And when he made love to her that night, he seemed more tender, more loving than ever.

Her climax brought tears of joy, marred only by the realization that he still had not spoken the words of love she so desperately wanted to hear.

The following day Eric came home for lunch. He did that as often as he could, and Laura found herself looking forward to his company. They'd talk about his work and whatever gossip he'd picked up around town. He'd spend a few minutes playing with the twins if they were awake.

She had just slid a plate in front of him at the kitchen table, a roast beef sandwich stacked high and a side of fruit and cottage cheese when she heard a car arriving out front.

She glanced out the window and her heart plummeted.

Russ Ungar hadn't given up his quest to claim the twins. He was back.

This time he'd brought a friend with him, a man wearing a dark suit and carrying a briefcase.

Chapter 13

"Eric!"

At Laura's soft cry of alarm, Eric looked up from his sandwich. Her face had gone as white as a winter snowstorm, her eyes as wide as if she'd seen a ghost.

"What's wrong?"

"Ungar. He just drove up with a friend."

Eric cursed and shoved back from the table. "Take the twins upstairs. I'll handle Ungar."

"No matter what, don't let him have the twins."

She scooped Becky out of the playpen that was set up in a corner of the kitchen, and Eric handed Mandy to her.

"He won't take them anywhere."

Not unless Ungar had gotten a court order, which seemed unlikely without a hearing. Since they hadn't been notified of any proceedings, and Laura was still the twins' legal guardian, Eric figured they were safe for the moment. But out of a need to protect the twins, he retrieved his revolver from the safe and strapped on his holster before answering the knock on the front door.

He acknowledged Ungar with a nod.

"Afternoon, Sheriff." Ungar's sneering smile revealed one broken tooth and another that had gone gray with decay. "I brought along my attorney this time. Meet Henry Smedling."

The man in question whipped out a business card, which Eric took but didn't examine. Instead he sized up the attorney—frayed shirt collar, a tie spotted with residue from more than a few meals, a cheap knock-off watch. Not a big-time player in the legal world and very likely the only lawyer in the state who would agree to represent Ungar. If he was an attorney at all.

"Are you gonna let us in or make us cool our heels out here again?" Ungar asked.

"Why should I let you two losers in?"

"We have a proposition for you, Sheriff Oakes. And your wife, of course." The attorney's voice was so sniveling, a jury would vote against his client on general principles as soon as the lawyer finished his opening statements.

Eric lifted his brows. These two guys had to be up to something. He needed to know what.

Opening the door wider, he stood back. "Don't bother to sit down, gentlemen. You won't be staying long."

As he ushered them inside, Laura came downstairs.

"Well now, there's the little lady of the house,"

Ungar said. "You taking good care of my sweet little babies, honey buns?"

A muscle flexed in Eric's jaw. "Mr. Ungar brought his attorney along this trip," he told Laura, introducing Smedling.

Her gaze darted to the stranger and back to Eric. "What do they want?"

"Mrs. Oakes," the attorney began, "we appreciate you've become attached to the twins. Who wouldn't? I'm sure they're a delight to you. However, my client's paternal rights supersede yours when it comes to—"

"We haven't seen any proof your client is the father of the twins," Eric pointed out.

Putting his briefcase on the coffee table, Smedling opened it and removed a sheet of paper. "I have here an affidavit from my client stating his relationship with Ms. Amy Thorne. It provides details of where they lived and for how long, their cohabitation and conjugal activities during the period in which Ms. Thorne became pregnant with the twins."

"I can hardly wait to read the details about that," Eric said derisively.

Ungar barked a laugh. "She was one hot mama, I'll tell you that!"

"You beat her, you…you scum!" Laura cried.

Gesturing for Laura to be quiet, Eric took the affidavit from the attorney. At a quick glance he realized the form didn't offer any evidence that would stand up in court in a paternity case.

"This is bull, gentlemen. What are you after?"

"As it happens, Sheriff Oakes," the smarmy attorney said, "my client is sympathetic to your situation and to your desire—and that of Mrs. Oakes—to raise the twins yourselves."

"Then you can leave and never come back," Laura said, practically lunging toward to the door to let them out.

Eric gestured for her to be quiet. He intended to handle Ungar...in his own way.

Smedling continued. "On the other hand, if Mr. Ungar were to give up all parental rights, it would cause him great mental suffering. These two precious little girls, who are the subject of our dispute, might be the only children he ever fathers. To never enjoy their affection and love would be a great loss to him."

Eric was beginning to see a very clear picture emerging, and it looked like a scam to him.

"What sort of consideration are you looking for in order to ease his...mental anguish?"

"It is hard to set a dollar value on that kind of pain," the attorney countered self-righteously.

"How does ten thousand dollars sound?"

Ungar was quick to say, "Make it twenty."

"No deal."

"Eric! If all it takes is money—"

"No deal, I said." What Eric needed was proof that Ungar wasn't the twins' father. Nothing less would free them of the man, no matter how much or how often they tried to pay him off.

Getting in his face, Ungar said, "You'd better listen to your old lady, Sheriff."

Laura grabbed Eric's arm.

"Trust me, Laura." He glanced away from Ungar to meet her frantic gaze, hoping she'd believe he knew what he was doing. "We're not going to give this scumbag a dime. The twins are ours until a court says otherwise."

A snarl rose from Ungar's throat. "You know damn well if I get those babies away from her, there's no way in hell you're ever gonna get a piece of her again."

His crude remark would have been enough for Eric to punch Ungar under almost any circumstance. In this case he had an even better motive.

Bringing up his fist, he landed a direct hit to the bridge of Ungar's nose.

"Yeow!"

"Eric, what are you doing?"

Blood gushed from Ungar's nose, and he staggered backward.

Quickly Eric produced a clean handkerchief from his pocket. "Sorry about that," he said mildly.

Ungar pressed the handkerchief to his nose. "I'b gunna sue you, Oakes."

Shrugging, Eric said, "Could I help it if you were crowding my personal space when I reach up to swat a bug?"

Smedling took his client by the arm. "Come on, Russ. These people are being unreasonable. We'll see them in court."

"Please, Eric, don't let him leave this way," Laura pleaded. "Tell him you're sorry. Tell him we're willing to discuss his terms."

"Nope. The only thing I want from this guy is my handkerchief back."

Ungar tossed the blood-soaked square of cotton to the floor. Carefully Eric picked it up, then blocked

Laura's way as she tried to follow the two men out the door.

"Are you sure you know what you're doing?" she asked, visibly shaken by the exchange.

"I hope so." Although, he had taken a risk and could end up in court on an assault charge—not an ideal situation for a sheriff. Still, based on his intuition, it had been worth the chance.

"He was going to sign over his paternity rights." Laura raced to the window to watch the pair leave. "I don't care how much money they wanted. I would give anything, the money from selling my condo—"

"And keep on giving year after year, if my guess is right."

She whirled. "What are you talking about?"

"He was trying to blackmail us. If we'd paid him off once, he would have come back for more, again and again. We'd never get rid of him."

"But now he'll take the children. I would rather—"

"I don't think he's their father."

She looked at him dumbfounded, then crossed the room to pick up the affidavit that he'd dropped on the coffee table. She scanned it quickly.

"How would he know all these details if he wasn't—"

"We're not even sure those details are accurate. You said yourself you and your mother were out of touch with Amy. He could have made everything up. Or maybe someone else told him where Amy had been living."

"Who?"

"I don't know." Taking her hand, he led her into the

kitchen where he found a plastic Baggie and slipped his bloodied handkerchief inside, zipping it closed.

"What are you doing with that?"

Setting the Baggie on the counter, he took her by the shoulders, caressing her, trying to calm her. "Listen to me. What's not in that affidavit, and what he didn't volunteer, is a blood test. That's the only way he can prove he is the twins' biological father."

"Maybe he recognizes he isn't in a position to raise the twins as well as we could, and he's willing to give up his rights for that reason."

"Plus twenty thousand dollars." She was so damn softhearted, she was willing to give the lowest of the low the benefit of the doubt. Eric wasn't. "Trust me, Blue Eyes. I wouldn't willingly give up my own kids for a million bucks. Twenty million. So ask yourself why Ungar seems so eager."

She hesitated, and he could see her good reason warring with her emotions. She wanted the twins at any price.

"Because he's lying," she finally said.

"That's what I'm counting on."

"And if you're wrong?"

"We'll still have a lot of ways to battle him in the courts, starting with him being an unfit father because he tried, in effect, to sell his kids to us."

She still looked skeptical but she nodded her head. "What do we do now?"

"Do you know the twins' blood type?"

She thought for a moment. "It's A. A-positive."

"That's pretty common but maybe we'll get lucky." He nodded toward the Baggie on the counter. "I'm going to take my handkerchief over to Kristi and Doc Justine at the clinic. We'll see if Ungar's blood type matches."

Her eyes widened. "That's why you hit him, isn't it?"

"Among other reasons." It had felt damn good, too. He didn't have patience with any man who physically or verbally abused a woman. Ungar had deserved what Eric had laid out.

"And if Ungar's blood is A-positive?"

His forehead tightened. "Then I'll ship the handkerchief off to the lab at Great Falls that does DNA testing. They'll be able to tell us if Ungar is the twins' father—or a fraud."

"How long will that take?"

"A few days. Meanwhile I'm still investigating, trying to find a connection between Ungar and Amy. Or Ungar and some other man Amy had been living with. That so-called affidavit he provided is going to give me some new leads to follow."

Crossing her arms, Laura hugged herself as though a winter wind had slipped in through an open window. "You do realize if you find someone else, the girls' real father—if it's not Ungar—you may create a bigger problem than we already have."

Yeah, Eric knew that. But he didn't have much of a choice. He either had to prove Ungar wasn't the twins' father—or deal with the man the rest of the girls' lives. He wasn't about to do that voluntarily.

"All right. You're the cop. You must know what you're doing."

Her words were slow and hesitant but they said that

she trusted him. Under the circumstances, that was a lot.

Eric hoped to God she was right.

The bell on the clinic door jingled as Eric stepped inside. He was greeted by the faint scent of antiseptic and a mother with her two children in the waiting room. Eric walked right on by them into Doc Justine's office area.

"You got an emergency, Sheriff?" she asked. "Or do you always bust in here without an appointment when folks are waiting?"

"I've got an emergency." He produced the Baggie with the bloody handkerchief. "Have you got the equipment to determine blood type?"

Kristi appeared. "Whose blood is it?"

"The guy who's trying to take the twins away from us. I'm hoping to prove he isn't their father."

"You cut him?" the doc asked.

"Punched him in the nose."

"Wish I'd had the pleasure myself." Coming to her feet, Justine took the Baggie from him. "Kristi, you do the Jamison boys' physicals. I'll see what we've got here."

Kristi stopped Eric before he could follow the doctor. "Is Laura all right?"

"She's upset, but she'll be fine if it turns out the guy doesn't have the same type blood as the twins."

"I'll drop in later this afternoon, see how she's doing."

"Thanks, Kristi. She'll appreciate it."

She gave his arm a squeeze, then released him to

find Justine in the back room she used as a lab. Fussing with her medical equipment, the doc was sitting on a stool in front of a microscope on the table.

She didn't look up when he arrived. "It won't speed things up if you hover over my shoulder, you know."

He stayed near the door. "We're kind of anxious to know the answer."

"I'll have to get a blood sample from the twins to compare."

"They're A-positive."

"So are about half the people in the country."

"Then let's hope Ungar is in the minority."

The seconds ticked by so slowly that each beat of the clock felt like an hour. If Ungar was any blood type besides A-positive, his gamble would pay off.

Eric couldn't stand still. He began to pace. Damn, what was taking so long?

Doc Justine spun around on the stool. "Sorry. This blood is A-positive."

Eric blew out a disappointed breath. "Can you package up the handkerchief for me? I'll have to take it to the lab in Great Falls." He could overnight express it via the postal service but it would be faster if he drove into town himself. He wanted answers as soon as possible, and he knew people who worked in the forensic lab.

"When Kristi's done with the Jamison boys I'll send her over to draw some blood from the babies. The lab will need to compare the samples."

"Thanks." Doing an about-face, he marched out of the lab, past the display cases in the front hallway that held an array of antique medical equipment and out the front door.

He hated to think he'd guessed wrong about Ungar, hated even more the possibility that his half sister had been hooked up with a man like that. If only he'd known she existed, he could have taken care of her. Given her a home. Convinced her she deserved better than a lowlife like Ungar. Every woman did.

Worse, he didn't want Laura to feel as though she had misplaced her trust in him.

Laura had wrapped Eric's mostly uneaten sandwich in plastic wrap, washed up the lunch dishes, scrubbed the kitchen sink and counter until they shone and was considering using her nervous energy to do the same to the floor when Eric returned.

"What happened?" Her heart lodged in her throat at his worried expression.

He shook his head. "Life's never easy, is it? I'm going to have to drive to Great Falls."

"Ungar has the same blood type?"

"Kristi's going to come over in a few minutes to draw blood from the twins for DNA comparison."

Laura covered her mouth with her hand to prevent herself from crying out. Her whole body trembled. The fear that she might lose the twins had never been so strong. She felt as though she was being torn asunder atom by atom.

Sensing her terror, Eric wrapped his arms around her. His khaki uniform shirt was smooth against her cheek, his body warm against the chill of dread that filled her heart.

"Don't fall apart on me now, Blue Eyes. Ungar isn't going to get the twins. I promised you, didn't I?"

"I'll go with you to Great Falls. We'll take the twins." She wanted to be with him, needed his reassurance.

"I'm going to drive there and straight back. No sense messing up the twins' schedule. I'll be home by bedtime."

She hated that he was being so logical when her emotions were in a turmoil, but she nodded her agreement. He knew what he was doing.

"I'll get Rory or Kristi to stay with you," he said.

"No, I'm fine. I'm keeping the doors locked." She wasn't fine, of course, but she couldn't allow Ungar to turn her into a frightened mouse.

He lifted her chin. "Have you ever used a pistol?"

"My father taught me to shoot, but it's been years since I've—" Her stomach knotted on a new fear. "Why?"

"I don't think Ungar will show up while I'm gone, and he wasn't armed the other day when he came to call. Still, I'd feel better if I knew you could protect yourself and the twins."

God, things seemed to be spiraling out of control. "I think I remember enough to use a gun if I have to."

His fingers slipped through her hair, and he tucked a few strands behind her ear. "I'd like you to be a little better than that. I've got a short practice range in the barn that I use so I can keep qualified. After Kristi comes, I'm going to take you out there and give you a refresher course. I need to know you're safe with a loaded weapon."

She couldn't argue with his reasoning. Her father had drilled gun safety into her. She would expect nothing less from Eric.

The shooting range was twenty-five feet long, the target small and backed by piles of hay. The ten-shot semiautomatic pistol and ammunition clip Eric handed her, the extra weapon he kept in the kitchen safe, felt heavy in Laura's hand.

"You remember how to load the clip?" he asked.

She nodded, never more aware of Eric's occupation and the danger it represented. She trembled a little as she slipped the clip into the grip, cocked the pistol and felt the first bullet slide into firing position. The scent of gun oil mixed with the elemental aromas in the barn and Eric's heady masculine scent. Everything about him spoke of rugged virility. And courage. Yet he was the same man who could gently cuddle a baby or love a woman with such tenderness it brought tears to her eyes.

She could not imagine loving any other man with the same depth of feeling that she loved Eric. Or wish more desperately that she could give him the sons he deserved.

"You okay?" he asked.

She blinked back a sheen of tears that blurred her vision. "You don't really think Ungar will come back, do you?"

"I think it's smart to be prepared."

She swallowed hard and took a deep breath. "I'm ready."

Standing behind her, his warm breath barely a caress across her neck, he lifted her right arm. "Use your left hand to steady your aim."

"You sure the bullet won't go through the back wall and hit one of your horses?"

"I'm sure. Besides, they're in the side corral."

"Good planning."

"Okay, line up on the target and squeeze—don't pull—the trigger."

It sounded like a cannon had gone off, and the gun jerked in her hand. Dust blew up from the bale of hay well above the still-unmarked target.

"Looks like I'm a little out of practice."

"You'll be fine. Just remember it's going to kick on you. Keep the nose down. Try it again."

She'd never been fond of guns or shooting even though her father wanted her to be familiar with using a weapon. Now that she might have to safeguard the twins from Ungar, she was well motivated.

Her second shot hit the target in line with the bull's-eye but several inches high. Her third try found the inner ring.

"Good. That one will slow a man down."

She shuddered. "I'm not sure I could actually squeeze the trigger with the pistol pointed at a person."

"I think you could, if that was the only way you could protect the twins."

Or protect you, she thought, knowing she'd do any-thing within her power to keep Eric out of harm's way, as well. She could only wonder if he felt the same way about her.

She finished the magazine clip and Eric took the

pistol from her. Half the bullets had found the target if not the center of the rings.

He caught her under her chin. "You did good, Blue Eyes."

"It's scary to think I may actually have to use a gun on someone."

"Scary for me, too. But I want you to promise you'll mean business if you have to use that weapon. The worst thing that could happen is to have a perp take the gun away and use it on you."

"I know."

"I can count on you?"

She nodded, whispering, "Yes."

He lowered his head and found her mouth in a deep, searing kiss that sealed their bargain. Heat spiraled through her. Her blood roared through her veins. She moaned, instinctively reaching for him. Wanting more.

She nearly sobbed aloud when he broke the kiss.

"I've got to get the samples to Great Falls."

"I know." They were both breathing hard. "You'll come right home after you drop off the blood at the lab?"

His lips quirked ever so slightly. "That's a promise I won't have any trouble keeping."

In her heart of hearts, his eagerness thrilled her. "I'll wait up for you."

Eric spent the better part of the next day on the phone. He talked with the police chief in Helena, and even managed to reach the officer who had responded to a domestic dispute call at the address Ungar had listed on his so-called affidavit.

With a single call to the state bar association, he'd discovered Henry Smedling wasn't an attorney at all. The guy was no more than a jailhouse lawyer, who'd learned his way around a few law books while he'd been in prison himself for fraud. A sure sign Ungar's effort to claim paternity rights was nothing more than a poorly conceived con job.

But the most productive call he'd made was to the warden at the state prison.

By late afternoon when he locked up the sheriff's office, he was feeling optimistic and impatient to share his latest theory about Ungar with Laura.

As he swung into his patrol car for the short drive home, he realized that before his marriage he'd never been in a hurry to go home. The empty house had held little appeal and no welcome.

Now when he walked in the door, more often than not there was the scent of something baking in the oven or cooking on the stovetop. There might be a vase of wildflowers in the middle of the kitchen table, collected while she took the twins for a stroller ride. She'd set out place mats and silverware, napkins.

In the rest of the house dust didn't pile up like it used to, though he didn't know how she found the time to clean and dust when she had to care for the twins. When he was doing the child care that's all he could manage, and then he seemed to be pulled in two different directions at once and desperately wished he had two sets of hands.

As easily as a duck takes to water, she'd turned his house into a home.

He'd never experienced that before. Not really. Sure,

Chapter 14

"Looks like Becky may have a future as a gymnast."

Laura started at the sound of Eric's voice. She hadn't heard him come in and, as usual, her heart responded with a jolt of pleasure to have him home.

"I don't know," she said. "She gets such terrible giggles, we may be looking at a circus clown instead."

Sitting on the couch nearby, he extended his hands for the baby. "I think I'd rather have her be daddy's little-stay-at-home girl."

Laura passed Becky to him, smiling as he settled the baby in the crook of his arm like the experienced daddy he'd become. She rolled to her feet, wincing a little at a niggling pain in her side.

"I've got bad news for you, Eric. I intend to raise two independent young ladies who'll make their own decisions about their future."

Oliver Oakes had been a damn good fath[er] ways that mattered. But he'd had a hard ed[ge] not soft and caring in the way Laura was twins.

And with him.

As he pulled the cruiser into the garage f[or] night, he realized no one had taught him anyt[hing] about love. Except for the gut-wrenching love he[] for the twins, he'd never experienced anything b[ut] temporary relationship with a woman. He'd been afra[id] to try, afraid in the long run a woman would find him lacking in some way—as his mother had.

He didn't want to be abandoned again so he didn't develop attachments. As easy as that.

But maybe he ought to reconsider his strategy.

Unlocking and walking in the back door, he tossed his hat on a peg in the mud room and strolled into the kitchen.

He sniffed the air. Chocolate-chip cookies! A plateful sat on the counter. He snatched one before strolling into the living room.

His breath caught in his lungs at the sight of Laura stretched out on the floor playing with Becky, lifting the infant over her head, bringing her closer to nuzz[le] her and pressing her up again. The baby loved it, h[er] mouth wide open, giggling with excitement.

Maybe Laura, with all the love she had to give, [was] capable of teaching him to love, too.

He chuckled. "Maybe so, but they'll always come home to Daddy, won't you, Tinkerbell?" The baby blew a juicy bubble in response.

Home to both of us, Laura wanted to say but swallowed the words that would give away too much of her heart.

Picking up Mandy from her playpen, Laura sat down across from Eric, jiggling the baby on her knees. "Were you able to find out anything about Ungar today?"

"I was. And about his phony attorney, too."

"Phony?"

"As much a crook as Ungar, which lends a whole lot of credence to my theory their whole deal is a scam."

She exhaled in relief, brushing a quick kiss to Mandy's forehead. "Thank heavens. But what about Ungar?"

"For a time he had a cell mate named Christopher Barry. He was a young guy, not much older than Amy, with a big mouth and a violent temper. He got into a brawl a couple of months after he was sent to state prison. Somebody slipped a homemade shiv between his ribs."

Laura gasped. "Someone killed him?"

"Right. I'm thinking if this Christopher guy was Amy's boyfriend, he might have told Ungar about her. The details of their relationship. At least enough to fill in some blanks on that affidavit he gave us."

"So if he was their father, he's dead now. He'll never be a part of their lives?"

"That's what I'm thinking."

She ran her hand over the blond crown of Mandy's

head. "I'm not sure how to react. It's terrible, in a way, that the girls will never know their father. But he was a violent man and a criminal. I can't feel badly that he'll never have any influence over them."

"If I'm guessing right and Christopher Barry was their father. Not Ungar."

"We may never know, will we?"

"Maybe it's better that way, for us and the girls."

"Almost anything would be better than finding out Ungar is their biological father." Holding Mandy with one hand, she rubbed at her side again. She'd been achy all day, as though she was coming down with something. Her immune system was probably on the fritz due to too much stress in her life.

"I talked to the police in Helena, too, but there was no record of a domestic dispute call regarding Amy. I was hoping to get a description of the guy she was living with."

"She probably never called the cops. Whomever it was had convinced her she deserved what she got."

He grimaced and shook his head. "I wish I could return the favor."

That was one of the many reasons Laura had fallen in love with Eric. He was protective of those he loved. Even though he'd never met his half sister, he'd automatically included Amy within the circle of those he felt obliged to defend.

"How soon will we hear on the DNA tests?" she asked.

"The technician said he'd rush it." He shrugged as though he was unable to predict a time. "It may depend if he gets a rush order for a criminal trial or something."

"I understand." Which didn't make the waiting any easier.

Deciding it was time to fix dinner, she passed Mandy to Eric. He was so comfortable with the twins, she had no qualms about letting him take over the parental duties with both babies.

In the kitchen, she got down a bottle of aspirin and swallowed a couple of pills. If she'd picked up a flu bug somewhere, she hoped she wouldn't give it to the twins.

Realizing she wasn't the least bit hungry, she forced herself to prepare a chicken breast, some squash and a baked potato for Eric. He could fill up on chocolate-chip cookies and canned peaches for dessert, if he wanted.

About the time she was ready to serve dinner, the sounds of fussing babies rose in volume, so she fixed two bottles, zapping them in the microwave. She'd feed the twins while Eric ate. Her uneasy stomach rebelled at the thought of food, anyway.

"Dinner," she called.

"Hope you've got something for these famished youngsters. The way they've been eating lately, neither one of them is going to fit into their prom dress." Juggling Mandy, he slipped Becky into her car seat. "Not that I'm going to let either of them date until they're thirty, of course."

Laura smiled but she couldn't find enough energy to laugh at his joke. Her face felt clammy and her stomach was threatening rebellion.

"Eric, I don't think I should—"

The phone rang. She rolled her eyes. Just once she'd like to have dinner without crying babies or Eric being called out on the job.

He got the phone while she got the bottles out of the microwave. To quiet Mandy, she propped her bottle then fetched Becky from Eric's arms. He wasn't talking. Just listening intently. Laura hoped it wasn't an emergency, because she was going to have to go to bed early. So far the aspirin hadn't done much.

Sitting down at the table, and trying not to breathe on Becky, she slipped the bottle into the baby's eager mouth. Despite feeling miserable, she couldn't stop the smile that curved her lips or the feeling of maternal love that welled up in her. She'd never be so sick that the emotional high the twins gave her would vanish.

Eric touched her shoulder. An emphatic smile lit up his face, and his pale blue eyes glistened. "We're home free, Laura."

She cocked her head in question.

"That was the guy from the lab. Ungar's blood doesn't match the twins. He's not their father."

Her eyes fluttered closed and her shoulders sagged in relief. "Thank God!"

"Man, I'd really like to get my hands around Ungar's throat for the worry he put us through. That phony attorney, too. All they wanted was money. They both ought to be locked up, and I'd personally be willing to throw away the key."

"Eric!" She thrust the baby into his arms. "I've got to—" Hand over her mouth, she raced for the bathroom.

Startled, Eric tightened his grip on the baby and grabbed for the bottle before it dropped to the floor. "What's wrong?"

He hadn't expected Laura to react to such good news by bolting from the room. He'd been thinking of a celebratory kiss. A good long smooch followed by an even more interesting activity after the twins went down for the evening.

He'd been dead wrong.

With a quick glance at Becky to see that she was okay on her own, he carried Mandy to the downstairs bathroom where Laura had disappeared. During the past couple of days, he'd realized he could finally tell the twins apart—the shape of their brows, the different sounds of their cries and mostly their personalities.

He rapped his knuckles lightly on the bathroom door. "You okay?"

Her moan sounded miserable.

Hesitating only a moment, he shoved the door open. She was sitting on the floor, her arm draped over the commode, and she looked as sick as a dog. A panicky fist gripped him in the chest.

"Laura, honey, what's wrong?"

She shook her head. Her hair looked lank, her forehead damp with sweat. "Flu, I think."

"What can I get you?"

She tried to wave him off. "The twins, you take care of—"

"I will. But I can't leave you here like this."

"Just go. Go. I'll be fine."

She wasn't fine, and he was helpless to know what to do. Dammit, he'd dragged broken, bloodied bodies out of crumpled cars. Rescued people who'd been stranded on a cliff three hundred feet high. Pulled people out of fiery buildings.

But he'd never felt like this. Powerless to help the woman he'd come to care about, and more than a little bit concerned.

From the other room he heard Becky cry.

"I'll be back," he promised, edging reluctantly out of the bathroom. Laura looked so weak, she could barely lift her head. "Should I call Doc Justine?"

"No." She waved him away again. "Babies."

"Right." He hurried to Becky, determined to get the twins fed and down as soon as possible. Then he'd see to Laura.

Maybe it was just a bad case of the flu, he told himself. Nothing anyone could do about that. A cold cloth on her forehead. Broth when she was feeling better. Lots of liquids, he remembered as he patted Becky's back and brought up a giant-size burp, making her feel instantly better. No need to panic.

Laura screamed.

Frantic, Eric managed to get both babies into the living room and in the playpen, giving them a quick, "Your mom needs me," before hustling to Laura in the bathroom.

"What's happening?"

Holding her belly, she was practically rolling on the floor. "It hurts. Oh, damn, it hurts! I'm sorry." She groaned in an apparent effort not to scream again. Her face was as white as bone, her lips twisted into a grimace.

That didn't look like flu to him. "I'm calling the doctor."

His fingers shook as he punched in the phone number. It took three rings before Kristi answered.

As coherently as possible, Eric told her what was going on.

"Can you bring her over here?" Kristi asked.

"The twins. I can't—"

"We'll both be right there," Doc Justine said on the clinic's extension phone.

Barely hanging up and without saying goodbye he raced back to the bathroom. He sat on the floor and cradled Laura's head in his lap. Sweat poured off her forehead, her cheeks were flushed. Grabbing a silly little fringed guest towel from the rack above him, something Laura had brought with her from Helena, he wiped away the dampness from her face.

"It's okay, sweetheart. Doc's coming. Kristi, too. They'll know what to do."

"I feel like such a wimp. It's got to be just a bad case of the—"

"Naw. Think of this as an exercise to make me feel like a hero."

"You are, you know." Her whole body shuddered in his arms. "A hero."

God, what was taking the doc so long? The damn clinic was only a block away. By now they could have driven to Great Falls and back.

One of the twins started to fuss again. But Eric wasn't going to leave Laura. Not now. Both babies were safe. He'd seen to that. Laura wasn't.

"That's Becky," she whispered hoarsely. "She can be so fussy—"

"She's fine. The doc will be here soon. Then I'll see to her." It figured Laura would be worried about her baby instead of focusing on her own pain. Whatever heroics he'd ever managed in his entire life paled in comparison to her maternal instincts. "Try to relax," he urged her.

Distress shadowed her beautiful eyes and etched lines of tension across her face. "If anything happens to me—"

"Shh, nothing's going to happen. You've got a nasty bug of some sort. Doc will give you a magic shot that will hurt like hell and you'll be fine. You'll see."

She didn't look convinced, but by now he'd heard the local medical team arrive. The crying baby hushed a moment before Doc Justine squeezed her way into the bathroom.

"Okay, young man, let me take a look. You go see to your babies."

Doc virtually shouldered Eric aside. He had no choice but to leave the room. Among other things, there wasn't enough space for three adults to fit in the guest bathroom.

Feeling drained and weak in the knees, he staggered out of the bathroom to find Kristi and the twins. She seemed to have the babies under control.

"You look awful, Eric. Sit down." She gestured toward the couch.

He sat as ordered. "Laura's real sick. I don't think it's the flu."

"Justine will know what's wrong."

God, he hoped so. Leaning over, he buried his face

in his hands. What would he do if he lost Laura? It would be like the sun not coming up in the morning, spring not following winter.

"Eric!" Doc called.

He sprang up from the couch, racing back to the bathroom. "What?"

"I want you to carry Laura into the living room, put her on the couch. I can't examine her properly here."

Ignoring Laura's protest that she could walk, the doc moved out of the way and Eric picked up his wife in his arms. The moan she stifled against his chest nearly drove him to his knees. She was hurting, and it was something he couldn't fix.

Once he had Laura on the couch, the doc poked and prodded at her abdomen, more times than not drawing a cry or wince from Laura.

The examination didn't take long. Doc Justine sat on the edge of the coffee table keeping an eye on her patient.

"We could do a blood test," she said, "but it's not likely to change my diagnosis. Laura, you've got an acute case of appendicitis. You need to get to a hospital right away."

"But the twins—"

"You don't have any choice," Doc insisted. "If your appendix ruptures—and it may—you'll be in worse trouble than you are now."

Forcing himself to stay calm, to handle the emergency, Eric said, "I'll put in a call to the medi-vac helicopter in Great Falls."

"It'd be faster to drive her yourself," Doc said. "The weather's good, the roads clear. The helicopter would take almost as long to get up in the air and here as it would for you to do the trip yourself with your lights flashing."

"Okay. Sounds good." Hell, nothing sounded good when Laura was in danger of a ruptured appendix.

Kristi said, "One of us should go with them."

"You know," the doc said with a wink, "I've been itching to get my hands on those twins to give 'em a good cuddle." She glanced at Kristi. "You're more agile than I am these days and can pretty well do anything I could do. Hustle on back to the clinic, get an IV set to go. While you folks are off to Great Falls, I'll indulge my grandmotherly instincts and give those twins lots of lovin'." Taking Laura's hand, she gave her an encouraging smile. "If that's okay with you."

"At this point, I'm not exactly prepared to argue with anything you say. Just take care of—"

"They'll be fine," Justine assured her. "And so will you."

Kristi said, "I'll be back in under five minutes. I'll let Rory know I'm going with you."

Eric wasn't quite as confident as Doc Justine as he readied the SUV cruiser to act as an ambulance. He was supposed to be strong; the thought of losing Laura made him weak. Never before had he known this feeling of sheer terror.

He could only hope he'd be able to hold himself together, keep his emotions under control, until he got Laura safely to the hospital.

He'd alerted the hospital that he was bringing in a patient, and he'd driven as if he was on an Indy racecourse, lights flashing, siren wailing. Even so, it seemed like an eternity before he whipped his police cruiser up to the hospital Emergency entrance and brought it to a halt.

He bolted from the car just as a couple of orderlies with a gurney and a nurse appeared. With a quick, professional summary, Kristi brought them up-to-date on Laura's pulse, blood pressure and the pain medication she'd been given. The hospital staff placed Laura on the gurney.

Eric held her hand as she was wheeled inside.

She looked up at him with a sleepy smile. "That was some wild ride, Sheriff."

"I wanted to get you here in a hurry."

"You did fine. I knew you would."

Her words filled him with an unexpected sense of awe. She'd trusted him to get her safely to the hospital—just as she'd trusted him to be the father of the twins she dearly loved. And to be her husband, in sickness and in health, until death do them part.

Emotion clogged his throat. *Don't die, Blue Eyes. Please.*

"We've got her, Sheriff," the nurse said as a doctor arrived to examine Laura. "You can wait in the lobby. We'll keep you posted."

He couldn't seem to let go of her hand.

She gently squeezed his fingers. "I'll be fine, Eric. Let the doctor do her work."

Nodding, he bent down and brushed a kiss to her lips. "I'll be right outside if you need me."

"I know," she whispered.

Kristi took his arm, gesturing that they should leave

the examination room. He still didn't want to go, but he didn't have much choice.

In the lobby, a half-dozen people were waiting in various stages of boredom and anxiety, watching the flicker of a TV set mounted on a faux marble post.

Kristi said, "You go move your cruiser away from the emergency entrance, then check at the admissions desk. I'll wait right here. If anything happens, I'll be able to keep you posted."

"Right." Feeling muddled, as though he'd been the one getting a heavy dose of painkiller, Eric followed Kristi's instructions.

At the admissions desk, he discovered he didn't know Laura's social security number or her date of birth, which she must have listed on their marriage certificate but he hadn't been paying attention. Or if she had any allergies, though she hadn't mentioned any. She would have told him about that, he was sure. Well, mostly sure.

Damn it! Laura was his wife and there was so much he didn't know about her. She liked flowers because she was always picking a few wildflowers and putting them in a vase on the kitchen table. She could cook and bake like a whiz, and probably knew more about history than he'd ever wanted to know. And she had a tiny mole on the side of her neck that he loved to kiss.

But he didn't know her favorite color or what kind of music she liked. Where she liked to go on vacation. If she hated going to the dentist as much as he did.

By the time he finished with the admissions clerk, he was mentally kicking himself around the block.

Don't die, Laura. There's a lot I want to learn about you yet. It may take me years to get all the answers.

Kristi stood when he returned to the lobby. "They took her up to surgery a couple of minutes ago."

A painful, hollow sensation filled his stomach. "I should have been here. Gone with her."

"They'd already given her a light anesthetic. She was sleeping when they took her up." She placed a reassuring hand on Eric's arm. "We can wait upstairs, if you'd like."

"Maybe we should call her mother," he suggested. "Let her know what's happening. Information probably has her number."

"I'll take care of it after I get you settled. I'd just as soon not have a big guy like you pass out on me. You're looking a little green around the gills."

Eric couldn't argue with her judgment. He felt as bad as if he were the one about to have surgery.

The upstairs waiting room was small and unoccupied at the moment, which left Eric alone with his thoughts while Kristi made the call to Laura's mom.

He sat on a narrow couch, elbows on his knees, head in his hands, picturing Laura, willing her to be okay. He never should have put her in the bind of *having* to marry him in order to be the twins' mom. That hadn't been fair. She'd had her life all planned out. Her teaching. Her curriculum job.

Then he'd turned stubborn and selfish, not wanting to give up the twins himself.

Kristi joined him on the couch. "Her mom's going to drive over. She'll be here as soon as she can."

"Thanks for making the call." He sure as hell was in

no shape to hold a coherent conversation with Laura's mother or anyone else.

"I certainly hope Laura knows how much you love her."

Slowly he turned his head to look at Kristi. The lamplight haloed her reddish-gold hair.

"A guy like me? I'm not exactly capable of love."

"What makes you say a thing like that?"

"You know something about my background. Dumped by my mother when I was—"

"You love your brothers, don't you? Rory and Walker?"

"Well, yeah, but that's—"

"How about the twins? You worked so hard to keep them, to be their dad, you must love them as much as I love Adam."

"They're babies. My only living blood relatives. Sure I love 'em." What the hell was Kristi getting at?

"And yet you're out here, dying a thousand deaths yourself because Laura's having a relatively routine surgery, and you're trying to tell me you don't love her? Give me a break, White Eyes. You Oakes boys have to be as dumb as dirt when it comes to women and your emotions." She rolled her eyes in exasperation. "Rory was exactly the same way with me."

Eric stared at her for a long minute. *He loved Laura?* Rolling the idea around in his brain, he decided it fit. It fit comfortably, in fact. He wondered how long the thought had been hiding somewhere in the cracks and crannies of his brain without him being aware it was there.

He loved Laura. Somehow when he wasn't paying

attention, he'd actually fallen in love with her—despite his background and his fear of not having the capacity to love a woman.

He grinned. *Well, I'll be damned!*

"I get the feeling a lightbulb just went on in that male brain of yours."

"Yeah, it did." His smile broadened.

"Then I suggest you share your new insight with Laura at your earliest opportunity."

"I'll do that." He swallowed hard as he had a second thought. Given that they had married for the sake of the twins, he wasn't all that sure how she would react to the news that he loved her. She might prefer to keep things as they were—a marriage that didn't carry a lot of emotional baggage.

Maybe *she* didn't love him.

What the hell! Not only didn't he know Laura's favorite color, he didn't know how she felt about him.

"Maybe I'd better hold off on telling her until she's feeling better," he muttered.

"Eric Oakes, if you love a woman you *have* to tell her. Anything else is cruel and unusual punishment, for heaven's sake."

He blinked again, recalling a conversation he'd had with Rory not that many months ago. His brother had been afraid to tell Kristi how he felt about her, and it almost cost him the woman he loved.

God, now he knew why Rory had been so scared. He was sweating bullets.

Patting his shoulder, Kristi said, "Tell her, Eric. I promise she loves you back. It's in her eyes every time she looks at you."

Chapter 15

Eric picked up Laura's hand, curling her fingers over his palm. "How you doing, Blue Eyes?"

A lazy smile curved her lips. "A little woozy still, but I'm okay."

"Yeah, you're more than okay. The doctor said the surgery went perfectly. You'll be home in a day or two, and then I'm suppose to pamper you."

"That sounds nice. Remind me to thank the doctor for suggesting that."

"She didn't need to. I'd already figured that part out." He smoothed back a few damp strands of hair from her forehead. "I brought you flowers, too. From the gift shop downstairs."

She glanced toward the end of the bed where he'd placed the floral arrangement on the nightstand.

"They're beautiful. I love daisies and chrysanthemums. They always look so cheerful."

"I'll keep that in mind for future reference." He'd keep her in flowers, too, for the rest of her life, if she'd let him.

"Where's Kristi?" she asked.

"Waiting outside. She wanted to give us some time alone. She also called your mom. She's on her way here, by the way."

Laura nodded. "She'll be worried."

"She'll be okay once she finds out that you came through surgery with flying colors." Taking a deep breath, he said, "There's something else I've figured out, besides the pampering part the doctor recommended."

"What's that?"

He tried to lick the dryness from his lips without much success. "I was so scared when you got sick, and then during that miserably long drive into town. And again when they took you into surgery. I was afraid I was going to lose you, Laura."

She looked surprised by his admission. "You didn't have to worry. I knew I was in good hands."

"The thing is... I hadn't realized..."

A tiny frown stitched its way across her forehead, and her eyes cleared with concern. "What's wrong, Eric? Tell me."

"Nothing's wrong, exactly. It's just that I... I love you, Laura. I don't know when it happened or quite how, but it did. And the thing is, I don't think I'm ever going to stop loving you."

She brought the back of his hand up to her face, rubbing it across her soft cheek as she smiled. "How nice..."

"I know I practically forced you to marry me so you could be a mom to the twins. I'd understand if you decide you don't want to stay married to me. I wouldn't even fight you for their custody, if that's what you want. They need you."

Laura strained to break through the residual fog of anesthetic to understand what Eric was telling her. Hadn't he just said the words she'd longed to hear—that he loved her. And now he was giving her custody of the twins? "Don't they need you, too?"

"Seems to me that mothers are extraimportant."

"So are fathers. Amy wanted her babies to have both a mother and father. That's what you and I wanted, too."

"Yeah, well, I thought maybe if I gave you a choice—"

"That I'd choose to stay with you?"

Looking more uncertain than she'd ever seen him, Eric glanced away. "Something like that," he said.

Her old worry resurfaced, and she trembled on the inside. "Even though I can't give you children of your own?"

"You and the twins are all I could ever want. If you decide to stay with me, later on—if it seems like a good idea—we could talk about adopting another kid or two. I mean, that's worked out pretty well for Walker—if you'd be willing."

"I think I would." She'd been afraid no man would ever consider that option, that he would reject her because of her inability to bear the children he deserved. "In which case, I have this really good idea. You do love me?" His quick nod of agreement thrilled her. "And I love you."

He brightened. "You do?"

"With all of my heart. Which is why it makes a lot of sense to me that we stay married for the next fifty years or so, raise the twins together, add a few more babies along the way however we can and maybe even bounce a few grandchildren on our respective knees before we're too old and creaky to enjoy them."

"Oh, God..." Without letting go of her hand, he dragged a chair closer and sat down heavily. "Grandchildren, huh?"

"When the girls are ready to start their own families."

"It better not be too soon," he said sternly. "I mean, teenage boys can be pretty—"

She laughed, which pulled the muscles in her abdomen, and tears of happiness filled her eyes.

He was instantly on his feet again. "What's happening? Are you hurting? I'll call the doctor."

"No. Just tell me again that you love me."

"I do." Bending over, he brushed a sweet kiss to her lips. "I love you, Laura Oakes. I always will."

She smiled, and tears squeezed out of the corners of her eyes. "I love you, my beloved husband. I'll love you forever, until death do us part." This time she knew the vows they were sharing came from two hearts that had found each other and their new promise was meant to last a lifetime.

A light rap on the door preceded her mother's appearance. "I'm sorry to interrupt, but I was worried. I came as soon as—"

"Come in, Mrs. Cavendish." Giving Laura's hand a quick squeeze, Eric stepped away from the bed. "Your daughter's fine. In fact, we're both fine."

Without hesitation, Barbara Cavendish gave Laura a gentle hug and was quickly reassured that all was well, or would be soon. Kristi came into the room to add her own best wishes for a swift recovery.

Laura was feeling quite overwhelmed by all the attention—and the depth of love she saw in Eric's eyes—when her mother pulled an envelope from her purse.

"Bill Williams—our family attorney," she noted for Eric's and Kristi's benefit, "dropped by the other day. It seems Amy left a letter in his care at the time she was making plans for the twins if she should—" She halted, her chin quivering slightly.

"It's okay, Mom. We understand how much you loved Amy."

Barbara steadied herself. "Apparently Amy wanted you to have this letter on the twins' first birthday. But since Bill is retiring at the end of the month, he wanted to pass it on to you now so that it wouldn't be lost in the changeover at his law firm." She handed Laura the envelope with the attorney's return address.

"Do you want me to open it now?"

"I think so," her mother said.

Laura glanced at Eric, who gave her a shrug that said, "Your choice."

Opening the envelope, she unfolded a single sheet of paper covered with Amy's almost childish scrawl. Slowly she read her foster sister's last message.

No one could have had a better sister than you were to me—or a better mother than Barbara was. If I disappointed you, I am sorry and wish I could have been a better person. I hope my babies, who I love with all my heart, will make it up to you by giving you all the love you deserve.

I know you think it strange that I insisted you try to locate my half brother. But you see, ever since I learned of his existence I've had this dream that you and Eric, wherever he is, would raise my babies together. Without knowing a thing about him, I'm hoping he'll be the kind of man who could love you and be kind to you, as a man should.

Forgive me if this was a silly dream. If it didn't work out as I had hoped, forgive me for trying to play matchmaker from the grave.

I love you and will be watching over you and the twins.

Amy.

Laura's hand trembled, and she couldn't stop the flow of tears that ran down her cheeks.

Concerned, Eric took the letter from her nerveless fingers. "What is it?"

"It's perfect. Your sister sent me to find you because—"

She couldn't finish the thought, the swell of love she felt for Amy filled her throat and made her chest ache.

Eric scanned the letter. "I'll be darned," he said, passing it to Barbara, who let Kristi read it over her shoulder. There were tears shining in his eyes, too.

"She got her last wish," Laura whispered.

"Yeah, she did."

He bent over the bed railing to kiss her again, and Laura knew that somewhere Amy was looking down on them, smiling through her own veil of tears.

* * * * *

Teresa Carpenter believes that with love and family anything is possible. She writes in a Southern California coastal city surrounded by her large family. Teresa loves writing about babies and grandmas. Her books have been rated Top Picks by *RT Book Reviews*, and have been nominated Best Romance of the Year on some review sites. If she's not at a family event, she's reading, or writing her next grand romance.

Books by Teresa Carpenter

Harlequin Romance

Her Boss by Arrangement
Stolen Kiss from a Prince
The Making of a Princess
Baby Under the Christmas Tree
The Sheriff's Doorstep Baby
The Playboy's Gift
Sheriff Needs a Nanny
The Boss's Surprise Son
A Pregnancy, a Party & a Proposal

Visit the Author Profile page at Harlequin.com for more titles.

Baby Twins: Parents Needed

TERESA CARPENTER

To Jill Limber, critique partner,
writing buddy and lunch companion,
I'm lucky to have you in my corner. And to
Michelle and Gabrielle, my favorite
twins in the whole wide world.

Chapter 1

Rachel Adams was at war. And the enemy outnumbered her two to one. Hands on her hips she surveyed two plump-cheeked, hazel-eyed cherubs smeared head to foot in baby lotion.

"Cody Anthony Adams," Rachel admonished the unrepentant ten-month-old, "if you can't keep your hands to yourself, I'm going to duct tape them to your diaper during your naps."

The sight of the greasy mess acted like scissors to nerves already frayed thin by exhaustion. Inhaling a calming breath, she reminded herself she was a mother now. That it had happened by default didn't matter. She'd made a vow to provide a home for her orphaned niece and nephew.

But boy did she have a lot to learn.

Already she'd discovered that children, like animals, sensed fear.

God knows she'd had little time to mourn the sister she'd barely known. Instead, Rachel had learned that messes happened. Literally. And repeatedly. And if she didn't keep things far enough out of Cody's reach, creatively. Usually with food, jelly, bananas, potatoes whatever he could get into when she turned her back. He liked to finger paint. And his favorite target was his sister.

Yuck, yuck, yuck.

Armed with rubber gloves and a tub of wet wipes she went on the attack, cleaning bodies, fingers and toes. And hair. Both babies needed a bath to complete the job. She made a mental note to move the crib another six inches from the changing table.

It struck her suddenly; this must be love. When forbearance overshadowed disgust and exasperation, letting affection rule, there could be no other explanation.

Sometime over the last six days she'd fallen in love. And it was huge, bigger than anything she'd ever experienced.

The feeling terrified her.

One thing was for sure, if her co-guardian ever deigned to show his face, she'd fight with everything she had to keep her niece and nephew.

"That's right, kiddos, you're stuck with me. I'm wholeheartedly, irrevocably a goner. And I'm keeping you. I promise that you will always know you are loved. You'll never have to worry about simply being tolerated or that you're here only because of a sense of duty.

"We're a family now," she whispered around the lump in her throat.

Stripping off the rubber gloves, Rachel ran her fingers through the slick darkness of Cody's hair. She kept looking for signs of her sister in the twins, and caught the occasional expression. But they must have gotten their dark hair and eyes from their father, because Crystal had brown eyes and light brown hair.

Crystal had gotten her coloring from her father. Rachel took after their mother with white-blond hair that she kept short and manageable and eyes that couldn't decide if they were blue or green.

A sudden knock at the front door interrupted her musings.

Rachel tensed. "Who could that be?"

Wearily blowing a strand of hair from her eyes, she looked at the naked babies and considered ignoring the door. Whoever it was couldn't have come at a worse time.

Jolie began to cry. In the week the twins had been in her care, Rachel had learned that Cody liked to be naked but Jolie didn't.

A loner who preferred animals and plants to most people, Rachel didn't usually get visitors; not even her neighbors. But whoever banged on her door meant business, pounding again almost immediately.

Leaving the twins in the safety of the crib, making sure nothing else was within Cody's reach, Rachel made her way to the door reminding herself she wasn't a loner anymore. Through the peephole she saw a man half-turned away from her with hands tucked into the pockets of his dark jacket.

Hmm. Could this be Ford Sullivan, co-guardian of the twins? A Navy SEAL, his commanding officer had explained that Sullivan, aka Mustang, was out of the country when the twins were orphaned but he would be in touch as soon as he returned from assignment.

As far as she was concerned he could stay away.

She opened the door a few inches.

The man appeared bigger and broader than his image through the peephole. Much bigger. Much broader. Dressed in jeans and leather with dark glasses, biker boots and a five-o'clock shadow as accessories, his stance warned he wasn't someone to mess with. Snow fell from a gray sky, landing in white clusters on wide shoulders and dark hair.

This man bypassed bad and went straight to dangerous.

A sucker for a good action movie, the sight of this tall, dark and menacing man sent unexpected, and unwanted, tingles down the back of Rachel's neck.

She crossed her fingers he was a motorist who'd run out of gas.

"Yes?" she said. She purposely did not ask if she could help him. Or smile. She'd found smiling only encouraged people to linger when most of the time she preferred her own company.

"Rachel Adams?" he asked. His deep baritone slid as smoothly as hot coffee through the icy afternoon air.

And just as smoothly and potently down her spine.

"Yes." She shifted restlessly, thinking in the back of her mind that she needed to put her SUV in the barn.

"Your sister was Crystal Adams?"

So much for him being an anonymous motorist. Her

head went back, and she narrowed her gaze on him. "Ford Sullivan I presume?"

He cocked his head in acknowledgment. "Yes. I've come to collect the twins."

Hackles bristling, Rachel planted her hand dead center of his chest when the military man attempted to cross her threshold.

"Hold it, big guy. I don't know you. And so far, I don't like what I'm hearing."

Sullivan didn't give an inch, but his eyes narrowed and she felt the flex of muscle under her fingers, silent warnings of strength and resolution. He reached inside his jacket and came out with a wallet. He handed her his military ID.

She knew of Navy SEALS. They were elite, Special Forces who were dropped into hot spots all over the world. Granted, her knowledge came from movies and books, but there was no denying it rated as very high security stuff.

After a moment, he plucked his ID from her chilled fingertips. "Lady I've driven a long way, and it's cold out here."

Damn him. She didn't want him in her home, not when he talked about taking the twins away. Not when she wanted to keep the twins herself. But he had legal rights she couldn't ignore.

Reluctantly she stood aside and let him come inside. His commanding officer had said Sullivan was an honorable man. Right. His edges were so rough he practically chafed her skin as he stepped past her.

Blowing out a pent-up breath, she closed the door. Then clenched her teeth against the sight of him framed by the hearth fire. His big body made her blue and gray living room seem entirely too small.

And more disorderly than she'd realized. The babies came with a lot of clutter, and a lot of demands. Picking up was a luxury that came right after sleeping and showering.

Jolie's cries from the bedroom reminded Rachel where she'd left off. Grim amusement lifted the corner of her mouth. She'd just been thinking she was at war and here stood a warrior.

He wanted the babies? She knew just how he could help.

"I'm so glad you're here." Pretending not to see the disdain with which Sullivan viewed her home, she hooked her arm through his and drew him into the bedroom. "Because the twins need a bath."

To his credit Sullivan didn't flinch. He took off his sunglasses revealing sharp blue, expressionless eyes. He tossed the glasses along with his leather jacket onto the bed.

Jolie immediately stopped crying to stare at Sullivan. Rachel didn't blame her. Soft black cotton defined muscular shoulders and hard pecks. His arms were strong and browned by the sun. He heated the room better than a fireplace.

Something she shouldn't be noticing. Still, she empathized when she cleaned the drool from Jolie's chin.

"What happened?" he asked as he stepped up to the crib.

Rachel took perverse pleasure in explaining Cody's little habit.

He hiked a dark brow. "You might want to check on them more often."

"Wow, why didn't I think of that?" Jerk. She lifted Jolie into her arms. "Grab Cody. The bathroom's through here."

Rachel flinched at the sight of dirty towels and overflowing clothes and wastebaskets. Half the contents of her medicine cabinet littered the sink. And— she cringed—was that a fork?

Ignoring the mess, and the rush of embarrassment, she bent to start the bathwater. Once it ran warm she set the stopper and knelt on a towel still folded next to the tub from the babies' last bath. Then she set Jolie in the warm water.

Sullivan knelt next to her, so close his arm brushed her shoulder as he lowered Cody into the water. Rachel jumped away as if singed by steam.

She shot to her feet. "Watch the babies, I'll grab clean towels."

"Clean would be good," he said, making no attempt to hide the derision.

Stunned she swung around to confront him, but his attention remained on the twins. She waffled for several seconds on whether to appease or challenge him on his concerns regarding the condition of the house.

On the one hand, the house was a mess; on the other, she'd been handling their wards on her own for six days. How dare he judge her?

She'd like to see him do better.

No, she turned away to get the towels, that wasn't true. That would mean he'd have the twins and she needed to care for them, to be there for them, because she hadn't been there for her sister.

If he thought she'd simply step aside and allow him to take them away, he could forget it.

"How did you know Crystal?" she asked as she returned to the tub.

Making sure to leave plenty of room between her and Sullivan, she knelt next to him. She glanced at him, then away, pretending not to notice how the twins' excited play had dampened his T-shirt causing the fabric to cling to his impressive chest.

"Eeey!" Cody shrieked in joy and slapped the water with both hands, splashing everyone. Jolie shied away, the movement causing her to slide sideways. Rachel reached for her, but Sullivan got there first, catching Jolie in his large, competent hands.

He held her with such gentleness, righting her and making her giggle. He appeared so calm despite his obvious frustration with the circumstances.

"It wasn't Crystal I knew." He finally answered her question as he scrubbed Jolie's tummy. "At least not well. Tony Valenti was my friend. We worked together."

"The twins' father?"

"Yeah."

"He was a SEAL, too?"

"Yeah." A short pause. "He saved my life."

"I see." Yeah, she did. And the picture didn't look good. An honorable man, he'd feel all the more obligated to take the twins because of what he felt he owed his dead friend.

An hour later the babies had been bathed, dressed and fed. Lowering Jolie into the playpen and tossing in a few plastic blocks, Rachel had to admit having an extra pair of hands had made everything easier. And faster. It would have taken her nearly twice as long to complete the tasks on her own.

She turned to where Sullivan sat on the sofa with Cody. The little boy looked up at him and smiled showing two bottom teeth. The man ran a gentle finger down the baby's cheek then bounced him on his knee.

Cody reached up and grabbed a handful of dark hair. Sullivan calmly freed himself.

They'd bonded quickly.

She crossed her arms over her chest, denying that his tenderness toward the baby touched her. She walked to the opposite end of the sofa and began folding the clean clothes mounded in the corner.

"What are your plans for the twins?" she demanded.

He lifted a dark brow at her directness. "I plan to honor my friend's request by taking them back to San Diego to raise them."

Her heart clenched as he confirmed her worst fear. "Right. And what about me?"

"Simple. I plan for you to sign over your custody."

"Simple?" She nearly choked on the word. "How can you hold that baby in your arms and call this simple?"

He frowned, shifting the baby. Cody tipped back his head and looked up at the expanse of black fabric, to the man's face. Silent communication passed between them as once again, Sullivan pulled the baby's fist from his hair.

Sullivan focused his blue gaze on her. "I understand this isn't easy for you. But it's for the best."

"You don't understand anything, Sullivan. I failed my sister once. I'm not going to fail her now. Her dying wish was that I raise her children. And that's what I'm going to do."

He eyed her for a moment before cocking his head in acknowledgment. "Your sister never intended for you to raise her children."

Rachel's head went up and back as if she'd taken a blow to the chin. It couldn't have hurt more if Sullivan had actually hit her.

Old guilt rose up to choke her. Resolutely she shook it off. She and Crystal had put the past behind them when their parents died three years ago and Crystal had come to stay with Rachel. And when Crystal had left for San Diego State University, they'd stayed in touch by phone and e-mail.

Rachel was the only family Crystal had had left in the world. Through all of her uncertainty and exhaustion this last week, Rachel had held on to the fact that her sister had trusted her to take care of Jolie and Cody.

She caught herself rubbing her arms as if to ward off a chill. When she felt Sullivan watching her, she clenched her hands into fists and dropped them to her sides.

"Why would you say something so hateful?" Rachel demanded.

"Look I only know what Tony told me. Crystal didn't like it that Tony made a will naming a guardian for the twins without consulting her. So she made her own will and named you as guardian."

"Which just proves she wanted me to raise her children." Something deep inside her eased.

"No, you were leverage. No offense, but Tony didn't want someone who ran away from life and responsibilities, who couldn't maintain a relationship to raise his kids."

Everything in Rachel screamed a denial of his claim, of this whole situation. But it was here; *he* was here, standing in her living room and not budging by the look of it.

"I don't believe you." Believe? Not likely. "If this is a joke, it's in very poor taste."

"No joke." He hesitated, and she could practically hear the debate going on internally. Being free with information obviously wasn't part of his job description. "That would be cruel. Listen, I have a large, close-knit family that Tony was a part of. He wanted the twins to have that connection."

Sullivan bent to retrieve his jacket and withdraw some papers. He extended them to Rachel. "I have legal documents here for you to sign over custody."

She reluctantly lowered her gaze from him to the folded papers he offered. She didn't want to take them, didn't want to think he spoke the truth about her sister's motives. But she'd learned long ago no good came from lying to herself.

Or from avoiding reality.

He looked around the cluttered room then met her gaze. "Clearly you're out of your depth."

"That's ridiculous." She ignored the proffered papers to pick up a tiny set of overalls, folding them over and over. "I'm not overwhelmed. I just need time to adjust."

He rose and settled Cody next to Jolie in the playpen. "And while you adjust, the twins suffer."

Anger, simmering under the surface since she

opened the door to this ungrateful man, rose to a boil. She planted her hands on her hips and glared in outrage.

"How dare you? They have not suffered. So I'm behind in my housekeeping. So what? You caught me on a bad day. I usually pick up when they're in bed, but last night I had to write. I had a deadline."

He gestured to the cluttered room, his blue eyes flashing with impatience. "This is more than one day's filth. Make this easy on both of us. Sign over custody to me and you won't have to adjust and you won't have to pick up after them any longer."

"Okay, that's it!" Rachel had had enough. Filth? Oh, she'd had more than enough.

Stomping into her room she grabbed up the diaper bag. A quick glance inventoried the contents. Going to the changing table she stuffed in more diapers, two sleepers, a pack of wipes, some formula.

"You think you can do better?" She marched by Sullivan on her way to the kitchen.

"I think you need to calm down." Sullivan watched her efforts with an impassive expression that only fueled her anger.

She ripped open the refrigerator door, hissing when her thumbnail caught in the handle and tore. Tears rushed forward, but she blinked them away determined to show no weakness in front of the cold man watching—and judging—her every move.

"Oh, I'm calm." She quickly tore off the broken nail and stuffed her finger in her mouth as she held the door open with her hip and plucked two bottles from the refrigerator adding them to the other items in the red baby bag.

Glaring at her nemesis, she stepped up to him and thrust the overflowing bag into his arms. She half hoped he'd drop it, but he quickly controlled the bag.

"I'm just wonderful."

Adrenaline pumping through her, she brushed past him on her way to the playpen where she swooped Jolie up into her arms. From the edge of the playpen Rachel snagged two blankets. Folding one around Jolie, Rachel tossed the other to Sullivan who now eyed her with sharp-eyed wariness.

"Bring Cody."

"What's happening here, Rachel?"

"I'm doing you a favor." Finding her coat, she pulled her car keys from the pocket and headed for the door.

"You're going to sign the papers?"

A bitter laugh broke free. "Better than that. I'm not signing the papers."

He caught up with her at her Toyota SUV and swung her and Jolie to face him. "Where do you think you're going?"

She shook him off. "I'm not going anywhere. You are." She took the diaper bag from him, opened the front door and tossed it inside. "You wanted the twins? You've got them. For the next twenty-four hours."

"Excuse me?" Now his tone held a bite. "I'm not accustomed to taking orders."

"Yes, you are, you're in the Navy."

Let him argue that.

His expression didn't change; he was too much a warrior to give anything away that easily. But his shoulders went up and back, fighting ready. A clear indication she'd hit a nerve.

She should be ashamed of the satisfaction that gave her, but he threatened her on too many levels.

"You seem to think two babies are so easy to care for." Walking around him, she opened the door, put Jolie in her car seat and began to belt her in. "Right. Fine. You're going to get your chance."

Sullivan had left the door open. Cody didn't care to be left alone in the house, and he made his displeasure heard with loud cries. Flashing Sullivan a disdainful glare, she suggested, "You might want to start by getting Cody."

"Not until I understand what's going on here." Before her eyes he changed from civilian to warrior. His hands lowered to his sides, his chin jutted down and his blue eyes chilled by several degrees.

Climbing from the car, she closed the door with soft emphasis. She instinctively kept her distance, out of reach of his sensual appeal. What was with her that this stranger's dangerous edge affected her so easily?

"The first thing you have to learn is you don't get to take the high road when a baby is crying."

He spiked a hand through his dark hair. "You're right." Turning he loped into the house and came back out a few moments later with his jacket under his arm and Cody wrapped in a blanket.

Okay, so Sullivan got points for common sense.

She reached for Cody, but Sullivan held him fast. She lifted one eyebrow and waited.

"We need to talk first," he stated.

"No, we'll talk after." Facing him, she propped

hands on hips. "After you've tried to feed and change two babies. After you've spent a sleepless night trying to get them both to sleep at the same time. After you haven't brushed your teeth before noon and your best shirt's stained beyond repair. Then we'll talk."

The sound of grinding teeth reached her across the two feet separating them. He shook his head. "What's to stop me from taking them and driving on to San Diego?"

She narrowed her eyes at him, and this time when she reached for Cody she refused to be cowed.

"Honor. Integrity. I spoke to your commanding officer. He assured me you have both in spades." She walked around the SUV and set Cody in his car seat. Kissing his dark curls, she tucked the blanket around him.

Bending, she gathered a few scattered toys and handed one to each baby. They immediately tried to take a bite. Her heart turned over. How trusting they were. At ten months old life wasn't that complicated.

"I'm doing this for you guys." She told them. "Have no mercy."

She rounded the SUV to rejoin Sullivan.

"Plus, I haven't signed the papers." She held out her hand, palm up. "Keys."

"I thought you meant for me to take them." None of the tension had left those truly impressive shoulders.

"To your Jeep. You're taking my vehicle, I'll need to keep yours."

Silence stretched while she met those compelling blue eyes head-on. The scowl creasing his brow revealed his displeasure at the situation.

"Look, I'm not giving these babies up without a fight, but I'm exhausted, dirty and hungry. In no shape to have an important discussion. And until you've spent some quality time with the twins, you're in no shape for the discussion, either. So we trade keys and regroup tomorrow."

He hesitated for a heartbeat.

Time slowed. Breath misted on the air. Her nerves jumped.

Finally he handed over his keys and took hers in exchange.

"I hope you realize what you're doing," he said as he climbed inside the vehicle and adjusted the seat. "Honor and integrity don't make me a gentleman." He closed the door and turned over the ignition, rolling down the window a crack. "I'm a SEAL. And we never leave a man behind."

Rachel watched the taillights disappear down the driveway, praying she hadn't just made the biggest mistake of her life.

Chapter 2

Ford pulled into a slot in front of his hotel room, slowly turned the ignition off, eased back in his seat and closed his eyes. Twenty hours after leaving Rachel Adams's house and he was ready to run back to her door with head and tail tucked low.

How humiliating.

Using all the stealth learned over eight years in the SEALS; he risked moving to check on the babies in the back seat. Jolie, as tidy and neat as when he'd strapped her in, slept with her pink beanie on her head and her bottle nestled close. Cody, who'd long ago lost his hat and shoes, had a catsup smear on his cheek and a French fry clutched in his fist.

They'd finally fallen asleep an hour ago.

Ford settled back in his seat. He planned to sit right where he was for as long as they slept.

Time well spent finding an appetizing way to eat crow. Only sheer stubborn will had kept him from running back to Rachel's place hours ago. How had she managed on her own for six days?

A call home netted him lots of advice from Gram, and other family and friends, but the twins were having none of it. Nothing he'd done, or said, or sung— yes he'd sung to them—had done any good. Talk about logistical nightmares, he'd rather plan a two-team infiltration any day than repeat the last twenty hours.

Clearly they wanted Rachel.

Hell, he wanted Rachel, and it had nothing to do with the soft curves hidden under her burp-stained sweater. Okay, that was a lie. No man could look at her trim little figure and remain unaffected. But her sweet butt and perky bosom were beside the point. He'd misjudged her big time. For six days she'd cared for the two babies with patience and devotion.

He knew that because they were clean, well fed and distraught without her.

With one or the other, or both, of the babies awake most of the night; he'd gotten about two hours sleep. And she'd had them for six nights. No wonder her pretty sea-green eyes had dark bruises shadowing them.

She was one feisty woman. A blond wildcat determined to stand between him and her cubs. But for all her attitude, she was a lightweight. Barely five foot five, six at the most, her sweet curves scarcely filled out her jeans or rounded out her gold sweater.

Obviously she'd been ignoring herself to care for the twins. Protective instincts had flared when he should have been thinking of ways to convince her the babies were better off with him.

He'd told her a SEAL never left a man behind, which was nothing less than the truth. He could no more leave Tony's twins in the care of another than he could leave a teammate on the battlefield.

He tensed and turned to the window just before the local sheriff rapped on the glass. He held up a hand and eased from the car.

"Officer." Ford addressed the man who looked like Mr. Clean in a uniform. Sheriff Mitchell according to his badge. "What can I do for you?"

"Sir." The sheriff crossed his arms over his massive chest and nodded toward Rachel's SUV. "Problem?"

"No." Ford made sure to keep his hands in plain view as he leaned against the SUV, not wanting the officer to feel threatened. Had the hotel owner called the law? He'd been to Ford's room twice in response to complaints about the babies' crying. "No problem."

The last thing he had time for was trouble from the local law enforcement.

"This is Rachel Adams's vehicle." Sheriff Mitchell took two steps to the side and looked into the back seat. "Those are her wards."

"Yes." What game was Rachel playing? Did she regret sending him away with the twins? "Has she called with a complaint?"

"Well now—" assessing brown eyes were turned back on Ford "—we don't need a complaint to take an interest in the citizens of Scobey."

"I'm sure your citizens appreciate your diligence." Having grown up in a small town, Ford took the sheriff at his word. Which didn't mean he intended to tell the other man anything.

"What's your business in town?"

"That's between me and Ms. Adams."

"I've heard there have been complaints about the babies crying."

Ford's tolerance for the questioning dried up. He opened the back door next to Cody. He gestured inside. "Look for yourself, they're fine. They're still adjusting to the loss of their parents. They have the right to a few tears."

"I suppose they do." The sheriff hiked his pant legs and crouched to look in at the babies. Satisfied he rose to his standard six one. "Why are you sitting out here?"

Ford frowned to see Cody starting to stir. He quietly closed the door. "They aren't sleeping well, we took a drive to settle them down."

"Right. I'll let you go." Mitchell sounded disappointed he had no reason to detain Ford, and his next words held a clear warning. "Just take heed, Rachel Adams isn't alone here in Scobey."

"It's been snowing here for about an hour." Rachel frowned at the view outside the window. Dark clouds obscured the sun. Snow fell, pushed around by whistling gusts of wind. This weather had better not keep Sullivan from bringing back the twins. Maybe she should call him and tell him to come now.

"I can stop by on my way home." Sam Mitchell offered. "Make sure you're all right." He'd called to warn her an unexpected cold front was moving in fast and heavy.

Uh-huh.

He'd already mentioned running into Ford Sullivan in town. She bet. He'd probably hunted Sullivan down at his hotel.

"Mitch, I'm fine. There's no need to waste a trip out here."

She'd broken things off between them nearly two years ago, but the sheriff continued to take an interest in her affairs. Or lack of them, in the hope of reigniting the ardor between them. For an intelligent man, no one buried his head in the sand better than Mitch.

"I heard they're really missing you over at the clinic."

"Hmm."

"Mrs. Regent's Poopsy nipped a couple of the techs during her clipping."

"Rough."

"Yeah. Poopsy doesn't care for anyone but you. Rumor is Mrs. Regent won't be scheduling Poopsy again until you're back from maternity leave."

"Oh joy."

Rachel opened up a new e-mail, wondering, not for the first time, at the man's ability to basically hold a conversation on his own.

Only half listening, she sent her latest article off as an attachment, then closed down her computer. When she looked up, she spotted her SUV pull past the window.

Her glance immediately went to the clock. Sullivan was early. By almost three hours.

Yes!

"Mitch, I've got to go. Sullivan just pulled up with the babies."

"I still don't like the idea of you dealing with him on your own. You call me if you have any problems."

"He's a SEAL, Mitch. I'm either in great hands, or you'll never find the body."

"That's not funny."

"You're telling me." Not that she feared for her life. No, she feared for her peace of mind. Not only because he'd threatened to take the twins from her, but because she'd dreamed of exactly how great those hands would feel against her skin. Her blood heated with the memory of gentle caresses and not so soft strokes. Oh my.

A knock sounded at the door.

"Mitch, I'll be fine. Gotta go." She disconnected and headed for the door fanning herself en route. No way she wanted Sullivan to know he got her hot and bothered.

She opened the door and leaned against the threshold. Sullivan stood alone on the porch. "Sullivan. You're early."

He ran a hand through already mussed hair. The gesture was the first sign of vulnerability he'd displayed. Behind him snow fell from a gray sky— heavier now than a few minutes ago. White clusters covered wide shoulders and dark hair. It did her heart good to see him disheveled.

Red rose high on his cheeks. Rachel blinked, surprised by the sign of discomfort. But was it temper or embarrassment that lit up his features?

"Call me Ford, or Mustang if you prefer. Let me just get this out right up-front." He met her gaze straight on. "I'm sorry. I made assumptions I shouldn't have. You've done a phenomenal job handling Cody and Jolie alone over the past week. Thank you for being there for them."

Oh, unfair. Here she'd hoped for a moment of weakness and instead he showed his strength with a sincere apology. And he wanted her to call him Mustang? The picture of the beautiful range horses came to mind. Proud and wild, free and reckless, she had no problem seeing how he'd earned the nickname that played off his given name.

No, she'd stick with "Sullivan," much less intimate, more distancing.

"Enough already. In another minute you'll have me weeping." She pushed past him. "Let's get the babies inside out of the snow."

She dashed to the nearest door, freed Jolie from her seat and quickly returned to the house. Teeth chattering, because she hadn't bothered with a jacket, she arrowed straight for the fire.

She spread a blanket in the middle of the floor and set Jolie in the center with a couple of Matchbox cars. Then Rachel stepped back and watched Sullivan lower Cody to the blanket.

Moving away, she curled into the corner of the sofa while Sullivan stood taking in the room.

Nothing to be embarrassed about this time. She'd been busy for the last twenty-one hours. Well, okay, she'd slept for the first part of that time, but the rest had gone toward housework and laundry. Plus she'd gotten a couple of articles written for her syndicated column on animal manners.

"Place looks great."

"You don't." Jolie soon gave up on the toy cars to crawl across the living room carpet straight for Rachel. She lifted the girl into her lap. "How much sleep did you get last night?"

"I've had less." He shrugged away her concern. "It's not the lack of sleep that got to me. It's the helplessness. I'm a man of action, but nothing I did was right."

"That's how it was for me for the first three days, then they finally began to calm down." Okay, this conversation wasn't so bad.

He even made her laugh when he told her how he'd found the cereal in the bottom of the baby bag, but since he didn't have high chairs he'd taken the twins out to their car seats and fed them in the SUV. Smart actually, but she'd had no doubt of his intelligence since the moment she'd first opened the door to him.

"At least they stopped crying long enough to eat." Sullivan bent to pick up Cody who was trying to climb his leg.

"They take comfort from each other." Rachel ran her fingers through Jolie's soft hair.

The look he sent her spoke volumes. "You mean they feed off each other's emotions. One starts crying, and they try to outdo each other."

"You have to remember they're traumatized." She defended her niece and nephew. "They've lost their parents. That's going to take time to get over."

"Yeah." The fire popped and shifted. Sullivan walked over to tend it, easily handling both Cody and the fire poker. "The sooner they're settled the better. Have you considered signing the papers?"

Disappointment washed through Rachel. Back to square one. But she wouldn't be signing any papers. Now or later.

"I'm thinking you should be the one signing the papers," she challenged.

Before he could respond, the lights flickered. Once. Twice. Then they settled.

"Shoot." Holding Jolie close, Rachel leaped to her feet and headed for the front window. A wall of white fell heavily. Actually it blew sideways, the wind's force strong enough to blow the snow horizontal, confirming her worst fears.

The storm had become a blizzard.

"Looks bad." Sullivan stood behind her.

She smelled the clean scent of him. Musk, starch and man, an intoxicating mix. Almost distracting enough to take her attention from the storm.

But that would be a deadly mistake.

"Yeah. Blizzard. Damn, there was no mention of snow in the weather reports earlier." Obviously she should have paid better attention to Mitch.

"Won't be the first time they've been wrong."

The understated response startled a laugh from Rachel. "You've got that right."

Already her SUV was buried under several inches of snow and ice. It needed to be moved to the garage or the engine would freeze.

The lights flickered again. And again they came back steady.

That wouldn't last.

"Do you have a generator?" he asked.

She nodded. "Fuel is in the barn."

Lord, she hoped she had enough fuel to weather the storm. Living alone, she'd learned to be prepared, but a lightning storm in late September had hit a power tower east of Scobey, knocking her power out. She hadn't had a chance to restock before receiving the news about Crystal. Since then she'd been so busy with the twins, she hadn't thought about restocking her emergency supplies.

"I should leave. The hotel will probably let me back in without the twins."

"You can't drive in this." She handed Jolie to Sullivan and then moved to the closet to yank out her jacket and some boots. "Give me my keys."

"I've driven in worse."

"So you're looking to leave me alone with the babies again?" One boot on, one boot off, she propped her hands on her hips. "Look, I don't want you here any more than you want to stay, but I wouldn't send my worst enemy out in a storm this bad. Oh wait, you are my worst enemy."

He lifted a brow as he rocked the babies, but he only said, "We're only six miles from town."

"Only?" She stomped into her other boot. God save her from ignorant tourists. "Where are you from?"

"Southern California. But I've trained in all forms of extreme weather."

"I've no doubt. But there's no need to go all SEAL on me. Now, hand over the keys."

Sullivan frowned his displeasure as he glanced out of the window. "You can't go out there, either."

"I have to. If the SUV isn't moved, the cold will crack the engine block."

"I'll move it."

She shook her head as she wrapped a scarf around her throat and ears. "I need to get fuel for the generator, too. And bring in some wood."

He stepped into her path. "I can do it."

"Look, you're helping by being here to watch the twins." She pulled on her gloves, waiting for him to step aside. "I know what I'm doing."

Giving in, he juggled the babies to reach the keys in his pants pocket, which he handed to her. "Be careful."

"Always. Candles and matches are in the kitchen cupboard to the left of the sink. In case the lights go out before I get back with fuel for the generator."

Ducking into the closet again, she looped a heavy coil of rope over her shoulder.

"What's that for?" Sullivan demanded.

"Snow line. One end hooks to the front porch post, the other I hook around my waist. It acts as an anchor so I can find my way back to the house."

A grim look settled over his features. "This is ridiculous. I can't let you go out there alone."

"Didn't we just have this conversation? I live alone, Sullivan. I do what I need to survive. That doesn't change just because your macho self is here." She pulled a second pair of gloves from her coat pocket and donned them over the first pair. "And I don't have time to argue."

Not waiting for a response, she moved to the door, stepped out and quickly pulled it closed behind her.

Ford looked down at the babies in his arms. Their care and safety had to be a priority, but it didn't feel right letting Rachel struggle against the elements on her own.

He carried the twins to the playpen. Both babies immediately crawled to the side and pulled themselves up. He tossed a few of the plastic blocks in to keep them occupied. Neither Cody nor Jolie paid any attention to the blocks.

"Ba da da sa." Cody registered his complaint and lifted his arms to be picked up.

"Maa ga do." Jolie put her two cents in and held her arms up, too.

He itched to go to the window and check on Rachel's progress but moved to the fireplace instead. The fire had died down to mere embers. He tossed on a new log, then began to pace, wearing a path in the dove-gray carpet.

"What do you say, Cody, we're the men here. It's up to us to protect the women. And that's not happening with us in here and her out there."

"Mamama?" Jolie stuck her finger in her mouth.

Ford stopped midstride and stared at Jolie. How odd to hear her call Rachel mama or almost mama, he reasoned. But still, it sounded wrong. Felt wrong. And brought home to him how much life had changed in such a short period of time.

Tony and Crystal were gone, killed in an earthquake while visiting a Mexican resort.

Ford had been shocked to return from assignment to learn he was guardian of Tony's children. Yeah, he'd agreed to take on the responsibility, but he'd never really expected it to be necessary. Certainly not so soon. But prepared or not, Ford owed Tony. He'd saved

Ford's life; honor and friendship demanded Ford step up to meet Tony's last request.

Tony had always envied Ford his close family, so much so that he'd arranged for Ford to raise his kids. Which meant the twins went home with Ford. He'd be moving in with Gram, who had agreed to watch the babies for him. He'd also be hiring a full-time nanny.

Ford didn't want to hurt Rachel, but it couldn't be helped.

The storm, however, managed to delay the inevitable.

Rachel really surprised him. Her aquamarine eyes and white-gold hair cut short and sassy hid a depth of passion he'd bet few people saw.

Frustrating as her protectiveness was, he respected her spirit, her willingness to put herself on the line for the children in her care.

He just needed to convince her they'd be better off with him.

After he saved her from the freezing hell outside.

For all her feistiness and lean strength, she had to weigh next to nothing. She'd whip around on the end of that snow line like a kite in a hurricane.

It'd only been five minutes, but he couldn't take this. Gram had taught him better than to sit on his butt while a woman did the hard chores. Forget endangering herself in a storm of this caliber.

Checking on the babies, he found the sleepless night had caught up with them. Curled together they slept peacefully.

"Now that's what I call team players." He tossed a blanket over them. "You hang tight. I'm going to help Rachel."

* * *

Cold attacked Rachel from all sides, freezing exposed skin, slowing her down, making each breath cut like ice. Snow and hail pelted the windshield, making it hard to see.

The engine refused to turn over the first few tries. She worried it may be too late to move. Crossing her fingers, she gave it one more try and breathed easier when the engine fired up.

Thank God. She didn't want Sullivan stuck here any longer than necessary. Unfortunately necessary looked like several days at the moment. Just damn.

And to top it off, when the weather cleared Sullivan expected her to hand the twins over to him, never to be seen again. She couldn't even think about that without choking up.

So she wouldn't think about it.

As if.

While she waited for the engine to warm, Rachel rested her head against the steering wheel and worried about what she was going to do if Sullivan fought for custody of the twins.

She lived in a one-bedroom house in Scobey, Montana, population barely topping a thousand. And she worked as a veterinarian technician at a pet clinic because she liked dealing with animals better than dealing with people.

Wind buffeted the car as she worried about what she had to offer the twins besides cramped quarters and nonexistent social skills.

A home. A warm touch in the middle of the night. Someone in the world to belong to. The answers came from deep in her soul where she kept her secret hopes and dreams hidden from the light of day.

Belonging. It was no small thing. Rachel vowed she'd fight to give Cody and Jolie a sense of belonging. Because damn, she never thought she could love this deeply or this quickly.

And no one, not Sullivan, not anyone, was going to take them from her.

Lifting her head, she reached for the gearshift.

Next to her the door suddenly opened. She jumped and screamed.

Chapter 3

Sullivan stood framed in the opening of the SUV door.

"Jerk," Rachel shouted. "You scared me. What are you doing out here?"

"I came...help."

The storm stole part of his reply, but she got the gist. She yelled out her own concern. "Babies?"

He leaned down so he spoke directly into her ear. "Playpen. Sleeping. Scoot over so we can get this done and get back inside."

She shook her head. No way was she climbing over the gearshift in the bulky jacket and boots. "Go around."

Surprisingly he did so without argument.

Rachel drove the thirty feet to the old-barn-turned-garage at a crawl. She left the SUV idling while Sullivan braved the storm to open the big barn doors. Inside, she found an old blanket and they covered the vehicle.

"I could have handled this on my own." She advised him resentfully as she tugged on her end of the blanket.

"Pull in your claws, wildcat. This has nothing to do with your abilities." He didn't look up from anchoring his end. "I was raised better than to let you do it on your own."

Damn him for making her sound hysterical. "The babies aren't safe alone inside."

"All the more reason to work together so we can get back to them quickly." He came around from the front of the SUV. He wore her yellow raincoat, which dwarfed her but fit him just right.

He looked strong, calm, confident and a little amused as he grabbed his duffel bag from the back seat.

She moved away from him to where she stored the generator fuel. Her heart sank when she saw she only had enough fuel for a couple of days.

Sullivan crowded close to reach the fuel. "Is this it?"

Rachel bristled. "I don't usually let it get so low. I've been a little distracted since the twins came to live with me."

Her whole world had shifted with the arrival of Cody and Jolie. Luckily the pet clinic had given her maternity leave because she'd been so busy getting them settled, becoming accustomed to their presence and schedule, everything else, including her writing had suffered.

She hadn't taken proper care with her normal chores, which in this case could prove costly.

"Cut yourself some slack. You've had a big adjustment to make." He shook a can. "How long will this last?"

His simple understanding floored her. And deflated her snit.

"A couple of days, more if we're careful. We'll probably loose electricity, but we have plenty of wood and propane. And a well-stocked freezer."

If she had any luck at all, the blizzard would be over before they ran out of fuel.

Of course it would take another day or two for the roads to be cleared after the snow stopped. Extra time with a man hot enough to give Brad Pitt a run for his money and who had an unsettling habit of reacting in the way she least expected. And two babies still fretful after suffering the biggest tragedy of their young lives.

Oh joy.

"So we'll be careful," he said with a confidence that indicated he was used to handling difficult situations. "Do we need anything else from here?"

"Yeah." She opened a cupboard and took down a large flashlight. "This is it."

He took the flashlight from her and led the way outside. She stood shivering while he closed the barn doors.

Turning toward the house, she encountered a moving wall of white.

Teeth chattering, hands shaking, she pulled on the snow line until it grew taut, a chore made more difficult because she could no longer feel her fingers.

Sullivan's hand joined hers on the rope. He surrounded her with his strength and warmth, urging her forward. She started for the house.

The last of the light had gone so Sullivan used the flashlight; even so, she saw little beyond her own hands on the rope.

It was hard going, the exertion exhausting, the cold debilitating. Every step became a battle of will against nature. The protection of his bulk sheltered her from the worst of the storm and helped move them along. By the time she spotted the corner of the porch she was truly grateful for Sullivan's help.

The lights were out. She worried about the babies alone inside. Hopefully enough light would come from the fire that they wouldn't get too frightened.

She stopped and indicated the shed on the side of the house. "We need to fill the wood reservoir," she shouted. "We may not be able to get outside for days."

He spoke next to her ear. "I'll do it. You need to get out of this weather."

"I…help."

"Save the heroics. Your teeth are about to crack from the chattering."

He helped her the rest of the way to the porch and handed her the gasoline and flashlight. She leaned close to instruct him on the location of the reservoir door on the outside of the house.

He nodded his comprehension. "Get inside. Take care of the babies." He turned away.

She caught his arm, stopping him. "The rope." She found the hook at her waist and tried to release it.

"Don't need it. I'll be close to the house."

He started to leave again. But fear clutched her gut and she grabbed his coat. "No. Take the rope."

Rather than argue further, he threaded the rope through the layers of his clothes and clicked the hook to his belt.

Once he was rigged up, he stepped over to her rather than away. He tucked her scarf up around her ears. "Get inside where it's warm. I'll be back."

Half frozen, exhausted, and more worried about him than she cared to admit, Rachel let herself inside the house dragging the fuel and lanterns in with her.

She couldn't stop shivering. Even the marrow in her bones felt frozen.

Below the icy discomfort and the natural concern of being cut off from the rest of the world, she was just plain pissed at the quirk of fate that made her anxious for the safety of the man responsible for tearing her life apart.

But then why should life suddenly start playing fair?

After stripping off her soggy outdoor gear, Rachel breathed on her hands to warm them as she stumbled to the laundry room just off the kitchen. She kept a flashlight and candle on a shelf inside the door. She quickly got the generator going and then went to check on the babies.

Her heart melted when she found them cuddled together sleeping. She swayed in relief. Clutching the cushioned rail, she held on tight. She stood lost in awe at the sheer innocence and resourcefulness of them.

After a while she heard the door, felt an icy draft of air.

"How are they doing?" Sullivan appeared next to her.

Emotions more mixed than ever, she moved her gaze to him, noted his damp hair and skin still flushed from the cold. She'd never admit it to him, but she'd been really glad to see him out there.

"Fine. They're still sleeping."

"They look so peaceful."

"Yeah," she turned away to hide the tears in her eyes. "Too bad it won't last."

"What's that supposed to mean?"

Temper spun her back around. "I mean if you have your way, the little bit of normalcy they've found since losing their parents will be torn away from them by the very people they should be able to trust."

He scowled. "It's not like that."

"It's exactly like that, but you can forget it. I'm not giving them up."

"Hey, hey." He framed her face, caught an escaped tear on his thumb. "I know this is hard. But my friend and your sister entrusted their children to our care because they knew we'd do right by them. Even when it's hard."

The fight went out of her.

"It's not fair." She pulled away from his touch, from the pity in his eyes.

He easily stalled her attempt to distance herself and folded her into his arms instead.

"No." He agreed. "It's not. But you're not alone. We'll help each other through this."

She wanted to riot against him, to push him away and deny his reasonableness. But it felt too good to lean on someone for a change. Someone with a hard chest and muscular arms, who smelled like a dream and warmed her with the heat of his body. Giving in, she laid her head on his shoulder and closed her eyes so he couldn't see her anguish.

"I don't want to like you."

His chest rumbled under her ear when he laughed, and he stroked her hair like she stroked Cody when she held him. The tender caress both soothed and unnerved.

"Well hold onto that thought, tomorrow is another day. Listen, you're cold, tired and hungry. We'll postpone talk of custody for now. Why don't you go take a shower while I fix some dinner."

The truce, like the shower, sounded like heaven. "We should probably conserve the hot water."

"Not tonight. We need to thaw out. You go first while I check out the kitchen."

"The twins?"

His chest lifted and fell on a heavy sigh. "Let them sleep. They didn't get much rest last night."

"They haven't slept well over the last week." Which, except for last night, equated to the same for her. Maybe that's why she felt like she could sleep just like this, standing up with her head on his shoulder listening to the steady beat of his heart. "They've been through so much."

He gave her a squeeze. "It'll get better with time."

He gave out heat like a furnace, thawing not only the chill from her bones but also the frigid wall around her heart. How long had it been since she'd been comforted by a man like this?

Never. Certainly not by the man she'd called father.

The thought was enough to have her pulling away and backing up. She had no business leaning on any man, least of all this man. So he had a point with his argument that the babies' parents had trusted them to do right by their children. That didn't mean she could trust *him*.

His opinion and hers hadn't gelled yet when it came to the twins.

She debated whether to leave him alone with them but there was little enough he could do. The storm prevented him leaving and he'd proven his gentleness when dealing with them.

"I'll go take that shower." She turned toward the one bedroom. When she reached the door, she glanced back. "Thank you."

He'd been watching her, more accurately he'd been watching her butt. He raised his gaze to meet her eyes; no apology there for being caught enjoying the view, just simple male appreciation. He lifted his chin in a gesture of acknowledgment.

A small thrill warmed her, raising every feminine instinct she kept ruthlessly suppressed.

She closed the door between them, deliberately placing a barrier between her and the dangerous man who awakened feelings she preferred to keep buried.

Time to get a grip. How could she spend even a moment in her enemy's arms? No exaggeration. Anyone wanting to take the twins from her rated as an enemy.

Really she didn't understand why he wanted the

twins. As a SEAL and bachelor—his commanding officer had also shared that bit of information—taking on the twins could only be a hardship, even with family to help.

Or maybe he meant for his family to absorb the burden.

Family. Definitely her weak point.

In the bathroom she stripped down and stepped into the shower letting the cascade of hot water soak the cold away.

Her thoughts turned to Crystal. When Rachel had left home, her biggest regret in walking away was in leaving ten year old Crystal behind. But Rachel couldn't stay where she wasn't wanted.

On her seventeenth birthday, she'd learned that the man she'd always known as her dad wasn't her biological father. The news had devastated her, yet explained so much. Like why she'd always felt like an outsider in her own home.

Beginning to thaw out now, she reached for her favorite peach scented soap.

Dan had gotten a raw deal. Rachel had understood that. He'd been lied to, tricked into raising another man's child. Yet he'd fed and clothed her, never beat her. Plenty of other kids had had it worse.

Rachel blamed her mother. She was the one who had lied, who had traded one man's child for another man's pride. Who had traded her child's comfort for her own. Stella Adams could have given Rachel the things Dan denied her: time, attention, affection. But Stella chose not to rock the boat.

For that Rachel had never forgiven her.

After rinsing, she turned off the water and stepped out of the tub. Wrapped in a large towel, she moved into the bedroom.

Rachel had learned her lesson too well in childhood to easily change now. Rather than chance heartache, she preferred her own company. Sure, she'd had relationships, but they never really went anywhere. Her fault. She wasn't willing to put her heart on the line and risk being rejected by someone she loved.

Not again.

Unfortunately her relationship with her sister had been a casualty of that lesson. But contrary to Sullivan's allegations, they'd forged a new kinship after their parents' death.

Rachel refused to believe Crystal had been faking the rapport they'd shared.

Dressed in thick socks and old sweats, she entered the living room, stopping to check on the still sleeping babies before moving on to the kitchen. She'd expected Sullivan to open a couple of cans of soup, but she'd underestimated him. The scent of garlic and tomatoes made her stomach grumble.

"Smells good."

He looked up from where he was buttering bread. "It is," he said with confidence. "Spaghetti. I thought we needed something hardy."

He'd changed out of his wet clothes while she'd been in the tub. The jeans and gray T-shirt displayed his masculinity to advantage. The casual clothes should have minimized his appearance, instead they emphasized his broad shoulders, muscular thighs, firm butt.

A dark lock of hair fell forward on his forehead. She

fought an uncharacteristic desire to sweep it back, to feel the tactile softness against her fingers.

Remembering too well how it had felt to be in his arms, she moved to the refrigerator and pulled out a head of lettuce. She needed something to keep her hands, and her thoughts, busy.

"Why don't you grab your shower while the bread toasts?" She urged him. While she'd been dressing, she'd come to a decision. The less time she spent in his company the better. Not an easy chore considering they were stuck together in a one-bedroom house, but she was committed to the act of self-preservation. "I'll make a salad."

He washed and dried his hands. "Sounds like a plan."

Opening the preheated oven, he bent to insert the garlic bread.

Rachel's hormones, usually under strict control, chose now to go astray. She wanted nothing more than to walk over, plunge her hands in his back pockets and squeeze.

Luckily he straightened before she gave in to the impulse.

She cleared her throat. "I put a towel out for you."

"Thanks." He grabbed his duffel bag and disappeared into the bathroom.

She breathed a sigh of relief. He took up so much space in a room. His very presence energized the air. Her recent trip down memory lane served to remind her exactly why she needed to keep him at arm's length. She had everything to lose and nothing to gain.

He came from a different world, here only as long as it would take to shatter her life.

A whimper drew her to the playpen in the living room. Jolie stirred. Rachel tucked a blanket around the little girl and then gently patted her back until she settled down to sleep. Cody didn't stir.

Would they be better off with Sullivan? He'd mentioned a large family, supportive and close-knit. Everything she'd dreamed of as a child.

Yet it seemed a betrayal to the children she'd come to love to even think the question.

Hearing the water go off in the shower spurred her to action. She caught the bread while it was still golden-brown. The salad went together quickly with a course chopping of lettuce and chives and quartered tomatoes.

By the time Sullivan came out of the bathroom, once again dressed in jeans and T-shirt, she had the table set. "Dinner is ready."

"Great." Ford slicked his fingers through damp hair before moving to hold Rachel's chair out for her.

She frowned at the gesture, suspicion alive in those amazing aquamarine eyes. "Who are you trying to impress?" She demanded. "We're not on a date."

Now why did he find her prickliness so appealing? "Blame my upbringing. Gram believes in old-fashioned courtesies."

"Thank you." The words were grudging as she slid into her chair. "You were raised by your grandmother?"

He nodded as he claimed his own seat. "Since I was eight."

"Hmm."

"She raised my five brothers and me after my parents died in an automobile accident."

Her eyes flashed to his then away. "I'm sorry."

Okay, less grudging but still a conversational dead end. He got the feeling she was good at dodging discussion.

Watching the tines of her fork slide through plum-pink lips, Ford fought off the sensual memory of how sweet she'd felt in his arms. Another time and place and he'd be making major moves on her. But he was already guaranteed to bring heartbreak before he left. No sense complicating the situation by acting on the attraction he felt for her.

Which didn't mean he'd allow her to ignore him.

He sent her a chiding glance. "Let me know if I'm boring you."

The cutest thing happened. Her earlobes turned red! And though agitation came and went in her sea-foam eyes, she made an effort to participate in the conversation.

"That must have been a difficult childhood."

"It was tough losing my parents, but Gram loved us and we were able to stay together. That counted for a lot." He leaned forward on his elbows. "You're not very talkative, are you?"

She swallowed a bite of spaghetti. "No."

"Why not?" He speared a tomato.

Silence greeted his question. She obviously didn't want to respond but he waited her out.

With a sigh she finally answered. "Generally because I prefer my own company."

"And in this case?"

"I don't know much about this topic." As if that revealed too much, she added, "And I see no need for us to become all buddy-buddy."

He ignored the dismissal. "What did you mean when you said you'd failed your sister?"

Her eyes flashed. "I'm not talking to you about my sister. You're wrong about her."

What a fake she was. For all her cold facade, she was all heat and passion underneath. And so incredibly vulnerable. Whatever happened in her family, it had left her hurting.

"Crystal said you ran away from home. Why? Family is important."

"Yeah. And I'm all the family the twins have."

Stubborn woman. Yet her relentlessness demonstrated her protective feelings toward the babies. Much as he wanted to exploit her weaknesses, Ford couldn't fault her for that.

"Tell me why you left home," he said.

She cocked her head causing a white-blond lock of hair to fall into her eyes. A quick flick of her hand sent it back into place.

"I know what you're doing, you know."

He hesitated for a heartbeat. "And what is that?"

"Information is power." Rachel drew circles on the table with the condensation from her ice water; a small frown drew her light brown brows together in concentration. "You want me to tell you about my past so you can use it against me to get what you want."

She was right. "I shared my history with you."

"For a purpose." She slanted him a wry glance. "No

doubt I'm supposed to believe the twins would benefit from all the male influence tempered by the sweet
little grandmother."

"Maybe I'm just making conversation."

She cocked an eyebrow. "Please. All is fair in love
and war. And you're a warrior to the bone."

"Very clever." He raised his glass of water in acknowledgment.

"Now why do I feel that surprises you?"

Unabashed, he grinned. "Everything about you surprises me."

"Gee thanks." She clinked her glass against his then
sipped. "Considering you think of me as a lazy dead-
beat who can't maintain a relationship, I'll take that
as a compliment."

He laughed, enjoying the note of humor mixed with
the censure.

"I admit I had a few misconceptions. Your courage, patience and dedication were totally unexpected.
In my job we put emotion aside to complete the task."

Now *he'd* revealed too much, which hadn't been
part of his plan at all. Her quick wit and intelligent
eyes made talking to her too easy. And too dangerous.
Avoiding her speculative gaze, he stood and carried
his dishes to the sink.

She looked as if she wanted to pursue the topic, but
thankfully her habitual reticence kicked in.

"I'm beat." Feeling he'd dodged a bullet, he pushed
away from the counter. "What do you say we get these
dishes done and go to bed?"

Chapter 4

Go to bed. Go to bed. Go to bed. The words echoed and bounced around the room, bringing to mind images of bare skin, tangled limbs, clinging mouths.

Unnerving to say the least. More so because Rachel was less disturbed imagining him naked than she had any right to be.

Her nipples tightened and her loins clenched around an emptiness she longed to assuage.

Embarrassed by her reaction, because of course he didn't mean they should sleep *together,* she avoided his gaze by clearing the table. Even so, she felt the heat rise in her cheeks, staining them red. Her ire rose, too, because only part of the heightened color came from mortification.

The rest was desire, pure and sinful.

Just because she preferred her own company these

days didn't mean she didn't know what to do with a man when she got him in her clutches.

As she neared the counter, she noticed the clock on the oven: 7:03.

"It's only seven o'clock." She pointed out. So much had happened in the last few hours it seemed much later. "A little early for bed."

He checked his watch, then grinned wryly. "Is that all? Must be feeling the effects of yesterday's early start. And did I mention the twins didn't get much sleep last night?"

"You did." She started the water running in the sink, splashed in some soap. She supposed she owed him for her best sleep in days. "Why don't you—"

"Oh." She jumped when she turned and came face-to-face with Sullivan. Instinctively stepping back, she slipped in some water on the floor and she felt herself going down.

"Careful." Lightning fast Sullivan caught her against his hard length. "I've got you."

Startled to find herself in his arms again, she looked up and found only inches separated her from blue eyes filled with stark longing.

She blinked and met a gaze devoid of all emotion.

That fast. Which begged the question if he'd felt anything at all. Or if she'd projected her own longing onto him.

"Sorry," she said, quickly pushing away. He let her go, a little too easily for her ego. Chiding herself for the foolish pang, she hiked up her sleeves and plunged her hands into the sudsy water.

"Did you drive all the way here, or fly?" She latched

onto his comment about his trip, determined to maintain a conversation to dispel the awkwardness.

"I drove." Dishcloth in hand, he started drying.

She watched him out of the corner of her eye as they made quick work of the dishes. In her experience men avoided household chores. Likely she had Sullivan's grandmother to thank for his thoughtfulness.

Rachel appreciated his help, if not his proximity.

"Easier that way to pack them into your Jeep and take them home with you." She had no illusions about his strategy.

He lifted one shoulder, let it fall. "That's the plan."

Present tense. So he hadn't changed his mind about the twins even though his impressions of her had improved. Disheartened, she fell silent.

A whimper from the direction of the living room disrupted the moment. The babies were stirring.

"I'll go." Sullivan moved past her into the living room, headed toward the playpen.

Reminded why she kept her own company, she picked up the dishcloth, folded it over the drawer handle and slowly followed.

"Hey, Cody." He lifted the boy into his arms. "How're you doing? Are you hungry? It's time for dinner."

Cody stopped crying and laid his head on Sullivan's shoulder.

Jolie held her arms up for Rachel to lift her, too. Rachel swooped the girl into a big hug. And discovered a desperate need for a diaper change.

The next hour and a half was spent taking care

of that problem, feeding the babies and getting them ready for bed.

"There's only the one bedroom. Which is where the crib is." Rachel gave Sullivan the layout. She indicated the slate-blue, ultra-suede sofa. "You can take the couch. I'll get you some blankets."

"This will be fine." He eyed the overstuffed cushions dubiously. With good reason, considering the length fell short of his six-two frame by six inches.

Leaving him to the logistics, she gathered the extra bedding from the hall closet.

Back in the living room, the babies played in the playpen, and Sullivan had the wood closet open as he restocked the oversized basket near the fireplace. A nice blaze burned in the old grate.

The lights in the kitchen had been extinguished, and he'd lit the candles on the credenza behind the couch giving the room a cozy feel.

The whole scene smacked of domestic tranquility. Way too home and hearth for her. It struck her as wrong. Because it felt too right. Sullivan was a stranger, an interloper. They shouldn't be so comfortable with each other, so easy together.

Time for a tactical retreat.

"Here you go." She dropped the bedding on the end of the couch. He was a big boy; he could make his own bed. "I'm beat. And it's past the babies' bedtime. We're for bed."

He closed the door to the wood closet and dusted off his hands. "Thanks. Do you think the storm will be gone by morning?"

"Hard to tell." Did his question mean he felt as

antsy as she did? "We weren't expecting snow, but it was supposed to rain for several days."

"How long before the roads get cleared after a storm like this?"

"Why? You suddenly need to be somewhere?"

"Other than getting the twins home and settled? No." He ran a weary hand through his dark hair. "I was thinking of the fuel levels."

"Right. We need to shut down the generator. That's what we're short on. The heat is on propane, so we're okay there."

"And we have plenty of wood."

Amused, she propped her hands on her hips. "Listen to Mr. California"

He crossed to the couch and started putting his bed together. "We do get snow in California you know." With a flex of biceps the size of ham hocks, he tossed the pillows into the corner. "Paradise Pines is in the mountains east of San Diego. We usually get snow once or twice a year."

Carefully keeping her distance from Sullivan, because she was inordinately tempted to test the strength of those biceps, it took Rachel a minute to process what he'd said.

She blamed her distraction on him. Unused to having strangers in her home, especially tall, muscular he-men intent on taking her cherished wards from her, her normal instincts were off.

She laughed. "And it lasts for what, a day and a half? Please. We lose the refrigerator with the generator. I'll bag up some snow to put inside to keep things cold."

"Okay." He nodded toward the kitchen. "You take care of the snow, I'll get the generator."

Surprised and pleased by his easy acceptance of her opinion, she grabbed a flashlight and headed for the drawer with the extra large plastic bags.

Oh, yeah, he was a mystery. As was the way he made her feel.

Not willing to explore the thought, she made quick work of filling several bags with snow from the back stoop and placing them strategically throughout the refrigerator.

Back in the living room she watched him move his duffel bag from the end of the couch to the head of the couch, then toe off his shoes and place them next to the duffel. He nodded toward the playpen. "Those two are out for the count."

Rachel checked on the twins. Cody and Jolie were once again sleeping curled up together. They looked so peaceful.

"Darn. I hate to disturb them. I know from experience if I wake them just to put them to bed, they'll fight sleep like heavy-weight contenders fight for the belt."

"So let them sleep. I'll be right here if they wake up."

"I'm not sure that's a good idea." No, giving control to this man was definitely not a good idea. What if he took the twins in the middle of the night?

What, her more rational side scoffed, and hike six miles to town in a blizzard?

Not so strange, the mother in her argued, he was a SEAL after all.

Sensing her turmoil, he met her gaze straight-on and held up his right hand as if making a vow. "I promise, they're safe with me. Come on, Rachel, we all need a good night's sleep."

"All right, but I'll leave my door open to listen for them."

"I'm not going to make off with them, Rachel."

"Excuse me if I'm wary. I just met you." God, was it only yesterday? "What you say and what you do could be two different things."

"No, I'm a man of honor. My C.O. told you so, re-member?" His expression said he didn't like being doubted. As a SEAL, she'd think he'd be used to ques-tioning actions and motives and having them ques-tioned in turn.

Was it her? Did he care what she thought of him?

A tingle ran down her spine.

"Oh, yeah. Man of honor. I forgot." She turned her back on the titillating sensation and on him.

At her bedroom door she halted to face him but forgot what she meant to say as the words suffocated for lack of breath.

Sullivan stood folding his T-shirt, firelight danced on his naked skin, his sleek muscles. Boy was he ripped. Dark hair lightly covered his chest narrowing over his six-pack to low riding jeans.

When his hands moved to his zipper, she gasped, inhaling much needed air.

"Good night." Executing an abrupt about-face, she dodged into her room, one thought clear in her mind. She was in serious danger of falling in lust.

Rachel woke to a gloomy room and the smell of coffee. Under the circumstances, she'd feared she wouldn't be able to sleep, but the last thing she remembered was planning to work on her book à la Abe Lincoln style.

A couple of months ago a publisher, enamored with her syndicated animal antics column, approached her asking for a book on animal manners. She'd been intrigued enough to send out a proposal.

That was before she got the call regarding the children.

Catching sight of the time, eight-thirty, she bounded out of bed. She never slept this late. The babies never slept this late.

Spiking fingers through her tousled hair, she padded in her sweats and socks into the living room. And found the babies where she'd left them last night, sleeping in the playpen. A change of clothes proved they'd been up and about at some point.

Ford was doing double duty. Trying to soften her up by letting her sleep in again. Darn him for being considerate. It wouldn't change her mind.

A rush of love swelled her heart. She bent and ran her hand over Jolie's silky brown hair. More than anything she wanted to do right by Jolie and Cody. She prayed that wouldn't mean giving them up.

Before straightening she traced a finger over Cody's rosy cheek. Whatever happened, the twins were innocents.

A bang in the kitchen spun her in that direction.

Ford stood, arms braced on the granite counter, head hanging between those amazing biceps. Silhouetted by the window, the violence of the storm outside embodied his internal struggle.

Obviously a private moment.

Rachel back pedaled to give him his privacy. Until he reared back and slammed his fist into the granite, bloodying his knuckles.

Shocked, she stood rooted to the spot. The fierce action exposed a well of anger and grief. *Unresolved* anger and grief. She debated whether to go forward or leave him be.

He drew his arm back for another strike.

"Stop." Rachel lunged forward and grabbed onto his arm with both hands.

Not the smartest move she'd ever made.

Before she'd felt more than the flex of muscle, he'd hooked a foot around her ankle and taken her down to the floor. Blue eyes savage, his body blanketed hers, his forearm pressed hard against her windpipe.

Oh, yeah, he definitely had a dangerous edge.

By rights she should be terrified right about now. But fear wasn't the emotion sending shivers through her body.

He blinked then instantly relaxed his arm.

"Oh God." Unbelievably he lowered his forehead to rest on hers. "I'm sorry."

"Apology accepted." She lay completely still. "You can get off me now."

He didn't move. "I usually have more control."

She bet. "That's good to know."

"It's not smart to grab me."

"I'll remember that." Tentatively she moved her upper body, reminding him he still held her pinned. The movement rubbed her breasts against his chest. Her nipples responded to the contact.

So did his body.

She froze. And looked up into features drawn taut with desire. His gaze locked on her lips, and he began to lower his head.

A baby's cry broke the tension.

Reminded they weren't alone—how could she have forgotten his whole reason for being here? Rachel pushed Ford's shoulders until he rolled off her.

"Don't do that again." On her feet, she straightened her clothes and dusted her butt. And carefully avoided his eyes.

Sure, she felt the attraction between them, saw the want in his eyes. In another time or place, she might be willing to blow off some steam in a no-strings fling. But she had too much to lose with this man in this situation.

No matter how tempted she might be.

He forced her to look at him when he invaded her space. Towering over her, his gaze lingered on her mouth before rising to meet her eyes. "You have my word I won't attack you again."

She scowled at him. "That's not what I was referring to."

He crowded close to gently tuck a wild curl behind her ear. "It's the best you're going to get."

Ruthlessly squashing the thrill the warning gave her, she pushed past him to check on the babies. Not surprisingly they were awake and wanting to play. To keep them occupied while she dressed, she dumped a handful of toys into the playpen.

She escaped to her room to brush her teeth and change into jeans and a sweater. Mixed feelings kept her company. Such a luxury to go through her morning routine without feeling rushed or worried the twins would wake before she finished. Yet she felt bad for enjoying the indulgence because she loved Jolie and Cody, and they were totally dependent on her.

She both resented and appreciated Ford for giving her these moments of freedom. For allowing her a full night's sleep.

Back in the living room she spread a blanket on the carpet in front of the fireplace and let the babies loose to crawl around. And when they started to wind down, she picked out several of their favorite books then tucked a baby on either side of her on the couch and spent the better part of the next hour reading to them.

Ford spent the time roaming the room. She tried not to think of his big, long-fingered hands touching her things. The sound of the drawer opening and closing in the credenza told her he'd found the broken bit. One side had pulled free of the front of the drawer. It looked like it should notch together but a set of staples prevented the pieces from connecting. She hadn't scraped together two minutes to fix it.

As she read on, he went to the utility closet next to where the generator ran, and retrieved her toolbox. She heard the clunk of it hitting the ground near the credenza behind her.

She finished the story then let the wiggling babies free. They immediately popped up to look over the back of the couch to see what Ford was doing. Rachel moved so she could keep track of the babies, ensuring neither fell backward or climbed over the top.

The new position gave her a premium view of one prime butt as Ford bent to look at the credenza from the bottom up.

Ford? Since when did she start thinking of the enemy by his first name? Maybe since he'd proved he wasn't the enemy by helping her in the snow, cooking her dinner and letting her sleep in.

All signs of a good guy.

Or a clever way to throw her off. Combined with his penchant for touching her at every opportunity and the smoldering glances he constantly sent her way, the strategy was working.

She reminded herself of her plan to keep her distance from him.

"You don't have to do that," she told him.

Sitting back on his haunches, he shrugged, his attention fixed on the screwdriver he wielded. "It's no problem."

"You don't need to be doing things for me." She kept her tone cool. No need for him to know he was getting to her. "I can take care of my own children. Do my own chores."

"I like to keep busy." He eyed her over his shoulder. "It's not a crime to accept a little help sometimes."

"When you live alone, self-sufficiency is important."

"So is making friends of your neighbors."

"Baa da ha." Cody dug his toes into the cushion and pulled himself up.

"Oh?" She ringed Cody's ankle, pulled him gently down. "I've never found that to be the case."

"Ha da ca." Jolie bounced up and down.

Ford's gaze challenged Rachel. "Have you ever tried?"

She stiffened. No doubt his neighbors were nubile young things who brought him casseroles and apple pies.

"Why don't you tell me what the great benefits would be?"

"Well." He fitted the front of the drawer to the sides and tapped them together. "Having neighbors is like being on a team. They look out for each other, help out with big chores, take care of the mail or pets when you have to go somewhere."

"This is Montana," she shot back, this time harnessing Jolie who imitated Cody's stunt in climbing up the back cushion. "Security isn't a huge issue. I can hire someone to help with the big chores. I don't have a pet. And I don't go anywhere for anyone to need to pick up my mail. I don't need a team. They're overrated if you ask me."

"Overrated?" The question held disbelief and a touch of insult. "You're talking to a Navy SEAL. Teamwork means the difference between life and death to me."

She suppressed the urge to squirm. "That's different. That's the military. You have to work together."

"We're an elite team of highly trained officers that go into the hottest spots in the world to save strangers, help governments, retrieve sensitive information."

"You're twisting my words." Giving up fighting the two babies, she set them on the floor and gave them toy trucks to play with, and began pacing in front of the fire. "I respect what you do, but I'm not you. Becoming dependent on others is an invitation to heartache."

Flinching as she heard the revealing comment, she turned her back on the room to hide how much of herself she'd just given away.

She heard the drawer slide neatly into place, the clink of tools being replaced.

"Is that what you want for your niece and nephew? A life of isolation and loneliness?"

She whipped around, chest heaving with fierce emotion. "Don't make this about them. They'll have me. They won't ever be alone."

"Rachel." He came around the end of the couch.

"No." Palm raised she stopped him. "You want to help? Fine. Watch the babies. I'm making lunch."

She escaped to the kitchen, which wasn't much of an escape, but as long as she kept her back to the living room she didn't have to see Ford. Or continue the disastrous conversation.

Damn him for making her defend her lifestyle.

Gathering the makings for sandwiches from the refrigerator, she carried the lettuce to the sink to wash.

Who was he to put her on the defensive? So she kept to herself, what was the big deal? She didn't hurt anyone, and this way they didn't hurt her.

Of course Jolie and Cody would have friends. She knew too well how it felt to be an outsider when you craved to belong.

She plunged her hands under the running water and shivered at the icy temperature. She frowned as she realized there was a definite chill in here away from the warmth of the fire.

Propane fueled the heater and the water heater and ran independent of the electricity. The air in here should be comfortable. Getting a bad feeling, she went to check the thermostat, pushing the slider way up to see if it activated the heater.

Nothing happened.

Dread settled low in her stomach. If they lost the propane—and the heat it provided—her plan to keep her distance from Ford would go with it.

Chapter 5

"Damn." Irritation and trepidation sounded in the one word.

Noticing Rachel's agitation as she monitored the thermostat, Ford asked, "What's the problem."

Hands on hips, she waited, as if wishful thinking would kick-start the heater. Finally she conceded. "It looks like something has happened to the propane."

Now he understood her worry. Without the heater they'd be restricted to the fireplace for warmth. A huge gust of wind shook the windows, a timely reminder that the storm still raged outside.

"What makes you think so?" he asked though he didn't truly doubt her take on the situation.

"It's cold in the kitchen, and I haven't heard the heater come on in a while."

"Propane turns to vapor when it freezes." Ford

joined her by the thermostat. "It could be nothing more than that. Do you have an above ground or below ground tank?"

"Aboveground, but I've never heard of propane freezing and I've lived in these frozen wilds for thirteen years."

He lifted a shoulder, let it drop. "It has to be really cold."

She looked from him to the ice-encased window and back again. "Sullivan, I've known really cold, and never lost the propane."

"Then maybe something fell and broke the connection. I'd better check it out." Ford headed for the closet holding the outdoor gear. He took out the yellow slicker. "Where is the tank?"

"What makes you such an expert on propane?" She demanded from behind him.

Ford dug through the closet, finding gloves he thought might fit, and a warm fleece muffler, thankfully in a simple navy. It was cold enough that he'd have worn a froufrou color, but he wouldn't have liked it.

"If something can be used as an explosive, has ever been used as an explosive, or can be mixed with something to form an explosive, it's my job to know about it."

He surfaced from the closet to find her blocking his path. She scowled, something going on behind those sea-green eyes. But whatever brewed in her thoughts she kept to herself as she answered his question.

"The tank is behind the house. You can see it from

my bedroom window." Again she eyed the storm out the front window.

He knew exactly what she saw—nothing but swirling white. There'd been no abatement at all in the weather. If anything, the storm had worsened overnight.

"Let's go see what we can see." Losing the propane wouldn't worry him if it was just him and Rachel, but the babies upped the ante.

In the bedroom he pushed aside her smoky-blue curtains and pulled the cord to lift the mini blinds.

Rachel joined him, using a tissue to clear the condensation from the glass. She pointed to the left. "Over there."

They both looked out on a cloud-darkened world of white on white, with the wicked storm spewing snow and ice through the air.

"It's buried under snow," she said.

He took in the placement, the proximity to the house, the flow and depth of the snowbanks, the visible foliage, making note of the wind direction and velocity. "I see branches between the house and the tank. Do you have something planted there?"

"No. I keep it clear." She shivered. "If it's that cold, maybe you shouldn't be going outside. You don't have the proper gear. That Macintosh isn't going to protect you from the cold and none of my other coats will fit."

"I'll be fine. It shouldn't take more than a few minutes to check things out and decide if there's anything to be done."

Hugging herself, she unconsciously rubbed her upper arms in a warming motion. "It doesn't take long to get frostbite or hypothermia, either. If something happens to you out there, I'm not sure I can get you back to the house by myself. Maybe it's not worth the effort."

He tugged on a short wisp of her blond hair. "You're worried about me."

She ducked her head, pulling away from his touch. She backed clear up to the bed and abruptly sat when the back of her knees hit the mattress. In a flash she sprung to her feet and headed for the door, leading them away from the intimacy of the bedroom.

Over her shoulder she said, "I may be a loner, but I'm not a monster. Yes, I'm worried, especially if the risk isn't necessary."

He followed her to the end of the hall, propped a shoulder against the wall and watched her pace the living room carpet. For such a tough cookie, she had a marshmallow center.

"Even though I'm the enemy?"

She slanted a glare his way. He probably shouldn't take such pleasure in teasing her, but she riled so easily. Her shows of emotion just pulled him in.

"Yes," she hissed the word then stopped, crossed her arms and cocked a hip, the picture of indignation. "And I don't appreciate being made to feel concern when I'm trying not to like you."

"You might have to give up on that project. I'm a pretty likable guy."

Her eyes narrowed. "You're bossy, nosy and you're planning to take my family away. I think I can resist your questionable wit and charm."

Ouch. That stung more than it should. Time to get back on point.

"We're already low on fuel for electricity, if we lose the propane, too, it's going to get very primitive around here very fast." He notched his head toward the playpen where the twins played. "That would be tough enough if it were just you and me, but with the babies—"

As if cued, Cody's sneeze punctuated Ford's point.

Rachel held up a hand. "I get the picture. I'll go with you."

He started shaking his head before she finished speaking. "Don't even think it. I'll be out and back before you even realize I'm gone."

"Storms are unpredictable. What if something happens to you out there? It's best if we go as a team, like yesterday."

"No. When I went with you to the barn, the babies were asleep. They'll freak out if you leave them alone."

He knew he had her, but she didn't relent until he agreed to a signal system, which made a lot of sense. Every ten minutes she'd yank twice on the snow line and he'd yank back. If he didn't respond, she'd come find him. Then she insisted on giving him one of her large sweatshirts to put under the yellow slicker. He wore extra large so they had to cut out the sleeves to make it fit, but it gave him an added layer of warmth. And the feeling didn't just come from the sweatshirt.

As soon as the door closed behind Ford, time slowed so every minute lasted an eternity.

Rachel tried to convince herself her worry factor

would be the same for whoever was out there. The trouble with that was, she was no good at lying to herself. She'd stopped that practice a long time ago.

What insanity gripped her that she suddenly loved the whole world? Okay, that was an exaggeration. But not by far. Not by nearly far enough.

She'd allowed Sullivan to get entirely too close for comfort. As if by letting the twins into her heart, she'd left a breach for others to slide in, too.

Standing at the sink, her gaze trained on the path Ford would traverse back to the house, she made sandwiches and determined—absolutely—to shore up her defenses.

Just as soon as he got back safely.

He came into view and, breath hitching in relief, she went to the back porch to greet him. He burst through the back door along with a cloud of snow and sleet. She brushed at his head and shoulders as he stamped his feet.

"Good news. The connection is sound. A large tree limb fell, but the tank took the brunt of it." His large shoulders shuddered as his body combated the freezing elements.

"I have a towel and blankets here. Let's get you out of this wet gear." She reached up to help free him of the slicker, but he shook his head.

"I'm going back out. The gauge showed you're at a little over a quarter tank. That's probably why it's freezing. Less mass, and the tree dropped a load of snow and ice on and under the tank. I want to dig it out, create a windbreak to shelter it through the rest of the storm. Where's your shovel?"

"You're half frozen," she protested. "You can't go back out there."

"The exertion will warm me up." He spied her snow shovel in the corner of the porch.

While he gathered it and looked over her other equipment, she rushed to get the coffee she had heating up by the fireplace. She poured a mug and then filled a thermos, dumping in lots of sugar.

She reached the door at the same time he did. He carried a shovel in one hand, an ice hatchet in the other.

"Here—" she thrust the mug at him "—drink this before you go."

She got no argument this time. He drank the coffee in one swallow while she slipped the thermos into the deep pocket of the slicker.

"Be careful," she urged him.

"I will." He wrapped his hands around hers on the mug and squeezed. "Thanks."

The look in his eyes shot right through her, threatening her new resolution. Stepping back, she indicated the door with her head.

"Every ten minutes," she reminded him.

"Two tugs." He confirmed before sliding out of the door, tools in hand.

Rachel's gaze immediately went to the clock marking the time. She needed something to occupy her thoughts or she'd go crazy while she waited. First, check on the babies. Then, more coffee.

She threw another log on the fire before going to the playpen. Jolie slept on her side, a teddy pillowed her head and she still held a toy car clutched in her little fist.

Cody began to cry when he saw her. His nose was running and his eyes looked glazed. He held up his arms and she bent to pick him up.

"Poor tyke. You're not feeling well, are you?" Kissing his forehead, she felt the heat coming off him. "And you're a little warm. Let's get you some medicine. That'll make you feel better."

After cleaning Cody's nose with a tissue, she covered Jolie with a blanket, checked the time and headed for the medicine cabinet.

She spent the next hour cuddling a fussy Cody, tugging on the snow line and watching for sightings of Ford through her bedroom window. Once he had the tank cleared, the sightings became fewer and fewer, but the heater kicked in after forty-five minutes. So whatever he'd done, it had worked.

Thank goodness. Without the heater, the fireplace would have been their sole source of heat, which would have held them all captive in the living room. Tight quarters for four people, two of whom were at odds with each other.

Ford returned the shovel and ice hatchet to the corner of the porch then pulled off his gloves. When he turned toward the kitchen door, Rachel was there in front of him. Without a word she began helping him out of the wet clothing.

His fingers refused to work the buttons on the slicker. He welcomed her help and took the towel she handed him to dry his neck and hair.

"I've managed to boil enough water to run a warm bath for you." She removed the thermos, placed it on the washer then dragged the yellow plastic garment off his shoulders.

After the roar of the storm outside, the quiet inside struck him as odd and was offset by a low-grade whine. He finally realized the sound came from inside the house. A baby was crying.

"Wh-what's wrong with Cody?" he asked through chattering teeth.

"He's running a low-grade fever. His cold's come back. He'll be all right until we can get you into the tub. Sit." She pushed him into a kitchen chair.

A mug of coffee appeared in his hand, which shook so badly he wrapped the second hand around it as well. The bite of a brandy chaser sent heat rolling through his body.

"Oh my God." He savored the warmth of the brew, the invigorating burn of alcohol. "I think I love you."

She looked up from where she worked on his bootlaces. "Careful, Sullivan. Someone might think you're easy."

"An-anything you want," he stuttered. "Name it, and for another c-cup of this c-coffee it's y-yours."

"Really?" Her eyes turned wistful. "Maybe now is the time to talk about custody."

"Uh-huh." He shook a finger at her. "Truce, remember? No talk of c-custody while we're sn-snowed in."

"Right." Ducking her head so he couldn't see her eyes, she finished removing his boots and socks. Then she refilled his mug, including another shot of brandy. "We'll just put this on account."

She tugged him to his feet and headed him toward the bathroom. "Come on, you can drink that in the tub, you need to get warmed up. I've already put a change of clothes in there for you. The water's luke- warm now, but I can boil more and add it as you start to thaw out. At least until the propane kicks in and we have hot water again."

"Thanks." He stopped at the bathroom door. "I can take it from here."

"Right. Sorry." Color flowed up her neck and into her cheeks. She swung on her heel and crossed the room to a teary-eyed Cody.

A moment later Ford sank into the tub cursing as he lowered his frozen body into the water. His skin came alive with a million stinging prickles. He went from shudders to shivers to chills, which was when he reached for the kettle of hot water.

Sipping from the mug he began to experience a warm sense of well-being. Hearing the heater kick in, he sighed and relaxed back in the tub.

At least his efforts had succeeded. Heck, even if the heater hadn't come back on, the effort would have been worth it. He didn't do idle well. And consider- ing every unoccupied moment allowed guilt-ridden thoughts of Tony's and Crystal's deaths to worm away at his conscience, Ford prayed they'd see a break in the storm soon.

Logically he understood there was no way he could have predicted an earthquake when he purchased the tickets for his friends' vacation. But the bottom line was they'd still be alive if he hadn't bought the tick- ets, hadn't butted into their business.

And he'd never have met Rachel Adams.

Truthfully he hadn't made any such agreement not

to talk custody while the storm held them captive, but he was reluctant to bring it up when they were stuck in such close proximity with each other.

He expected the conversation would get heated, and they may both need fallback room.

The more time he spent with Rachel, the less he wanted to hurt her, but he had to do what was best for the babies.

Ford loved his five brothers, hell, as the youngest, he'd spent his life emulating them or competing for a place among them. It hadn't been good enough to match their efforts, he'd had to do more, do better. He'd earned their respect and a spot on the SEAL team because of the drive and ambition he'd learned early in life. Tony had been a brother of the soul. They'd worked the trenches together, saved each other's hides.

He owed Tony in ways the average person could never understand.

Tony had made it clear he wanted the twins raised with Ford's family, and Ford had had to agree an extended family with aunts, uncles, cousins and a grandmother was a better support team than a lone aunt.

Not to mention San Diego offered cultural, educational and employment opportunities unavailable in Scobey, Montana.

Plus, with the income Ford got from his share in the family jewelry store in addition to his military pay, he had the money to give the babies advantages Rachel wouldn't be able to provide. At least not without touching the life insurance from the loss of their parents.

No matter how he looked at it, he still thought the best plan was for the twins to come home with him.

If Rachel wanted to take them occasionally for holidays or vacations, he had no problem working something out with her.

Now he just needed to convince Rachel.

Dressed in jeans and a navy T-shirt and sweater he opened the bathroom door to a prime view of Rachel's heart-shaped butt as she bent to put something in the bottom drawer of her nightstand.

Flush from the tub, the vision of her lush derriere ignited his blood. The sight of a satin and lace fuchsia thong peeping over the top of her jeans shot him right to boiling point.

Making short work of the hallway and bedroom, he advanced on her so that when she stood and turned it was into his arms. Surprised, her gaze flew up to his. Slowly he cupped her cheek in his left hand, giving her plenty of time to pull away.

"I have to do this," he whispered, "I have to taste you." And lowering his head, he claimed her lips with his.

Oh, yes, so sweet, so hot, she fit against him perfectly ratcheting his blood pressure up another notch. He shifted his head and took the kiss deeper, longer.

Groaning softly, she melted into him and circled his neck with her arms, anchoring herself to his length. She opened her mouth and invited him in, tongues meeting and mating in a sassy dance of give and take.

The intoxicating scents of soap, baby powder and woman wove around him, teasing his senses so he longed for more.

"Closer." Spreading his stance, he pulled her between his legs, pressing her soft breasts to his chest and reaching down with his right hand to trace the flirty line of her thong.

Her breath hitched and a shudder ran through her body, rocking her against him. Murmuring her approval, she tightened her arms around him, and hiked up on her toes aligning her body with his.

He trailed his fingers up to the small of her back and found the softest patch of fine velvet skin. A low moan told him he'd discovered one of her sweet spots. So of course he played his thumb over it again and she went up in flames.

One second she was as lost in the moment as he, the next she'd pushed him away.

"I can't do this." Her voice shook. Taking a step back she tucked her hands behind her, an obvious move to prevent her reaching for him again. "Not with you."

"Rachel." He lifted a hand, needing to touch her, needing to ease the torment in eyes more blue than green.

"No." She sidestepped. "I can't. If you have your way, you're going to take the twins. And that's going to tear me apart. I can't give you this, too."

His hand fell to his side as he watched her walk away.

The next morning the quiet woke Rachel. For a moment she snuggled under her blankets and thought ahead to her day. She'd be done at the clinic by four. Maybe she'd treat herself to dinner at the diner tonight, save time and effort so she could get right to work on her book when she got home.

The sound of a whimper disrupted her thoughts bringing reality rushing back.

The twins.

The storm.

The wolf in hunk's clothing.

Remembering Ford, and the time spent in his arms yesterday, she groaned and buried her head under her pillow. What had she been thinking?

Problem was she hadn't been thinking at all. Tasting, touching, feeling, she'd been doing all of those and more. In fact, her senses had suffered overload at his first touch, and it became all physical after that.

Intensely, mind-blowingly, wonderfully physical.

And it had been sheer insanity.

Really. The man may smell like heaven, but giving into the temptation of his passionate embrace lay the direction of hell.

She'd never forgive herself if she let her libido interfere with her bid for custody. Because make no mistake, he was a warrior, and he'd use every weapon at his disposal to get his way. She'd be a fool not to think that included any perceived affection for him.

Already she'd given too much away by letting him know he possessed the ability to hurt her.

Last night the tension between them could have been cleaved with a hatchet. Cody's fretfulness kept them both busy but only added to the already tense atmosphere. The poor baby just didn't feel good. And she felt for him, but she'd also been grateful for something to focus on besides the blunder of letting go in Ford's arms.

The silence outdoors meant the conversation they'd both avoided could no longer be put off.

About time. In retrospect she wished it had happened before she'd gotten to know him, to like him, to want him. But she'd have to deal with it.

And no time like the present. Tossing aside her pillow, she threw back the blankets and climbed out of bed. She checked on Cody. Because of his restlessness last night, Jolie had slept in the playpen out in the living room with Ford.

Despite a restless night and the whimper she'd just heard, Cody slept peacefully in his cot. She brushed the back of her fingers over his forehead feeling for a fever. Pleased to find him normal, she tucked the blanket around him and escaped to the bathroom for a shower.

Twenty minutes later she left her room to find Ford and Jolie still asleep. Jolie looked like a little angel. Bare chested with dark stubble and a scowl on his face, Ford looked like a disreputable pirate. Oh, yeah, even sleeping he had that dangerous edge that drew her.

He'd let her sleep in yesterday, so he deserved a sleep in today.

In the kitchen she put on coffee and started pancakes. Jolie woke up first and Rachel snagged her up before she woke Ford. Then she heard Cody through the baby monitor. She changed and dressed both babies then set them up in their high chairs with bowls of pancakes cut into tiny pieces and dusted with powdered sugar.

She glanced into the living room, surprised Ford hadn't stirred yet. She'd heard him cough a couple of times but nothing more. He'd proven to be an early riser. And he didn't strike her as the type to sleep through all the morning activity.

Leaving the twins happily eating their pancakes with their fingers, Rachel slipped into the living room to stand over the couch.

Still sleeping, at some point Ford had pushed the blankets further down his chest so they ringed his waist. He'd also kicked his feet free. This worried her, because even with the heater working, a chill lingered in the air. She wondered if he had a fever? Perhaps he'd caught Cody's cold.

After yesterday morning's lesson in hand-to-hand combat, she knew better than to startle him.

"I'm awake," the words came out in a deep, raspy growl.

"Good, then you won't jump me when I do this." She brushed the backs of her fingers over his forehead and along his cheek, feeling the heat of his skin and the scratch of his beard.

"No promises." He reached up and grabbed her hand, pressing her palm to his cheek. "That feels good."

"You're burning up. How do you feel?"

"I'm fine," he said in the same gravel pit voice. "I don't get sick."

"Uh-huh, Mr. Temperature of 102. I'm going to get you some aspirin, some vitamin C and a cup of tea with Echinacea."

"Don't bother. I just need a shower and I'll be good to go." He sat up and the blankets pooled in his lap.

"No arguments. Think of it as preventative maintenance if it helps. I can't afford for you to be sick when I have two babies to look after."

"I said I'm fine." The denial held a bite.

She propped her hands on her hips. "Fever and grouchy. You'll take what I give you, or we're going to go a few rounds. Then I have pancakes if you're hungry."

"We lost the fire." His glazed blue eyes were angled toward the empty fireplace.

"Yeah. I put the last of the wood on about an hour ago. The good news is that it stopped snowing overnight."

"That's what's different. No wind." He stood and wrapped the blanket around his hips, ran a hand through his disheveled hair. "Good. I'll go out later and fill the wood reservoir."

She sent him a wry glance. "One of us will."

He lifted a dark brow and advanced on her. Suddenly there was nothing debilitating or tame about him. He was hard eyed, hard bodied, hard edged.

With an effort she stood her ground.

"Don't attempt to mother me, dynamite," he breathed against her ear as he walked by her. "That's not a relationship either of us wants."

Wow, she mouthed after he disappeared into the bathroom. Too bad all that male intensity was attached to a totally inappropriate man. The sooner the snow melted and she could send him on his way the better.

The twins belonged with family. She would care and provide for them not out of a sense of duty but out of a sense of love.

Now she just needed to convince Ford.

Chapter 6

Ford placed a piece of wood on the block and cleaved it in two with one swing of the ax. He then quartered the pieces and tossed them into his done pile.

After a morning moping around eating Rachel's cold remedies, he felt well enough—and desperate enough— to escape outside. Cutting wood fit his mood to a T.

Being snowed in gave a man too much time to think, too much time to admire the long, soft curves of his reluctant hostess. To admire her quiet strength and loyalty, her perseverance in the face of uncertainty and her infinite patience when dealing with the twins. Her tolerance of a stranger bent on tearing her world to pieces.

Instead of tasting those luscious lips, instead of dwelling on how he paid for the vacation that had claimed his friends' lives, Ford worked off his frustration and his guilt by swinging an ax.

The very idea of Rachel out here wielding an ax tore his gut to pieces. Not that she wasn't fully capable. That wasn't the point.

Not that it mattered. Because it was none of his business. The only thing that mattered was getting the roads cleared so he and the twins could get on their way to San Diego.

Another log went on the block.

He had arrangements to make. A nanny to hire, a nursery to set up.

Lift and swing.

He always figured he'd wait to start a family until he retired from the team. Now the decision had been taken from him.

But damn. He wasn't ready to hang up his wet suit. Crack.

Two months ago Tony had signed up for another four years. Ford had planned to do the same when his commission came up in another couple of months.

If the twins' dad could be a SEAL, Ford could be a SEAL.

New log.

All right so that theory held some flaws. Like the fact that Tony hadn't been living with his children. The twins had lived with their mother. And Tony had been in a bad place with Crystal when he'd reenlisted. She'd been adamantly opposed to his SEAL career, which in Ford's opinion had spurred Tony's recommitment for four years.

Lift and swing.

But there was no lying to himself. Ford had disapproved of Tony's decision.

Crash.

Ford believed if you had a family, you owed it to them to be around. Any military position involved risk to some degree. Obviously some more than others. SEALs were at the extreme end of that category. Which was why he'd been waiting to settle down.

And that brought him full circle.

Guilt, resentment, uncertainty and resolution made for a confusing jumble of emotions spurring on his efforts. In the end it came down to one truth. He owed his friend not only for his solidarity on the battlefield but because Tony would be alive today if Ford hadn't butted into his business.

Ford had a reputation for always following through. With the twins' future on the line, he couldn't fail now.

He stopped, braced the ax handle against his thigh and swiped the back of his wrist over his sweaty brow. The crunch of footsteps heralded the approach of someone.

Rachel was headed his way. Dressed in jeans and a brown parka she moved with athletic grace. In the sun her eyes sparkled more blue than green and the cold weather brought a flush out on her cheeks. Her blond hair contrasted against the fur of her jacket framing her face like a halo.

"Hey, that's quite a pile you have there." She greeted him. "I won't have to chop wood for a month."

"That's the plan." He set a new log on the block. "What about the twins?"

She pulled the baby monitor out of her coat pocket. "They're sleeping."

He nodded toward the monitor she'd tucked back in her pocket. "That's pretty handy."

"Yeah, it's been invaluable. The receptionist at the clinic gave them to me. Everyone's been incredibly kind. When I picked up the twins in San Diego, they gave me one diaper bag with the minimum of essentials included. I had to outfit a nursery from scratch. People at work, my neighbors, they gave me a lot."

"And that's hard for you."

She ducked her head, peeked at him through her lashes. "A little, yeah. I can't help who I am."

"No. We are who we are. Whatever good intentions we have."

Rachel glanced at the pile of wood that would have taken her days to chop. She'd say his good intentions had cost him quite a lot. Remembering his rage of yesterday, she hazarded a guess. "That sounds like guilt talking."

"Yeah." He picked up the ax, but his gaze moved off to the distance.

She went still, touched by his distress. He obviously felt the loss of his friend deeply. Whatever their differences she understood his sorrow. "I'm sorry about your friend."

His grip on the ax handle tightened until his knuckles whitened. "And I'm sorry about your sister. It's hard to believe they're gone."

Rachel swallowed a snowball-size lump. Her relationship with her sister had been so new. In a way, that added to her heartache.

"People say things happen for a reason."

"Eternal optimists." His words had the quality of crushed glass. "People who've never seen the horrific things I have... Death is nothing new to me."

"No, but it sounds like grief is." She gently took the ax from him, set it aside. Clearly she'd hit a raw nerve. "Your job must require a huge amount of skill and bravery, but I imagine in order to see the things you have you'd have had to develop a pretty thick skin."

"Impartiality is necessary, yes. That doesn't mean we don't care." He stood, fists clenched at his sides, his profile a portrait of stubborn pride.

"I can see you do care." No doubt more deeply than he let most people see, which spoke to the level of his torment. "But that's all part of the job. This was different. This was your friends, and there was nothing you could do to save them."

His jaw clenched. "I don't like feeling helpless."

The problem with not interacting with people very often was that she lacked the words to comfort him. So she just spoke from the heart. "We have to think of the babies now, that's what they'd want us to do."

"It's because of me the twins no longer have parents." The confession seemed torn out of him. "How am I supposed to face them every day for the rest of our lives knowing what I cost them?"

"What are you talking about? Tony and Crystal died in an earthquake in Mexico."

"Yeah, and I sent them there. Hell, I paid for the tickets and practically escorted them to their deaths."

He began to pace, snow crunching under the heavy weight of his boots.

She'd never seen him so agitated. "I don't understand."

He drilled her with an anguished glare. "Me. I'm the one who sent them to Mexico. Tony and Crystal were constantly at odds. They never agreed on anything to do with the twins. I thought if they could get away from the problems of everyday life for a while, be together as a family, they might settle some things. Come to an understanding."

"And instead they died."

"Yeah."

And he blamed himself. Which was ridiculous, but he'd brooded about it for so long that simply saying so would have little impact. So that's not what she'd say.

"Wow. No wonder you feel guilty."

He blinked at her, shock in his blue eyes.

"What?" She feigned innocence. "Were you expecting sympathy? This is my sister we're talking about."

"No. Right." He sank down on the chopping block, scrubbed both hands over his face "You're right, I deserve the recrimination."

"Damn straight." She purposely struck a hard note. "This whole thing is your fault."

"Now wait a minute." His head and shoulders went back.

"You owe me." Beginning to circle him, she laid on the guilt. "You owe the twins. Because of you our only family was taken from us. The only honorable thing to do is sign over custody to me so we can keep what's left of our family together."

"The hell you say." He surged to his feet, placing himself directly in her path.

"Hell yes." She propped her hands on her hips and met him chin to chin. "You can also give me the winning numbers for the lottery this week."

His dark brows drew together and he shook his head as if trying to clear his confusion. "What are you talking about now?"

"I'm talking about winning the lottery. The twins and I could use the money. I mean you are psychic right? Otherwise how could you know about the earthquake in Mexico?"

The tension went out of him. "No, I'm not psychic."

She pouted. "No lottery numbers?"

He stepped closer, lifted her chin with the edge of his hand. "No lottery numbers."

"And you're not to blame for Tony and Crystal's deaths?"

"As I have no psychic ability, I guess not." He stared into her eyes, and she saw a lightening of his spirit. "You think you're so smart, don't you?"

"Pretty much." She grinned, then grew serious. "You aren't at fault here, Ford. Don't let it haunt you."

He turned her toward the house, and draping an arm over her shoulders started walking. "We should check on the twins before Cody wakes up and finds something to finger paint with."

"At least I got smart and started separating them for naps."

"Good idea. Yeah, that boy gets into everything, nothing is out of his reach."

"He got you, didn't he?" She giggled and slanted him a look through her lashes. "When you had the kids the other day, he got you."

"I'm not admitting to anything."

"Coward."

"Hey, that there is a fighting word to a SEAL."

She bumped her shoulder into him. "I'm not afraid of you."

"No." He laughed. "You're one tough little cookie." They reached the front of the house. "Thanks for talking trash to me."

She stopped on the first step of the porch, which she'd shoveled clear before going in search of him. Facing Ford now she saw the pain still shadowing his fathomless blue eyes. "But you still feel responsible, don't you?"

"Let's say, you've given me something to think about." His gaze swept her face and he leaned forward.

She saw the kiss coming and lowered her head. "Don't."

"You're a special woman, Rachel Adams." Gently he lifted her chin, and touched her heart by pressing a warm kiss to her cheek. "I wish things could be different."

Ford came awake in an instant. Unmoving he scoped out his environment to determine what had alerted him. The first thing that struck him was the warm weight and sweet scent of the woman in his arms.

He opened his eyes to find he was reclined on the couch, not unusual, as that's where he'd been sleeping, but his bed hadn't been made up and he was still fully clothed. A pity considering the woman cuddled up to him, was—to his disappointment—also fully clothed.

He sure wouldn't mind seeing more of her colorful, sexy lingerie.

A log fell in the fireplace shooting sparks through the grate. He recognized the sound as the one that had awakened him. He should get up, stoke the fire, toss on another log.

He had no intention of moving.

Not while Rachel slept so peacefully against him.

They'd had a busy day between his chopping wood, her shoveling the porch and looking after the kids. After dinner he and Rachel had settled on the couch, a respectful distance apart, and watched Cody and Jolie play in the playpen while discussing the events of the day.

Cody's cold appeared to be on the mend again, and good-natured Jolie put up with his high energy antics with stoic patience. The conversation moved from the kids to films and books, current events and war stories. He told her of the time he'd night-dropped into foreign territory only to get treetopped fifteen feet off the ground. She shared some outrageous animal tales that had him laughing out loud.

It turned out she wrote a syndicated column about animal antics, and had even been offered a book deal she was waiting to hear on.

Yeah, they talked about everything under the sun but what really mattered.

Which was totally out of character for him. He lacked the patience for prevarication.

Tonight had been different.

He'd never spent a more domestic evening with a woman. Didn't usually want to. But tonight, with Rachel, he'd enjoyed a quiet, fun, invigorating and peaceful interlude. She had a biting wit that both challenged and amused him. Even the occasional silences had been comfortable.

During one of those silences they must have fallen asleep. And as the fire died down and the room grew chillier, they'd gravitated together for warmth. Now he was lying with one leg up, one foot on the floor and she lay tucked between him and the back of the couch.

She felt good in his arms, every breath she exhaled whispered over his skin teasing the hair at the opening of his shirt. Her silky hair feathered his cheek and smelled of peach blossoms. And he pillowed their clasped hands, her left in his right, on his stomach.

Giving into temptation he ran his thumb over the petal soft skin of her palm. He longed to touch more of her, all of her. To taste every inch of her and have her ignite in his arms like she did yesterday. Her responsiveness, so sweet and sassy, so genuine, undid him.

The tiny movement of his thumb finally penetrated her subconscious because her hold tightened into a fist around him.

He liked that feeling. He'd hold her close and let tomorrow take care of itself.

Rachel sighed as the tension drained from Ford's body. The even flow of his breathing meant he'd fallen asleep or was close to it.

The stirring of the fire had woken her. How surprising to find herself in Ford's arms. She should have moved, put space and sense between them. Just gotten up and gone to bed.

Instead she'd stolen this time. Illicitly taken advantage of the peace and safety of being held by a strong, gentle man. For these uncounted moments she pretended he didn't want something from her. That he wouldn't be leaving in a matter of days.

For these cherished moments she just lay in the strength of his warm embrace and let herself be.

When he'd started caressing her palm, she'd thought he might try to touch her further, might try to wake her and turn so she was under him.

Her body clenched with need as she imagined welcoming him into her arms and her body.

She inhaled, loving the smell of him, the scents of man and soap with a hint of wood smoke. Oh, how the woman in her wished he'd woken her.

But she couldn't make the move herself. The mother in her couldn't forget the babies even for the length of time it would take to shatter in his arms.

But the woman in her, the one who longed for a man's touch, the one weakened by Ford's thoughtfulness and the tender way he handled the twins, that woman would have succumbed to a midnight seduction.

It wasn't to be.

Sigh. Rachel closed her eyes, content to savor these unplanned hours.

Tomorrow was soon enough for regrets.

The next morning Ford walked the quarter mile down to the main road. The intermittent sunshine yesterday and this morning had started a thaw. He could see patches of the driveway and when he reached the road it had been cleared.

They'd be able to make it into town today to replenish supplies. And the way to San Diego had been opened up.

"I don't know how much longer I'll be," he said into his cell in answer to his older brother's question. "My commander gave me thirty days leave to handle the situation. Now the snow has stopped, I'll be able to get on the road once we resolve the custody issue."

"What's the hold up there? I thought you said she wasn't interested in taking on the twins."

"The picture Crystal painted of her sister was off. Way off. She's already bonded with the kids and she's refusing to sign off on custody."

"So if she's willing and able to take on the task, why don't you let her?"

"Tony made them my responsibility. I can't do my duty by them if they're in Montana and I'm in California."

"I know you don't want to hear it, but you can't do it by jet setting all over the world, either. Maybe they'd be better off in Montana."

"I'm not exactly hopping the globe on pleasure trips. It's my job. And you were singing a different song about responsibility when you took Gabe from Samantha. She was willing and able and you still went after custody."

"Different scenario. Gabe is my son. The twins are not your family."

"They are now. I owe Tony in ways I can't define. I can no more deny his request than I could if something happened to you and Samantha and you left your boys in my care."

"I've always admired your loyalty, little bro. You know we'll support you any way we can."

"Yeah, I know. That's what Tony was counting on." After promising to keep his brother posted, Ford disconnected the call.

He sighed, his breath crystallizing in the air. He and Rachel were long overdue for a conversation on custody. Today he'd get her to sign the papers and tomorrow he and the twins would be on the road.

No more excuses.

As he approached the house he heard a ringing. Sounded like phone service had been restored.

He opened the front door to see Rachel waving her arms in the air and shimmying her hips. A tantalizing strip of creamy flesh showed between her low-cut black jeans and the turquoise sweater that matched her eyes. She danced around the kitchen; making the twins who were strapped into their high chairs, giggle.

"Was that the phone I heard?" he asked.

She whipped around at the sound of his voice and he saw the smile lighting up her face.

"Yes, it was." She shimmied toward him, threw herself into his arms. "The phones are working."

"That is good news. And if you like that..." He waltzed her around the table, twirled her around once and dropped her into a dip. "You'll want to do a jig when you hear the road is clear."

Her eyes laughed up into his. He grinned, taking delight in her happiness. And unable to resist while he had her dipped and at his mercy, he cupped her head in his hand and lowered his head to claim her mouth.

She immediately opened to him. Tightening her arms around him, she returned the kiss with a passion to match his.

Reluctantly he pulled back, brought her upright and twirled her around again.

"Whew." She swayed on her feet, her cheeks burning red. She licked her lips and blinked away the lust glaze from her dazzling eyes. "They want the book."

"Your book on animal manners?" he asked.

"Yes." Excitement made her glow. "That was my agent on the phone. They want my book. The publisher made an official offer."

"Hey." Absurdly proud of her, he swooped her up and swung her around. "That's great news."

She threw her head back and laughed. Joy radiated from her.

The babies shrieked in glee.

Ford realized he'd seen little happiness in her. Passion, resolve, sadness, determination, anger, sorrow. He'd seen all those and more. And certainly love for Cody and Jolie. Yet simple happiness and joy had been missing.

Slowly he lowered her to the floor. When she reached eye level, she sobered. He expected her to push him away as her sense of self-preservation demanded every time he got too close.

She surprised him by throwing her arms around his neck and laying one on him.

The kiss didn't last long but held a punch. Because it was the first overture she'd made to him. When she pulled back, he let her slip the rest of the way to the floor.

She framed his face between her hands. "You made this moment more special by being here. Thank you."

"Hey, this is a big deal." Something bloomed in his chest at her words. Some feel-good emotion that he didn't recognize filled him up. He liked making her feel good even if it meant putting off talking about custody issues. It would take a lesser man than him to spoil her pleasure.

"In fact we need to celebrate. Let me take you to dinner."

"Oh." Flustered, and clearly pleased, a flush added to her glow. But she flittered away, began fussing over the twins. "That's not necessary."

"Of course it is. You deserve a party. And the twins and I are just the ones to give it to you."

She hesitated for another moment, but her excitement couldn't be contained. She grinned. "All right. It's a date."

Chapter 7

It's a date. How lame was that?

Rachel surveyed her reflection in the mirrorlike surface of the restaurant door. Looking beyond the little girl in her arms, she saw a woman dressed in a calf length brown suede skirt with brown boots and an ivory sweater under a black leather duster. Too dressy?

Not for a date. Oh God.

Stepping through the door Ford held open, she inhaled the spicy aromas of onion, garlic and tomatoes. Decorated in dark woods and red vinyl with a video arcade and jukebox for entertainment, the Pizza Pit catered to families, sports teams and bored teenagers.

She'd directed Ford to the pizza joint knowing the twins were likely to be excitable after being cooped up for days. And maybe the loud, boisterous crowd, with kids popping up and down and all around, would make it less like a date.

Where had her head been? Answer: In the stratosphere.

Oh, yeah, she'd kept her cool while talking to her agent. But let Ford suggest something simple like a celebratory dinner, and she blew it all out of proportion.

Proximity was the problem.

The enforced intimacy of the last few days gave her subconscious ideas. Working together, sharing the responsibility of the twins, sleeping in each other's arms all played into her dream of having a family.

Ford with his intelligent blue eyes, muscle-ripped body and dangerous edge spoke to every female particle in her. But even more than his skillful fingers and sinful mouth, she responded to his willingness to listen, his patience and generosity, his loyalty and sorrow for his friend and his stubborn sense of duty.

Ideal mating material, or so her subconscious would have her believe.

But it was impossible.

Even if she decided to act on the amazing attraction between them, too many obstacles blocked the goal. He lived a thousand miles away. He was big city, big family, bigger than life. She was small town, family-poor and self-contained. He was a warrior who traveled the world; she was a loner, comfortable in her little corner of Montana.

She followed Ford to a booth not far from the video arcade. Hitching Jolie higher on her hip, Rachel looked around for the high chairs. Spying them by the salad bar, she pointed them out to Ford.

"I'll get them. Here, take Cody." Ford set the boy in her lap next to his sister.

Bouncing the babies on her knees, she watched Ford cross the room, his stride long and graceful. Yum, he looked fine in black jeans, a black T-shirt and black boots.

Out of her league fine.

Heck, he probably had a whole slew of beach bunnies waiting for him back in California. A prime military man with dark good looks and fatal charm, he probably had them lining up and down the pier.

She'd be delusional to think they had a chance in purgatory of being together.

Not only did they not have a future together, he had every intention of tearing her world apart. She'd do well to remember that.

He came back with the high chairs and they got the twins settled. A waitress arrived and Ford ordered the pizza. Pasting on a smile, Rachel tried to keep up her end of the conversation, to get into celebration mode. It was her party after all.

And she did appreciate his gesture. More than she could ever say, but she couldn't pretend any longer.

"It's okay you know," she said after about twenty minutes. "We can talk about the custody plans for the twins."

Clearly startled, he sat back and eyed her. "No." He shook his head. "We're here to celebrate your book. I don't want to spoil it for you."

"I appreciate that, I do." Rather than meet his quizzical gaze, she picked up her discarded straw wrapper. "But I can't sit here and pretend you're not plotting the best way to get my signature on the custody papers so you can pack up Cody and Jolie and truck on back to San Diego."

His features tightened. He almost looked hurt. "Is that what you think I'm doing, sitting here plotting against you?"

"Yes. No. I don't know." Confused, she bought some time by digging in her purse for some crackers to give the twins.

But she'd started this conversation she needed to see it through. "Look, we both know you wouldn't be here with me if not for your interest in the twins, so we might as well deal with the issue."

"I'm in Montana because of the twins." He reached across the table and took her hand. "Tonight I'm with you because I want to be with you."

"Don't." She pulled her hand back, scattering shredded wrapper pieces, her emotions seeming to scatter in the same way. "Please don't say things like that. There's no point. Let's just decide what we're going to do about the twins so we can get on with our lives."

He set his drink aside and leaned forward with concern in his eyes. "Not until I understand what's happening here. Why are you so upset?"

I can't afford to care for you. And I'm afraid it's already too late. But she'd give him too much ammunition by admitting that out loud. "You want to take the twins from me, isn't that reason enough to be upset?"

"I'm not taking them from you," he said carefully. "I'm bringing them into my family. There's a difference."

"They can live with me and still be a part of your

family. They can visit you in the summer and on holidays."

"If I thought that would work, I'd go for it in a heartbeat. But we both know that they'd feel like outsiders visiting strangers. My family will embrace them, they'll have aunts and uncles and cousins. They've already played with my brother's boys. They'll have a grandmother. Love will grow and surround them but only by being in the midst of the family."

"I already love them." Her gut clenched in fear. Everything he said made horrible sense. "All of the people you mentioned are the strangers. I'm their family."

"And you can have all the visitations you want. The twins can come here. You can come to San Diego. We'll work it out."

"I don't know how." She glanced at the twins and her heart bloomed with such love she choked up. Swalmlowing with difficulty she informed Ford, "I won't sign away my rights. I won't. I've thought and thought on how we can make this work because obviously neither of us is going to give up full custody, but nothing makes sense.

"We live too far apart to share custody unless it's for six months at a time. I'd be willing to consider that but honestly I don't think it's best for the babies. It would be disorienting for them when they're this young, especially after losing their parents."

"And when they get older and start school, they'd have to change school every six months." He shook his head. "That's every kid's worst nightmare."

A shadow loomed over the table. Rachel looked up

into Sheriff Mitchell's chiseled features. "Evening, folks. Is everything all right here?"

"Sheriff." Ford acknowledged the other man. "I imagine you've been busy these last few days."

"Some." Mitch turned his attention to her, a question in his eyes. "Rachel, how are you doing?"

Rachel sighed; the last thing she needed was a macho contest between the two men. Summoning patience—no easy task—she flashed a smile.

"We're fine, Mitch. I hope no one was seriously hurt by the storm."

"No serious damage, no." His eyes narrowed suspiciously and his gaze shifted from her to Ford and back.

Oops. Maybe she'd overdone the friendliness a bit.

Cody chose that moment to make a grab for Mitch's shiny steal handcuffs.

"Cody, no," she chided and reached to grab his hand.

Too late. Feeling the pull on his belt, Mitch slapped his hand down, connecting smartly with Cody's fingers. Stung, the boy began to cry.

Lightning fast Ford shoved to his feet, shouldering Mitch aside. "Back off."

"I'm sorry." Mitch held up both hands in a conciliatory gesture. "He startled me."

Rachel tensed, ready to jump between the two men if necessary. But Ford simply nodded and picked up Cody, quietly murmuring to soothe the distraught boy.

Mitch quickly made his excuses and left.

"I'm going to go run cold water on his fingers." Ford hefted Cody to his shoulder. "We'll be back in a minute."

Left at the table, Rachel and Jolie looked at each other. Big eyed, the little girl chewed on a cracker.

"Get used to it, babe," Rachel advised. "Boys never change."

The pizza arrived just ahead of Ford and Cody's return to the table. By unspoken agreement they ate in silence.

After a few minutes Jolie began to fidget and whine. Rachel grabbed the diaper bag and escaped to the rest room. Besides being wet the baby had developed a rash on her butt and along the waistline of the diaper. Rachel lathered on ointment, finished changing Jolie and rejoined the boys.

She'd barely regained her seat before Ford tossed out a new suggestion.

"What about split custody?"

As soon as he said the words, Ford wanted to pull them back. For so many reasons. In the short time he'd been around the twins he'd observed how they drew strength from each other. His older brothers, Rick and Rett, identical twins, would beat him to a pulp if they'd heard him voice the suggestion. He couldn't conceive of them being parted and the same went for Cody and Jolie.

"Split them up? Like you take Cody and I take Jolie?" She sounded both appalled and fascinated by the prospect. Her gaze went from him to the twins. Without breaking stride she casually removed a paper napkin from Jolie's mouth and handed Cody another piece of crust.

"That would probably be the best division of custody." Why was he pursuing the outrageous option? "What do you think?"

But she was no longer listening.

"Ford." The urgency in her voice caused him to tense. She set her pizza down and nodded toward the video arcade.

He looked over, spotted a pretty brown haired girl about fourteen or fifteen playing a video game. He also noted the young punk, dirty blond hair, oversize clothes, hassling her. The girl tried to walk away, but the boy blocked her retreat.

"I'll take care of it." He slid to the edge of the booth.

"Wait." Rachel's hand on his arm stopped him. "Look."

Another kid—Ford could tell it was the girl's older brother by the resemblance between them—jumped into the fray. He stepped between the punk and the girl, said something that had the punk backing off, then he took the girl's arm and escorted her back to their table.

Ford settled back into the booth. The whole incident lasted only a few minutes. Such a small envelope of time to deliver such a huge emotional impact. How could they possibly separate brother from sister after witnessing such a scene?

He met Rachel's blue-green gaze, saw she'd come to the same conclusion as him. "If I believed in signs, I'd say fate just slapped us with one hell of a lesson."

She arched a delicate brow. "You think?"

"It was a bad idea anyway."

"At last. Something we agree on."

Back at the house, Ford put away the groceries while Rachel got the kids ready for bed. Because she'd been fussy on the way home, Rachel had given Jolie a bottle while she changed Cody and dressed him in his pajamas.

Once he was settled in the crib with his bottle, Rachel reached for Jolie.

"What's wrong, baby doll?" Though she'd taken the bottle the little girl had continued to whine the whole time Rachel had been dealing with Cody. Usually the mellower of the two children, Jolie's distress began to worry Rachel.

Once she'd stripped Jolie down and seen the raw red welts covering her torso and bottom Rachel's uneasiness turned to apprehension.

"Ford," she called as she inspected the nasty irritation. She felt awful that the baby had suffered all evening. "Oh, poor baby, I'm so sorry. I should have realized something was wrong when I saw the rash earlier."

Ford appeared in the bedroom doorway. "What's up?"

"Jolie has a bad rash. It was only a little red earlier. I thought it was diaper rash. But now she has red welts."

"Let me see." He moved to her side, his features tightening when he saw the livid marks on the girl's delicate skin. "Probably just an allergic reaction. But it looks so bad."

"I want to take her to emergency. Will you stay with Cody?"

He shook his head. "We'll go together."

"There's no need to take Cody out, too. It's better if you stay here with him."

"Forget it." He wore his stubborn expression. "I'm no good at waiting. And I'm not letting you go alone."

"Fine." She could have argued, but she saw the concern under his obstinate façade. And she really would welcome his company. "Let's get going then."

They quickly bundled the babies up and Ford drove them to Daniels Memorial Hospital, where despite Ford's aversion, they spent time waiting. Cody was out like a light in the stroller. Jolie dozed intermittently but the welts obviously bothered her as she woke often. At those times she wanted to be held and walked.

Time dragged, worry escalated, nerves were strung tight, while Rachel lashed herself with self-recriminations. She should have acted sooner. She should have known the rash meant something more.

But no, she'd been too caught up in denying her attraction to Ford and claiming her rights to the twins.

Maybe this was another sign. Maybe Rachel wasn't meant to raise Cody and Jolie.

She'd rather give them up than see them harmed in any way.

"Stop beating yourself up," Ford whispered, his breath warm on her temple as he wrapped his arms around her, helping her to support Jolie's weight. "Kids get rashes, upset stomachs and colds. It's nobody's fault."

Rachel nodded unable to speak for the tears that threatened. His reassurances warmed her icy core. He'd been a rock. For a moment she allowed herself to absorb his strength, to lean just a little.

When they finally got in to see the doctor, a slim woman with blue-black hair and horn-rimmed glasses, they learned Ford had been right. It was an allergic reaction.

Jolie announced her displeasure at being stripped and inspected by screaming at the top of her lungs and trying to twist away. It broke Rachel's heart to have to hold her still for the doctor's examination.

The cries woke Cody. Ford had his hands full keeping the boy from following his sister's example.

"Has Jolie eaten or touched anything new over the past twelve hours?" Dr. Wilcox asked.

"I've racked my brain trying to remember if I fed them something different." Rachel heard the waver in her voice. Determined to keep the tears at bay, she took a deep breath. "We've been snowed in, so we've been eating what we've had on hand. Nothing new."

"It doesn't have to be something she ingested," the doctor clarified. "It could be something applied to her skin or that she's worn. Like soaps, lotions and softeners. It could even be something in the air."

Rachel tried to focus her thoughts. "I'm sorry, Doctor, nothing comes to mind."

"I opened a new laundry detergent when I washed the sheets this morning," Ford said. "She took her nap on those sheets this afternoon."

"Yeah." Rachel wearily pushed her hair back from her face. "I've used that brand before, but not since the twins have been with me."

"You've probably found the culprit, but you should see her pediatrician for allergy tests." The doctor advised. "In the meantime, I'll give her a shot. The welts should go down quickly."

"Thank you, Doctor." Ford settled Cody against his shoulder. "Can I take my family home now?"

A miracle happened on the way home. The twins fell asleep and stayed asleep until Rachel and Ford tucked them into bed. In the playpen. Too late to re-wash the sheets tonight, so they'd decided to pile in a couple of blankets for padding and let Cody and Jolie sleep in the living room.

Rachel stood over the playpen watching the babies slumber peacefully. Thank God it hadn't been any more serious than allergies. Even so, she felt as though she'd been put through the spin cycle and hung out to dry.

Ford came out of the bathroom, ready for bed in pajama bottoms and a T-shirt.

"Thank you for coming with me tonight. You made a difficult trip easier."

His gaze ran over her as he rounded the couch. She tucked a strand of hair behind her ear, knowing any glamour she'd managed earlier had long disappeared. She'd already had her turn in the bathroom so she lacked a lick of makeup. And her flannel pajama bottoms and long sleeved thermal underwear were a long way from date material.

Undeterred he stepped right up to her, wrapped a hand around the back of her neck and laid his forehead against hers.

"I'm glad I was there, too." His fingers worked magic on the sensitive skin of her neck. "But you would have handled it. You're one tough lady. You were amazing."

"Oh heavens, Ford. I never want to go through that again." Too weak to resist the lure of his comfort and strength, she relaxed against him.

"Me, neither." He ran his hands down the backs of her arms until his fingers tangled with hers then he stepped back pulling her with him. "You've had a tough day. Come lie down. I want to hold you."

"Oh. I shouldn't." She let him go until their arms were stretched full-length, but her resistance stopped there. When he continued walking she followed step for step. Sleeping in his arms sounded like heaven. But oh, she shouldn't. "You said it yourself, I'm tough. I don't need to be held."

"I do." He drew her down to the couch and into his arms. "Just for a while. Hold me."

When he lay back and took her with him, she let him. And oh it felt so good, so right to lie in his arms. She snuggled her cheek over his heart, sighed and closed her eyes.

"All right. But just for a little while."

Chapter 8

For the second day in a row Rachel awoke on the couch alone. How Ford had managed to slide away without waking her she didn't know. The man had skills.

Not least of which was sneaking past her defenses.

The harder she tried to create distance between them, the closer he seemed to get. He'd claimed to be a likable guy and she had to agree. Damn it.

He'd be much easier to resist if he were a selfish jerk, which considering his insistence on taking the twins should have qualified him hands down. Unfortunately he carried his weight and more with household chores. His patience and gentleness with the twins never wavered. Heck, he even changed diapers without complaining.

His loyalty and sense of duty were the biggest bane

of her life. And confirmed the honor his commanding officer proclaimed he had in spades.

He made her think, he made her laugh, he made her want.

But she couldn't—wouldn't—give in to the insanity of falling for him. Of all the mistakes she could make, that would be the biggest.

Hearing giggles from the kitchen motivated her to get up and get going. She hopped into the shower, brushed her teeth, and then dressed in jeans and a flannel shirt over a navy T-shirt.

In the kitchen she found a fresh pot of coffee, Ford kicked back reading the paper, and the twins covered from the waist up in applesauce as they pounded the trays of their high chairs with spoons. The bigger the mess they made the more they giggled.

Rachel shook her head and moved to pour herself a cup of coffee. She leaned back against the counter and sipped.

"Having fun?"

Ford lowered the paper far enough to meet her gaze. "Good morning."

Approval shone in his eyes even after his gaze had swept her from head to foot. Here she stood without a lick of makeup, and he'd made her feel as if he'd never seen a more beautiful sight in the morning.

The man had to go, and the sooner the better.

Before she did something foolish, like do more than sleep in his arms.

Like fall in love.

She hitched her chin toward the twins. "They're

dangerous with those spoons. You know they haven't learned to feed themselves yet."

He folded the paper and set it on the table then flicked a glance at Cody and Jolie. "It'll wash off. And they won't learn if they don't try."

"Huh. It's good to hear them laughing."

"Yes. The welts are down on Jolie. She's looking much better." He got up and punched some numbers on the microwave. Next he dropped bread in the toaster. "Sit down, I made breakfast."

"You spoil me." She took a seat at the table just as he set down a plate of scrambled eggs and smoked sausage.

"You make that sound like a bad thing." He went back to the counter for the toast.

"It is. I'm used to doing things for myself. I prefer it that way."

"Maybe that's why I like doing things for you." He sat down and pushed a plate of buttered toast toward her. "Because it's not expected."

"Huh." She flashed him an exasperated glare.

He grinned. "Eat up. I have a surprise for you."

She lifted her brows at him. "All this and a surprise, too? Are you sure you don't want to quit the Navy and move to Montana?"

The levity left his expression and his eyes turned pensive. "My brother thinks I should give up the SEALs now that I'm guardian of the twins."

"And you're not ready to?"

"Honestly? I don't know. My current commission is up in a couple of months, so I don't have long to think about it. I do know I want it to be my decision. Not something forced on me by circumstances or told to me by my brother."

"That would be ideal, wouldn't it? If outside influences and well intentioned advice didn't play a part in our decisions."

The exasperation boomeranged back to her. "Very funny."

"You're just upset because you have to think about this before you were ready to. Let me ask you this, does your brother expect you to quit because he voiced an opinion?"

"No, if anything, he'd expect the reverse."

"Why's that, because you're the youngest of six and you've been bucking the system since the day you learned to say no?"

His eyes narrowed in speculation. "How do you know that about me?"

"Please, I've known you what, a week? And I already know you can find Ford as a synonym for stubborn in a thesaurus. You haven't accepted no for an answer since you got here and when you have compromised, it's been on your terms." She reached for the grape jelly for her last piece of toast. "Your brothers must know you are your own man."

"Yeah, we all know that about each other." He reached over, took her toast, bit the end off and handed it back to her.

A smear of jelly clung to the corner of his mouth. Rachel bit her lip to keep from acting on the impulse to lean over and lick the sweet treat from his skin. Instead she sank her teeth into the same end of the bread he had and lectured herself on forgetting the physical attraction to concentrate on the conversation.

"So the decision is yours to make. Whether you allow the circumstances to influence you or not is up to you."

He looked at her for a long moment, his expression giving nothing away.

"You're not going to suggest you keep custody of the twins so I can re-up as a SEAL? We both know you want to."

"You mean because it makes perfect sense for me to take the kids while you pursue your career?"

Yes, it had occurred to her. And yes, she wanted to keep the twins. But begging would weaken her position. She'd learned that lesson too well, and too early in life to forget it when it mattered the most.

"No, I'm not going to suggest that. You're smart enough to come up with it on your own."

"Right. My brother mentioned the arrangements for Tony and Crystal's memorial service were set for the week before Thanksgiving. Will you come?"

"Your family made arrangements for Crystal?" The thoughtfulness of the gesture staggered her.

"It's what I thought you'd like. If you prefer to make other arrangements, I can let my brother know."

"No. No. She'd want to share this last rite with Tony. Of course I'll come."

Jolie called for her attention, breaking the growing tension.

"Good morning, baby. You're feeling better aren't you? I'm so glad." Rachel grabbed a napkin and swiped at Jolie's face. "But oh my. Uncle Ford let you make one big mess, didn't he?"

"Da na da." Cody pointed his dripping spoon toward Ford and grinned showing two bottom teeth.

Rachel's gaze met Ford's. He looked shell-shocked for a moment before shutting off all expression.

She knew how he felt. The first time she thought the twins called her mama both broke her heart and mended it back all at the same time. The incongruity along with the inherent acceptance struck right to the core of you. And revived the sorrow of loss all over again.

"Just coincidence." She crossed her arms over her chest. "They don't know what they're saying yet." But she knew the day wasn't far away.

Thinking of Ford being called daddy made her gut clutch. She loved the idea the twins were starting to adjust, that they felt loved enough to accept her and Ford in their parents' stead. But that meant they would be hurt again by whatever custody settlement she and Ford decided on.

Sometimes life just sucked.

"Hey, bud, let's get you cleaned." Ford reached for a dish towel and wrapped it around Cody. Ford carefully didn't look at Rachel when he asked, "Bath?"

Rachel stepped out onto the porch, a bundled up Cody riding her hip, to find old Mr. Brown from next door sitting on the perch of a shiny red sleigh drawn by a well-groomed, gray speckled horse.

"Ms. Adams," he greeted her with a huge grin and a tip of his red plaid hat. "Beautiful day for a ride."

"Mr. Brown." Determined to be neighborly she answered his good cheer with a smile. "I hope you and Mrs. Brown survived the storm in tact."

"What ya say there? Sorry lass, don't hear as good as I used to."

Rachel walked to the top of the stairs and, raising her voice. repeated her question.

"That we did, young lady. The Mrs., though, she caught a chill. I've been feeding her chicken gravy and biscuits, so she should be feeling better right soon."

"Chicken gravy and biscuits?"

"Yeah, yeah. Chicken noodle soup is more than an old wives' tale. It really works to help cure a cold. Don't know how to make chicken noodle soup, but I can make chicken gravy and biscuits. I figure it's close enough."

"I'm sure she appreciates your efforts." Rachel didn't know how well his heavy meal worked on the cold but at least it wouldn't hurt the woman. Rachel made a note to send some Echinacea tea home with him.

"Oh, the Mrs. always appreciates my efforts," he said and winked.

"Mr. Brown." Rachel chided him.

He cackled, pleased to get a rise out of her.

"Here now, that little guy wants to come say hello to Betsy. You bring him on down here." Spry for a man in his sixties, he hopped to the ground. He took Cody from her to gently instruct the little boy on how to pet the horse.

"I had Betsy out for a ride this morning. Met your young man down by the road. He thought you and the little ones might like to get out of the house and go for a ride."

Her "young man" was simply diabolical.

"Yes, I think we'll all enjoy a trip through the snow. This is a beautiful sleigh."

"She is a beauty isn't she?" He beamed. "I got it out yesterday to get it cleaned up and ready for Santa."

She blinked at him. "Santa?"

"Yeah, I've driven Santa's sleigh in the Thanksgiving Day parade for the last eight years. I'm sure you've seen it."

She shook her head. "I'm not much for crowds. I don't go to parades."

He laughed. "Lass, there are more people in the parade than watching it. The little ones would enjoy it."

Ford joined them saving her from having to reply. But Mr. Brown had a point. From now on she had to think beyond her own comfort zone to accommodate the twins.

"John, thanks for giving us a ride." Ford shifted Jolie to shake hands with Mr. Brown. "The kids are going to love it."

"My pleasure. Let's get you folks loaded up."

The men continued to exchange pleasantries while they all got settled, Mr. Brown on the perch, Rachel and Ford with the twins between them in the back.

And then they were off, gliding over pristine snow to the merry jingle of bells. Tucked beneath blankets, the cool air invigorated rather than chilled.

The twins took in everything red cheeked and bright eyed. Rachel figured she looked much the same. It was beautiful and fun. And never before had anyone ever done anything so special for her. For the twins, too, of course, but she knew Ford had done this mostly for her.

The scenery shimmered into crystal brilliance as moisture swelled in her eyes.

"Hey." Ford cupped the back of her neck and ran his thumb over her cheek. His touch felt especially warm against her wind-chilled skin. "Are you crying?"

"No, of course not." She blinked away the tears. "It's just the wind."

"It's more than the wind." He insisted. "Talk to me, Rachel. This was meant to be a treat, to make you happy not sad."

"I am happy." She assured him. "This is wonderful. The twins are loving it."

"And you? Are you loving it?" The intensity in his blue eyes convinced her the answer really mattered to him.

"I am," she confirmed. Hearing the huskiness in her voice, she cleared her throat, met his gaze. "Thank you for arranging this adventure. Nobody's ever done anything like this for me."

"You mean planned a surprise for you?" He gently tugged on a lock of her hair.

"That, or done something for me just because they thought I'd enjoy it." The confession didn't come easily. She didn't talk about her childhood, ever. But Ford had shared his guilt and sorrow with her and he'd put together this lovely surprise. He deserved some consideration from her.

"I had a strict upbringing." Okay, slight understatement there.

"Is that why you left home so young?" he asked.

She hesitated, glanced at Mr. Brown. He hadn't tried to participate in the conversation. His poor hearing along with the cheerful bells ensured their privacy.

"Yeah, and because I learned I wasn't my father's daughter." Funny, she'd thought the words would be harder to say. But here, with Ford, she said them for the first time and felt lighter.

"Wow. Heavy. How'd you find out?"

"My mother told me. I had to get a job when I was fourteen to help with expenses. My expenses, as it turned out. I didn't get an allowance, but I got to keep part of my paycheck. My senior year of high school, I wanted to buy a car. I'd saved my money. It wasn't hard considering I was never allowed to do anything.

"Mom said I'd need the money when I graduated because I'd no longer be welcome to live with them. I was shocked. That's when she told me she'd been pregnant when she'd married my dad. She'd lied and told him I was his. He'd found out and their marriage survived the truth, but he never accepted me, never loved me."

"Your mom sacrificed you for her own comfort." Ford cut to the heart of her past, the harsh edge in his tone criticizing her mother's choices. Too bad she had no excuses for her mom.

"I didn't wait to graduate. I packed up and left the next day. I bought a one-way ticket to Scobey and started a new life."

"It must have been difficult." The simple sympathy almost undid her.

"It was a relief to be free. I never felt loved in that house. Except by Crystal." She looked down at her hands clasped together in her lap. "Why do you suppose she misled Tony about me?"

He caught her chin and turned her head to face him. Bending, he sealed his warm mouth over hers, telling her with lips, teeth and tongue of his admiration and affection. Sealing the kiss with his lips, he pulled back.

"Whatever her reasons, you have nothing to be ashamed of. You're a strong woman who's made a good life from a bad beginning."

"Thank you." She cupped his cheek in her hand and showed her gratitude with a soft kiss in return. "I know that's true, but it's easy to believe the worst when someone you love bad-mouths you."

"I can only speculate. Tony didn't talk much about his relationship with Crystal, but I know it was tempestuous. They loved each other, but they weren't compatible."

Rachel recalled the e-mails where Crystal poured out her fears of losing Tony. She'd despised that he was a SEAL. "I know she hated it when Tony went out of the country."

"Yeah, that was tough on Tony. Being a SEAL defined who he was. His parents were alcoholics and they really did a job on his self-esteem. He was one of the best men I knew, but he had no sense of self-worth except on the job."

"I told her she needed to make peace with his job or let him go. It wasn't fair for her to impose her fears on him."

Not that Rachel was an expert on relationships, but one lesson she'd learned, and learned well, was you couldn't make someone love you. And if you weren't true to yourself, you'd have nothing to hold on to when you realized the truth."

Ford nodded his agreement. "They did break up for a while before she found out she was pregnant."

"Really? I didn't hear from her for several months. Then she called to tell me she was expecting a baby. She was so happy. I thought she'd made her peace. Now I realize she probably just stopped sharing her fears with me."

"The pregnancy did bring them closer. Until Tony made out his will. I knew there was no love lost between him and his parents, which is why I agreed when he asked me to watch over the kids if anything ever happened to him."

He lifted his hand to cover hers. "Crystal was young, only twenty-one. She was in love with a man she didn't really understand and couldn't control. I've been thinking about it and I think part of it was my fault."

"How could that be?"

"She didn't like that Tony named a guardian without consulting her. She didn't like that he chose a bachelor, hated that it was another SEAL. I was her worst nightmare."

"Mustang, wild and free." Rachel began to see what motivated her sister's actions. She still didn't like it, but a mother's concern accounted for a lot.

"Pretty much." Ford agreed. "My guess is she set up her own will listing you as guardian then played up the negative aspect of your life to teach Tony a lesson, both for leaving her out of the process and for choosing an inappropriate guardian. Being so young, she probably figured they had plenty of time to deal with the whole issue. It's the only reason I can think of."

She gave him a sad half smile. "I guess we didn't get as close as I thought."

The twins objected to being squeezed between them by squirming and pushing against them. When Rachel settled back into her corner, Jolie pulled on Rachel's sleeve and hauled herself to her feet. The better view and the wind in Jolie's face made her grin and clap her hands. Soon Cody stood next to her.

Turning to better anchor Jolie in place, Rachel noted Ford did the same with Cody and they were suddenly facing each other. Rachel felt as if they were in an oversize snow globe, an intimate cocoon with the beauty of a winter wonderland passing in the background.

Too bad the intensity of the conversation didn't match the splendor of the scenery.

Jolie laid her head on Rachel's shoulder. The excitement had worn her out. As always the acceptance and trust of Jolie's slight weight resting against Rachel sent warmth flooding through her. She settled the sleepy baby in her lap and wished Jolie could have grown up knowing her mother.

"Poor Crystal and Tony, they just wanted to take care of their kids. But instead of working together they worked against each other and didn't resolve anything."

"That would be my take." Ford stopped Cody from climbing into Rachel's lap along with his sister. He lifted Cody into his lap instead. "Hey, buddy. Let's get you warmed up." Ford tucked a blanket around the boy.

"And now here we are," Rachel said, "trying to make sense of their mess. At least Tony's parents are out of the picture."

"For now anyway."

That sounded ominous. "What's that mean?"

"It means if we don't work out a solid home situation for the twins, it'll leave room for Tony's parents to sue for custody."

"But they couldn't win." Her heart sank at the thought of the twins in the hands of the abusive couple. "A court's not going to give custody of small children to alcoholics."

Ford shrugged, his expression grimmer than she'd ever seen it. "They're closet drinkers. As an established couple making decent wages living in a nice neighborhood, the courts may find them eminently better than two single people living a thousand miles apart splitting or sharing custody."

"Oh my God." Put like that their chances did sound bad. "Why didn't you mention this before?"

"Because I didn't intend to split or share custody. I intended to take the twins and surround them with the strength and support of my family."

Her heart latched onto one word. "Intended? Does that mean you no longer have that intention?"

"It means I want you to move to San Diego."

Chapter 9

The cold must be getting to her because she thought he'd just asked her to move to California.

She looked askance at him and pounded the side of her head a couple of times. "I don't think I heard right. Did you just say move to San Diego?"

"Yeah, think about it. It makes perfect sense."

"It makes no sense whatsoever."

His somber expression didn't lighten. "I'm serious."

"No." The cold must be getting to him, too. "You're delusional."

"That's a knee-jerk reaction. Don't dismiss the idea without thinking about it."

"What's to think about? This is my home."

"No, it's where your house is." He delivered the harsh decree with utmost gentleness. "You've built a life here, but by your own admission you've isolated yourself from the community. I haven't heard you mention another woman's name besides Crystal. Who's your best friend?"

Ouch. The question cut deep.

And then her spinning thoughts spit out the words, you are.

The instinctive response irritated her almost as much as his question. And how revealing that in the short time she'd known him, she'd become closer to him than people she'd known for thirteen years.

"Just because I prefer my own company doesn't mean I don't have c-connections here." Hating the break in her voice, she buried her nose in Jolie's soft brown curls.

Ford slid closer. Once again she felt the tensile strength of his hand on her neck. Massaging soothingly, he melted her.

"I'm not suggesting there won't be sacrifices, but this could be the solution to our custody dilemma. You're going to have to move anyway. The three of you won't fit in a one-bedroom house for long. You can write anywhere, and there are bound to be plenty of opportunities to work with animals in San Diego.

"Look, you don't have to make a decision right now. You're coming to California for the memorial service, right? I'm just asking you to keep an open mind. Check out the area and consider staying."

Mr. Brown pulled the sleigh to a stop in front of Rachel's house effectively ending the conversation. Between expressing her appreciation to Mr. Brown, running inside for the Echinacea tea for Mrs. Brown and getting the kids inside and settled down for their afternoon naps, Rachel kept busy.

But for all the activity, her mind revved around one thing. The possibility of moving to California.

But it wasn't the practicalities that snagged her attention. It wasn't even the fear of leaving the comfort and safety of small town Scobey for the cosmopolitan metropolis of San Diego.

Although those concerns niggled at her psyche, what occupied her mind was being so close to Ford. She'd known him a week and already her emotions were way too involved. And, much as she'd fought it, not at all platonic.

The attraction went both ways but that only made the situation more dangerous.

If it had been anyone other than Ford, she'd seriously contemplate jumping his fine bod and riding the electric blaze until it caught fire or fizzled out. But a fling with her co-guardian? Not a smart move.

It opened up too many options for sticky relations down the line.

Moving across country may well solve their custody issues, but could she live so near him and just be friends? Could she watch him date other women, cut their wood, surprise them with sleigh rides and still maintain a personal relationship for the twins' sake?

The part of her that had learned not to trust emotions saw no problems ahead. But every other feminine instinct she possessed shouted out a warning.

And were his motives for asking strictly to make things easier with the twins? Or did he have a more personal reason for wanting her in California? He hadn't inferred any kind of intimate relationship in his request.

Yet he hadn't exactly kept his hands to himself, either.

After taking all that angst into account, none of it really counted. The twins mattered. What was best for them mattered.

Like her, they'd fallen under Ford's charming spell. If a resolution to the custody issue let her keep the twins and allowed them to be closer to Ford, how could she deny them the opportunity?

Ford wanted her to think about moving? Ha, she'd be lucky if she could focus on anything else.

A cheerful fire crackled in the hearth. Soft jazz played in the background. A nice red wine was breathing on the counter. The furniture had been pushed back, and Ford had spread a plush blanket on the carpet in front of the fire. Rachel tossed down several overstuffed pillows.

A more romantic scene would be hard to find.

Until Rachel sprinkled the area with a handful of plastic toys.

Sighing, Ford lifted Cody from the playpen and set him in the middle of the blanket. He shouldn't be thinking about seduction anyway.

Rachel set Jolie next to her brother and then settled against one of the big pillows. Pretty in a soft pink sweater topping black jeans, she looked sexy as hell. She glowed in the flicker of the fire, her appeal due more to good health and hair that looked like she'd just climbed out of bed than makeup or hair gel.

On this, his last night in Montana, they'd decided on a fireside picnic. The twins loved it when he and Rachel got down on the floor and played with them. He wanted tonight to be fun and carefree.

Too bad he didn't feel in the least lighthearted.

A week ago he'd thought he'd come in, save Tony's kids from the clutches of their evil aunt and shoot back to San Diego where he'd leave them in the capable care of his family. Now he dreaded walking out the door, dreaded leaving Rachel and the twins behind.

"You're sure you'll be all right traveling with both kids? They're going to be quite a handful." He dropped to the ground and stretched out.

A flash of panic came and went in her incredibly expressive eyes. "Don't remind me or I may change my mind. I love them so much even though I've only had them a couple of weeks. And they're just two little babies, but they're a lot of work." She cringed. "I mean—"

He held up a hand, shook his head. "I've only been here a week." A ball bounced off him and he rolled it back to Cody, enjoyed the boy's laugh. "I understand too well."

"The idea of traveling with two babies is daunting, but the flight's only a few hours. And you'll be waiting at the other end."

"Right, piece of cake. You'll be in San Diego before you know it."

Again the flash of panic reached her eyes. To distract her, Ford offered to get their dinner, a fragrant stew she'd been slow cooking all day. She waved him off and immediately jumped up to get the meal.

Ford winked at Cody who'd pulled himself up to lean against Ford. "Works every time. Keep it between us men."

He rewarded Cody's cooperation with a cookie and handed one to Jolie. They'd already eaten pasta and peaches. The cookies were a treat that Rachel had set within reach to keep the kids occupied while the two of them ate.

She came back with two steaming bowls of stew, a plate piled high with golden brown biscuits and two glasses of wine. Setting the tray on the ottoman coffee table, she handed him a cloth napkin.

"Sit." He told her. "You did the rest. I'll serve you."

"Okay." She sank down across from him and smiled as he fussed over her dinner.

He liked doing things for her. Talking to her. Looking at her.

They finished the stew, and the wine. He polished off the biscuits and a couple of cookies. All the while chatting and watching the twins play.

Time flew when he wanted each moment to stretch into forever. There was a lesson in relativity for you. Put him in the middle of a nest of terrorists and every minute lasted an hour. Yet tonight, in a room with a lovely, intelligent, witty woman playing with his delightful wards and every hour rushed by in a blink.

He felt his departure looming closer and closer.

Jolie crawled over and he helped her to climb up. Leaning forward she gave him an openmouthed kiss.

"Ah, baby." He wrapped her in a hug, kissing her soft curls. She laid her head on his shoulder breaking his heart with her love and trust.

In the next moment she wiggled to be set free. He sat up and held her fingers as she walked to Rachel who held her arms up ready for the trade off.

Suddenly Jolie let go and took two steps on her own straight into Rachel's arms.

"Oh my God, Ford," Rachel exclaimed. "She walked. Did you see her? Jolie walked. How smart you are." She covered the baby's face in kisses.

"I sure did." Ford clapped to show his pride in the girl. "Isn't she clever."

Cody, seated on the blanket between Ford and the fireplace, clapped, too. And added a gleeful shriek for good measure. He didn't understand what happened, but he felt the excitement.

Proud of herself, Jolie pushed away and turned to face Ford wanting to repeat her new trick.

Grinning ear to ear, he held out his arms and wiggled his fingers. "Come on, baby, come to Ford."

She toddled three steps and he grabbed her before she fell. The game continued with love and laughter. Cody wanted to take his turn, too. He couldn't quite keep his balance, but Ford shared a look with Rachel, they both knew it wouldn't be long.

Finally Rachel called for bedtime. Working together he and Rachel made short work of bathing, changing and tucking the two exhausted babies into their crib. They were asleep before Ford and Rachel backed out of the room.

Back in front of the fire, Ford handed Rachel a second glass of wine. He tapped his rim against hers. "To Jolie."

"I'm glad you were here to share the moment." She sipped around a grin.

"Me, too."

"You're wonderful with the kids." She leaned back against a pillow. "How come some lucky girl hasn't dragged you down the aisle?"

He shrugged. "There have been some special women along the way. But I wasn't ready to give up being a SEAL and they weren't willing to wait."

"No room for compromise? Then it must not have been love."

He cocked a brow. "Don't look now, but your cynicism is showing. You say that like you don't believe in love."

"Hard to believe in something you've never known." She turned her gaze to the fire but not before he saw the wistfulness in the aqua depths.

"You're right, I didn't love them enough to be tempted to break my rule."

She eyed him over her wineglass. "What rule is that?"

"My friends call it Mustang's rule. Basically I've never thought it would be fair to commit to a permanent relationship while I'm a SEAL. Not only for the woman, but for me. I'm not the type to forget my family back home, which is necessary in order to get the job done."

"I suppose it's good to know yourself so well. Being a SEAL obviously means a lot to you."

The admiration in her voice bolstered his confidence. Naturally reticent, the closeness they'd developed encouraged him to share feelings he usually kept hidden.

"Yeah, it does. It means I'm one of the best."

"No," she waved her wineglass back and forth in a negative gesture, "the training did that. What does the job mean to you?"

Nobody had ever made such a distinction before. He had to think for a moment.

"Justice."

"Justice? In what way?"

"There's a lot wrong in the world. A lot of evil people doing evil deeds. As a SEAL, I make a difference. It's not black and white. But nothing ever is."

"You fight for those who can't fight for themselves." She toasted him. "Commendable. But you won't be a SEAL forever. What comes next?"

So intense. Her skin looked translucent in the golden glow of the fire. He traced the gentle curve of her cheek. "You ask some tough questions."

"They're only tough if you don't have the answers."

"Ouch." The woman pulled no punches.

She turned on her side to face him. Her fingers found his on the blanket between them. She traced and played, warming him with her touch.

"Have you thought about training?" She suggested. "I think you'd be very good as an instructor."

His commander had asked the same question. Disdain curled the corner of Ford's lip. "Haven't you ever heard the expression those that can do, and those that can't teach? In this case, those that no longer can, teach."

"You don't believe that." But after meeting his gaze

straight on, she changed her tune. "I see you do. Why? Do you have so little respect for those who trained you?"

Her question took him back to BUDS training, to the extreme tests of endurance, lack of sleep and larger than life trainers. He hadn't doubted their skill at the time, hadn't dared. So why did he now?

Because he didn't feel up to the challenge? Or because others would know he could no longer handle the heat of active duty?

"Hum." The low sound in her throat shouted a warning: facetious comment coming. "Surprising you got to be the best with such inferior teachers." She laced her fingers through his, anchoring him even as she challenged him. "Maybe your condescension isn't so much what you believe, but what you think others will believe."

How did she do that, zero right in on the heart of his fears before he'd even recognized them himself?

"You mean disparaging the job is a self-defense against considering it as an option for the future. The great subconscious at work."

"It makes sense. You're a man of action obviously torn about settling down. What better way to put off a decision than to find something wrong with your choices?"

He flopped down on his back. Self-examination was a bitch. "So basically, I'm being a wimp."

"Not at all." She crawled over so she looked into his eyes, compassion rained down on him. "It just proves you're human like the rest of us."

She traced the rasp of his beard with a curved

knuckle. For a sassy, standoffish loner, she'd become quite the toucher. He liked it.

"I'm pretty sure they don't let wimps in the SEALs."

He grinned. "Damn straight. You're right about one thing. It's wrong to disrespect my trainers. They put us through hell, but we were ready when we hit the field."

The concern in her eyes lingered. "Just remember if you decide to pursue training. When you were ready, the instructors let you go. What happens after that belongs in the field not in your conscious."

"Heavens." She was talking about his guilt over buying the trip for Tony. In this she was wrong. They weren't the same thing at all. SEALs were ready for anything and everything when they hit the ground. They planned and trained for best and worst case scenarios.

Tony hadn't been prepared, his training hadn't helped him because he couldn't know an earthquake was going to hit. He couldn't save himself or Crystal because an earthquake provided no warning before raining down horrific destruction.

Ford ran his hands over his face, trying to scrub away the senseless helplessness. *Tony couldn't have known an earthquake was going to hit.* So how could Ford?

If only letting go of his guilt was that easy.

He looped his arm around Rachel, tucked her into his side. "How did you get to be so wise?"

"I don't know about wise." She placed her hand on his chest, and he covered it with his, pressing her palm over his heart. "I admit I'm a loner. But I'm also an observer. People and animals, we're not so different. We give love and loyalty until we learn the pain of rejection, we fight when cornered, and we shy away from what scares or hurts us."

Maybe that was Ford's problem, he'd never run scared. From the day he was born sixth in a family of sons, he'd been fighting for his place in the world. Which explained why he didn't recognize his subconscious at work.

And why he kept finding ways to put his hands on Rachel.

He understood the sense in keeping their interaction platonic. But in learning to fight for what he wanted, he pretty much got what he aimed for. Everything in him demanded more than the feel of her in his arms.

He desired all of her, and not for the sake of the twins.

When he got her to San Diego, she'd be his. And he wouldn't let her go until she agreed to stay.

Chapter 10

A new storm came in delaying Rachel's flight by a day and a half. She fretted all the way to San Diego. Thankfully the twins behaved beautifully because nothing else was going as planned.

Because of the delay they'd have to go straight to the memorial service. There'd be no time, or place, to change once she arrived so Rachel wore the new black dress she'd bought onto the plane. She counted it a blessing she'd be attending in wrinkled splendor. Better that than not attend at all, which had been her worst and most likely fear until the wheels of the aircraft had left the tarmac.

The past week had been harder than Rachel had ever anticipated. The kids missed Ford, especially Cody. The two had really bonded over the last week.

What Rachel hadn't expected was that *she* was missing Ford just as much.

How quickly she'd become accustomed to his presence, his help, his touch.

I wasn't that she hadn't had contact with him. She'd talked to him on the phone every day, sometimes more than once. And Ford had talked to the twins. Okay, so the kids couldn't talk and they usually tired of the conversation long before the adults disconnected, but she and Ford had had things to discuss, travel arrangements to make. They'd done a lot by e-mail but it wasn't the same.

Not the same as hearing his voice, his laugh, his concerns. She liked that he felt able to talk to her. Especially since she'd become a regular Chatty Cathy around him.

This week had taught her two things. One, she loved Cody and Jolie too much not to be a part of their lives. Whatever it took, she'd find a way to retain custody. And two, she was already way too attached to Ford. If she were smart, she'd forget her promise to think about moving to California and hotfoot it back to Montana as fast as possible.

Two insights and both put her heart on the line. Too bad they were at complete odds.

With the airline's help she made it through the San Diego airport with little trouble. A young sailor with a Southern accent and a shy smile met her in the baggage claim. He had a picture of her and an e-mail from Ford introducing Dawson as her driver. He took control of the luggage, and they were soon on the road to Paradise Pines and the memorial service.

Flying in, the plane had seemed to dodge skyscrapers. Now pulling out of the parking lot she saw those buildings across a harbor view framed by palm trees and a bright blue sky.

The third week of November in San Diego looked, and at seventy-eight degrees, felt a lot different than Scobey, Montana.

"Thirty minutes before the service starts." Rachel checked her watch, pulled it off to reset the time. "Mr. Dawson, how long before we get to Paradise Pines?"

He shot her a grin. "Ma'am, no need for the Mr. It's just Dawson."

"Okay. Please call me Rachel. Do you think we'll make the service on time?"

"We're sure going to try. It's early enough we'll miss traffic, and the church is in Alpine, which is about twelve miles this side of Paradise Pines. You just sit back and relax. I'll have you there in a jiffy."

"Thank you, Dawson. Do you have a cell phone so I can check in with Ford?"

"You don't have a cell?" He sounded shocked.

"No." Not much need for one in Scobey. Heck she rarely used her house phone. "May I borrow yours?"

"Sure, but when I tried Mustang twenty minutes ago to tell him your plane was on time, I got an out of service message. It can be sketchy close to the mountains."

Rachel received the same message. Disappointed, she returned the phone to Dawson.

Once on the road both babies fell asleep. Rachel used the time to freshen her makeup and hair. Dabbing perspiration from her temple, she realized her plan to hide the worst of the wrinkles in her dress under a fitted sweater jacket were out the window.

"Y'all want the air on?" Dawson pressed a few buttons on the console, and blessed cool air flowed from the vents.

"Thanks, I'm overdressed for this heat. It was ten degrees when I left Montana this morning. It sure is beautiful here."

Forty minutes after leaving the airport, they pulled to a stop in front of Queen of Angels church in Alpine.

"Here ya'll go. You want help with the little ones?"

"Please." Rachel climbed from the SUV and removed Jolie from her seat. Still sleepy, she laid her head on Rachel's shoulder and whined quietly.

"Shh, baby. It's okay." Rachel soothed Jolie while Dawson came around the car with Cody. When he saw her, Cody held his arms out to Rachel. She quickly distracted him with a teething ring.

Tears stung the back of her throat as she approached the church doors. Sadness welled up inside her. Focused on the logistics of the trip, the purpose had receded to the back of her mind. Now it rushed forward intensified by her disappointment in being too late to sit with Ford.

She'd so wanted to get here in time for the twins to be with Ford. For the four of them to be together to support each other in this time of sorrow.

It touched her to see the small church almost filled to capacity. Quaint colored light filtered down on the mourners from beautiful stained-glass windows.

Ford sat on the aisle in the front row. Rachel longed to go to him, but the service had begun. Not wanting to disturb the ceremony, she directed Dawson into the last row of chairs across the aisle from Ford. At least she could take comfort in seeing him and knowing he was near.

A lot cranky and a whole lot less impressed by the proceedings, Cody immediately protested with an annoyed wail.

Ford knew Cody's cry. He swung around, and across the expanse of the small church, he met Rachel's aqua-blue gaze.

Immediately something in him eased. She was here. Finally. It felt as if a lifetime had passed since he'd last seen her.

And here, mourning the loss of his friend, reliving his part in the untimely deaths of these young, vital loved ones, he needed her by his side.

Nobody understood like Rachel. Nobody was as close to the departed as they were, except the twins. And today more than ever he and Rachel stood for the orphaned siblings.

Uncaring of the assemblage, he rose and went to her, watching as Cody, not content to stay with Dawson, climbed into Rachel's lap so she held both twins.

He stopped in front of her. Jolie looked up, saw him and practically leaped into his arms. Rachel rose with a struggling Cody in her arms. Holding Jolie against his heart, Ford drew the other two into his embrace. For a moment he closed his eyes and rested his forehead against Rachel's, absorbing the peace of her presence, the sheer rightness of them being together again.

This, the four of them standing as a family, was the

biggest honor they could bestow on Tony and Crystal's memories.

When the quiet of the church registered, Ford looked up to realize the priest had paused out of respect for them. Taking Rachel's hand, he led her to the front row where his family had shifted to make a seat for her.

"This is my grandmother." He whispered the introduction of the petite, gray-haired woman with alert blue eyes.

"My dear." Gram reached for Rachel's hand, squeezed and held on. "I'm so glad you made it."

Ford held Cody in one arm and placed his other around Rachel's shoulders. She held Jolie on her lap. With his family linked in love and support, he nodded to the priest to continue.

A reception at the Sullivan estate in Paradise Pines followed the service. Many of the mourners, plus a few who couldn't attend the service flowed over to Gram's place. A soft blue color with white gingerbread trim, the large Victorian manor sat on a couple of acres of lush green grass and flowering gardens.

A crush of people filled the living room, parlor and kitchen. Rachel quickly lost track of names and faces. She made an effort to note Ford's brothers, a chore made easier by the resemblance between them. She'd met and liked his sister-in-law, Samantha, a green-eyed blonde, who Rachel learned was a school nurse.

The twins were swept away, oohed and aahed over and pretty much spoiled by everyone.

A self-proclaimed loner, Rachel felt a little out

of her element and a lot overwhelmed. If not for the twins, she'd have found a quiet corner to escape to. She felt a tug on her hand and turned to find Ford.

"Come, walk with me." He drew her toward the kitchen and the back door. "Samantha has agreed to watch the twins for a while."

"Oh—" she hung back at that news "—I can't let her do that. She has her own boys to watch. It's too much."

"Look around you." He swept a hand out to indicate the crush of people in the kitchen and beyond to the parlor. "She has plenty of help."

Seeing the babies bouncing on the knees of their uncles, she conceded he was right. The twins were in good hands. With them taken care of, the thought of spending time with Ford held great appeal.

"Okay, for a little while."

He grinned and led her outside. "The last time you said that, you slept in my arms."

"Oh snap." Laughing, she chided him. "That was your fault. You were supposed to wake me." Better to make light than to dwell on the peace and rightness she had felt being in his arms.

She'd found she had little impartiality when it came to him.

"Now you tell me." Stopping in the middle of a garden pathway, he wrapped an arm around her waist and pulled her close. "Let me warn you right now, if you're leaving it up to me to watch out for your virtue, there's an old adage that covers this situation."

"Oh?" Breathless at his nearness, at the intensity in his eyes, she was reminded of his dangerous edge. His sexy, seductive, uncompromising appeal. "What's that?"

"All is fair in love and war." Dipping his head, he claimed her lips in an urgent melding of their mouths. Unlike the slow and dreamy kiss he'd stolen on her porch before leaving Montana, this kiss demanded a response. She answered by rising onto her toes and opening to his sensual assault.

He angled his head, cupped her neck in a sure hand and took the caress deeper. The heat of his passion, the desperation of his touch showed her how much he'd missed her.

She savored the moment as she conveyed her own fierce loneliness.

When he stepped back, she blinked up at him slightly disoriented. His blue eyes were dilated and a red flush stained his earlobes. He glanced behind him, and she realized they still stood in the middle of the garden in full view of the house.

"This way." He led her past the garden and across a green lawn to a small cottage tucked into the back corner of the estate.

"What's this place?" she asked as he foraged for a key in the planter beside the door.

"Guest house." He opened the door and drew her inside. Overstuffed furniture and neutral colors offset with splashes of deep wine gave the room a comfortable feel. "We can talk in here."

Despite his predatory stance and the heat radiating from him, for all his body's readiness to finish what they'd started in the yard, he made no move toward her. Out of respect, she knew, for her. Because she'd made it clear how insane a physical relationship would be in their situation.

Right, sheer lunacy, she thought, as she advanced on him. Just call her crazy.

"Talk?" she asked as he watched her warily. "I think I'm ready to do more than talk."

"It's not that simple between us." He caught her hand when she would have touched him. Holding their clasped hands to his heart, he fought for clarity. "Are you sure this is what you want?"

"Yes." She turned her hand to press against his heavy pounding heart. "I feel alive when you touch me. I feel connected like I never have before." She pushed him toward the couch conveniently located behind him. "I need to feel alive today."

Six feet two inches of hard muscle and bone-deep honor, he didn't budge an inch. "All the more reason I shouldn't take advantage of you."

His resistance should have brought Rachel to her senses. After all, she'd been the one to fight against the attraction between them from the beginning. Except she hadn't lied. Sitting through the memorial service had opened a raw emptiness in her.

Her parents were gone. Her younger sister was gone. Yes, she'd walked away from them in her youth. She'd had her reasons, and she wouldn't really change her decision if she had it to do again. But she'd always known they were there. That she had family out there somewhere. Now she was alone, except for two young babies.

Her sister's children. Crystal had been young but she'd taken chances. She'd lived, she'd loved, she'd created life.

Today Rachel wanted to take chances, she wanted

to live, and she wanted to make love with Ford. If that meant seducing him, she was up to the challenge.

And she promised herself, no regrets.

"You won't be taking advantage of me," she assured him as she slipped behind him where he couldn't hold her off with his superior strength. Twining her arms around his waist she leaned into him, her breasts flat against his back, her cheek between his shoulder blades. "I intend to take advantage of you."

He laughed and she smiled as she felt the rumble vibrate through his body. She wanted this man, this body, this moment more than she'd ever longed for anyone else in her life.

"Am I going to have to get rough with you?" She let her hands wander, enjoyed touching him, thrilled at the tactile contrast between soft silk and hard muscles. He caught her hands when they reached his belt buckle.

He turned around, caught her face in his hands and kissed her with burning urgency.

"Rough can be fun," he whispered against her open mouth, "but it's not necessary. As long as you're sure."

Satisfaction and anticipation ignited her blood. Melting against him, she met his mouth, sank into the kiss. She felt more than alive in his arms, she felt energized, vitalized.

"Ford, we said goodbye to Crystal and Tony today. If life were fair at all, they would have lived to see the twins' first steps, to walk them to kindergarten, to teach them to drive. Tony would have escorted Jolie down the aisle and coached Cody on the finer points of throwing a football.

"But life isn't even close to fair. It's a kick in the

teeth. So instead of Tony and Crystal, the twins are stuck with us. I love the twins. I can't even remember what life was like without them, but I'd give them up quick as a heartbeat if it would bring my sister back."

"Shh." Ford pressed a finger to her lips, followed the gesture with a soft kiss. "Don't go there. It's useless speculation, and you're the one who kicked my butt about second-guessing fate."

"I know. I'm sorry." She wiped away a tear she'd sworn to keep locked away and almost lost it when he captured her finger to absorb the tear with his kiss. She cleared her throat. "I didn't mean to get maudlin. My point is I'm beyond sure. I want to be with you. More, I need the comfort and escape I'll find in your arms."

To show him just how certain, her fingers went to the buttons of her new black dress. She'd been looking for a reason to get out of the dress since she landed in San Diego. No better reason than this.

"Make me forget that they're gone, Ford. Let me remind you why it's good to be alive."

She released the third button, revealing the first rise of cleavage before Ford took over.

"Dynamite, you did that the minute you opened your door in Scobey." He made short work of the rest of the buttons. "Lucky for both of us, I'm a SEAL. The Boy Scouts have nothing on us for being prepared."

He was talking about birth control, telling her he had it covered. His assurance warmed her. She'd been running on emotion, hadn't thought that far ahead. Thank goodness his cool head ruled.

The heat of his breath caressed the curve of her neck

as the dress fell off her shoulders and to the floor, leaving her in nothing but a black bra and thong.

The sexy lingerie was another new purchase. Obviously her subconscious at work.

His eyes cherished her before his mouth began the same downward journey. Time slowed and lengthened while desire bloomed.

Suddenly her clothes were gone and he lowered her to the downy softness of a bed. Sensation replaced all else as he took her to heights she'd never known before. Precious, he made her feel so precious, using his mouth, fingers, and body to worship every inch of her.

She reciprocated touch for touch, kiss for kiss, stroke for stroke, thrilling when she drew groans of satisfaction from him. Wrapping her arms around him, she clung on tightly and followed him to the explosive realm of completion.

Ford sighed, contentment flowing through him along with the soft peach scent of Rachel's shampoo. He tightened his arm around her and buried his nose in her hair.

She smelled so good, felt so good. He'd known they'd be volatile in bed, but he'd been wrong. Oh, there'd been explosive chemistry between them, bursting gratification. But what they'd just shared went beyond the physical.

He cared about her and that infused the act with a special sense of fulfillment. She'd talked about being connected. He now knew what she'd meant. He couldn't remember the last time he'd felt so close to another human being.

She slipped past his defenses with her sassy attitude and fragile vulnerability. Yet he hadn't realized how much he missed her until she hadn't made it to the church before the start of the memorial service.

Even surrounded by family and friends, he'd felt as if he were all alone. Then she arrived and seeing her and the twins had grounded him, allowed him to make it through the emotional ceremony.

Now more than ever he wanted her to move to San Diego. With her here he wouldn't worry about Cody and Jolie. He'd have felt good about leaving them with his family, but as she'd pointed out, Rachel was their family. The twins wouldn't have to earn her love. She gave it unconditionally.

And he liked the thought of her being here when he came home between assignments. It was the best of both worlds.

This time Rachel slid away from a sleeping Ford. She barely breathed until she'd retrieved her clothes and ducked into the bathroom.

No regrets. That's what she promised herself. She'd taken a chance and received glorious results. Being with Ford exceeded all her fantasies. And revealed a scary new facet to their relationship.

She loved him.

She loved his honor, his gentleness, his generosity. She loved that he knew the sound of Cody's cry, that he had shed tears at the loss of his friend, that he loved and respected his grandmother. She loved his tough as nails exterior and soft as marshmallow interior. Through him she'd discovered that duty and responsibility weren't always used to squash down those in your care, but sometimes meant dealing with compromise and hard decisions.

All these soft feelings scared her to death. Because she'd be a fool to mistake his passion for anything more than casual affection. She knew the sad truth of unrequited love too well to risk rejection when the twins' future hung in the balance.

No doubt about it, her best course of action was to pretend this little incident never happened. She slipped out of the bathroom and made it all the way to the front door, when Ford spoke behind her.

"Don't go."

Her hand tightened on the doorknob. Two seconds more and she'd have been on the other side of the door.

"I don't just mean now. I mean for good." She felt his heat as he came to stand behind her. Snuggling close to her back, he ran his hand down her arm to link his fingers with hers. "Please stay."

The words seemed to echo in the stillness. His request brought her dilemma front and center.

Electing to remain turned away in case any of her newly acknowledged emotions showed on her face, she responded, "I promised I'd think about moving. I know it's the perfect solution to the custody issue, but it's a big decision. I need time."

"I don't mean just move to San Diego." He gently turned her to face him, traced the curve of her cheek with a knuckle. "I mean stay with me, move in with me."

Stay with Ford? The thought both terrified and exhilarated Rachel. Yes, she loved him and she longed to be with him, but her life was in Montana, what she had to offer the twins was in Montana. She could write anywhere, but her home was in Montana.

Dare she give up the life she'd made, which until a month ago was all she'd had to define herself?

"I'm so glad you made it in time for the service." The huskiness in his voice revealed emotions close to the surface. "I was lost until you got there."

"Oh, Ford." His unexpected vulnerability tore her apart.

"It was important to me that you and the twins were there because we've become a family." He kissed her ear, her neck, the corner of her mouth. "Let's make a home together, you, me and the twins. We can move in here until we find a bigger place."

She looked into his eyes, gauged his expression. She saw earnestness along with affection, determination, and desire in his sapphire gaze.

But love? Could what he felt for her grow into something stronger?

She'd taken a huge chance by making love with him, and suffered no regrets. Could she take it one step further?

"It's too complicated. We have to think of the future."

His mouth teased hers. "We won't let it get complicated. We'll take it one day at a time. As long as we're honest with each other and put the twins first, we keep it simple."

Her mind urged caution, but her heart wanted to believe. She threaded her fingers through his silky, dark hair and pulled him down for a kiss.

Against his mouth, she whispered. "I'll stay."

Chapter 11

Rachel followed Ford into the kitchen of the main house. Only the family remained. His brothers sat around the huge butcher-block table while Gram and Samantha watched over the four children from armchairs near the fireplace in what used to be the parlor. Ford's cousin Mattie stood at the counter making a new pot of coffee.

Laughter and chatter filled the room, happy sounds compared to the somber gathering they'd left behind earlier. The rich scent of brewing coffee added to the homey feel of the room.

"I'll take a cup of that." Ford opened a cupboard and took down a mug. He looked at Rachel and at her nod grabbed a second mug. While he waited for the coffee to finish, he faced the room.

"I have an announcement. Rachel has decided to

move to California. We're going to get a place and raise the twins together."

Silence greeted his statement. For five full seconds. Then pandemonium broke out. Everyone started talking at once, well wishes overlapped questions of concern, and advice on buying versus renting.

Unused to such chaos Rachel just let it wash over and around her until Gram came forward and squeezed Rachel's hands.

"My dear, welcome." Gram kissed Rachel's cheek.

Rachel gave her a hug. "Thank you, Mrs. Sullivan. I also want to tell you how much I appreciate all you, and your family, did in arranging the memorial service today."

"Call me Gram." The older woman waved away the formalities. "I was happy to help honor Tony and Crystal. Tony was dear to me. Crystal, I only met a couple of times, but she was full of life, and she loved those babies. Such a loss, for them, for you, for the world."

The simple sympathy caught Rachel unawares. Tears swelled up and overflowed. She'd done so well at maintaining her cool through the day, keeping her tears to the service. But then it all suddenly caught up with her. So much had happened, not least of all discovering her love for Ford, that Gram's words of comfort tipped Rachel over the edge.

"It's okay, you go ahead and cry." Gram pulled Rachel into her arms and rubbed her back soothingly.

Instantly Ford appeared at their sides, but Gram shooed him away. "I've got her, she just needs a little cry is all. Why don't you put together a plate of food to heat when she's ready? I noticed she didn't eat much earlier."

Ford kissed her hair and whispered, "Take your time. I'm here if you need me." Then went off to do as directed.

So gentle, so sweet. Rachel just sobbed harder.

Gram led her to a couch in the quiet of the living room. "I've got you," Gram said, holding Rachel in her arms. "Go ahead and cry."

Unable to resist the comfort of a motherly embrace, something she'd known so little of in her life, Rachel clung to Gram and let the tears flow.

"I like it." Rachel glanced around the medium-size kitchen of the prospective rental in Alpine. She'd insisted on renting at this point. Everything was moving so fast, falling so easily into place, she didn't completely trust it.

She and Ford had looked at houses with larger kitchens, but she liked the openness of this one. It reminded her of the setup of her home in Montana. No island, but a breakfast bar separated the kitchen from the family room. Like Gram's parlor, the family room had a fireplace.

Cautiously optimistic, Rachel could see the four of them spending lots of happy moments in these two rooms.

"I like it, too." Ford opened a pantry door, nodded and closed it again. "Only three bedrooms, but that's enough until the twins get older. The master suite is huge, great walk-in shower."

"We don't really need three bedrooms. We could find a two bedroom for less."

Shaking his head, Ford came to her, curved his arm around her waist and pulled her close. "We're only going to have two bedrooms and an office. I want you to have your own space to write."

"Ford—"

"Shh." He stopped her with a kiss. "I know the rent seems high compared to Scobey, but money is not a problem. We can afford any place we want."

Money wasn't a problem for him. He'd explained he held an interest in the family jewelry store, Sullivans' Jewels. Which apparently did quite well. She found the family's net worth somewhat intimidating.

She had decent savings, by Montana standards, but she couldn't help thinking she'd have been in real trouble if she'd had to fight Ford for custody.

"Money does matter." She wouldn't be a slouch in this relationship. Her independence had been too important to her for too long for her to change now. "I want to pay my share."

"You will." He promised, sweeping his mouth across hers. "You already have with all you bought for the babies. And I promise to let you pay for the utilities."

Her tension eased at his assurances and the look of understanding in his eyes.

"Okay, then." She leaned against him and looked around the kitchen one more time. "So, shall we put in an application for this place?"

"Yeah. We can take it with us to fill out tonight, and you can drop it off tomorrow."

He'd gone back to work the Monday after the memorial service. And she missed him so much. Gram, Samantha and Mattie kept her company and helped with the twins so Rachel got plenty of time to write.

Yet she still lived for the end of the day when he returned home to her arms.

"Sounds like a plan." She agreed. "The ad said available for immediate occupancy. Do you think we'll be able to move in over the long weekend?"

"That's the beauty of city life, babe." He tucked a stray lock of hair behind her ear. "Except for Thanksgiving the rest of the weekend is business as usual."

"Great, then we can move this weekend." She made to move away, but Ford held her in place.

"About this weekend. There's something I have to tell you."

Her heart started to pound, her mouth went dry, and dread grew heavy in her gut. She knew. By the seriousness of his expression and the leeriness shadowing the blue in his eyes.

"You're leaving on assignment."

"Yeah." He rubbed his forehead. "We're already on call. When we go in tomorrow we'll go into lockdown for planning and prep. I don't know when I'll see you again."

Wow, here it was.

Fear for him rose up in a tidal wave. She wanted to scream out a protest, to say no he couldn't go. He couldn't leave her and the twins. But she'd known what she'd been signing up for when she'd agreed to stay, to be a part of his life.

He supported her independence; she owed him the same respect, the freedom to be who he was. It's the advice she'd given Crystal; Rachel would be a fool not to take it herself.

Of course, that didn't stop the emotions from roiling through her. But she refused to give into the worry and dread, instead she chose to make the most of the time she had before he left tomorrow morning.

"Let's go home." Lifting onto her toes, she kissed the frown from his mouth. "Do you think Alex and Samantha would baby-sit? I want you to myself tonight."

In the predawn light Ford stood quietly next to the bed. Already packed, his duffle waited by the front door.

Time to say goodbye.

He didn't want to do it. Which set up all kinds of conflicting emotions inside him, satisfaction at being able to rejoin his SEAL team but reluctance at leaving Rachel. And regret that he'd miss a moment of the twins' development—he just knew Cody would walk any day now.

Ford stood gazing down at Rachel. Her short blond hair curled softly around her face while her long dark lashes fanned across her creamy skin. She looked like an angel tucked beneath the sheets. The last of the moonlight slanted a dim glow over an alabaster shoulder.

He grinned. A naked angel.

She'd slept little if at all during the night. His smile lingered at the corner of his mouth. They'd spent hours making love, from hard and fast, to sweet and sassy, to heart wrenchingly slow.

Only when they were both exhausted did he wrap her in his arms to sleep. Even with all the expended energy he knew she'd slept little. She'd pretended to sleep, as she was doing now.

To save them from the moment of goodbye.

He'd done that in the past, slipped out after a sensuous farewell. Because it was easier for everyone that way. More anonymous, less intense, especially when the emotions didn't run that deep.

Rachel deserved better than a hit-and-run. Standing over her, with death a true possibility on the other side of the door, saying goodbye rated as the hardest thing he'd ever done.

For that reason, it had to be face-to-face, eye-to-eye.

As if her thoughts brought her to the same conclusion at the same time, her stunning aqua eyes opened. All the anxiety and uncertainty she felt showed in her gleaming gaze.

"Hey," she said softly, sitting up so the sheet pulled tight across her breasts.

"Hey." Ford sat down next to her. Needing to touch, he cupped the back of her neck and ran his thumb over the silkiness of her cheek.

Because the words wouldn't come, he bent and put his feelings in a kiss, all his adoration, passion and torment. Her response equaled his in emotional impact.

When it reached the point where he needed to climb into bed or pull back, he lifted his head. "Promise me you'll let my family help you."

That earned him a wan smile. "I promise."

Knowing the time had come, he stood. He held out a hand. "Walk me out?"

She slipped out of bed, wrapped the sheet around herself and laced her fingers through his. He led her to the front door where his duffle waited.

Pulling her into his arms, he pressed his nose into her mussed curls. "Kiss the twins for me."

"I will." She looked up, framed his face in trembling hands. "Wild Mustang, come back to me."

I will, the words were on the tip of his tongue, but they both knew it was a promise he couldn't make. Instead he gave her one last, hard kiss and stepped out the door.

"Oh my goodness, Cody is walking," Samantha called out, drawing everyone's attention to where she and Rachel were sitting on the floor in front of the parlor fireplace.

Gathered together for Thanksgiving Day. Rachel sat among Ford's family in Gram's house and clapped along with the others as Cody wobbled from her hold to Samantha's. Her pride in Cody's accomplishment only suffered from Ford's absence. She knew he'd regret missing this special moment.

"Hey, little buddy, walk to Uncle Cole."

The Sullivans were a rowdy crowd, boisterous and giving. They'd welcomed her and the twins into their midst with warmth and generosity. The twins thrived in the loving environment, which showed in Cody's zigzag journey around the room as he walked from uncle to aunt to uncle.

Rachel did her best to fit in, but too many years on her own gave her a reticence that couldn't be shrugged aside so easily. Ford's brothers, bless them, gave her both space and casual affection.

Gram, Samantha and Ford's cousin Mattie drew her in and made her one of the crowd. No distance allowed here. Rachel accepted their good-hearted advice and interference with surprising tolerance.

Leaving the twins in the capable hands of the family, Rachel slipped out to the front porch. Last week's heat had given way to a cold front, and the nip in the air made her wish she'd grabbed her sweater.

In moments like this one she missed Ford all the more, not just for her sake but for his as well. His excitement when Jolie had walked had matched Rachel's. She knew he'd be disappointed to miss this milestone in Cody's life.

The door opened behind her and Ford's oldest brother Alex stepped out on the porch. Tall, dark and broad, with the Sullivan blue eyes, the resemblance between him and Ford was striking. But there were differences, too. Alex carried more weight and showed the beginnings of gray in his hair and he lacked Ford's dangerous edge.

"I guess you're missing Ford about now." Alex came to stand beside her.

"Yeah." She leaned her hip against the railing and faced him. "And I guess you've come out to give me the third degree."

He shrugged and propped a shoulder against a post. "What makes you think that?"

"I know animals. This is your pack. You need to check out the new member."

"I won't apologize for protecting my family." Totally confident, neither his stance nor his expression changed.

"I don't expect you to," she assured him, though she didn't back down. "Now I'm responsible for the twins, I have a whole new respect for what a parent will do to protect their family."

"And how far will you go for the twins, Rachel?"

A half smile tugged at the corner of her mouth.

"Somehow I don't think you're referring to the distance between Montana and San Diego."

"Once Ford sets his mind to something, it takes dynamite to change his course. He left here intending to bring the twins back, to raise them within the family. And that's exactly what he did. But you, you're a surprise."

She lifted a brow. "And you want to know if I'm taking advantage of him?"

"You've known my brother for little more than a month, yet you're living with him, raising children together. That's damn fast work."

"Do you think it would be so easy to make Ford do something he didn't want to do?"

He rolled his eyes. "You're a beautiful woman, what's not to want. You should know Ford isn't ready to settle down. For a commitment. He's not called Mustang for nothing."

"I don't think you give him enough credit, which is a shame, because I know your opinion matters to him." She crossed her arms over her chest. "Ford is the most generous, caring man I know."

Alex cocked a dark brow. "He's my brother, I think I know him better than you."

"You should, but you don't. You ought to know by now he doesn't like to be told what to do. The two most important things in his life are the SEALs and his family. He's committed to both. Having to choose between them is tearing him apart. A little support from you would be helpful, and I'm not talking about giving advice. I'm talking about supporting whatever decision he makes regardless of whether you approve or not."

By Alex's stark expression she saw she'd hit a nerve, had given him something to think about. Rachel drew in a deep breath, breathed out. She needed to compose herself. Being with Ford meant being a part of his family.

"It's hard as hell," she said more calmly. "But that's what I'm offering him, because it's what I'd want from him, and I respect him too much to force my fears on him." She forced a smile. "It may reassure you to know no promises have been made between us. None are necessary."

Pensive, Alex stuffed his hands in his pockets. He frowned as he focused on her.

"Is that fair to you?" he asked.

Now she smiled for real. "You can't help yourself, can you? You have to take care of everyone." She moved to him, watched the wariness come into his eyes, but all she did was give him a kiss on the cheek. "You're sweet, but this is where Ford and I are right now. As you said, we've only known each other for a month. We'll work it out."

"And that's good enough for you?"

"Oh, yeah. Mustangs are famous for being wild and free, but they make great domestic animals if you don't break their spirit." And because she'd reached the limit on what she felt comfortable revealing to him, she turned to the house. At the door she stopped and glanced back at him. "Alex?"

He looked over his shoulder at her, one dark brow lifted in query.

"Ford has a nickname for me, do you know what it is?"

Alex shook his head. "What?"

"Dynamite." With a wink and a grin, she stepped into the house.

* * *

Rachel spent Friday and Saturday packing and shopping for furniture. Before he left, Ford had arranged for the baby furniture at her place in Montana to be packed up and shipped to Alpine. The rest of the stuff could wait until she had time to make a trip.

In the meantime Samantha volunteered to help so they left the children in the care of Sami's regular baby-sitter and set out to put a home together.

The first course of action was to inventory Ford's condo in downtown San Diego to see what they wanted to take and what they'd need to buy new.

"I like this dining room set, but I think I prefer using the living room furniture from the cottage to this black leather." Rachel stood hands on her hips surveying the setup.

"I agree and Gram said you were welcome to use whatever you need." Sami swept a long length of blond hair behind her ear. "What's Ford going to do with this place?"

"He talked about renting it. I told him we could stay here, but he wanted the twins and me to be closer to the family when he was gone." Rachel walked down the hall into the master bedroom. "Oh, this is beautiful."

A lovely king-size mahogany framed bed dominated the room. Matching bedside tables and a large bureau completed the set. The comforter was a scrumptious red satin with oriental motifs.

Rachel loved it, but only one thing came to mind when she looked at it. She met Sami's gaze.

"New bedroom set," they both said at the same time.

Chapter 12

By sheer force of will and instincts honed by years of experience, Ford made it through the assignment without getting anyone killed. Himself included.

Rachel invaded his mind every minute of every day. And the twins, he couldn't help wondering whether they were all safe and sound.

While the team worked to rescue a politician's daughter from a hostage situation, he worried about his little corner of the world.

Lord, he thought, he'd missed Rachel in the week between leaving Montana and her arrival in San Diego. The whole world had seemed dimmer that week.

He'd known before she'd even got to San Diego, he wouldn't be letting her leave. He'd been prepared for a fight, and to do whatever it took to win.

Instead she'd surprised him with a soft and giving

acceptance he knew had cost her hugely in trust and independence. The next week he'd literally and figuratively lived in Paradise.

Everything fell into place. He went back to work. Gram helped Rachel with the twins during the day so she had time for her writing. And at night they'd been together as a family until they closed the bedroom door and he had Rachel all to himself.

"Hey man, how you doing?" Hoss, massive, dark skinned, bald headed, and a straight shooter on and off assignment sat down next to Ford.

"Not good." Ford bent his head, scrubbed at his eyes with the heels of his hands. "I was a mess out there."

"You held it together."

"Barely. And that kind of distraction gets people killed." A SEAL always knew danger was an inherent part of any assignment, but they put that out of their mind and did the job.

In the past Ford had embraced the impartiality needed to accomplish the task. This time he couldn't forget he had people at home counting on his safe return. People he longed to see again, to hold in his arms, to cherish.

"So what *are* you going to do?" Hoss asked.

Ford summoned a grin he didn't feel. "I called ahead, got a meeting with the CO to explore my options."

"You know Intelligence would scoop you up in a heartbeat."

Ford rubbed a weary hand over the tight muscles of his neck. "Yeah. Man, you remember BUDS training?"

"Hell, yeah. You thinking of training? Those instructors are tough bastards." Hoss eyed Ford thoughtfully, nodded. "You'd be great."

"You think? Rachel suggested it. The idea is growing on me."

"Woman knows her man." Hoss held up his hand and they bumped knuckles. "Good luck, Mustang."

When he reached the base, Ford went straight to the commander's office. He knocked, and then stepped inside at his CO's wave.

Ford saluted. "Sir. I'm here to request a transfer."

With all the excitement of the move and ending the day in a new house, the twins were over excited and refused to settle down on Sunday night. Rachel glanced at her watch. After nine. She'd hoped to get some unpacking done, instead she threw pillows down on the living room carpet and let the kids loose.

Restrained most of the day both of them immediately climbed up to practice their new favorite thing, walking.

"You two are tired, so be careful." Rachel perched on the edge of the sofa ready to spring into action if needed.

Jolie grinned and walked straight to Rachel.

"Hey, beautiful. You're getting good at this aren't you? Cody has some catching up to do doesn't he?"

Hearing his name Cody turned from where he stood by the coffee table and waved his arms. His weight shifted and he started to fall.

"No." Rachel saw it happening, saw it and couldn't stop it. She jumped up but couldn't reach Cody before he fell hard against the edge of the hardwood table.

He twisted trying to compensate, but instead of saving himself he hit the table hard splitting his forehead open.

Cody screamed.

Blood spurted everywhere.

Jolie began to cry.

"Oh God. Oh God." Heart in her throat Rachel scooped Cody up in one arm and Jolie in the other and rushed to the bathroom. She put Jolie in the dry tub and took Cody to the sink.

"It's okay, baby, it's okay." God she prayed it was okay.

She tried to wash the wound but the gash was deep and wouldn't stop bleeding. Her mind spun as she considered what to do. She tore a new pillowcase into strips and wrapped a makeshift bandage around his head.

The hospital, she needed to get Cody to the hospital.

Grabbing a baby in each arm she carried them both to the crib, and then went to the kitchen to call Alex and Samantha. They'd left an hour ago. She hated to drag them back, but she didn't know where the hospital was, and if they could watch Jolie…

"Shoot." No answer. And no time to keep trying. She tried Cole's number, but again received no reply. She elected not to leave messages because they'd only worry and there'd be no way for them to reach her.

Damn. First thing tomorrow morning she was getting a cell phone.

It was after two when Ford reached home. He'd decided to stop off in Alpine in case Rachel had managed to arrange the move over the long weekend as she'd wanted to do. And sure enough lights blazed from several rooms.

He didn't have a key yet so he knocked. Then knocked louder. No answer. Utilizing skills he usually restricted to national security, he unlocked the door and stepped inside.

He immediately spotted the blood in the hall, in the living room. Adrenaline shot through his system.

"Rachel," he called out, following the blood trail down the hall. His stomach flipped when he spied the mess in the bathroom. "Rachel!"

He pulled out his phone, called Gram. She hadn't heard from Rachel since early evening. Next he tried Alex and Sami. Alex reported they'd left Rachel and the twins around eight-thirty. Everyone had been fine. They had a missed call from her a little after nine, but she hadn't left a message.

"Grossmont is the nearest hospital," Alex reasoned.

"I'm on my way." Ford was already climbing into his Jeep.

"I'll call and see if I can learn anything. Don't worry, Ford, we'll find them. Was Rachel's SUV in the driveway?"

"No." Ford cursed. "And I didn't stop to check the garage."

"It was in the driveway when we left, that means Rachel was able to drive them wherever they went. That's something at least."

"Yeah." Ford disconnected. His stomach churned. Bloody scenarios raced through his head. The fact that

Rachel had been able to drive offered little consolation. He just wanted to find them all safe.

Then he'd talk to Rachel about taking off without letting anyone know where she was going or what had happened.

He made the twenty-mile drive to Grossmont Hospital in twelve minutes. He stormed up to the nurse's station. "I'm looking for Rachel Adams. Are they here?"

"Ford?" The voice came from behind him. "Ford!" He turned in time to catch Rachel as she launched herself into his arms. "I'm so glad you're here."

"Rachel." He breathed her name, more a prayer of thanksgiving than a greeting. He squeezed her to him, buried his face in her hair. "Tell me you're all right."

Rachel wrapped her arms around Ford and held on tight. For the first time in hours her world felt right. Tears held at bay for so long broke free. She clung to Ford, wanting nothing more than to burrow into the safety of his arms.

"Rachel!" He pushed her away, held her at arm's length. Concern bleached his features of color. "Talk to me. What happened?"

Swiping tears from her face she struggled for composure. "Cody—" She hiccuped and a fresh wave of tears flowed as she remembered her panic and fear when he hurt himself.

"What about Cody?" Ford walked around her to get to the twins in their double stroller. Both babies slept. Cody sported a white bandage across the length of his forehead. "My God." Ford crouched down by the boy. "Tell me what happened."

"He fell." Her breath hitched; again she brushed the wetness from her cheeks. "It was after everyone left. Th-they, the twins wouldn't settle down so I l-let them out to walk around."

"Cody is walking?"

She nodded, breathed deep. "On Thanksgiving. He fell tonight, hit his head on the coffee table. It took six stitches to close the gash."

"Good God." Ford shot to his feet and rolled the stroller outside. He stopped and confronted her. "Alex said you were moving all weekend, that they didn't leave until after eight. You all had to be exhausted. How could you be so careless?"

Stunned Rachel backed up a step. She blinked away the last of the tears. "What?"

Ford's cell phone rang. He took it out, flipped it open. "Hi, Alex. Thanks, I found them. Cody fell and cut his head. We're taking him home now." He listened. "Yeah, she's fine. Hey can I give you a call tomorrow? Thanks."

He flipped the phone closed, pocketed it. "Let's go. I'll drive. We can leave my Jeep here and pick it up tomorrow." He held out his hand. "Give me your keys."

Chilled inside and out by his cold and accusatory attitude, she led the way to her SUV, helped put the children in their seats, stored the stroller in the back, but when it came to climbing in next to him the tension broke her.

"I don't think so." She crossed her arms under her breasts. "Not until you explain your accusation."

He stalked around the vehicle to confront her. "You're the one that needs to explain a few things."

He paced away, then back, his movements jerky, out of control.

"Do you know what it was like to walk into the house tonight and find blood everywhere? To call my brother and find out you couldn't be bothered to leave a message about what happened or to say where you were?" He raked both hands through his hair, shook his head. "On top of that selfishness I find out this could all have been avoided if you'd used a little common sense."

"Enough," she demanded. Not since he'd first landed on her doorstep had he been so critical of her. So cold. She'd spent the last hours wishing he were here to help her, to hold her. To make everything all right. How cruel of fate to grant her wish only to deliver this antagonistic stranger.

"I've just spent four hours beating myself up over Cody's accident, but I'll be damned if I'll stand here and take criticism from you when you don't know what you're talking about." She shook with anger, with disappointment, with betrayal.

She spread her arms wide, exhibiting the rust-colored bloodstains on her blue shirt and jeans. "Yeah, there was blood in the house, lots of it, so excuse me if I chose to get Cody to the hospital rather than chase down your family, who'd already spent the weekend helping us move. And no I didn't leave a message because I couldn't wait for them to respond, and I didn't know where I was going so why worry them unnecessarily?"

Beyond weary, she swayed where she stood.

He'd gone still and quiet during her diatribe, now

seeing signs of her weakness, he reached for her arm. "Come on, let's go home, we'll talk about this tomorrow."

"I'm not going anywhere with you." She dodged his touch, rounded the hood of the SUV and got behind the wheel. He followed her, but when he reached for the door handle she hit the locks.

"Rachel, open the door." He knocked on the window. A frown drew his dark brows together. He looked tired and drawn. "You're upset. Let me drive."

Tears came back, blurring her vision. She blinked them away and put the car in gear. She drove away without a backward glance.

Rachel was greeted for the empty streets—it compensated for the fact that her full attention wasn't on the road. On a lonely stretch of Freeway 8 at 2:55 in the morning reality hit her square in the face. Ford only asked her to stay so he could leave. By agreeing to stay she'd only set herself up for a repeat of her childhood, to live where she was valued more for what she did— care for the twins—than for who she was—a strong and independent woman.

A strong and independent woman foolishly in love.

Shame on her for dropping her guard, for believing, even for a moment, something special had developed between her and Ford. Love of the self-sacrificing, unconditional variety didn't exist between men and women.

Giving up her home, setting aside the protection of her loner ways had earned her nothing more than a broken heart.

Disillusioned, angry with him and herself, she realized she couldn't stay in San Diego. When Cody was well enough to travel she'd take the twins and fly back to Montana. With the decision made she went numb, her emotions and subconscious shutting down to protect her from the too familiar sense of loss and betrayal.

Aware of Ford following behind her, she almost didn't go to the house in Alpine, the house she'd taken such joy in preparing for their family, but it took more energy than she possessed to think where else to go.

She parked in the driveway, released Jolie from her seat and carried her to her crib, carefully avoiding any sight of the blood throughout the house. Cleanup could wait until later.

Ford arrived with Cody, gently lowering the baby into his crib. Rachel felt his gaze as she changed Jolie and got the little girl situated. She ignored him, unable to deal with him any further tonight.

She breathed easier when he moved to the door without speaking. She'd be even happier if he'd left the room entirely, but he lingered by the door watching her.

Forcing herself to focus, she went to Cody and woke him as instructed, checking his pupils and level of alertness. Both seemed fine so she changed him and then lifted him and pointed to Ford, because regardless of what was or wasn't between the two of them, she knew he cared about the twins.

"Look who's here," she said.

A grin broke across Cody's face and he held out his little arms.

Ford cradled Cody against his chest and felt something click into place deep inside. Cody and Jolie had pulled on his heartstrings until his heart had grown big enough to embrace them both. He had a lifetime love affair going on here.

Trailing Rachel to the kitchen where she prepared a bottle, Ford knew she was part of the package. More, she was the heart of it.

Boy he'd blown it big time tonight. An overload of adrenaline had caused him to come out blazing when he should have provided a strong, comforting refuge in the face of her ordeal.

Rachel had told him how she'd left home at such a young age because she'd felt unwelcome within her own family, and what did he do but make her feel an outsider again by putting more importance on informing his family of the emergency than of praising her for her handling of the distressing incident.

"I'm sorry," he said to her back as she stood waiting for the microwave to heat Cody's bottle.

Her shoulders tensed; otherwise she gave no sign of hearing him.

"I'm an idiot. No, that's not strong enough." He crossed the room to stand behind her. "I'm an insensitive ass."

"If you're waiting for an argument from me, you won't get it." The microwave dinged. She made no move to remove the bottle. Or to face Ford.

Not a problem, Cody was already sleeping on Ford's shoulder.

"I've decided to return to Montana." With the declaration, Rachel turned to look him in the eye. "And I'm taking the twins with me."

"No." The hurt and lack of hope in her gaze tore him apart. He'd done that to her.

For a man of action he'd sure been slacking. He'd failed to tell her of his feelings, been afraid to admit his love just as he'd been afraid to give up the excitement of his job. It was time he stepped up. "You can't go. I won't let you leave. I love you."

Rachel frantically shook her head, sidestepped away from Ford, and wrapped her arms around herself.

"You have no say." She completely disregarded his declaration of love as too late, too convenient. "I'll pay for the month's rent. The furnishings can be returned. You're right, your family is special, the twins are lucky to have them in their lives, but I'm keeping them until you leave the SEALs behind. And you're going to let me because it's the decent thing to do."

Her throat tightened before she finished, a sure sign tears threatened. Refusing to break down in front of him now, she started for the kitchen door.

"Please put Cody in his crib. I have to wake him every hour but first I have to get out of these bloody clothes."

"Rachel, wait—"

"No, just no." She escaped before he tempted her with his easy charm.

In her room she grabbed clean clothes and locked herself in the bathroom where she let the shower wash away the tears. She'd started the day with so much joy, with such anticipation of finally living her dream of love and a family. Hearing Ford announce his love should have been the ultimate high of the day instead of a devastating betrayal of everything good between them.

Unable to stay hidden forever, she dressed and opened the door.

Ford leaned against the doorjamb. He held up a packet of folded papers.

"What's this?"

"Transfer forms. I talked to my CO when we reached base. A master chief instructor at the training facility is retiring next month. I'll be taking his place."

"Why?" She took the papers, opened them to read. "I thought you wanted to finish on your own terms."

"These are my terms." He led her over to the bed, sat down beside her. "I was a mess in the field. I couldn't get you or the twins out of my head. I love you, Rachel. Nothing is more important to me than building a life with you, Jolie and Cody. And maybe a baby of our own someday."

Oh, unfair. Longing and fear battled inside her. "I can't. Tonight—"

"Tonight I overreacted. I was so scared. When I found you all safe I went into an adrenaline crash and I lashed out. But I was wrong. You were smart, and brave, and you made all the right choices."

She shook her head, she wanted to believe but she didn't dare.

"It's no use, you know." He brought her hand to his mouth and kissed her palm. "I know you love me."

That burned her; she snatched her hand away. "You think you know what?"

"You don't fool me. Not once during the argument at the hospital did you throw my job up at me. No reference to missing the twins' first Thanksgiving, to having to handle the move on your own, or to blaming me for not being there when Cody fell. All kill shots. But you didn't make them, why not?"

She looked away from him. "It was already ugly enough."

"Uh-huh, my little piece of dynamite. You never held back when it came to protecting the twins. You could have decimated me, but you didn't." He lifted her chin, forcing her to meet his gaze. "For two reasons. First you love me, and second because of your past. Subconsciously you believe all the nonsense I was spewing. But I was wrong, so wrong."

She swallowed the lump in her throat as she realized she'd fallen into her old familiar role. Drawing in a deep breath, she let the tension go. She refused to give the past power over the future.

"You truly think I was brave?"

"Very brave." He leaned in for a kiss, keeping it slow and gentle. "I'm the SEAL, but you're the one with all the courage. You gave up your home to move here, to be with me, to make a home for the twins. Don't give up on us now."

"If you're transferring to training, you'll be here for the twins. You don't need me to stay."

"I never needed you to stay for the twins. It was always for me."

"Really?"

He pressed her back into the bed. "Oh, yeah."

Rachel looked up into his blue eyes; saw the love shining there for her. "I stayed for you."

"I know." He claimed her mouth, and her love with

a passionate sweep of his tongue, deepening the kiss when she wrapped her arms around his neck and lifted into his embrace. "Let's make it permanent."

She pulled back, threaded her fingers through his silky hair. He made her feel so cherished. Yet… "Ford, we didn't make it through our first day in our own home."

"Because I didn't respect what we have. Love is both simple and complicated, easy and hard. Heartache and joy. As long as we stay true to love, as long as we don't give up on each other, we'll make it together. Forget one day at a time, I want forever. Marry me."

Oh God, she wanted to believe him. In truth she'd changed over the last month. Ford and Cody and Jolie had collectively shattered the barrier she had used to buffer herself from the rest of the world. She was stronger because of the love they'd brought to her life.

Her mind urged her to run, but her heart begged her to stay. Deciding to take a risk on love, she pulled him down for a kiss.

"Yes," she whispered against his mouth. "I'll stay. Forever."

* * * * *